Magic Landscapes

❧ Magic Landscapes ❧

A Mary Wesley Omnibus

Containing
Haphazard House
Speaking Terms
The Sixth Seal

J. M. DENT & SONS LTD
LONDON

This collection first published in 1991

Haphazard House first published in 1983
Copyright © Mary Wesley, 1983

Speaking Terms first published in 1969
Copyright © Mary Wesley, 1969

The Sixth Seal first published in 1969
Copyright © Mary Wesley, 1969
Revisions copyright © Mary Wesley, 1984

Cover illustration copyright © Peter Melnyczuk, 1991

Typeset at The Spartan Press Ltd, Lymington, Hants
Printed in Great Britain by Bath Press Ltd, Avon.
for J.M. Dent & Sons Ltd
91 Clapham High Street
London SW4 7TA

British Library Cataloguing-in-Publication Data
Wesley, Mary, 1912–
Magic landscapes.
I. Title
823.914

ISBN 0-460-880950

❧ Contents ❧

Haphazard House

'Life is a stair up which Death beckons.'

Anonymous

I

Josh and I sat at the top of the stairs listening to the voices below.

'You were very keen when he suggested it in the first place.' Our mother had said this several times.

'Well, I'm not keen now. The whole thing is idiotic, pretentious, and a waste of my time. I shall not go; it might kill me.'

'Josh and I enjoyed ourselves.'

'I don't approve.'

'Darling, Sandy knows what he is doing; he's a very good agent. You'd see if you'd take the trouble to go.' Our mother's voice rose. Josh put his head on one side and began to conduct an imaginary orchestra, a Biro in his right hand, his left outstretched with fingers spread.

'Sandy just wants to make money.'

'Some money would be nice.' Ma's voice dropped a note.

'Money, money, money.' Josh waggled the Biro.

'Next you'll say that's all I think about!' Her voice rose, suddenly harsh. Josh threw up his arms, holding them stiff.

'Oh, don't let's quarrel.' The key was low. 'You know my principles.'

'I'm not quarrelling. I just think you should go.'

'I'd be recognized.'

'Why not?'

'People would ask silly questions.'

'Rot.'

'You know they would. It's a racket, a racket, a racket.' Josh emphatically waved the Biro.

'It's Sandy's job. The pictures are beautifully framed, you said so yourself; and they are well hung. Do go.'

'I won't.'

'You must.'

'Why should I?'

'Out of common politeness.'

'Politeness!' Very low growling. 'Rallentando,' murmured Josh.

'No. No. No.'

'Presto,' whispered Josh.

'Darling – please go. Take Lisa. She only didn't come with me because of you.'

'Very sensible child.' Josh raised an eyebrow.

'For your father's sake then.'

'How does he come into it?'

'He's old; he hasn't got much longer.'

'I know that.'

'It would give him a boost; make him proud to see your success.'

'What success?'

'A one-man show is success.'

'Not if it's a flop.'

'It won't be a flop. Go for his sake. Let him see your success before he dies.'

'We are all dying.'

'He is nearer to it than you. He's a lonely old man.'

'He doesn't believe in my painting; he scoffs.' Josh held the Biro still. I held my breath.

'He lives in peril of eviction.'

'He's been in peril of eviction ever since he moved into that flat when my mother died.'

'It's much worse now, and he's that much older. Please go.'

'The Council will find him somewhere.'

'It won't be the same and he won't be allowed to keep a cat.'

'What has my father's cat got to do with the exhibition of my paintings?'

'Oh! You are exasperating! I could massacre you!'

Josh waved the Biro and clenched his left fist.

'You can only massacre a lot of people. I am alone.'

'She's winning,' I whispered.

'Never mind my grammar!' Ma was furious.

'I love your grammar. I love you. I love our horrible children.'

'Oh, darling – '

'I hate exhibitions. I hate commerce. I hate living here. I just want peace to paint.'

'Then you'll go?'

'All right.' Very quiet, muted.

'Good. I've found a suit at a jumble sale you can wear. Nobody will know you.'

'A suit!' Pa's voice sounded like a runaway trumpet blast. 'I never wear suits.'

'That's why it's so perfect. You can see for yourself how well the pictures have been hung. I shall make Lisa presentable, too.'

They burst out laughing. Josh brought the concert to a close. I mimed clapping hands.

'*How* stupid articulate adults can sound!' Josh grinned.

'I want to go, really,' I said as I got up from the stairs.

'Of course you do.'

'Do people make remarks?'

'Nothing nasty. I was surprised how good it was. He makes out he's not marvellous but other people – '

'What?'

'You go and see. Goodnight.' Josh went off to bed.

In the morning Pa looked clean and tidy and I did, too. Ma had achieved the impossible; Pa looked ordinary, like other people. He still stood very tall, six-foot-four but, in a pepper-and-salt suit, polished shoes and blue socks, he might have passed for anyone other than an unknown painter going to see his first one-man show in London.

'A hat?' Pa suggested timidly.

'No. They are not worn except by parsons and people like that.'

'Who are like parsons?'

'Don't be difficult; you know what I mean. Lawyers, parsons, etc.'

Pa shut up.

Ma looked at me, her eyes travelling from my well-brushed head to my feet in school shoes. She suppressed a smile.

'Nobody will know you.'

'Sure?'

'Absolutely.'

Ma and Josh stood in the doorway and watched us get into the beat-up Mini – for Pa an athletic feat. When driving, the curious would turn and stare as his head touched the roof and, even with the seat as far back as it would go, his legs had to be folded so that they did not get in the way of the driving wheel.

'Off we go then,' he cried. I waved. Ma and Josh waved. Pa drove down the road and headed for inner London. Ma had told me to keep Pa happy and calm.

'Ma says nobody paid any attention to her or Josh and that no one said anything derogatory.'

'Derogatory?'

'Unsuited to your dignity.'

'What dignity?'

'You look very dignified in that rig.'

'Ah, Lisa, I am glad to have you with me. Perhaps if I got a hat people would just think I was some country parson up for the day with his little girl having a dekko at modern art on the way to the dentist.'

'Ma said no hat, and I *am* on the way to the dentist.'

'I know. I can't think why you and Josh make such a fuss; neither of you has ever been hurt.'

'We will be one day. Perhaps today is that day for me.'

'Lisa. I'm sure your mother told you to keep me calm and cheerful. This is no way to set about it. Let us plan,' said Pa, reversing our roles and making an effort to console me for the visit to the dentist which lay ahead. 'Let us plan what to do with the money if I have sold a picture or two. Let's be wildly optimistic.'

'I should think you'd like to put it on a horse.'

'What would your mother say?'

'We needn't tell her if it doesn't win.'

'Isn't that a bit, er, dishonest or something? It's against her principles, is betting.'

'She wants a Hoover or a colour television.'

'Well, that's against my principles, as you well know. I am against gadgets, and television in particular. The money on a horse. I agree to that. You shall choose the horse.'

'Today is Derby Day.'

'Is it indeed? How very suitable.'

Driving into London from the south, we reached Waterloo and crossed Westminster Bridge. Pa drove through St James's Park and brought the Mini to rest in an empty space in St James's Square. We were delighted to find nearly an hour left on the meter and Pa gave me a tenpenny piece instead of putting it in the slot.

'That's time enough for us,' he said. 'We shan't be long.'

The sun shone; the traffic did not seem to smell quite as terrible as usual as we walked up to Bond Street.

'You must admit,' Pa said, pausing by Scotts, 'that it is tantalising.'

We stood looking at the hats. There was a black, a brown and a grey bowler. A fine grey top hat was placed away from the bowlers; the only swan in a gaggle of geese, next to a restrained check-cap and a deerstalker.

'Not really; I expect she is right, she usually is.' Pa took a step forward, hesitated, turned, and went quickly into the shop. I waited on the pavement, sure he would come out muttering some excuse, but he did not. After a few anxious minutes, I went into the shop. Pa stood wearing a Panama and was about to write a cheque.

'Pa!' I protested. 'Really!'

'Just the job isn't it?' Pa turned the brim down all the way round. 'I should be wearing my dog collar.'

'Many of the clergy don't nowadays, sir; just a black polo-neck.'

'That is so.' Pa wrote the cheque and we left the shop with him wearing the hat and holding me firmly by the hand.

'Don't speak,' said Pa, 'my heart is going pit-a-pat; we are nearly there.'

'Not a soul will recognize you. There is no need to be so scared, Pa.'

'But I *am*. I know it is illogical, but this show is far, far worse than your visits to Mr Heath are for you.'

'None of your self-portraits is of you wearing a hat and none is really like you.'

'So you all say, but I don't look like me now, do I, and nor do you look like my lovely pictures of you, but the people, if there are any people, may twig; they just might.'

'No, Pa, they won't. They none of them recognized Ma or Josh. She said you walk round, look at the pictures, and walk out.'

'My knees are knocking together.'

At the gallery the notices said this was the first one-man show of Andrew Fuller's work and a lot of blah about his special talent for depicting family life. I sneered inwardly at that, having heard Pa complain often enough that we were all rotten models. I gave his hand a jerk and we went in.

Pa pulled his sun-glasses out of his pocket and put them on. 'Better be safe than sorry.' He squared his shoulders and we advanced into what I think of now as a magical day.

Apart from a girl with very short hair wearing a lot of make-up (which showed she was not as young as she dressed) sitting at the table selling catalogues, there were only two other people besides ourselves; a short man in jeans and a sweatshirt with 'Bonnie Dundee' stencilled on it, and an immensely tall girl with spectacles, long hair, long skirts and lots of bean necklaces. The man had his arm round the girl's waist, holding his arm high to do so. They swayed round the gallery. 'I like the one of the hipbath.' The girl peered. Pa held my hand and we paused, as though looking at the full-length portrait of Ma in a deck-chair. Pa gave my hand a squeeze.

'Can't say I like that one.' The girl swayed on.

'Somebody did.'

'Sure somebody did. Wish I had that kind of dough. Just look at that! That's alive. That handstand's great. The greatest, isn't it?'

They stood in admiration in front of the picture of me. The framer had framed it upsidedown. Pa had said, 'Let it go, it won't make any odds; nobody will appreciate it in any case.'

'I sure appreciate that one,' said the girl, her bean beads making a gritty noise as they swung across her chest. 'The whole effect is vertigo, sheer genius. Any other painter would have the skirt fall over the kid's face, but not this one! It sure puts a pin in Newton's eye.'

'That's a good expression, the one about the pin. Where did you get it?' Pa was unable to restrain himself.

'Some Western, I guess.' The girl took off her spectacles and looked Pa up and down, smiling. 'Reverend.' Without the glasses her eyes were lovely. She turned away, her skirts trailing, the short man hanging on. She put the glasses back on her nose to peer again at the picture of Ma.

Pa, still holding my hand, moved to the middle of the room and let his eyes rake the walls. His hand began to tremble.

'Is your heart going pit-a-pat?' I was anxious.

'It certainly is. Let's get out of here.' Pa made for the door. I ran after him.

'Got to telephone. Let's go to the Ritz.'

'The Ritz?'

'Lots of telephones. Here, buy a paper.' Pa grabbed an *Evening Standard* from a paper seller.

'You've never been to the Ritz.'

'What's that to us? Lord, Lisa, mind that bus, it nearly got us.' He dragged me through the swing doors, down the hall to the telephones. 'Hold my hat and study the form.'

'Study what?'

'The form, Lisa. Choose a horse, pick the winner. Turn to the racing page. I have to telephone. There's a pin in Newton's eye!' He quoted the girl in the gallery.

I shrugged my shoulders and opened the paper. I had never been in the Ritz and wondered whether the people behind the reception desk knew that we were totally out of place. Then I remembered that we were not looking like us but like a country parson up for the day with his little girl. I turned up the brim of the Panama, put it on and applied myself to the list of horses. In the telephone booth Pa was talking excitedly. I chose a suitable horse: False Start. This horse would win.

Pa came out of the booth. 'Found one?'

'Yes.' I pointed with my finger, noticing without surprise that since leaving home it had grown dirty.

'I can't back a horse called False Start. Let's see the list.'
He snatched the paper from me. 'Really, darling, False Start
is fifty-to-one. It won't get round the course. Ah, here's one,
False Modesty, relation I expect. Oh, it's the favourite.
That'll do, have to, we haven't much time. I've got to get the
money. We'll have to ring Sandy again.'

'But Pa – '

'What now?' Pa was suddenly furious. I began to cry.
'Oh, all right, it's all some frightful joke anyway, none of it's
true. False Start it is. Very apt, I daresay.' He spoke
haughtily, grabbing the telephone; talking to Sandy he
raised his voice to an angry shout. 'Yes, I know it's mad. In
the Ritz. I know it's not my line. No, you wouldn't
recognize me. My wife's disguised me as a parson. No, I
have not been drinking. Do as I say or I'll fire you.' Pa
banged down the receiver.

'Mop up,' he said, handing me his handkerchief. 'We'll
buy some lunch and watch the race on your grandfather's
television in glorious colour.'

'It's against your principles.'

'So is success, money, all the rotten lot. We should be
living in a barn in the country, not in a suburban semi with
"Success" on the gate. Hah!'

When he cried 'Hah!' it was time for silence. I was silent.

'Blow the lot,' said Pa. 'Let it blow away as quickly as it
came. It is much healthier, better for the soul.' When Pa
spoke of The Soul the storm was over. 'Lunch, and a pin in
Newton's eye for a False Start. It will entertain my father,
it's his kind of joke.'

'What is?' We were walking along King Street by now,
heading for St James's Square.

'He will laugh like a hyena when he hears about my
pictures.'

'Hears what, Pa?'

'That I've sold the lot.'

The blood rushed to my face. 'Pa!' I wailed.

'Yes.'

'You sold them?'

'Yes. Didn't you notice all the red blobs in the corners?'

Pa stopped outside Spinks and looked down at me. 'Don't worry,' he said kindly. 'It's all on the horse. There may be enough left over to give your Ma a treat, but not to buy her a colour TV.'

'Oh, Pa.' I began to cry bitterly. 'I didn't know. I didn't see. I so hated that girl – '

'Darling, do stop. What a day! First me then you getting strung up. What would you have done if you'd won?'

'Bought a house in the country. Oh, I would, I would.'

'Nothing is as easy as that, love,' said Pa. 'This is real life, with idiotic girls thinking a portrait of my lovely wife is a hipbath and – oh look – we have a parking ticket – ' Pa broke into a run, his legs scissoring along like Dr Roger Bannister in an old replay to engage the traffic warden in argumentative protest.

'I have written the ticket,' said the traffic warden. 'Can't go back on it but I'll make a note of the time: only half an hour. Usually people take three for lunch and then the fine mounts up.'

'But we haven't had lunch,' I said.

'Must be hungry then.'

'Not very. We were backing a horse, that's why we overran our time.' Pa tipped the hat onto the back of his head.

'Which one?' asked the traffic warden.

'False Start.'

'Don't you mean False Modesty? He's the favourite.'

'We know.'

'Got a tip from Above?'

'My daughter chose him.'

'This isn't the pools where you just give the baby a pin.'

The warden spoke severely. 'You have to study the form, his breeding and that; do a lot of research.'

'Have you done that?' Pa enquired.

'Of course, in the library here. The London Library, number fourteen,' he prompted.

'Oh.' Pa looked thoughtful.

'Don't think I'm fit to belong to such a posh place, I suppose, holy gent like you. Well I am. That library's a democratic institution, all sorts belong, gents like you, students, lads on bicycles who look like they need a wash – squatters some of them I wouldn't be surprised – chain their bikes to the railings, don't trust nobody and why should they? The world treats them rough.'

'Hold on, hold on,' said Pa meekly. 'I'm in disguise. I'm not a holy gent, I'm a painter.'

'So was Hitler,' said the warden nastily.

'I don't believe I am quite as bad as he was.'

'Ah well, why didn't you say so.' The warden snapped his book shut

'What's your subject?' asked Pa.

'Toads,' said the warden. 'Very interesting animals. Not many round here, though.'

'When False Start has won we are going to buy a house in the country. Come and stay with us,' I said.

'Okay, I will.'

'What's your address?' Pa asked.

'I'll write it here.' The warden wrote with his finger on the dusty back window of the car: John Bailey, 12 Harrow Buildings, Islington. 'Long way to come to work, but when I go off duty I go into the library; it's handy.'

'Must be.' Pa looked fleetingly envious of the man's good fortune. 'We must go. It's been nice to meet you.' He began to insert himself into the Mini.

'Good luck with your painting,' said the warden, smiling for the first time.

'I've had that,' said Pa. 'It all depends on the horse.'

'Forgive a horse laugh,' called the warden as Pa drove off.

Tears of anger welled up.

'Oh, Lisa, it's not serious.' Pa dodged a large Mercedes. 'If we hurry we can buy some grub and get to your grandfather in time for the parade.'

We stopped in Soho long enough to buy a tin of tunafish, an onion, a carton of cream, and strawberries. We reached the tattered house in Bloomsbury where my grandfather lived on the top floor, defying all efforts of landlords and developers to evict him. 'Only death will get me out,' had been his cry for years, and the vultures, as he called his landlords, waited.

There was no meter free. Pa, careless now, left the Mini under a notice which said 'No Parking', leapt out and pressed the bell.

'He won't be pleased,' I said, clutching the parcels.

'No. Probably won't let us in.'

'Who's that?' Grandpa's aged voice came from a window, high up.

'Me, Grandpa.' I stood out in the street so that he could see me.

'Lisa. What are you doing here?'

'Want to watch the Derby,' I yelled. Then, more tactfully, 'Come to see you.'

'Wait a moment.'

'Oh dear, he takes hours to get downstairs.'

We stood on the steps in the dusty sunshine. The strawberries were getting squashy. Inside the house which, apart from Grandpa's eyrie, was empty, we heard the clatter of shoes as somebody ran downstairs. The door opened.

'Sandy, what are you doing here?' Pa looked surprised.

'Thought you might come here. Thought I might be in time to stop you.'

'Well, you are not.' We trooped inside, the door clanged, echoing up through the empty house. I ran ahead of Pa and Sandy.

'Hullo,' said Grandpa, when I reached his flat. He sat with his back to me, facing the television. I could see the frill of white hair hanging over his collar, the light from the television glinting on his bald head. The curtains were drawn, the room stuffy.

'Just in time,' said Grandpa. 'What have you backed?'

'False Start.'

'Very suitable.'

'The traffic warden who booked us said False Modesty would win.'

'That's the favourite. There's an animal called Embattled I fancy, but you may be right. I also like Iron Duke.'

'Pa said you'd laugh.'

'Why?'

'He's sold all his pictures and put the money on False Start. I didn't know. I chose the horse. I thought it was a joke.' This came out in a rush.

'So that's what that Sandy fellow is fussing about.' Grandpa chuckled. 'Thinks he may lose his commission. No wonder he's sweating.'

I groaned.

'No need to shed tears over him,' Grandpa sniffed. 'He knows he's on to a good thing with that boy.' By 'that boy' Grandpa meant my father. 'What would you have done if your beast had won,' He spoke as though the race were already in the past.

'Bought a house in the country.'

'Very sensible. You are stranded in Croydon. Not that I don't like the place — learnt to fly there.'

'Learnt to fly?'

'Why not? I haven't always been a poor man besieged in his home by vultures. If your animal wins I'll come with you. A sniff of fresh air might clear my pipes.'

At this moment Pa and Sandy, who had obviously quarrelled for they looked studiously calm, came into the room.

'Sit down if you can find a chair, but don't talk. I want to watch this.' Grandpa did not turn his head.

'Lisa, are you starving?' Pa took the parcels of food from me.

'I couldn't eat.'

'After the race then.' Pa took the strawberries into Grandpa's kitchen and the room's usual smell of tobacco, garlic and oil reasserted itself. I could hear my father muttering as he searched for a cool place to put the food, 'He really should have a refrigerator, this cream will curdle – '

'Thought you were against electric gadgets,' shouted Grandpa who, like many old people who pretend to be deaf, had the hearing of an animal. 'Turn up the sound you, Sandy Whatsit, and sit quiet.'

Pa joined me on the sofa, feeling with his hand in case he sat on Old X-ray, Grandpa's cat.

'She's here,' I said, 'in my arms.' I laid my cheek for comfort against her stout flank. Old X-ray moved off my lap on to the floor with a plop.

'Do I *have* to go to Mr Heath?'

'You do.' Pa gritted his teeth. Neither of us was having an easy day.

'The traffic warden said you were like Hitler.' Rage against the injustice of the world beset me. I was glad my pa was going to lose all that money – delighted.

'He meant Hitler was a bad painter. That's what he did before his glorification bit. We might ask him to stay.'

'He's dead isn't he?'

'I meant the warden, stupid.'

'Stay where?'

'In this barrack you are going to buy in the country.'

'So False Start will win?'

'Would be a pin in Newton's eye, wouldn't it?'

3

As you will have guessed ever since you read that famous horse's name, False Start won the Derby by five lengths. Embattled came second, Iron Duke third, and False Modesty trailed in last. None of us – except Sandy – actually saw the drama when False Start cast his jockey to the ground, kicked his trainer in the teeth, and bit the lad who was leading him in the arm so badly that it later had to be amputated, before whirling to win. Sandy was the only one who sat through the confusion and noise caused by Old X-ray's ghostly shriek indicating that she was about to give birth to the first, and indeed last, kitten she ever had.

With my grandfather, Pa and myself in attendance, Old X-ray produced one tiny kitten in Grandpa's bed. After licking the kitten dry, she ate a large part of the carton of cream we had bought to eat with our strawberries, then settled, watchful, to rest.

Sandy's garbled description of the race took a little while to penetrate after this extraordinary episode, if such a belittling word can be used for the birth of Old X-ray's progeny, Angelique.

Grandpa, having heard Sandy's story and made sure that all was well with Old X-ray, tiptoed out of the flat and disappeared, while Pa, his head buried in his arms, listened to the television commentators who replayed the race twice. We were too bemused to speak. When Grandpa returned, panting from the long climb up the stairs, carrying a bottle of champagne, Pa revived and was able to mix tuna and chopped onion and fix bowls of strawberries with what was left of the cream.

We felt better after that. Grandpa had backed both Embattled and Iron Duke for a place and won a lot of money which made him very happy. Even Sandy, who had backed False Modesty, was pleased for our family and especially so after an expedition to the nearest telephone to ring up his bookmaker. Pa, by backing False Start with the entire proceeds of the sale had made, as Sandy put it, 'a bomb, oh BOY!' For the sake of Old X-ray who, Grandpa said, would need quiet, we ate and drank almost in silence until, laying down his spoon, Sandy ventured to say, 'Why do you not have the telephone, sir?'

'I do not have the telephone' – Grandpa raised his voice to a harsh shout, forgetting Old X-ray and her kitten – 'because fools like you might ring me up, my landlords might make threatening calls, my friends might invite me to their deathbeds – we have all reached that age – I might be tempted to invite people here; I would lose the use of my legs – '

'Your legs?'

'Staggering up and down that appalling flight of stairs is the only exercise I get. Young people are fools.'

'Sorry, sir, I truly am.' Sandy was stupefied by this outburst.

'Now you have assured yourself that my son is able to pay you, perhaps you will leave. Nobody invited you here. Take yourself off. Go elsewhere. Find some other door to put your foot in.' There was silence as Sandy left. We heard his feet tapping down the stairs and the street door close.

'Do I *have* to go to the dentist?' I asked in the vacuum which followed Grandpa's rudeness.

'Yes, you do,' cried Pa, catching Grandpa's rage like a virus infection. 'You do indeed, you spoilt brat, eating strawberries and cream like a pig, betting,' – he made it sound like a mortal sin – 'watching television. Hah!' He sprang to his feet, seized the television, lurched to the window and cast it out.

We watched, holding our breath, as the television, missing our Mini by an inch, smashed into smithereens in the street.

'Sorry, Father.' Pa spoke very mildly.

Grandpa grinned. 'Worth it, dear boy. I like a man of principle. Besides, you can afford to buy me another.' He stooped to kiss my forehead. 'Off you go to the dentist. I shall come and stay with you. Why are you wearing those clothes, dear boy? You look like a cleric. I rather like the hat though. Will you give it to me?'

'No,' said Pa. 'This hat is mine; it's a lucky hat.'

A thought struck me as we trotted down the stairs.

'Pa, it must be a lucky hat. I was wearing it when I chose False Start.'

'You were?'

'Yes.'

'Magic?'

I nodded.

〜 4 〜

Driving to Hampstead, where Mr Heath lurked, I saw, reflected in the driving mirror, the tracings of the traffic warden's finger. 'Shall we invite John Bailey to stay?'

'The fellow who said I was like Hitler? Why not? He will get on well with my father and, if he likes toads, with you and Josh.'

'May I choose the house? There are lots in the *Country Lifes* in the waiting room.'

'It makes me ill to look at all those stately lots.'

'Some of them are quite small.'

'You know I can't even afford to look.'

'You can now you are rich.'

'So I am.' Pa let go of the wheel and patted the Panama with both hands. A car driving beside us swerved and the driver let down his window to shout. 'Made your will?'

Pa pretended not to notice. 'Where do you want to live?' he asked.

'As far from Mr Heath as possible.' The heights of Hampstead were growing near.

'Ungrateful child,' said Pa, quoting my school dentist. 'One of the few juveniles to have the Heath process from milk teeth to molars.'

'Ugh!'

'It would be sad if his trouble was wasted and my trouble too, bringing you here every three months.'

The dreaded Mr Heath, I shall have to explain, as I have not had time to before, was carrying out an experiment on children's teeth, painting them with his own anti-rot invention from the moment they pushed through infant gums to the time they reached adulthood. The process was painless, but before painting on his 'brew' as he called it, Mr

Heath would explore our mouths with sharp instruments and podgy fingers. The brew was bright red and after each application we looked as though we had chewed betel nut.

The parents of his volunteers, as we were called, were able to claim a small travel allowance, and Mr Heath averred that this enabled many children to go to the pantomine who would otherwise have missed it. This laughable theory made us wonder whether the experiment was not a fraud of some sinister kind.

'We could also have Mr Heath to stay.' Pa parked the Mini. 'And kill him off.'

The waiting room was full of leather-covered chairs and tidy piles of *Country Life, Vogue* and *Private Eye*, to show, Josh said, Mr Heath's sophistication. I sank gloomily into a chair while Pa gave my name to the receptionist who knew it perfectly well but pretended to have forgotten.

'And how is Mrs Fuller?' she asked.

'She was all right when we left home,' said Pa.

'Oh good.' The receptionist's voice was high.

'She won't be when we get back.' The receptionist, not sure whether this was a joke, gave a half smile. 'Mr Heath won't keep you long.' She always said this. We always arrived early and there was always time for *Country Life*.

'Lend me the hat,' I whispered. Humouring a fractious child, Pa handed me the Panama. Though it reached my nose in front and the nape of my neck behind, I could, as I had found when looking at the *Evening Standard* in the Ritz, balance it on my ears.

I concentrated on *Country Life*, turning the pages slowly. A Georgian manor in Hampshire, a grange in the Cotswolds, a Tudor manor in Kent, an abbey on the Welsh border, desirable residences all over the British Isles. I sighed, turning up the brim of the hat. Perhaps no residence desired us, the Fuller family.

In the corner of the last page was a blurred photograph of a house, one end of which looked kind, the other, partly hidden by a tree, cross. As I peered at it from under the brim of the hat I thought someone called my name, 'Lisa, Lisa', from a long way off, 'Lisa'. The call seemed to come from the house in the photograph. I suppressed the idea as idiotic. All the same, 'This is it,' I said to Pa, handing him the magazine.

'Haphazard House?' Pa queried, holding the photograph up. 'Darling, too grim for words – we'd hate it.'

'Put the hat on.' I handed him the Panama.

'Dearest, it will be sold. This is a year old.' He waved the magazine.

'Put it on,' I said. Pa perched the hat on his head and looked again.

'I see what you mean.' Pa smiled. The receptionist called. I went meekly to my doom.

Mr Heath had a new chair. One sat, swung up one's legs and lay back. I felt helpless.

'Ah, Lisa Fuller, aged ten.' The plump voice throbbed from a throat buried in a thick neck.

'Eleven,' I said.

'Ah yes, eleven of course. Age is so important when one is growing up. Open wide. Let's have a look at your gnashers.' He sounded eager. I opened up. 'No trouble of course.' This was a statement. 'What a happy little girl you must be.'

I closed my mouth.

'Open o-o-pen wide. Your lovers will bless me for my care.'

Rage and affront gripped me. His impertinence pried my feelings as his pick explored my teeth. 'I have no lovers.' I clenched my jaws.

'But you will have. That's what it's all about, you must know that, dear.' Fruity reproof.

'I am not *dear*.' My face was red, tears close.

'Oh, sorry. I must remember that. The acids released by bad temper affect the teeth. I have told you that before.'

'No, you haven't.'

'Come on, Lisa. I haven't got all night.' He sounded almost human. I unclenched my jaws. My mouth was full of spit.

'Rinse,' Mr Heath said patiently. He had a new rinse instead of the pink I was used to. This was orange.

'Nice, isn't it?' He noticed my surprise. 'Come on, Lisa.' I submitted. The sharp steel pick tiptapped round my teeth, pausing, probing. With his left hand reaching round my neck from behind, he held a mirror pressing roughly down on my lower lip. He was getting his revenge; he always did.

'You will be grateful to old Heath one day.' He always said this.

I closed my eyes. He was using a new kind of soap, more expensive than the one I was used to. He released me.

'Do you have private patients? What do you charge them?'

'Pry, pry, pry. None of your business. Open wide.'

'It's immoral.'

'Been reading the papers, eh? Open, please.'

'I'm a guinea pig. I'm entitled to know.'

'Come on, Lisa. I want to paint on my brew; it's a new colour.'

'What?'

Mr Heath deftly wedged my jaws open with a wodge of gauze. 'Now keep still,' he said grimly. 'Your brother behaves much better than you.' The painting began.

Suddenly anxious to get the whole stupid business over, I lay back. Mr Heath was silent, earnest and concentrated. At last he said, 'There. That wasn't so awful was it? See you in three months. Oh, just a teeny fraction left out; you distracted me by your naughty talk.' He pulled the light down on its stalk.

I caught sight of a weird reflection in the burnished steel of the light shade – Mr Heath's nose bending over me, his podgy fingers painting the last teeny bit of tooth – blue.

I snapped my teeth, tasting the expensive soap, and blood. He shrieked. Pa gave a roar of laughter when he and the receptionist dashed in in answer to the shriek. After delightedly watching the application of elastoplast, we got a frigid farewell.

'Well,' said Pa, slamming the Mini door which was apt to stick. 'That is the end of that panto. Let us make the day complete with a visit to Squire, Close and Sword.'

'Who are they?' My feeling of triumph was short-lived and regret was creeping on.

'Is your soul troubled with remorse?'

'A bit.'

'Don't give it another thought; the man's a charlatan. On, on to the faithful Squire etc. They, too, like the famous library, are within reach of St James'. Perhaps we shall meet the warden again. We could tell him we won.'

'Who are – ?'

'The house agents of course. Through them we buy the house, Haphazard.'

5

Squire, Close and Sword were shut when we reached them at five-past-five. We had left the Mini in St James's Square and as we walked back to it we saw the traffic warden sticking something under the wiper. He waited for us. Pa took the paper – a short note. 'Did you win much?'

'A tremendous lot,' I said.

'Thought that somehow. What will you do with it, if it's not rude to ask?'

'Buy a house in the country, but the agents are shut. We are going to ask you to stay.' I smiled at Mr Bailey. He rocked back on his heels.

'Whatever have you done to your teeth?'

We explained. We told him about the race, the kitten, the dentist and how I had bitten Mr Heath. The traffic warden laughed a lot and agreed that I was not cut out to be a guinea-pig.

'What about this house, then?' he asked.

'We shall have to come back tomorrow – if my wife agrees.'

'If I was you I wouldn't tell her,' said the warden. 'Present her with a *fait accompli*. I study French, too.'

'Ma speaks French. You can talk to each other when you come.'

'I should like that, but would she?'

We assured him that she would and, promising to meet next day, set off home.

We arrived late for tea and too early for supper. My mother gave an exclamation of pain when she saw my teeth. 'What on earth has he done this time?'

'She bit the man. That is the stain of his blue blood.'

'Ma, we – '

'And *where* did you get that hat, Andrew? You look quite weird.'

'Bought it to wear at the show.' Pa took it off and handed it to Ma.

'Really, darling.' She handled the hat with curious fingers. 'It's a real Panama; a fearful waste of money.'

'Put it on,' I said, taking it from her and placing it on her head. She made as if to refuse, but a funny look came over her face and the expression of tired exasperation left her. She seemed far away. She put her hands up and felt the hat, her eyes astonished.

'What's the matter?' Josh who, at fourteen, was as tall as Ma, took the hat and put it on.

'It's,' she began. 'I was – I thought – no, I *saw*. It was a bit vague, but – '

We heard Josh give a grunt of surprise and watched his face as he, too, wearing the hat, put his hands up to it.

'What a super house.' Josh's voice was joyous. 'Where is it?'

Pa was as surprised as I by Ma, Josh and the hat, for when Pa and I had worn it we had seen nothing, only felt.

'Try it on Bogus,' I suggested. Bogus was a sad, uneasy dog who had never forgotten that he was a lost dog until Josh visited Battersea Dogs' Home one winter afternoon. We lavished love, walks, treats of all kinds on him, but Bogus had always been a faraway dog, looking upon us kindly but not with devotion. He made us feel we would do until his lost master turned up, but no more. He was standing a little apart from us, his tail neither up nor down, his eyes tolerant.

Ma knelt down. 'Come here, Bogus, look at this.' She took the hat from Josh and gave it to Bogus to sniff. He backed away. She held it a little above him and he cringed as though she were going to hit him. Then, suddenly, as she stood holding the hat, Bogus went wild. He gave a yelp which turned into full throttle barks. He threshed his tail, he jumped up and down, greeting each one of us in turn as though he had waited long years for us. He ran in circles; he lovingly licked our hands and faces; he grew visibly younger and tremendously jolly. The sad, thoughtful, lost dog from Battersea had gone.

The scene with Bogus lasted quite a long time and we moved into the kitchen, a poky room looking on to a strip of garden where nothing grew.

Ma put the hat down and, taking Pa's hand, said, 'And now begin.' Still whimpering in his throat, Bogus pressed his chin on Pa's knee. The tale came out disjointedly. Pa told and I told. We told about the traffic warden and the pictures. Josh interrupted.

'But the *hat*? And where – is – that – house I saw?'

'It is Haphazard House,' I cried. 'Did it look kind on one side and not on the other?'

'Well the other side is hidden by a tree – '

'We are going to buy it,' I said.

'Money?' Ma was ironical.

'False Start won at fifty-to-one, didn't he?'

'You bet? Where did you get the money?'

The whole story came out, the sale of the pictures, the money put on False Start, the parking ticket, Old X-ray's kitten, *Country Life*, my biting Mr Heath and the tragic moment when we found Squire, Close and Sword shut. 'Mind you, I don't believe any of it really happened,' Pa ended rather sadly.

'Yes, it did. Look at Bogus. You bought a magic hat and solved our problems. We move to Haphazard House and live happily ever after,' said Ma.

'That magazine was over a year old. The house will be sold.'

Ma snatched up the hat and put it on Pa's head. He smiled and said, 'You are right of course.'

'Oh, I'm so hungry.' Josh let out a cry. 'Starving.' We had been sitting talking until supper-time was long past.

'I wish tomorrow would come,' I said as I helped get supper. 'I won't feel safe until Haphazard is ours.'

'If it has been bought by someone else we will buy it back.'

'You talk as though you know all about it. *I* found it,' I said.

'But *I've* seen it,' said Josh.

'What about Bogus,' said Ma peaceably. 'If that dog could talk I believe he could tell us all about it.' As we sat down to supper Bogus reached up and took the hat off the table to his basket where he lay with it, his nose resting blandly on its crown.

'Darling,' said my mother to Pa, 'be an angel and take off that suit before you eat. You might spill something down your front.' She held a china ladle she had found in a junk shop over the saucepan of soup.

'Does it matter?'

'Well – yes.'

'You said you bought it for forty pence at a jumble sale.'

'A white lie. Do please take it off.'

'Then where did you get it?'

Josh and I listened, grinning, to this exchange. Pa's clothes were always jeans and jersey in winter and jeans and tee-shirt in summer. To avoid recognition at his show Ma had produced the suit from, she said, a jumble sale. 'The soup will get cold if you don't buck up.' Ma was brisk.

'You insist I change my clothes before supper?' He was belligerent.

'Well, yes.' She was firm.

'Why?' Pa's voice rose.

'Because,' said Ma, putting the ladle back in the sauce-pan and returning the saucepan to the stove as though preparing for a long argument, 'because I hired it from Moss Bros.'

'You did *what*?'

'Where else would I get a suit for a man of your height?'

'My principles – ' Pa gasped. 'You'd think I had gone to a levee, to the Royal Academy. Hah!'

There was a long pause while they glared at each other. Then Ma said mildly, 'Well, love, you bought a hat to go with it. You were glad enough of the disguise when I provided it, so take it off now and we can get on with supper. You seem to have forgotten your principles when you wanted to watch the Derby on your father's TV.'

'Suppose I say that giving my principles a rest is good for my soul?'

'I'd still say look sharp and change because we are all hungry and want to celebrate your success. I bought a consolation bottle. Now we will celebrate with it.'

'All right, you win.' Pa stood up. 'And that reminds me – I have to buy a television.'

'A television?' Our mother looked astonished.

'What's happened to him?' asked Josh, but Pa had left the room.

'Is it for us?' Josh asked me. I shook my head, thinking it more tactful that Pa should explain his action at Grand-father's himself. He was capable of a version of his own. He, too, might tell a white lie; find it expedient to say the television had fallen out of the window by itself. If his painting of Ma could be mistaken for a hipbath, he might see his action of the afternoon differently from me.

'What's a hipbath?' I asked.

'Before H & C, stupid,' said Josh, 'people sat in hip-baths in front of a roaring fire and washed in parts.'

'Oh,' I said, none the wiser.

'Why did you want to know?' Our mother stood by the stove, gently stirring the soup.

'There was a tall girl at the show who thought the portrait of you was a hipbath. She was pretending to be American. She was with a short man. They were the only people there.'

'Oh.' Ma stirred. 'It would be nice to know who bought the pictures. Did your father ask?'

'No.'

'Soup.' Pa came back wearing jeans and a jersey, his hair ruffled. 'Soup.' He carried the pepper-and-salt suit reverently like a fireman carrying an unconscious child from a blaze. 'Where shall I put it?'

'Put it on the hall table. We can return it tomorrow.'

'I forgive you. That was a very wicked thing to do, tripping me by my principles.' Pa was happy now in his old clothes.

Bogus in his basket gave a satisfied groan and settled himself more comfortably. 'I would love to know – ' Josh looked at Bogus, 'where he came from.'

'A hat shop, obviously.' Ma ladled out onion soup and passed round toast and grated cheese.

'It might be something about the hat,' I agreed.

Bogus, like many lost dogs, was of unknown breed. When Josh visited the Dogs' Home he came away with Bogus. Why not some other dog? Why this particular one, we had asked. How could he bear to go to such a place?

Josh had looked at the dogs, poodles and terriers and mongrels galore. They had all been very eager to come. They asked by whining and yelping and wagging their tails, standing against the bars. They had begged to become gladly, obligingly, Josh's dog. Josh, who was thirteen at the time, had found the choice impossible. He knew that he could only have one dog, one which was not too large and expensive to feed. A dog who was, if possible, young. Josh had had no idea what all those dogs wanting him for a master would do to him; the pressure of having to make a choice was great. He burst into tears and turned to leave, to get away from that hopeful barking, those wagging tails.

But then he saw Bogus. Bogus had not barked, yelped or wagged his tail. 'He was sitting there,' Josh told us, 'just sitting there looking at me, and then he turned away, as though I wouldn't do.'

27

Josh wiped his tears, paid the money and got the man in charge to ring up Ma to confirm that the dog would have a responsible family. He led Bogus home to Croydon and not once did Bogus look pleased or grateful. We made him welcome and he tolerated us. His coat was long and silky like a collie and his tail abnormally long. His ears could never make up their mind whether to stand up like an Alsatian's or to flop across the top of his head like the flaps of a deerstalker. His paws had been worn when he was brought in, the Dogs' Home man said, the nails raw. He had only one claim to beauty – his eyes. Bright, intelligent eyes which, undoglike, outstared us from under a fine fringe. When, that evening, we settled down to supper, and Bogus in his basket groaned, we realized that if by selling all the pictures and putting the money on False Start our lives had changed, Bogus's life had changed, too.

'Tomorrow,' said Pa, holding out his bowl for more soup, 'tomorrow we shall all go to Messrs Squire, Close and Sword to buy Haphazard House and take Bogus with us.'

'Hear, hear,' said Josh, and Bogus, hearing his name mentioned, groaned again.

'Did you say – ' our mother gave our father more soup, 'did you say you had to buy a television? Not like you, is it?'

'I threw my father's out of the window.' Pa accepted the soup.

'You know, love, your manic exaggerations are a fearfully bad example to the children. More soup, Lisa?'

'Yes, please,' I said and passed my plate.

We set off, squashed into the Mini, parents in front, Ma driving, Josh, Bogus and me behind. Pa wore the hat.

Ma drove into London, via Chelsea, Eaton Square, down

the Mall and up into St James's Square; not as Pa had driven
the day before, over by Westminster Bridge, his favourite.
Driving round the square, we passed the warden sticking a
ticket under the wiper of a Rolls. Ma found a space.

'Morning,' shouted Pa.

The warden looked up and scowled. 'That meter's out of
order,' he said.

'Oh, good,' I said.

'Oh, it's you,' said the warden, relaxing the folds round
his nose in a smile. 'Didn't recognize you in that get-up.
Going slumming or something?' He looked at our parents.

'No, no, this is the real me,' said Pa. 'What you saw
yesterday was a disguise. May I introduce my wife? Darling,
this is Mr Bailey who we told you about.' Ma held out her
hand. 'And my son Josh, and our dog Bogus.'

The warden shook our hands and stooped to pat Bogus
who endured it. 'Going to buy your house then?'

'Yes,' we nodded.

'Come and stay, Mr Bailey. I hear you are interested in
toads,' said Ma.

'I am. Toads and grass snakes. I'm a bit of an ornitholo-
gist, too, but you don't get much opportunity in London:
sparrows, thrushes, blackbirds, mostly.'

'Will the car be all right here?' asked Pa.

'I'll keep an eye on it. Can't give you a ticket if the
meter don't tick over, can I? This one,' he smacked the
Rolls, 'been here hours. Some people are made of money.
I forgot, you're rich yourself.' He grinned at Pa and
moved away.

'That job represents power,' said Pa. 'Come on.'

We trooped in single file to Squire, Close and Sword, just
off the square. The office had thick pile carpet. A young
man sat at a desk with three telephones on it, and a girl sat at
another, typing – tip-tap-tippity-tap.

'Can I help you?' The young man rose, his eyes – taking in
our group – took us for people who had come in to ask the
way. He looked with distaste at Bogus, and aloofly at Pa in
his jeans. He clearly thought our mother pretty, Josh and I
not worthy of attention.

29

'I want to buy a house called Haphazard House.' Pa spoke from a foot above the young man's head.

'Haphazard House?' The young man – little more than a youth – shook his head. 'I don't think – ' he began.

'Ask someone who knows.'

'Oh yes. Will you wait a moment? Take a seat.' He indicated an armchair near the door. We remained standing. 'I'll ask.' He picked up one of the telephones. 'Mr Spruce? There's – er – a person here asking about a house – Haphazard House. Is it on our books, sir? Shall I? Oh – yes sir, certainly, at once.' He looked dismayed. 'Will you come this way, please?' We followed him.

'What name, please?' he asked dubiously.

'Fuller. Andrew Fuller.'

We reached a door with 'B. Spruce' written on it. The youth knocked, a voice said, 'Come in'. The youth said, 'Mr Andrew Fuller, sir,' and stood aside to let us pass.

A very suave man stood up behind a grand desk and catching sight of Pa, sprang forward, exclaiming, 'Fuller, Not *the* Andrew Fuller?'

'Well,' said Pa, 'I'm not Fullers' cakes. I just paint.'

'That's what I mean. I am thrilled to meet you! I was at your exhibition only two days ago. Alas, for me – of course not for you – every picture was sold. I had hoped, well hoped – ' His voice trailed as his eyes took in our group. 'What an extraordinary dog! Oh, I beg your pardon, and is this Mrs Fuller?' He shook hands with Ma.

'We are the little Fullers,' Josh introduced us.

'Won't you all sit down?' Mr Spruce ranged chairs in a semicircle.

'Thanks.' We all sat down. Bogus remained standing, staring at Mr Spruce from under his eyebrows.

'Haphazard House,' said Pa. 'I want to buy it.'

'You advertised it in *Country Life*,' I said.

'In what issue?'

'An old one.' Pa was patient.

'Oh, I see.' Mr Spruce smiled. He obviously saw nothing except us, and we were not the kind of people he was used to. He pressed a button. 'Elizabeth, look up Haphazard

House – yes, that's what I said.' His voice grew acid. 'These girls – ' he said to Ma. 'One cannot get a good secretary these days. The turnover in a firm like this is so big the name had slipped my mind.'

'Is it sold?' asked Josh. Mr Spruce, who obviously had no wish to do business with children, gave an irritated frown. 'If it was advertised in an old issue – '

'At the dentist,' I said.

'There you are. They hang on to their old mags until they fall to pieces. People don't mind what they look at when they are waiting for the chair.' Pa looked stony.

'I read *Private Eye*,' said Josh. 'The dentist's called Heath.' Mr Spruce ignored him.

A girl with red hair walked into the room. 'This what you want?' She plonked a pile of papers in front of Mr Spruce and walked out. 'You see what I mean?' Mr Spruce looked at Ma.

'Like to paint her,' said Pa. 'You don't see many of those Burne Jones types.'

'But she can't even spell.' Mr Spruce looked again towards Ma for sympathy.

'Nor can I,' said Ma, giving none.

'Well,' Mr Spruce pulled himself together. 'Let's see now. Haphazard House. Great hall, one half demolished in 1949, kitchen, eight bedrooms, barns, walled garden – '

'Where is it?' I asked.

'On the Devon and Cornwall borders. Rather remote, I fear. Ah yes, let's see. Twenty acres, mostly woodland. Would make unusual gentleman's residence.' His eyebrows rose. 'That might have been better put.'

'I'm an unusual gentleman,' said Pa. 'Is it still for sale?'

'Well, yes it is. I must in all honesty tell you this house needs a lot doing to it. It has no electricity.'

'Suits me.'

'No main drainage.'

'Don't mind that.'

'It's own water supply.'

'Fine. No filthy chloride.'

'No road to it, just a track.'

'We don't mind that,' Josh and I chorused.

'The house was struck by lightning in 1949 and partly burned down. Nothing has been done to it since.'

'Why not?' I was curious.

'Well, the owner died and, I remember now, the cousin who inherited it put it in our hands to sell.'

'Fine, fine,' Pa fidgeted. 'I'll buy it.'

'We will have it,' I said. 'We said so.'

'Yes, you did.' Mr Spruce didn't seem to like children, but that was okay by me.

'The house,' – Mr Spruce addressed himself to my parents – 'is furnished.'

'What with?'

'Well, beds, tables, chairs. You have to take the furniture with the house.'

'I expect it's worm-eaten,' said Josh.

'We can sell it if we don't like it,' I said. Mr Spruce looked pained and sucked in his breath.

'If it had been valuable the cousin would have flogged it,' said Josh.

'Of course he would,' I agreed. 'It's probably very ugly.' I looked round Mr Spruce's office. I didn't think much of his taste – characterless and respectable. I wondered how he could have liked my father's pictures.

'Where did he come from, this heir?' asked Josh.

'Los Angeles, I believe.' Mr Spruce looked at Pa, not caring for Josh any more than me.

'Have you seen it?' I asked.

'No.' He looked at Ma like a witness in court answering to the Judge when questioned by Counsel.

'We'll have it,' said Pa.

'I'll give you an order to view, of course.'

'We'll have it, I said.' Pa was growing irritable.

'I must tell you, Mr Fuller, we must be strictly honest, that the house is supposed to be haunted.'

'Hah! I said I'd buy it. Why beat about the bush? You want to sell it, don't you? How much? I'll give you a cheque and have done with it.'

'It's not as easy as that. You have to have the documents drawn up – '

'Look,' said Pa ominously. 'I have the money, right? You get on with the legal side. You settle with my wife. She may not be able to spell but she's not stupid. Just tell me how much.' He produced his cheque book with the panache of a villain drawing his gun.

Mr. Spruce mentioned a huge sum. Pa wrote a cheque, handed it to Mr Spruce, rose to his feet and said, 'Thanks, Spruce. You settle with my wife. All right, darling?' Ma nodded. 'Then we'll meet you at my father's flat. I want to see Old X-ray. Giving birth at her age isn't easy, when it's for the first time.'

We trooped out. 'She'll soon settle his hash,' said Pa. 'Come on, we'll take the car. She can take a taxi.'

'A ghost, how super!' Josh jogged towards the Mini with Bogus.

'Just a selling point. When a property won't move they throw in a ghost to give it something it hasn't got.'

'Haphazard hasn't got a lot of things.' Josh waited while Bogus sniffed at a lamp-post.

'Haphazard will be all right when it's got us.' Pa began to sing. 'I had plenty of money, I poured it down the drain – ' He leapt into the air and did an *entrechat*. 'I don't believe that fellow liked us, Lisa. I don't think he took to Bogus or your teeth, your true-blue Tory teeth.' He caught my hand in one of his and Josh's in the other and we danced in a circle round Bogus's lamp-post. Bogus stopped what he was about to do and began to bay.

'Come on, for goodness sake, we will attract a crowd.' Pa ran to the Mini as though pursued.

'Did you get it?' asked the warden, who was prowling by.

'Yes,' said Josh. 'It's got a ghost.'

'That's nice.' The warden didn't believe him. 'And toads?'

'Forgot to ask. Sorry,' said Pa.

'Sure to be toads.' Josh began pushing Bogus into the Mini.

'Dog will like it there.' The warden looked wistful.

'This is the address.' Pa snatched a parking ticket from a nearby windscreen and wrote, Haphazard House, Coldharbour, Devon/Cornwall border.

'Coldharbour? You being funny?'

33

'No, that's on the prospectus. It's half-burned down, a ruin more or less.'

'Toads like ruins.' The warden memorized the address and put the ticket back under the windscreen.

'So do birds,' said Josh, getting in beside Bogus, 'and snakes.'

'Will you tell my wife when she comes to take a taxi?'

'Okay,' said the warden. 'You left her any money to pay for it?'

Pa clapped his hand to his head. 'No, I haven't. Oh Lord!'

'I'll advance it,' said the warden, already a family friend.

'That's very good of you.'

'You repay me when I come and stay. I'll ring up from Coldharbour.'

'I don't know whether there's a telephone. There's no electricity, no drains and no road.' Pa pressed the starter and the Mini leapt to life.

'You sure there's a house?' The warden was sarcastic.

'Quite sure.' Pa settled the hat firmly on his head and shot backwards into the traffic.

When we reached Grandpa's house Josh rang the bell while Pa eased the Mini into a gap beside a van painted with nymphs and daisies. This odd conveyance housed the neighbourhood cats when it rained and served as a place to chat on summer evenings for a squatting community befriended by our grandfather. Though refusing to leave his flat, he felt an affinity towards the squatters since they, too, were threatened with eviction.

While we waited on the doorstep the owner of the nymph-and-daisy van came up carrying a plastic bag.

'You going up to old Mr Fuller?'

'Yes, if he'll let us in.'

'His cat's ill.'

'Old X-ray?'

'Yes. This is for her. Will you take it up. I'm late for a date.'

'What is it?'

'Chicken livers to tempt her appetite. She's refusing food.'

'All right,' I said. The young man ran off. 'Pa, Old X-ray's ill.'

'Doesn't he answer the bell?' Our parent was impatient. 'I'm not surprised she's ill, having a kitten at her age.' Pa stepped back into the street, cupped his hands and roared, 'FATHER!'

A window opened and a bunch of keys shot down to clink in the street. Pa opened the front door and we raced up.

Grandpa sat hunched in his armchair with Old X-ray in his arms. His face was all lines and furrows, tears coursed down beside his nose to drop on his chest. His veined and bony hands held Old X-ray stretched across his knees, her eyes shut, body limp. She looked like a sad, little body swept to the side of the street after failing to make the necessary dash to safety. Grandpa did not look up. In one hand he held the kitten close to Old X-ray's flank. It made futile swimming movements with its paws. Its eyes were still shut.

'We brought the chicken livers.' Josh held out the bag.

'Too late I think.' Grandpa was gruff.

Pa took off the hat and knelt beside Grandpa to look closer. Old X-ray's breathing was so frail we could hardly see it.

'She used to romp in that van,' Grandpa muttered. 'She seemed to enjoy herself. Not much of a life for a cat of spirit, living alone with an old man. She was bored so I let her romp.'

'Father.' Pa gently removed Old X-ray from Grandpa, holding her, kitten and all, close to his chest.

'Is she dead?' Grandpa's eyes were so full of tears he could not see. I heard Josh gulp. He smacked the bag of livers angrily down on the floor. Bogus stood up on his hind

35

legs against Pa. He took Old X-ray from Pa and carrying her – tail and legs limp, head nodding in death – put her into Pa's hat on the floor. Then he came back and removed the kitten and put it, too, into the hat, nosed it against Old X-ray and stood back, his tail wagging, staring hopefully. Nothing happened. Bogus barked loudly in Old X-ray's ear. Old X-ray opened her eyes, sneezed, shot out a paw and scratched Bogus, turned to the kitten and licked its head roughly. The kitten began to suck, and Old X-ray to purr. We let out our breath.

Old X-ray looked at us with contempt, curled herself comfortably in the hat and finishing with the kitten, lifted a back leg and began to wash.

'One would almost think,' Grandpa blew his nose hugely, 'that hat had some special quality.'

'I bought it at a perfectly respectable shop,' said Pa defensively. 'I didn't want people to recognize me at my exhibition. A hat seemed better than a false nose. I'm a shy man.'

'What do you want a false nose for?' In his relief, Grandpa was more than ready to pick a quarrel.

'I didn't want a false nose.' Pa rose to the bait.

'Now, now.' Ma came into the room. 'What's going on? There's a girl downstairs who says Old X-ray is ill.'

'Well, she isn't.' Grandpa was belligerent. 'How on earth can you live with a man with a false nose? You should have more sense. I told you what he was like when you agreed to marry him.'

'You've been crying.' Ma attacked in her turn.

'Hay fever,' said Grandpa.

'The girl said something about chicken livers. Has Old X-ray had any?' Ma had made her point.

'Not yet.' Grandpa looked contrite.

'Shall I chop some?'

'Yes, please.'

Ma took the livers and went into the kitchen. I followed.

'What's all this in aid of?' said Ma.

I told her.

'Well,' she said, slicing livers. 'Well, why not?' She

expected no answer and we took the liver to Old X-ray who ate it noisily. Since Bogus was drooling, he got some, too.

'Have you heard,' said Ma, after giving Grandpa a searching look to assure herself he was all right, 'have you heard that we are on the move to the country?'

'That fellow,' said Grandpa, after listening to the story of our buying Haphazard House, 'that fellow who bought these livers – saved the cat's life.' Ma quelled us with a look. 'That young fellow does moving jobs, owns the van outside, the one painted with daisies and birds. He could move your furniture. He and two people I know at the "squat" can help,' said Grandpa, revived.

'It doesn't move,' exclaimed Josh. 'It just sits there.'

'That's what you think.' Grandpa laughed like a concertina with a tear in it. 'Doesn't move! They put spare tyres on and whoops, off they go!'

'Who are they?'

'Tall girl who pretends to be American. And a short chap, and that young David. You could put the odds and bobs like your easel in that.'

'Thanks.' Pa was huffy.

'I bet it's the man and the girl we saw at the exhibition,' I said. 'She called Pa "Reverend", Grandpa, she – '

'What would she have called him if he'd worn his false nose? Coco?'

'Don't start that again.' Ma was firm. 'You'll wake Old X-ray.'

'Got room for me in this chateau of yours?' said Grandpa, unrepentent. 'I'm coming, too. Seems to me none of us can do without this Panama so we'd better stick together,' which was as near to admitting the magic of the hat as he was prepared to go.

'We'd love it,' I said.

'Right. I'll travel in the van with my cats.'

'I wonder what the village of Coldharbour will say when they see us arriving,' Josh pondered.

'Don't make difficulties, boy. They will think we are strolling players, especially if your father wears his false nose. Or a pop group.'

Ma put her arms round Grandpa and kissed him. 'Just stop, darling,' she whispered. 'We've all had rather an exhausting day. I'll make some tea and we can watch your lovely television.'

'You can't. That clown threw it out of the window.'

When it was time for us to go home to Croydon, Ma gently lifted Old X-ray out of the hat and put her on Grandpa's sofa. Old X-ray's sides began to heave and she gave a pitiful mew.

'She was happy in the hat; what do you want to disturb her for?'

Pa put Old X-ray back in the Panama where she instantly revived.

We looked at one another. Nobody spoke for a while. Grandpa gazed into some faraway land. Pa, with his hands behind his head, stretched his long legs, arched his back, and finally said, 'Ahem.'

Josh and I clattered downstairs with Bogus. When Pa or Ma said 'ahem' it meant they would rather discuss something without us being there. Propping open the front door with an empty milk bottle, we sat on the steps to watch the world go by, with Bogus between us on his hunkers. People passed carrying parcels, lurching on aged legs. Neither Josh nor I was prepared to speak first.

Presently we heard voices and, from the basement occupied by squatters, two figures emerged. I recognized the tall girl and the short man who had been at the exhibition.

'That's the girl and the man who thought Pa's portrait of Ma was a bathtub,' I said.

'Thought you said hipbath. It's not the same thing.'

The man reached up and put his arm round the girl's waist. She laughed. 'Edward, don't do that.'

'Makes me feel dependent,' said the man. The girl laughed again. They walked across the street to the van.

'Time it had a wash,' said the man who, though short, looked strong, with thick arms and legs and a bushy beard.

'It looks okay. It would be different if we were going to use it. Picturesque is what it is.'

Unable to restrain himself, Josh got up and went across to them. Bogus and I followed. 'Our grandfather says you might help us to move,' he said abruptly.

The two looked startled. 'Is that old man the Council are evicting your grandfather?'

'Yes.'

'Oh dear.' The girl looked sympathetic. 'He's lost the battle. Got to move. Like us in the squat. It's final. Any day now we all go. But where, one asks? Where?'

'He hasn't told us.'

'He's valiant. He wouldn't want to upset you. He has to go to alternative accommodation. He'll hate it. We all like him. He invites us up to watch his television and see his cat. Some vandal threw his telly out of the window. Can you believe it?' The girl swayed in her long skirt. She no longer talked American. 'It smashed to bits. Might have hit the van.' Edward patted it, his hand leaving marks on its dusty bonnet.

'Don't you ever get a parking ticket?' Josh wished to change the subject.

'The character who shares the van, David,' – Edward waved his arm – 'told someone, who told someone else, who let it be known to the police, that there's a voodoo on it.' He laughed.

'Or in it.' The girl laughed. 'My name's Victoria,' she said. 'What's yours?'

We introduced ourselves.

'Do you ever drive it?' Josh, I could see, was checking.

'We did, but we can't afford to tax it any more.'

'Would you hire it if we got it taxed?' I asked.

'Sure, but who to and what for?' Edward thought we

were joking. 'It's nice for the cats, that's all. Your grandfather's old cat used to frolic about with the Siamese from
the papershop.'

'She's had a kitten,' I said. 'It nearly killed her; she's
twelve.'

'We heard. David told us; said she wasn't well. She all
right now?'

'We met him. Yes, she's fine.' Josh was measuring them
in his mind. 'Would you and your friend David rent the
van? We are moving to the country. Grandpa says why
don't we all go – he's coming, too – in your van, if you'll
take us.'

Victoria and Edward stared. 'Who are you?' Victoria
said. 'I've seen you somewhere.'

'We met yesterday at Pa's exhibition.'

'So we did, but you looked different.'

'Well, Pa's shy. You called him "Reverend". We were
incognito,' I explained.

'The guy in the funny hat, your father, is he the painter?'

'Yes. It's not a funny hat, it's a Panama. It's funny in
another way, it's – '

'Josh,' I warned.

'How do you mean? How funny?'

'Pa threw the television out of the window,' I said
desperately. 'He hates television and "progress". He's an
artist. He's being driven mad in Croydon, that's why we are
moving. We've bought a house with the money he got from
his pictures – ' I paused. Why was I telling our business to
total strangers?

'He put all the money on a horse,' said Josh boastfully,
'and it won. He bought Haphazard House where we're
going. Will you take us, and will your friend help with the
van?'

'Why not? We all have to move.' Edward sounded
unsurprised. 'Did your father paint your teeth blue?'

'No,' I said indignantly.

'I only meant that if he is a painter who chucks televisions
around he might have a go at your teeth.'

'Well, I'm blowed!' Pa had crept up on us from behind.

'Here's a pin in Newton's eye.' He shook hands with Victoria. 'And who are you, really?'

'A furniture-removing team,' said Edward. 'Your kids are hiring us.'

'And will you do it?' Pa seemed to like the look of Edward and Victoria.

'The van isn't taxed; otherwise it's no problem.'

'What problem can't be solved?' said Pa. He was looking at Victoria as a suitable model, weighing up the contrast of flowing skirts and angular elbows.

'A holiday in the country,' she said. 'Super! The last we had was in a grotty place in Portugal where we got diarrhoea and nearly died. That's where we met David and bought the van. No more "abroad" for us now we have Baby.'

'We have a baby,' explained Edward.

'One baby won't make much odds. There are four of us and my father,' said Pa.

'And Bogus,' I said. 'And Old X-ray and her kitten.'

'We should all fit in all right.' Pa looked very pleased. 'By the way, would you like to come to supper? My wife seems to think we should stay the night and keep an eye on Old X-ray. She sent me out to buy food, so why don't you come, too? Only makes two more.' I had never seen Pa so expansive to strangers.

Victoria gave Edward's arm a little tweak. 'Say yes. May we bring Baby? He's called Arnold.'

'Arnold!' Pa looked aghast. 'What a name!'

'It's a family name. We just call him Baby.'

'Then bring him.'

'Thanks, we will.' They moved away, Victoria taking long strides in her trailing skirt, Edward hurrying to keep up with his short, thick legs.

'Now then, you two.' Pa sat down abruptly on the kerb. 'I have to talk to you.' He paused.

'Go ahead,' said Josh encouragingly, folding his legs under him and sitting beside Pa. The pause lengthened.

'Go on,' I said, standing above them. One could sit anywhere in the country, I thought. Pa, when he stood up,

might find he'd been sitting on some bubblegum or worse.
'Go on, do,' I said.

'Sit down, then.'

I crouched beside them, an inch above the pavement.
Bogus lolled indolently against the railings.

'It's – ' said Pa. 'Well, it's – oh Lord, it's so *ridiculous*. It's
the hat! I mean, it's mad, it's illogical, but your mother and
grandfather and I, well – um – we all – um – think – '

'Know,' said Josh quietly.

'The animals know,' I said.

'Well, if you all know I needn't explain.' Pa looked
relieved. 'We've got ourselves a magic hat and there it is.'

'Yes,' we said.

'Well then, let's go and buy some supper. We had better
keep it quiet or we will find ourselves psychoanalysed or
something. All we do is keep our traps shut until we take
refuge in this Haphazard House, if it exists.'

'Oh, it exists.' Josh got up, smacking the dust from his
bottom. 'We all saw its specification in writing, didn't we?'

'Never believe all you read,' said Pa, rising up tall.

'Shall we tell Victoria and Edward?' I asked.

'No, no, no. They might not trust us with the van.'

'What about the lad, David?' Josh liked calling people
older than himself 'lad'.

'No, certainly not, he might think we were liars, to say the
least.' And Pa began to sing to an improvised tune, 'Liars,
lyres, tooraliah.'

'I think,' said Josh as we headed for the supermarket, 'I
think he is afraid of getting out of its orbit. He can't wear it
while Old X-ray is in it and he's not brave enough to go
home without it, so we stay the night.'

'What are you two whispering about?' Pa called from the
corner of the street. 'Lies to the sound of a lyre,' he sang.

10

By the time Old X-ray's kitten opened its eyes, Pa had taxed the van and got Edward, who was practical, to check the engine. Grandpa gave his kitchen utensils and furniture to the squatters who were moving elsewhere. In Croydon Pa ordered that we travel light. Ma ruthlessly stripped us of all our possessions.

'I want,' she said, 'to have nothing to remember Croydon by.' Now that we were leaving, we admitted none of us had ever been happy there.

Pa, wearing the hat which Old X-ray had left after one night, settled up with our landlords, paid bills and packed his painting things.

Bogus was the only member of the family who, having nothing to do, was able to lounge about watching. He seemed better able than anyone to grasp a situation none of us was prepared to discuss. We had bought Haphazard House. We had made three new friends – Victoria, Edward and David; if you counted Baby, four. As soon as we were ready we would all travel west in the Mini and the painted van. There was little discussion, somehow – it seemed better not. We decided to start at dawn. Josh and I had washed and polished the van. Pa repainted some of the daisies and added some buttercups. We tidied up the Mini. Both vehicles were full of petrol and the tyres checked.

From their basement Victoria helped David bring four brass figures which they screwed into sockets at the corners of the van's roof. The first was of a girl in flimsy draperies, trailing a garland of flowers. Next a fat lady, arms folded across her chest, in the 'They shall not pass' attitude of French war memorials. Then Death carrying a

43

scythe, and a dancing Harlequin. Edward fetched a rag and some Brasso and gave them an energetic polish.

David grinned at our surprised faces. 'This van was a hearse when I bought her. Nothing like a repaint job.' He ran a friendly hand over the floral work. 'Be back as soon as I can.' He ran off.

'Home, and we've never seen it,' I said to Josh who looked at me strangely, about to speak, but changed his mind.

'You must rest,' said Ma, passing us on her way up to Grandpa. 'We have far to go and need all our strength. The journey may be terrible. Lend me the hat, Andrew. You can't wear it all the time.' She took the hat; Pa parted with it reluctantly. 'A dawn start will save us all the holiday traffic hassle,' she said, pressing the hat on to her head and closing her eyes. 'That's better.' She handed me the hat. 'Take it in turns,' she said as she left us.

Victoria, with Baby asleep in her arms, came along the pavement with Edward. They sat on the steps without speaking, and we watched Pa pacing the street.

'I can't rest,' said Josh. 'I feel something might go wrong. There's an ominous feel in the air. Don't you feel it? Ominous.'

'Oh, shut up,' I said, and passed him the hat. 'Your turn.'

'Mine next.' Victoria was nervous. Edward put his arm round her. 'Silly,' he said gently. 'It's a *holiday*.' He pressed his bushy face close to hers so that his beard tickled her nose. She sneezed; laughed apologetically. 'Something might go wrong,' she whispered. Josh handed the hat to Edward who held it above their two heads, smiling.

'Where is David?' I asked anxiously.

'Gone to fetch his girlfriend,' chorused Victoria and Edward.

'There isn't room for another person.' Josh looked worried. 'As it is we shall be a tight fit. He never said – '

'Here he comes,' Victoria exclaimed as David rounded the corner of the street walking fast. 'Got her?' she cried.

'Yes,' David looked triumphant. 'They never count heads accurately.'

'What's he on about? He hasn't got anyone with him. David, they say you're bringing a girl. There isn't room for anyone else. Pa said it's a tight fit.'

David stood looking up at us on the steps. He put his hand carefully into his pocket and held it palm upwards with a white mouse in it.

'There's room for Mouse,' he said and stroked the mouse with his finger. The mouse sniffed towards us, twitching her nose, whisking her whiskers in curiosity, then began to wash her ears with brisk movements of her paws. In the lamplit street the little animal looked ghostly, her pink eyes catching the light like tiny torches.

'I've stolen her.' David sat beside me carefully. 'I've been working for a hospital. The people use mice for experiments. Mouse has had four families, all gone.'

'Disgusting,' I said. 'I'd rather die than Mouse.' I felt anger.

'That's as may be. Vivisection's not nice. Mice don't ask to help humanity. I've grown very fond of this particular mouse and decided she shall have a natural death.'

'She won't have a nice death if she meets Old X-ray.' Josh peered at the mouse who was looking about her with interest.

'That's where you're wrong.' David put the mouse into his pocket. 'This mouse terrifies cats.'

'Tell us another,' Josh jeered.

David smiled. 'You wait and see.'

The stuffy night seemed to go on for ever. The pubs closed. People and cars grew fewer. The great orchestra of London faded to a rumble; its menacing noise jollied by the occasional blast of a police car. Some sleepless person let a radio play till it went off the air. Pa stopped his restless pacing and joined us to sit on the steps.

'The street air is stale. It smells,' Josh grumbled.

'Tomorrow will be different,' I said.

'You are looking very pretty, Miss Pin,' said Pa. He had lately taken to calling Victoria 'Miss Pin' in memory of our first meeting. 'Where, by the way, are those thick glasses?'

'Those are my picture-show glasses. I wear them to minimize the shock.'

Pa looked uncertain whether to take offence. David laughed, stroking Mouse gently.

'It's just her way,' said Edward, taking Baby from Victoria. 'Isn't it, Baby? Your mum's a funny girl.' Baby began to dribble on Edward's beard. 'She doesn't need glasses.' Pa looked suspicious. 'It's just her way.'

'Is everybody ready?' Ma came out with Grandpa carrying Old X-ray and the kitten, Angelique.

'Yes,' we all cried, springing to our feet. 'Yes, we are,' we answered joyfully. Whatever had been stalking the streets paused. The dawn was a gleam in the east bringing hope, fending off fear.

A sudden yell from Grandpa and Old X-ray flashed past and was gone.

'Oh no!' Ma cried. 'Oh no!' she wailed. 'Who let her out of the basket?'

'Oh my Lord!' David pocketed Mouse. 'Which way did she go?'

'It's still dark, she may be quite close. If everybody would stop making such a noise – '

'Stop the row, it will only frighten her more.' Grandpa, trembling with anger, stood small and old on the pavement. 'She isn't used to going out.'

We looked under the Mini and the van. We looked under all the cars in the street. No Old X-ray.

'Puss, puss, puss,' called Victoria.

'She hates being called Puss,' shouted Grandpa.

'Don't shout, Grandpa, you'll scare her.'

'I'll shout if I want to. She's my cat. She likes me shouting.'

'Surely she will turn up,' said David.

'Nothing sure about it.' Grandpa, in the half-light, looked wizened with anxiety.

'What shall we do?' Josh asked.

'Keep calm,' Ma answered. 'The most difficult thing in the world.'

We stood on the doorstep and conferred. We decided that

Grandpa, with the kitten, should wait on the doorstep while
we searched.

I had never realized until that morning what a lot of cats
there were in Grandpa's neighbourhood. Black cats, white
cats, tabbies, gingers, Siamese, all out and about in the
streets, but no sign of Old X-ray, no sign whatever; and
nobody had seen her, not the milkman, the postman, nor
the police.

'What does it look like?' people asked.

'A calico cat: tortoiseshell with black ears, white tummy,
golden eyes, white face.'

'No,' they said. 'Sorry.' And went about their business.

It grew light and the streets filled. We came back to
Grandpa to check, but each time he just shook his head. 'No
sign,' he said. Angelique, becoming hungry, mewed.

After my sixth search I came back to find a small crowd
gathered around Grandpa. My spirits soared but soon fell.
Someone had asked him what we were all doing. Why were
we leaving London?

'To bury ourselves in the country. To get away from the
noise, the people, the smells, the aggression. If it were not
for that cat we would be well on our way.' Pa was desperate.

'I shan't leave. Wild horses won't move me. We should
have known the portents. False Start, indeed!' Grandpa
suddenly nipped back through the front door, slammed it
and was gone, cat basket and all. David came along the
street. I saw Victoria speak anxiously to him. Usually so
calm, he clutched his head, then threw up his arms and flung
back his head like some medieval martyr. He remained in
that attitude, his finger pointing. High above our heads,
looking down from the parapet of the house, peered Old
X-ray, her eyes yellow in the morning sun, her ears back,
pink nose querying. Very slowly she stretched down a
tentative paw then withdrew it. Above us the top window
opened and Grandpa, white faced, stared down at us.

'Look out!' cried Josh, as Old X-ray sprang, landing
neatly on his head, scrambling along his back into the flat.

'She has nine lives.' Ma was weeping with laughter. 'We
had forgotten that.'

'I had not.' Pa inserted himself behind the wheel of the Mini.

'It was my fault. I'm sorry.' David spoke confidentially to Ma. 'The cat must have seen Mouse. Sit quiet now,' – he patted a small bulge in his pocket – 'or you'll be causing more trouble.'

'Hurry,' shouted Pa from the Mini. 'Hurry. We are late.' He started the engine.

A chill wind blew down the street filling me with fear. The others were affected, too. We pushed Grandpa with his cats into the van. Victoria, looking pale, clambered in carrying Baby. Edward and David slammed the doors. David got behind the wheel. As Josh got into the Mini, Bogus leapt in with the hat in his jaws. Pa snatched it and put it on. 'Follow,' Pa called to David, 'follow me.' David shouted something and waved his arm. Sitting on the back seat with Bogus pressed against me I heard a voice calling, 'Lisa, Lisa,' but the street was empty when I looked back. I could have sworn it was the voice I had thought I heard at Mr Heath's, the dentist.

We drove through the afternoon into the evening and into the night until we stopped in the square of a sleeping village and Pa said in a voice I had never heard before,

'This is Coldharbour.'

Stillness. We gathered close together in the road. I had never experienced stillness. The quiet was awesome. My tired ears, full of the sound of traffic and the Mini's engine, took a while to adjust.

Then I heard the cooling engines click, and Victoria sigh. There was a full moon. The shadow of a church tower fell across our group. The church clock ticked, the minute hand jerked, the clock whirred, then struck twice.

The square was small; four roads led from it. On tiptoe Josh and I explored. There was a post office and general store, and that was all in the way of shops. The village was very small, the church of cathedral proportions. We went back to the others.

'Which way now?' Even Grandpa didn't speak above a whisper.

'I don't know.' Pa tipped the hat to the back of his head.

'We cannot wake anybody at this hour,' whispered Ma.

'Why not?' Grandpa looked worn out.

'Darling, just look at us.' Ma grinned. I could see her teeth in the moonlight. 'We'd make an awful impression. We look like a pop festival in this van. Or refugees.'

'Maybe, but we must ask where Haphazard is. We can't spend the rest of the night here.' Pa spoke reasonably enough.

'Doesn't the – ' I began.

'No, it *doesn't*,' Pa hissed. He tipped the hat forward. '*Nothing*.'

'Oh.' I felt betrayed. I believed magic worked best at night. With this moon the night was magical.

'Look!' Edward spoke low. 'What's wrong with your dog?'

Bogus was leaping about, jumping and bowing, his ears flapping, tail wagging, he growled and whined throatily. He ran a little way down the road and looked back.

'That creature wants us to follow it.' Grandpa spoke emphatically. Bogus pranced back then ran off again to look back, invitingly. From the van Old X-ray dropped down to the road and, with tail high, went leaping to join Bogus. The two animals set off side by side.

'Push the cars down the slope, then we won't wake the village.' Pa scrambled into the Mini and Ma gave it a shove, then jumped in as it moved.

Victoria gave the van a heave, helped by Josh. We rolled down the slope clear of the village before starting the engine.

Ahead, Bogus and Old X-ray trotted, Bogus steadily, Old X-ray in the manner of cats, in dashes and stops. After a while the animals stopped and Old X-ray jumped back into the van. Bogus quickened his pace, running hard, ears and tail streaming back. Josh and I sat with David in the van.

At a crossroads Bogus turned left. The road grew narrow. By the light of the moon I had my first glimpse of Haphazard: a low house, lying under a hill at the top of a valley on the far side of a wood.

'That's Haphazard. I recognize it.' Josh was crying.

'Josh, you're crying.'

'I'm not. I'm happy.' He wiped tears away with the back of his hand.

'It's a trick of the imagination,' said David. 'That house is hidden by the wood.'

'But you saw it, too.' I looked sidelong at David.

'Sure I did. I've worn that hat, haven't I?'

'Oh,' I said, digesting this fact.

We followed the Mini into the wood. 'Lovely wood!' I was excited. The wood was dark, mysterious, a wood we were to know later to be full of oak and beech, hazel and holly, here and there a wild cherry and at one end thickets of blackthorn and briar. The track wound twisting through the trees, dipping to a stream which we forded. Then we were out of the wood and had arrived. Looking up at the house, I thought somebody watched us from a window, but the moon went behind a cloud. When I looked again there was no one.

Bogus was battering at the door with his paws, whimpering, snuffling, growling.

'Who has the key?' Grandpa got down from the van, holding the kitten. Old X-ray wound herself in and out between his feet, purring and arching her back. 'I have,' said Ma and gave a clumsy key to Pa.

Pa put the key in the lock, turned it, pushed. The door swung open and we all crowded in.

We walked into a long room with a stone floor. The moonlight pouring through the windows gave light. The walls were white and bare, the ceiling moulded; at the end of the room a large fireplace, a sofa on either side of it. Against the walls stood chairs and tables. There were doors in the inner wall. There was a smell of wood smoke. The effect in the moonlight was grey and muted white. Gentle.

One door led into another room, the walls lined with bookshelves. Above the fireplace hung a mirror which reflected our tired faces. There was ash in the grate. Oak chests stood against the wall, armchairs in the middle of the room; the windows looked into a cobbled courtyard.

A second door led into a cloakroom with a washbasin and lavatory in willow pattern. Ma pulled the chain and water rushed in an enthusiastic surge. 'That works, at least,' she said.

The third door led to a kitchen with a range such as I had seen in picture books, a tall dresser on which was a dinner service; pots and pans hung by the range.

'Nice job for somebody,' said Pa. 'They are copper.'

Beyond the kitchen was a scullery with a sink and wooden plate rack; in the corner a pump.

'Exercise for all.' Edward pumped, and below our feet water gurgled. Victoria turned on a tap and, after a few hiccups, water ran.

'How do we get upstairs? I want to go to bed.' Grandpa wheezed with fatigue. We looked for the stairs.

'In a house like this they would go up from the hall.'

We went back to the front of the house. Once the stairs had indeed gone up from here, but no more. The charred remains of a staircase went up the wall; no framework remained, just the black marks of fire.

'The fire was in 1949, the man said.' I remembered Squire, Close and Sword.

'Perhaps we were impetuous,' said Ma hesitantly.

'We can climb up,' – Josh pointed – 'up here. Look.' Against the house grew a magnolia. Josh and I began to climb it. The branches were tough; shiny leaves clattered as we climbed.

'Oh,' I exclaimed, 'it's in flower.' I touched a white flower which nearly overpowered me with its scent. Josh forced a casement window and we were soon looking down at the others from where the head of the stairs had been.

'So I can't go to bed.' Grandpa was furious. He turned, left the house and climbed back into the van.

'Perhaps there are back stairs,' said Pa below us. We searched and found back stairs but they had many treads missing. 'These can be repaired.' David examined them.

'How many rooms are there? I'm coming up.' Pa began to climb. 'The first thing we must get is a ladder.' He manoeuvred himself in at the window.

We found the bedrooms, a large bathroom with a fireplace in it; the bath and lavatory had mahogany surrounds. Every bedroom was empty except one in which furniture was piled, all heaped higgledy-piggledy.

'Deal with that later. Let's get down and see what more there is.' We followed Pa down the magnolia. 'Haphazard it certainly is.' He jumped the last six feet to the ground.

'Andrew, come here,' Ma called. We followed Pa.

'Look,' said Ma. She was kneeling by the hearth in the hall. 'This fire is still warm. The ash is glowing.'

'How peculiar.' Pa held his hand over the ash. 'See whether you can find some wood,' he said to us. 'Look in the outhouses.'

We found logs by the back door and soon the fire in the hall was ablaze. Ma looked puzzled. 'Let's get the other fires going.'

In the room next to the hall the ash was easily lit. We brought Grandpa in and he fell asleep with the kitten, stretched out on a sofa. The rest of us unloaded the van and the Mini before they were driven round to the yard at the back of the house.

Josh and I explored, moving away from the house across the grass.

Josh pointed. 'That's the tree which hid one part of the house when I first saw it, when you and Pa came home with the hat.'

An enormous oak with spreading branches stood fifty yards from the house. A bit awed by its size, we stared. An owl cried in the wood and we watched as one, and soon another, flew across the space from the wood to the tree. 'They must live there.'

'Josh – '

'Yes?'

'Nothing.' I had nearly mentioned the person at the window.

The grass sloped down to the wood. I sat down. I was tired. The grass was soft; I closed my eyes and lay back. I did not sleep for long. A wren's loud song awoke me; a rabbit thumped its feet. Far off a cock crowed and I heard the church clock strike. I kept my eyes tight shut. This dream was too good to leave. I had never smelled anything in my dreams before.

'Has anyone seen Lisa?' my mother's voice called in the house.

'No,' voices answered. 'No.'

'Perhaps she went with your father.'

'No, he was alone.'

'Ask Bogus to find her.'

I listened sleepily to their voices. In the wood a cock pheasant let out a warning 'cackcack'. Bogus licked my face and scraped at my shoulder with his paw. I opened a reluctant eye and he snuffed.

'Oh, Bogus, such a dream!'

'Lisa,' Ma called.

'Coming.' I sat up. The sun was up and I was hungry. I followed Bogus to the house. There were sounds of activity. Someone was working the pump. David came round the house pushing a barrow full of logs. I smelt bacon and coffee and followed my nose to the kitchen. Ma, wearing an apron, was at the range frying bacon, making coffee, laughing and talking. She looked so happy I stopped in the doorway and stared.

'Lisa darling, come and have breakfast.'

'Ma.' I went and kissed her. 'Ma.'

'What is it?' she asked.

'I don't know. I can't say.' She handed me a plate of bacon and fried bread. 'Go and sit by your grandfather. Eat it before it gets cold.' Grandpa, a cup of coffee in his hands, gave me a sharp look from under beetle brows. His fingers looked like knotted hawthorn twigs.

'You don't know what a hawthorn looks like.' He spoke low. I blushed. 'Nor could you recognize a wren or a pheasant.'

'No,' I whispered.

'Then hush,' he said.

'What did you say?' asked Ma.

'I told Lisa to hush.'

'The poor child said nothing.'

'She was about to.'

'Really, you are unfair!' Ma exclaimed.

'Only taking precautions.'

Ma smiled and heaped a plate with food for David who had just come in. 'Hungry?'

'Starving.'

'Where's Pa?' I asked.

'Gone to the village.'

'Is he – has he got the hat?'

'No, it's hanging in the hall,' Grandpa hissed.

'Where are Edward and Victoria?'

'Exploring.'

'And Josh?'

'He's had breakfast; he's gone to the walled garden.'

'Oh, the walled garden. I'd forgotten there is one.'

'Yes,' said Grandpa, stroking Angelique who had scrambled up his leg, 'a fine walled garden. Somebody's cultivating it.'

'Who?'

'Your father will ask if he remembers. Now shut up.'

'Aren't you being a bit stiff with Lisa?' My mother looked annoyed.

'Cautious.' Grandpa gave her a benign smile. 'He will also, one hopes, bring a ladder. I can't climb magnolias, but I might manage a ladder until we get a staircase built.'

I ate my breakfast, wondering at Grandpa's knowledge and awareness.

'A circular stair would be nice,' said Ma, joining us to eat. 'I dreamt I bought one in a sale.'

'You dreaming too,' Grandpa looked at her suspiciously.

'Yes. You are not the only one to dream.'

I left the house and set off to explore. The cobblestones of the yard humped under the soles of my feet. The painted van was under cover in a coach-house. It looked smaller than it had in London, the brass figures more relaxed than I had remembered. The fat woman looked contented and the figure of Death more like a man about to cut grass than life. During the journey the Harlequin had swung round in his socket to face the girl. I climbed up to put him straight but I could not move him.

A door in the wall led into the walled garden. I went through, closing it behind me. There were rows of vegetables, well tended, along the walls, fruit trees. I picked a peach and bit the sweet flesh, feeling the furry skin on my tongue as the juice ran down my chin. I listened. Blackbirds in the raspberry canes shrieked and flew away noisily; a bullfinch piped near me. There was a loud noise of insects; bees buzzed, flies hummed, butterflies on a buddleia rustled their wings like tissue paper. The garden centred on a well. I saw my face looking up from dark water. High above me a buzzard shrieked. I stood watching as he wheeled with his mate in the morning sky to disappear over a hill. At my feet there was a scraping sound; a large toad pulled one slow leg after the other, crossed the flagstones around the well to move out of sight into a clump of iris. My mind flew back to St James's Square and Mr Bailey sticking tickets under the windscreen-wipers of the rich, his heart full of longing. I left the garden by another door to find myself in the open behind the house. I climbed a slope to a point where I could look down. All the windows on the ground floor were open and presently I saw my mother, Victoria, David and Edward climb up the magnolia. I wondered where Grandpa could be and spied him sitting with his back to a tree with Old X-ray and Angelique sitting prim beside him.

Upstairs windows flew open and I heard my mother talking to the others. They were moving furniture and setting up beds. In the still air I could hear their feet shuffling as they carried heavy beds, then light as they ran from room to room. Not far from Grandpa a kestrel swept down to hover a few feet from the ground, before catching sight of Old X-ray and winging off. I wondered where Josh was and set out towards the wood to look.

The ground under the trees was springy, the sun pale green through the beeches. I found the stream and followed it. Fish darted in pools and a heron flew up, trailing long legs. I listened to the noise of the stream as it passed over stones, round rocks, cutting deep under high banks. Rounding a bend, I came on a long, deep pool, almost black at the edges and perfectly clear in the middle.

'Come in and swim.' Josh and Bogus were sitting on the opposite bank. 'It's quite warm. The water is marvellous; it's like swimming in beer.'

I undressed and dived in. I had never felt such water. After London's harsh product this was silk. I let my hair trail like weed. Josh joined me and we swam until we tired, then climbed out on the bank to sit by Bogus in the sun.

'I went up the hill through the wood,' said Josh. 'I followed the stream. It comes down the hill in falls, and in all the pools there are trout. I saw a fox. I've never seen one before.'

'There might well be,' I said.

'And badgers, I'm sure. There are lots of deep holes halfway up the hill. You must come and look.'

'I will.' I felt the sun drying my body and shook my wet hair.

'You know the garden, the walled garden?'

'Yes.'

'It's locked. I couldn't get in but I looked over the wall.'

'No, it isn't. I've just come from there.'

'The door is locked, silly you.'

'No, I'm not.'

'Very, very silly.'

I hated being called silly. 'I'm not. I've just been in there. I ate a peach.'

'Oh rot!' Josh mocked. I slapped his face. We fought, slipped and fell into the water. Bogus barked, bowing to us from the bank. I surfaced, my hair streaming over my eyes. I was furious.

'I'll show you. I've got the peach stone in my pocket.'

'You can buy peaches anywhere.'

'Come with me. There's a toad there, too.'

Josh came sulkily to the garden and stared. 'It must be another garden. This was locked.'

I said, 'If you look from up the hill you can see there's only one.'

Josh looked along the wall to the peach trees, went and picked one and bit. 'All right, now where's the toad?' He looked embarrassed.

'You look embarrassed,' I said, taunting.

'Well, I am. The door was locked against me. Why? It's not the sort of thing that happens every day.' He paused. 'I don't suppose it happened every day in fairy stories.'

'We are too old for fairy stories,' I said. We ate more peaches, thoughtfully. 'Shall we take some to the house?' We picked the fruit and put it in rhubarb leaves.

'Did you notice Bogus last night?' Josh pushed open the door to the yard.

'Didn't we all?'

'Nobody commented.' Josh patted Bogus. 'Nobody said nuffink, did they Bogus?' Bogus wagged his tail.

'Oh look,' said Josh, as we came round the front of the house, 'here comes Pa with one of the village lads and a ladder. Now Grandpa can get up to bed.'

We watched Pa drive up in the Mini followed by a truck with a ladder in the back. The driver was a grizzled man in blue jeans with a beret on the back of his head. He had blue eyes set in a brown face. Bogus went up to him, wagging his tail.

''Ullo, 'ullo, if it isn't Rags! 'Ullo, boy, where 'ave you been then?'

14

'This is Mr Pearce, darling. He is very kindly lending us a ladder.' Pa introduced Mr Pearce to our mother who shook his hand. 'It's very kind of you, Mr Pearce, to help us.'

'Well, you have to get upstairs.' Mr Pearce looked down at Ma. 'I hear you climbed the magnolia; won't do it no good to do that.'

'No. It's such a beautiful tree, it must be very old.'

'Not all that old.' Mr Pearce let go of Ma's hand. 'It was sickly until the fire, then the fire set it up!'

'How?' I asked.

'Magnolias like heat. When the stairs burned the walls grew hot and the magnolia pulled herself together and grew. But she won't like you climbing up and down her.'

'We'll use the ladder.' Ma tried to reassure.

Mr Pearce forced his eyes away from Ma's and took a long look at Josh, then me, then Grandpa, his eyes large, blue, unblinking. 'This all of you?'

'All the Fullers. I told you about our three friends.' Pa was enjoying the inspection.

'So you did. Well, let's set up the ladder.' Mr Pearce started to untie the rope which held it. 'This should do you.' He eased it to the ground. 'Funny you should have brought Rags along with you.' He fondled Bogus's head.

'He's called Bogus.' Josh was polite.

'He was Rags when he left.'

'When was that?' Ma asked.

'After Mr Hayco died, after the fire. Hung about a bit, poor dog, then he left. Wouldn't live with nobody else, would you Rags?' Bogus wagged his tail.

'But you said the fire was in 1949. Bogus can't be Rags; it's nearly forty years.'

'Forty or so,' agreed Mr Pearce.

'A long time,' said Pa.

'Time's a funny thing. This is Rags.'

'Well,' said Pa in the awkward silence which followed this statement, 'let's see how the ladder goes.'

The ladder reached from the hall to the landing. Mr Pearce fixed the foot with a heavy wood block and wedged it at the top. 'There,' he said to Grandpa, 'you try it.'

Grandpa climbed halfway up with agility followed by Old X-ray and Bogus. They squeezed past him. Grandpa hesitated.

'Can't do it. Won't do it,' Grandpa grunted.

'Go on, Father, you are doing fine,' Pa called from below.

'I'm not ready.' Grandpa lowered himself down the ladder, clutching the rungs as though he were afraid of falling. 'Not ready.' I got the impression he was not so much afraid of the ladder as of reaching the top. There was something up there he was afraid of. I met his eyes as he reached my side. 'Not afraid, just not ready,' he muttered.

'Who is up there, Grandpa? D'you know who it is?'

He looked sly. 'Don't know what you're talking about.' I didn't believe him. The others were all watching Bogus and Old X-ray.

'Rags was always good up the ladders, used to come up the hayricks. Lots of dogs can climb ladders, but Rags, he doesn't mind coming down. That's what makes him different, ain't it boy?' said Mr Pearce looking up.

Bogus peered at the ladder then came down without hesitation. Mr Pearce laughed. 'Now Mr Hayco's nephew what sold this house, he never thought to borrow a ladder.'

'What did he do?' David had joined us, coming quietly into the house.

'Stayed for a few days, liked it not and left.'

'Liked it not and died,' murmured David.

'But he didn't die, did he? Put the place on the market.'

'Lucky for us,' I said.

'Maybe.' Mr Pearce gave the ladder a shake to make sure it was firm.

'What do you mean, "Maybe"?' I asked curiously.

'Maybe. Well, maybe if you come to terms?'

'Come to terms?'

'That's what I said.' Mr Pearce spoke rather smugly I thought. Ma invited him inside. He followed her into the kitchen. 'A cup of tea?' asked Ma.

'Thank you.' Mr Pearce sat down at the table and looked at the range. 'You don't want to be bothered with that range,' he said. 'What you need is an Aga.'

'Need?' Ma grinned complicitly. 'I can manage with this, Mr Pearce.' Mr Pearce smiled at Ma. Ma filled the kettle, smiling. 'The front stairs – that's different.'

'I can fix the back stairs for you.'

'How so?' Grandpa had come to join us.

'Very expensive, if you don't stay.' Mr Pearce's eyes met mine, then glanced away.

'But of course we shall stay, stay for ever.' I spoke angrily.

'Steady on,' said Mr Pearce. 'Steady on, my beauty.'

'I thought – ' Pa was lounging in the doorway, wearing the hat. 'I thought just now when we put the ladder up how beautiful it would be to have a spiral stair made of glass. It would give an elegant dimension.'

'How did you know?' Mr Pearce gave a sudden roar. 'Who told you? That stair was his, his great idea, not yours – not – not – not – yours. NO.'

There was a long, awkward pause. I felt very frightened.

'I don't think I can tell you because I'm not sure I know, but I think I have come to terms.' Pa spoke softly. 'Could you tell us where the staircase is?'

'Oh, Mr Pearce!' Ma gave a cry. 'Oh, Mr Pearce, don't.' She rushed across the kitchen. 'Please don't cry.' Tears were oozing from his blue eyes.

'I thought you'd never come. It's a shock.' Mr Pearce gulped. 'An 'orrible shock, *'orrible.*' Ma wiped Mr Pearce's eyes with a corner of her apron.

'Catch the aitch, Mr P.,' she cried boldly. 'Here,' she snatched the hat from Pa's head. 'Wear this for a few minutes and you'll find it all tumbles into place, whatever it is.' She put the hat on Mr Pearce's head and her arm round his shaking shoulders. We were watching this scene when Victoria, wearing her long skirt and bean beads, strode into the room, followed by Edward. 'Give me my specs,' she exclaimed. 'This I have to see. The poor man's hurt. There, there,' she said. 'Don't cry. Please don't.'

Victoria's arms were full of lilies, large cream flowers, spotted with brown, their stamens heavy with yellow pollen.

'Where did you find those?' Mr Pearce, the tears wet on his cheeks, stared at Victoria as though she were an apparition.

'Growing in the wood.' Victoria laid the flowers on the table, her beads making a gritty noise as they swung against her chest. 'There are lots of them and the smell is fantastic.'

'I should get them out of the house if I was you, double quick.'

'Oh.' Victoria handed the flowers to me. 'Why?'

'They won't do no good. They don't belong to the house.'

Victoria looked at Mr Pearce doubtfully, then she took Baby from Edward and held him out to Mr Pearce.

'Like to hold him?' Mr Pearce took Baby. ''Ello, 'ello, 'ello,' he said, 'if it ain't young Arnold.'

'Mr Pearce – ' Only Ma was brave enough to speak. 'How do you know his name is Arnold?'

'It is, isn't it?'

'Yes,' said Victoria, taking off the pebble glasses through which she had been staring at Mr Pearce and straightening up so that the beads clattered. 'But we call him Baby most of the time.'

Our visitor tossed Baby up and down on his knee and took stock of Victoria. After a time he said, 'If you stay and think of getting the garden back in order, you might plant them beans.' He stretched out a hand and fingered the necklace.

'But it *is*,' Josh and I chorused. 'It is in order.'

'Nay.'

'Yeah!'

'Nay.'

'Yeah!'

'What's this? A Bible class?' Grandpa had been silent up to now.

'Garden was famous once.'

'The garden's in perfect order,' I said.

'Nay!'

'Yeah, Mr Pearce. There are beans, peas, spinach and a toad.'

'Somebody's kept it in order then,' said Pa.

'Nobody would. People don't come here much.'

'Why not?'

'Well – ' He drew out the word.

'Because it is haunted, I suppose,' I said.

Mr Pearce looked uncomfortable.

'A useful ghost.' Pa looked cheerful. 'Left warm ash in the fireplace, and digs the garden.'

'That so,' Mr Pearce handed Baby back to Victoria. 'Those lilies should go – they ain't for you,' he said. 'I must be going or Mrs Pearce will give me stick.' He shook hands with Ma and, giving the rest of us a wave, drove off.

'Who is he?' Ma watched the van vanish into the wood.

'Local builder,' said Pa. 'He says.'

'Funny he should know both Bogus and Baby.'

'Baby looks like most babies and there are lots of mongrels like Bogus.'

'No, love, there are not. And Bogus knew him; he greeted him.'

'He knows a lot,' I said. 'Mr Pearce and Bogus, too.' I stroked the silky ears. 'If Bogus could talk he could sort out everything for us.'

'Pity he left so soon. I wanted to ask about the stairs.' Pa looked thoughtful. 'He seemed to imply that there are stairs, glass stairs.'

'He seems to be in a bit of a muddle. Bogus, Baby, whether we are staying. Why doesn't he expect us to stay?' Ma looked at Pa.

'Possibly we won't be able to.' He smiled at her then gave her a kiss. 'Don't worry, darling. This is different from London. Let's get settled in. I've found a splendid loft to work in, quiet, with the right light. That's a great blessing.' Ma smiled, a little sadly.

'We've escaped,' said Pa. 'The noise, the crowds, the smell, the traffic, the people, the violence, Father's fear of eviction, the terrible hurry, the aggression, the dreary existence.'

'School,' said Josh.

'You'll have to go to school here.' Ma was brisk. 'You aren't in quarantine for imaginary measles any more. No doubt there's a school.'

As I came down to reality with a bump, I wondered whether the person I had seen at the window when we arrived would stay on with us. Whether he/she was of school age like us, or like Baby and Bogus seemed to be to Mr Pearce – ageless.

'May I borrow the hat please? I want to see whether I really saw a toad in the garden.' I looked at Pa.

'You'll see them at night, but by all means try.'

'We must write to Mr Bailey,' I said.

'Perhaps Mr Pearce knows him, too.' Ma seemed to be accepting Mr Pearce with serenity.

I shivered as I put the hat on. Everything seemed out of focus, and I was frightened. I wondered how Haphazard House had got its name and what the hazards were. The sky was overcast. I took the lilies into the yard, wondering what to do with them. She shouldn't have picked them, I thought. It would have been better to leave them growing. A bucket lay on its side by a tap. I righted it and turned on the tap. The scent of the flowers was fearfully strong. I put them in the bucket. Perhaps Mr Pearce had meant the smell was too strong indoors, that it would give Baby snivels. I arranged the flowers.

In the coach-house David's van looked young and jolly though it was almost a vintage machine. The four figures on the corners of the roof shone in the gloom. Bending to arrange flowers, the hat tipped forward over my nose. I picked up the bucket, climbed on the van's bonnet and pushed it to the centre of the roof. The lilies looked right up there. I went on my way.

When I reached the garden it was silent and there were no toads to be seen. I sat down and listened to the silence, my heart uneasy. I laid the hat beside me and stared at the clump of iris into which the toad had crawled. The flowers were over and the seed pods bursting with red fruit. As I sat studying the jointed stalks and the butcher's knife leaves, I heard the clink of a hoe working through the earth and the breathing of a man working, breathing which now and again became a low whistle ending with a cough and a sniff. I hoped the man who kept this wonderful garden would not mind our intrusion. I stood up to introduce myself but there was nobody there. Snatching up the hat I ran.

I raced into the house to shout 'Ma!' but terror made me dumb. I stopped by the door to listen and put the hat on the hatstand. There was nobody on the ground floor. I ran from room to room, each one still and empty. I scrambled up the

ladder from the hall trying to call out for Ma. My voice
was a tremulous bleat, 'Ma-a-a.'

'Everybody's out.'

David lay on the landing floor facing the wall. I could
see his feet, bare, rather dirty and his foreshortened body
at the top of the ladder. 'Don't be so noisy,' he said
irritably.

'What are you doing?' Though not my mother, David
was a person I knew. I felt better, less panicky.

'Hush. Can't you be quiet. I am launching Mouse.'

'Launching?'

'That's what I said.' By David's hand Mouse crouched,
twitching, and hesitating, whiskers bristling, her ears alert.
Presently she moved, stretching out her body towards the
wainscot, every nerve strained.

'Oh,' I said. 'I see.'

'Interesting,' David stated.

'Not very.' My heart still thumped. Fear made me rude.
How could a white mouse compare with an invisible
gardener?

David lay still. Mouse, on a level with his nose, remained for a few moments then, at some secret signal, she
moved her tiny feet, scratching on the boards, and vanished into a crack in the wainscot. David sat up. 'There,'
he said happily. 'She never thought that could happen to
her.'

'Why not?' I sat beside him. My breath came normally
now. It was safe sitting by David with his bare feet and
torn jeans.

'She was bred for experiments, not to have fun. She can
try her own experiments here.'

'Won't she be missed?'

'Possibly.' His voice was flat.

'So she'll become a house mouse,' I liked David a lot.

'She will.' David sat up and looked at me. 'What's been
happening to you? You look het-up.'

I told you about the invisible gardener. I spoke as lightly
as I could. 'It's nothing really, not as important as Mouse.
I was frightened. I expect you will laugh.'

'No I won't. It's a bit like Mouse. Now you see her, now you don't, but she's there in that wall and your sniffing gardener is there, too. You heard him. Let's make some tea.' We climbed down the ladder.

'I shall put food up there for her until she can fend for herself.' David's thoughts were with Mouse. 'She'll have a life of adventure.'

I pictured Mouse exploring the secrets behind the walls of the house.

'Where are all the others?'

'They went to the village to check on the time and so on.'

'Ma and Pa have watches.'

David looked pitying. 'Time.' He stressed the word. 'They've gone to meet the village, find the shops, find their feet, find a school for you. What's known as "high time".' He laughed.

'Or time to know better. Why?'

'They were rattled by friend Pearce.'

'What he said about Bogus and Baby and the stairs?'

'Right, and an Aga instead of the range.'

'That sort of time? Modern?'

'Right again.'

'Why didn't you go, too?'

'I don't give much for time. My hold is tenuous. Any time suits me.'

'What do you mean?' We had reached the kitchen and David was filling the kettle while I pumped the water.

'Your Grandpa's time, your Ma and Pa's time are all different. Take Mouse, her time's short, your Grandpa's long. Time used to be pretty steady – it isn't now.'

'It's not steady *here*,' I heard myself say. David glanced at me, warmed the pot, put in tea, poured on boiling water. 'People feel they have to check on Greenwich Mean Time,' he said, 'to start with.'

'I don't understand.' I took the cup he handed me. I felt uneasy again.

'Keep your cool. No need to get scared.'

'I'm not, not really.'

'Don't make me laugh. You're as scared as Mouse but she's making use of her time. You'll be okay if you do, too.'

I warmed my hands round the cup. David sat silent. He had said all he had to say. I went and sat on the front step and waited for my family in the sun. Within reach of the hatstand I felt safe and calm though I had had the hat with me when I had been so frightened. Along the front of the house clumps of thyme and lavender grew between the flagstones, sweet alyssum gave off whiffs of scent. I got up to explore. Growing against the house, as well as the magnolia we had climbed, were roses and jasmine rising from a froth of Mediterranean daisies. The house was roofless where the fire had destroyed it. In the ruins grew buddleias and syringa, a self-sown garden with butterflies and bees feeding on clumps of Michaelmas daisies. It was very peaceful. I decided to find the room from which we had been watched when we arrived. David lay on a sofa in the hall, reading. If I shrieked he would hear me. I climbed the ladder and walked from room to room. My mother had done marvels. Beds were ready, chests of drawers, cupboards, chairs set about. Mirrors shone, wood glowed, rugs and carpets were soft underfoot, no spiders' webs, no dust, no smears.

I wandered from room to room guessing which one was whose. The bedrooms all opened on to a passage; it was more proper to call it a gallery. This must be for Grandpa I supposed, and this, with a fourposter, Ma and Pa's. Josh's room had his jeans and shirt lying on the floor. This room, also with a canopied bed, mine, as Bogus's basket was in a corner – a token, since he usually slept across my feet. 'For form's sake,' Pa had remarked when Ma bought the basket in the Portobello Road.

In another room Baby's things were neatly arranged, and Victoria's bean necklaces on the bedside table. Two more rooms – David's, and another ready for a guest. If Mr Bailey would desert his post and visit us he would be happy.

I remembered the watcher and went to find the window above the front door. However, whichever window I looked out of was either to the left of the porch or the right.

There was no room above the porch, no window from which to observe. I felt teased and angry, the more so as Old X-ray and Angelique followed me from one room to another, purring, waving contented tails. I gave up and leant out of the window of Ma and Pa's room, looking across at the wood. The cats jumped up on the sill and sat, blinking. I listened to clocks ticking and furniture creaking in the house and the sounds of birds and insects, so different from the noises of London, usually full of menace.

My family came out of the wood: Pa, Ma, Victoria carrying Baby, Edward and Josh, their arms full of parcels, Grandpa and Bogus strolling slowly. I went to meet them, running, my heart light.

'Poor old Mini gave her last gasp as we reached the village,' said Pa, bending to kiss me. I was horrified. We had had Mini ever since I could remember. 'From now on Shanks's Pony,' said Pa.

'Who was that with you at the window?' asked Victoria.

'The *next* window; she had the cats with her,' Josh corrected her.

'I was alone,' I said.

'Don't be silly. He was wearing the hat and he waved like this.' Josh made a regal gesture rather like the Queen Mother but more hearty.

'David?' Pa asked casually.

'I was alone,' I repeated.

'He was leaning out of the window above the porch, stupid.'

I stared at Josh, my insides churning. 'There isn't one. David's downstairs and the hat's on the hatstand.' I felt resentment as well as fear.

They said, 'Ah' thoughtfully, looking kindly at me.

'Did you find out the time in the village?' I wanted to change the subject.

'Yes.' Pa's voice was reassuring. 'Plenty of time to get settled before school starts, if it starts.' I felt time swinging down round my shoulders like a hoop.

'The school must be in another village,' said Ma.

'Grandpa found time to buy a false nose,' said Josh, 'in the shop.'

'He rides his jokes to death, let's hope this one doesn't last as long as poor Mini.' Ma sighed.

'I heard you.' Grandpa came up to us. 'I'm hardly likely to last as long as that machine, however cruelly you drive me.'

'Darling.' Ma looked at Grandpa with affection. The ruts and creases of his face crinkled into a grin.

'Give me some of your parcels.' I took them from her. 'Ma, I must speak to you.'

'All right.'

Grandpa walked on towards the house, bald head, shapeless jersey, old flannel trousers. 'So like the hind legs of an elephant.' Ma, watching him, was loving.

'Ma.' I laid my hand on her arm.

'Yes, What's bothering you?'

'There's someone working in the walled garden. I can hear him but I can't see him.'

'Really?'

'Yes. I was scared to death. I ran.'

'You mustn't be frightened, you really must not.'

'But I was. I am.'

'Listen.' Ma sat down on the grass, giving it a little pat so that I sat beside her. 'Listen to me. This morning we went up and sorted the furniture upstairs, the beds and so on.'

'I know. I heard and saw you.'

'We sorted the furniture into different rooms, beds, chairs, chests of drawers and so on, and then came down to the kitchen and had coffee. Then David, Edward and Victoria went out.'

'So?'

'I went up again to sort out sheets and blankets and – '

'And?'

'I found – ' Ma gave a helpless shrug – 'the furniture had all been rearranged, the beds were made up, the floors, the furniture. the windows were polished; it had all been very dusty but suddenly it was spotless. So when you tell me there is an invisible gardener I accept it.'

'Weren't you frightened?'

'Why should I be? It is a good thing and the furniture looks happy.'

'Furniture happy?'

'Furniture can look absolutely furious if you put it in the wrong place. It knows where it belongs.'

'It can't polish and dust itself.'

'One had always imagined so.' Ma stood up. 'Come on.' I told her about David's mouse.

'She will meet a Supermouse.' Ma looked younger and more cheerful than I had ever seen her. 'Poor Old X-ray,' she said. 'Lots of tiny Supermice.'

'Old X-ray doesn't seem to worry about the time,' I said to test her.

'Nor do I. Race you to the house.' Ma ran, reaching the house before me, running like a young girl, which she was not.

That night, before getting into my four-poster, I wrote by the light of a candle to Mr Bailey

Dear Mr Bailey,
We have reached Haphazard House. Please come. There is a toad. Your room is ready.
Love,
Lisa Fuller.

Mr Bailey, I felt, would understand; he of all prople, whose job was to watch time passing on meters. I found an envelope and a stick of sealing wax. I melted it in the candle and, licking my thumb, pressed it on the hot blob. As I settled my head on the pillow I recollected that some meters went out of order, stopped, but I was too tired to care.

🍃 16 🍂

I told Ma at breakfast that I had written to Mr Bailey.

'I'm glad. I must remember to pay him for that taxi.'

Pa gulped down the rest of his coffee. 'Come on, Miss Pin, I want to paint you, catch you while I can.'

'Sure.' Victoria resumed the American accent. 'Sure, anything you say. D'you want my glasses?'

'Yes, the elbows and the beads.' Pa measured her with his eyes.

'I'll take care of Baby.' Edward took Baby from Victoria.

'Don't lose sight of him, honey.'

'I won't.' Edward watched Victoria follow Pa. He carried Baby away on his shoulder. Grandpa, sitting with Old X-ray on his lap, watching Angelique treading delicately among the breakfast cups on the table, grunted. 'Our Coco, *now* he can paint.' He held Old X-ray's ears between finger and thumb, stroking them.

'Anyone want anything in the village?' I asked. 'I'm going to explore.'

David looked up from his book. 'See if there's a paper.'

'There won't be.' Grandpa went on caressing Old X-ray. She shut her eyes. Ma picked up Angelique, about to lick the butter, and put her on the floor.

'There won't be a paper,' said Grandpa.

'Why should there be no paper?' Ma leant close to Grandpa and kissed his cheek. 'You haven't shaved.'

'There's plenty of time for that.' He stroked Old X-ray's nose, pressing gently up from her pink nose to her forehead.

'Why no paper?' Ma's voice was low.

'Nobody to read it.'

'There's us.'

'You sure?'

'Of course I'm sure; well, pretty sure.'

Grandpa laughed. 'You're not sure, and who in the village wants a paper?'

'I don't know. I've only met Mr Pearce and his wife.'

'Guardians of village news.'

'It's funny we've only met *them*.'

Old X-ray climbed slowly down Grandpa's leg, letting her tail slide through his fingers.

'You said there was a school in the next village,' I said.

'Well, I suppose there is as there isn't one here.'

Grandpa looked at me from under wrinkled lids. 'Time for you to trot off,' he said. 'Enjoy yourself.'

'I shall,' I said, feeling brave, and set off to discover Coldharbour. I would post my letter and explore.

It had rained in the night and walking through the wood drops fell on my head. The air smelt of grass and leaves. Pigeons cooed, jays chattered, out of sight. In a clump of hazels long-tailed tits hunted in a flock. When I reached the road I saw the church tower, rearing like an Egyptian dog, ears pricked. Swallows dived and swooped round the pinnacles. The churchyard was crowded with headstones in long grass; tall stones, short stones, plain stones, stones decorated with curlicues; in the grass, poppies and columbines swayed. I read the inscriptions: died aged 96, died aged 70, died aged 6 months, 9 years, 4 months – there was no rule. The stones leaned north, south, east, west, bowing and tilting in a dance. A nice place to lie, I thought, and remembered my letter.

I pushed open the door of the post office. A bell fixed to the door made a horrible noise. Behind the counter a grey-haired woman observed me through fancy spectacle frames. I said, 'Good morning.'

She said, 'Good morning.' We paused, she sizing me up.

'Might I have a stamp, please?'

'A stamp.' She spoke emphatically. 'A stamp.'

'Yes, please.' I produced my letter.

'First class?' She reached for the letter and looked at it. 'First class for Mr Bailey of Islington, London.'

'Yes, please.' I was nettled.

'No need to be nettled. I am Mrs Pearce.' She opened a folder, extracted a stamp, licked it and placed it in the corner of my letter then gave it a thump. 'There.' She looked satisfied. 'You put it in the box. What's your name?'

'Lisa.'

'And your brother?'

'Josh.'

'Short for Joshua?'

'I suppose so.'

'You suppose?'

'Well, it is.'

'Then you should say so.'

I fidgeted from one foot to another, staring at Mrs Pearce.

'And your ma's a lovely lady and your pa paints pictures, the modern variety.'

'Yes.'

'Mr Hayco was given that way.'

'Old Mr Hayco who died? He painted?'

'Not exactly.'

'Not exactly dead or didn't exactly paint?' Two could play this game.

'Artistic.' Mrs Pearce was not giving in. 'A collector. And there's a young man called David who owns that van.'

'Yes.' I felt she wanted me to defend the van, those jolly nymphs and daisies, so I just said 'Yes'.

'And two young people with a child.'

'Yes.'

'They won't be staying.'

'Why won't they?' Mrs Pearce eyed me without deigning to answer. I decided to outstare her; take an inventory of Mrs Pearce as she was taking one of me. She had an upholstered front down which cascaded row on row of pink pearls. I began to count them.

'And you brought a dog.'

'And a cat and a kitten.' I was tired of saying 'Yes' like an idiot.

'That would be Rags.'

'His name is Bogus. He comes from the Battersea Dogs' Home. He was lost.'

'I should just think he was, poor Rags.' Mrs Pearce showed emotion, her eyes shining through the spectacle frames which were pink like the pearls. 'Poor, dear Rags.'

'His name is Bogus.'

'So you say.'

'Why won't Victoria and Edward stay?' I latched on to her remark like a dropped stitch.

'They can't, dear; not that lot.'

I had counted up to nine rows, hesitated and started again from the top of her chin.

'Mr Pearce thought Bogus was Rags, too.' I attacked boldly.

'Couldn't be, could he?' Mrs Pearce smiled mockingly. Her pearly teeth were almost pink. 'Disappeared after the fire.'

'That was in 1949,' I said.

'That's right, that was the year.'

'Were you here?'

'Oh yes, we are always here, George and I.'

'As postmistress and builder?'

'You can call us that if you like.'

'Oh.' We eyed one another. I didn't feel I was getting much information. I couldn't make out whether there were nine or ten rows of pearls on that vast bosom.

'There are ten, dear.' Mrs Pearce grinned. Then, putting out a plump hand, said, 'Another stamp?' in the tone people use when they offer another cake as though one had eaten too many already. 'And your pa has a hat.' She looked slyly at me. 'Perhaps you will like it here.' She folded her hands on the counter.

'We do,' I said, disliking her. 'What do people do here?' I would not discuss the hat.

'I run the post office and George has his business.'

'But other people?'

'There aren't other people, not often; they don't do anything as they aren't here.'

'There's us.' I spoke more bravely than I felt.

'Yes, there's you. Sure you won't have another stamp?'

'Quite sure, thank you. I must go now. Goodbye.'

'Goodbye,' said Mrs Pearce.

I paused by the door, curious. 'In what way was Mr Hayco artistic?'

'In various ways – a bit untimely.'

'Unsuitable, d'you mean?'

'My husband thought so about some things. They fell out.'

'Quarrelled?'

'What, dear?'

'You said Mr Hayco and your husband fell out. What about?'

'Did I, dear? I don't believe I did. We were talking about Rags. He *was* a nice dog – followed his master everywhere.'

'Dogs do,' I said coldly, angry that she would not tell me about her husband and Mr Hayco.

'And the baby is called Arnold. Isn't that nice.'

'It's an awful name,' I said.

'If you say so.' Mrs Pearce seemed to dismiss me. I opened the door and the bell clattered above my head. 'Thank you.'

'Goodbye and thank *you*,' Mrs Pearce called after me.

I sat on the churchyard wall. The village was very quiet. In villages in France people stood in groups talking, cats sunned themselves, dogs scratched their fleas; here there was no sign of life. I supposed everybody went off to work in the place Ma said we would go to school. The post office was the only shop. It seemed funny that I should be the only person to be seen. A sign outside a gate said, *George Pearce, Builder and Decorator.* Our Mini stood forlorn by the side of the road. I averted my gaze. It was stupid to be sentimental about bits of metal, but in her day Mini had been a car of character, especially when driven by Pa, as witnessed bumps and scratches on her bodywork. Poor Mini. I waved to her, kicking my heels on the wall.

Up the hill, walking slowly, came Grandpa and Josh. Bogus was with them, feathery tail aloft. I went to meet them.

'What news?' asked Grandpa.

'The village seems empty.'

'Then I shall fill the pub. I have a great thirst.' Grandpa stepped into the pub. Josh joined me on the wall and looked about him.

'Not much going on.'

'Nothing,' I said. 'Did you go into the post office yesterday?'

'Yes. Ma did her shopping there; it's run by Mrs Pearce.'

'I bought a stamp from her. She asked me a lot of questions.' Remembering my letter, I crossed the road and put it in the letterbox. As I rejoined Josh a bus lumbered up the hill and stopped. No one got in or out and it moved on out of sight.

'Coldharbour isn't exactly a hive of activity. Let's visit the church.' Josh kicked his heels against the wall and dropped beside me. We walked round the church and went in. 'What about Bogus?' Josh asked.

'Don't be boring,' I said. 'God made Bogus. He can come in.'

There was a beautiful screen and pulpit, and several nice tombs. 'Sacred to the memory of Hugh Hayco and his beloved wife Susanna who departed this life in the year of our Lord 1666.'

'They must have had the plague,' I said, staring at the prostrate figures carved in marble. 'I wonder whether he really loved her.'

'They couldn't put that they hated each other's guts. Look, a butterfly.' Josh pointed to a butterfly fluttering in a shaft of light. 'Let's get it out.'

We pulled some cords and opened a window. Josh moved away. I stood watching while the captive fluttered from one shaft of light to another, wishing it towards the open window. Bogus climbed into the pulpit and, standing on his hind legs, looked down on me, ears aflop. The butterfly flew out into the open air. I heaved a sigh of relief.

'Hey, Lisa come here,' Josh called from the foot of the tower. 'Look at this.' He had found a door to the crypt.

'Look, coffins.' Josh ran ahead, examining large, small and medium coffins ranged round the walls.

'There's even one for an infant,' said Josh, 'quite posh handles.'

'They're rather horrible,' I said.

'I like them. D'you think this suits me?' Josh lay down in a coffin, closed his eyes and crossed his hands. Bogus climbed in on top of him.

'Stop fooling, Josh. It's not funny to be dead.'

'How d'you know? We may die and, oops, we'll hear the Last Trump and be at a party.'

'Don't invite *me*.' I backed away up the stairs.

'We are all invited,' Josh called after me. I ran out and was glad to see the pub door opening and Grandpa come out. His step was sprightly, he was laughing, throwing back his head. He looked a lot less bald than usual, his trousers less baggy.

'Grandpa – '

'Where's that boy?'

'In the crypt. He's lying in a coffin with Bogus, pretending to be dead.'

'Is he indeed, morbid boy.'

'There are a lot of coffins ready. Grandpa, get him out of there, please.' I pulled at his hand nervously.

'Nothing to worry about.' Grandpa raised his voice and shouted, 'Out, come out,' very loudly.

'I've never heard you shout so loudly,' I said in astonishment.

'Coldharbour air's cleared my pipes.' Josh and Bogus came out of the church. 'Don't make bad taste jokes, boy.'

'Sorry.' Josh looked at Grandpa. 'What's happened to you?'

'Had a good pint of beer.'

'You are taller,' said Josh.

'More hair, less wrinkles,' I said. 'There's something funny about this village.'

Grandpa started briskly down the hill towards Haphazard. 'He looks younger,' I said.

'Don't be absurd,' Josh crushed me. 'He's just feeling cheerful.'

I ran to catch up with Grandpa. 'Was the pub nice?'

'Yes. Landlord is that Pearce fellow. Made himself agreeable.'

'Anybody else in there?'

'No, just me. Had the place to myself.'

'Grandpa, there is nobody in the village except Mr Pearce and Mrs Pearce. Don't you think it strange? No cats, dogs, women or children. The bus stopped and no one got out. I didn't even see a driver.'

'You talk too much,' Grandpa snarled. I stopped in my tracks and waited for Josh.

'I heard.' Josh grinned at me. 'He was beastly.'

'Mr Pearce reminds me of someone we know and Mrs Pearce, too.'

'I know,' said Josh, breaking into a trot to keep up with Grandpa. 'The Lollipop lady and the Lollipop man in Croydon.'

'The ones Pa called Mr and Mrs Charon and said, "look it up in the dictionary"?'

Josh nodded. 'He had something to do with a ferry.'

Grandpa waited for us to catch up. He looked amiable again. 'It's time for lunch.'

'Mr Pearce and Mrs Pearce behave as if they knew Bogus,' I said.

'A long time ago,' Josh stressed, 'and they knew Baby.'

'All babies look alike. Like Chinese,' Grandpa mocked.

'No two Boguses would.' We all laughed at this.

'So if they knew Bogus in 1949 that time was the time that it is now – '

'I am content with time for lunch,' Grandpa stated, 'for today at least.'

We came out of the wood and looked across to the house waiting for us. From the window above the porch the person waved before retreating into shadow.

'Did you see?' Josh and I spoke together. 'Grandpa, did you see?'

'Yes, yes,' he said testily. 'Don't fuss.'

Ma came out of the house to meet us. Walking beside her was Mr Bailey, smiling broadly. 'Soon as I got your letter I came. No time like the present, I said. Time to be off, I said. I downed my book of parking tickets and here I am. What's the matter then?' He stared at me gaping. 'Don't want me after all then? Ain't there no toad?'

'Of course there is.' I grabbed his hand. 'Come, I'll show you.' I led him to the walled garden. How could I tell him I had only posted my letter half an hour before?

17

'How did you get here, Mr Bailey?'

'Hitched a lift down the M4 to Bristol in a Jag. I knew the driver, booked him last winter. He didn't recognize me out of uniform. In Bristol I had some fish and chips. Then down the M5 in a Ford, a lorry to Coldharbour, then a bus dropped me by the village.'

'We saw the bus but we didn't see you.'

'Then I walks through the wood to the 'ouse and meets your ma. Where's the toad then?'

'This way.' I led him to the wall and pointed to the clump of iris. 'He went in there yesterday.'

'Couldn't have been yesterday. That's when I got your letter. You just try and be accurate. In my job you have to be accurate otherwise it's unfair. You keep a strict account of time, see?'

'Just try here!' I exclaimed. 'Time is absolutely haywire, Mr Bailey, it's gone mad.'

'How's that?' Mr Bailey squatted, peering down among the iris leaves. I told him about posting my letter, about Mr Pearce and Bogus, Grandpa's odd appearance coming out of the pub, Mrs Pearce's conversation; and while I was about it I told him about the person who watched and waved. Mr Bailey's eyes were on a level with the spiky leaves.

'They burrow,' he said. 'He may have burrowed. They hibernate, though it's early in the year yet.'

'Are you listening to what I'm telling you?' I was indignant that he seemed unmoved.

'Yes I am. Ah! There he is! See 'is eye? See it blink? He's the very colour of the roots, the clever chap.' Mr Bailey sat back on his heels, elated.

'Mr Bailey, I'm trying to tell you things about time. Are you deaf, or what?'

'I'm not deaf. If you'd heard as many versions of time as I have you would be unmoved. Unmoved,' he repeated, not taking his eyes off the toad. ' "No time at all, Mr Warden," ' he mimicked a woman's voice. ' "Just time to change my books at the library," ' – a man's voice. 'Oxbridge, that one, they're the worst. "Just time to collect my mail from the Club." Superior officer type, greatcoat and bowler 'at. "Time to slip into Fortnum's." "Time to trot into the Haymarket." Trot! I give 'im trot. They all talk about time as if they knew, but the blooming meter knows the time until she goes wrong and then nobody knows, so what's the fuss?'

'Aren't you surprised?'

'Not really, no.'

'And what about the person in the hat. We've all seen him.'

'Wot sort of 'at. Not a bowler?'

'No. A hat like Pa's.'

'Something funny about that 'at, ain't there?'

'Well, yes.'

'So this person wears it?'

'A hat like it – another hat.'

'Shouldn't worry. Ain't no law about looking out of windows; no meter, no time limit, no law about 'ats, either.'

'You got the letter I posted to you this morning, yesterday. Aren't you surprised, even a little? Don't you think . . .' I stopped. Mr Bailey was tickling the toad's back with a long grass.

'Likes that, don't 'e?' I could happily have hit him.

'You shouldn't monkey about with time.' He observed my rage.

'It's monkeying about with us.'

'Pity the dog can't talk.' Mr Bailey picked his teeth thoughtfully with the stiff end of the grass.

'So you believe me?'

'Oh, yes. We've got away from meters here so maybe it's more lax. Nothing to grumble at.' He prodded hard at a tooth. 'You got your teeth done blue; how are they?'

'It wore off,' I said haughtily, 'in no time.'

'No call to be snooty.' He leaned down again to poke the toad. 'Eh, look at that, 'e's got a mate.' Interested, in spite of myself, I looked and saw indeed that beside the toad was a smaller one.

'Marvellous camouflage those roots. Wonder how old they are. No bigger than your fingernail when they stops being tadpoles. Lose their tails like your 'umans coming out of nappies. They're beautiful,' Mr Bailey crooned.

'Grandpa's getting on but he looked years younger when he came out of the pub.'

'Is that so?'

'Yes, more hair, his trousers weren't so baggy, and less wrinkles. It was rather peculiar.'

' 'E's a peculiar old gent.'

'He's not!'

'Nicely so. Looks a bit like them toads. They all 'ave wrinkled necks. That's praise coming from me.'

I laughed. 'It's not normal to grow suddenly – well, younger.'

'I wonder what normal is.' Mr Bailey straightened up and turned towards the house. 'I'm hungry, that's normal. Now them toads, when they're hibernating they don't eat for months. That's normal for them. It's a matter of time between meals.'

'You don't seem to realize,' – I followed him along the path – 'that time is hopping about like your toads.'

'Toads don't 'op, it's frogs that 'op.'

'I suppose so.' I was sulky.

'So there's time like toads and time like frogs and time like 'umans, and here it's got into a *mélange*. That's French for time for dinner.' Mr Bailey laughed. 'Or what happens to your dinner when you've ate it. *Mélange* is French for mix, see? That's a joke, you should laugh.'

'I don't think it's funny,' I said, feeling prickly fear set my

fingers tingling, tightening my chest. 'I'm frightened,' I said.
'There's something very peculiar – '

'Nah!'

'Yes, there is.'

Mr Bailey looked at me curiously.

'To me, anyway.' I put my hand in his for safety. 'Also,' I
said, feeling better, 'the female toad is larger than the male.'

'Believe you're right.' Mr Bailey's hand felt dry like the
toad. 'Take a tip from me, young Lisa.' Mr Bailey held my
hand firmly. 'When you're afraid you say to yourself, "I'll
forget that". Repeat that after me.'

'I'll forget that,' I said, feeling comforted.

'That's right, you forget it.'

The shriek we heard as we approached the house stopped us
dead. It came clear and high from Pa's studio, a top note
worthy of Maria Callas, such absolute terror that I felt my
hair crackle. Shriek followed shriek. Ma and David rushed
out of the house jostled by Grandpa. Victoria, long hair
streaming, raced to the house, her skirts held high. She
bounded into the house and began scrambling up the
ladder. Halfway up she met Edward, carrying Baby,
hurrying down. For a moment they swayed in a group, then
the ladder slipped sideways and decanted them. We were
picking them up and trying to see whether anyone was hurt
when Pa arrived, breathless, holding a paintbrush.

'What did you do to her?' Ma stopped brushing Victoria
down.

'Nothing,' said Pa furiously. 'I was painting the girl, told
her she could rest. She took a look at the canvas and let out a
yell. I must say I've put up with some harsh criticism in my
life but never a model who had the vapours. Hah!' Pa was

shaken. Victoria was clinging to Edward, clutching Baby, at the same time squeezing him so hard that he began to whimper and then to yell. She pointed a trembling finger at Pa. 'You, you, you were – ' Her voice trailed. 'I, I was – '

Pa threw down the paintbrush and stamped his foot. 'I was doing very well, got those spiky elbows and goofy glasses. All I needed was your idiotic beads and skirts and I'd have got you. Hah!' He raised his fists in the air and stamped. He also cried 'Hah!' for the third time. There was a silence.

'Nobody hurt?' David gave the ladder a little shake.

'Coco is hurt.' Grandpa let out a guffaw. 'His artistic pride.'

'Grandpa.' Ma spoke very quietly. 'Will you please shut up?'

'Glad to oblige.' Grandpa made a bow and walked away.

'Come for a little walk.' Edward drew Victoria away, reaching his arm up to her waist. Victoria shook herself free.

'I'm sorry. I don't know what came over me. I've hurt your feelings.' She turned to Pa who still stood with his fists in the air.

'That's quite all right. Criticism's good for the soul – ' Pa's face cleared.

'I was about to call you for lunch. I've something I want to say to you.' Ma asserted her authority. We followed her into the kitchen.

'Where is Josh?' Ma looked round.

'Here,' Josh appeared, out of breath. 'I heard shrieks so I came to see who's been murdered.'

'That'll do.' Ma quelled him. 'Will you all sit down.'

We sat round the table waiting for her to begin.

'Well now. I daresay some of you have noticed things which are out of the ordinary, but first I suggest that we need a staircase from the hall to the first floor. Either we buy one or make one. We don't want Baby who is young, or Grandpa, who is old, falling down, though people seem to be able to fall in a heap and come to no harm – ' She was interrupted by laughter. 'So will you all be careful with the ladder until we get some stairs?'

'We could ask Mr Pearce,' Josh suggested.

'You can ask but he won't.' Pa stood up. 'I must get back to work.' He left the room.

'I'll sit for you tomorrow,' Victoria called after him.

'What upset my little pet?' Edward looked into her face protectively. Ma supressed a smile.

'I'd rather not say, not now.' Victoria was still tremulous.

'Then let's give Baby an airing.'

'Yes, let's do that.'

Ma sighed. 'Who is left to eat lunch?'

'I'm ravenous,' I said.

'Me too,' said Josh.

'I am in need of sustenance and so is Mr Bailey after his journey, and David.' Grandpa sat down at the table. 'Smells good.' He nodded towards the stove.

Ma brought food from the range, putting the dishes on the table.

'Help yourselves,' she said, sitting down beside Grandpa.

'Where did all this come from? We didn't bring it from the village.' David helped himself to beans and peas.

Ma smiled. 'That's one of the things I wanted to say. I found them in the scullery this morning: beans, peas, tomatoes and strings of onions hung on the beams, and garlic.'

'Who brought them in?'

'Your guess is as good as mine,' said Ma. 'Lisa has heard someone at work but we haven't seen him.'

'The fellow who waves?' Grandpa spoke as though to be waved to from above the porch was the most normal thing in the world.

'Anybody seen him clearly?' David spoke with his mouth full.

'You are unlikely to see him clearly,' said Grandpa. 'Some may not see him at all.'

'You sound as though you knew him,' I said.

'Better than most of you, if he is who I believe he is.'

'I wonder what he means by that.' Josh spoke low. 'Ask him.'

'I don't like to.' We ate our meal in silence.

Looking at Ma, sitting with the sun shining on her, I was puzzled. She sat relaxed and easy. In Croydon she had been tense and drawn. Now her hair showed no grey and her face was smoother than I had ever seen it. She and Grandpa had shed years. I looked at David and Josh. Neither was in any way different. Nor was Mr Bailey.

'Who brings in the veg then?' Mr Bailey asked suddenly. 'Fairies?'

Ma got up and began to gather plates. 'Put these in the scullery.' She handed a pile to Josh who took them out.

'Ma,' Josh called. The plates clattered as he put them down.

'What is it?'

'Masses of strawberries, Ma, but masses!' Josh came back carrying a basin full of fruit.

'Well, I would like to thank whoever it was,' Ma exclaimed. 'I heard nothing. Did any of you?' We shook our heads. 'Not a sound,' said Josh.

'Somebody must be pleased to have us here,' said Ma. 'The furniture is arranged for us, wonderful stuff brought in from the garden, the ash in the fireplace warm. I am so grateful, so happy.'

Pa came in. 'Any lunch left? Inspiration has left me. That girl's shrieks drove it away.'

'Not for ever, I hope.' Ma got up to get Pa food.

'One can never feel safe,' said Pa soberly, accepting a plate. 'Have you all finished?'

'No.'

'Good.' Pa ate in silence for a while. 'Did those two leave for the afternoon? If she'd come back I could recapture her.'

'She didn't like what she saw,' said Ma. 'What did you do to frighten her?'

Pa was morose, pushing away his plate. 'I was working; it was going well. I told her to rest; she looked at what I'd done and let out those yells.' He looked up. 'Hush. Here they come.'

Victoria and Edward could be heard talking as they came in. 'Lunch?' said Ma quickly.

'Thanks – if we aren't too late.' Victoria, calm now, sat down with Baby on her knee, Edward beside her. Ma and Josh dished out food. Pa looked at Victoria surreptitiously. Victoria, aware of this, pretended not to notice. A small awkward silence grew into a larger one.

'We miss the telly.' Edward spoke, suddenly aggressive. 'We miss electricity.'

'Victoria gave out some pretty electric yells.' Grandpa chuckled evilly.

'Oh, please.' Ma put her hand on Grandpa's. 'Do resist.'

'I find the candlelight beautiful.' David, not given to voicing an opinion, did so now. Edward and Victoria looked at each of us in a worried way.

'Why don't you go to the pub?' asked Ma gently.

'Bad for Baby.' Victoria's arm tightened slightly round Baby's waist so that he turned and looked up into her face.

'I'll mind Baby if you leave him with me,' Ma offered.

'Thank you, but we'd rather not. It's better not to leave him. He wouldn't be safe.' Ma raised her eyebrows.

'Come on.' Edward spoke roughly. 'We must hurry if we're to catch the bus.' He jerked Victoria to her feet.

'They had hardly any lunch.' Ma watched them go.

'That's how she gets those elbows.' Pa helped himself to strawberries. 'Doesn't eat enough.'

'You'd think they were afraid of losing him.' Ma was amused. 'They think he might get stolen.'

'Stolen!' I exclaimed. 'Babies only get stolen by frustrated girls outside supermarkets. Who'd want to steal Baby?'

'They are catching a bus to see a supermarket. That will make them feel safer.' David got up and left the room, followed by Josh.

'They will wander along the High Street and look at the shops. They will find a television shop and watch colour TV through the glass. They will be reassured. Come on, Father, let's have a go at you.' Pa and Grandpa went off, leaving me with Ma.

'You started off about the stairs,' I said as I wiped the plates.

'I did.'

'Why didn't you go on then?'

'I don't know. There's some mystery. Remember Mr Pearce's reaction that first morning?'

'That first morning it was – ' I paused, wondering when that first morning had been. 'How long have we been here?' I looked at Ma.

'I don't know,' she said. 'Ten days? Weeks? Does it matter? I don't think it matters much.' I watched her go back to the kitchen. She began collecting the copper pots and pans so that, afraid of being asked to help clean them, I left her. 'There will come a time when you stop being allergic to Brasso,' she called after me.

In the walled garden Mr Bailey sat by the well contemplating the clump of irises. 'Hello,' I said.

'Sit down and be quiet.'

I sat down beside him, waiting for the toads.

'Night-time's the time they move around,' he said. 'In summertime.'

'You sure they know the time?'

Mr Bailey did not deign to answer.

I watched Old X-ray strolling along the top of the garden wall, followed by Angelique. 'She's grown,' I said.

'Who?'

'Angelique. She was born the day we met you. Look at her now.'

'Looks full grown.' Mr Bailey glanced up at the cats then back at the toads' hideout.

'Angelique's only a few weeks old,' I said. 'She was born on Derby Day, don't you remember?'

'Quite a time you had that day. Bought an 'at, backed an 'orse, won a fortune, 'ad your teeth painted, but you're right, that cat ain't 'ad time to grow so big.'

I looked at Angelique, beautiful and shining, nearly as elegant as Old X-ray and just as large.

'You call her "Old X-ray" but she don't look old.' He watched Old X-ray suddenly rush along the wall, followed by Angelique. 'There now, they've gone. Here one minute, gone the next, like my aitches. Have you noticed I drop them?'

'Sometimes.'

'My old ma wore stays and sometimes when she was tired she'd loosen them, made 'er feel easy, see. Now I do the same with my aitches; verbal instead of physical. When I'm tired, see. I'm tired now. I'm off to 'ave a nap.'

'It's all that time you spent on the road; such a long time, Mr Bailey.'

'Enough of that. It's too dodgy. You leave time alone.' He nodded towards the clump of irises. I peered down at the toads and wondered how much time must pass before one of them moved. The sun was hot on my back, the garden very quiet.

I bent over the iris leaves and studied the toads. The larger toad blinked. I picked it up. I liked the feel of its skin, cool and dry. She sat on my hand, sides pulsing, body stout below her shoulders, legs folded on either side of her narrow waist. I held her against my cheek. 'Like a swim?' On impulse I leaned over the side of the well and let her plop into the dark water. Shocked, she began to swim. I was filled with remorse. There was no toehold on the smooth side. She scrabbled futilely. Her neck looked dreadfully like Grandpa's.

I ran to the toolshed, snatched a hoe and, running back, held it down to the toad. 'Climb up,' I whispered, afraid of somebody discovering my cruelty, afraid of frightening the toad still more. The toad swam away from the hoe then rested, its legs sinking in the water.

I swung my legs over the side and let myself down into the water. The cold made me gasp; my feet touched slippery bottom, then slid and my head went under. As I came up the toad was level with my nose. I put my hand under its stomach and she rested quietly, drawing in her legs. The water reached to my armpits. I stretched up with my free hand. The top of the wall was out of reach. I attempted to jump, my feet slid again and I lost the toad who swam, scrabbling at the sides. I put my hand under it again. I stood in the dark water and wondered how much time before I drowned. 'Not much time,' I said to the toad. She blinked. I put my free hand over her, and held her caged lightly between my fingers. She felt warmer than the water. I drew a deep breath and shouted 'Help! Help! Help!' My voice sounded odd, bouncing off the side of the well.

'Help!' I roared. The air was very still. The insects hummed loudly, and the sound of a bird's wings as it flew across the garden was clear, the displacement of air with each flap of wings distinct. I wondered where everyone could be. How long since Mr Bailey had left me? I would be missed at the next meal. How much time did it take to die of exposure? 'Help!' I cried, pitching my voice high so that it would carry like Victoria's. My cry sounded pitifully weak compared with hers. 'Help!' I tried again and listened.

I heard the tinkle of metal on stone, a scratching in the earth, a cough. The invisible gardener was working, his hoe scraping through the earth. He cleared his throat, whistled. I was so terrified I let out a yell which beat Victoria's. The toad stirred uncomfortably between my hands.

When I heard someone above me I hardly dared look. Bogus was hanging his head over the parapet.

'Oh, Bogus.' I began to cry, sobbing and hiccuping. Bogus became excited and barked into the well, whining, trying to reach me. 'Careful, careful!' I screamed. 'You'll fall in.' He lost his balance, fell in with an almighty splash, thrashing the water, scratching my chest with his paws, out of his depth. He will drown, I thought, and so will I.

'If only you were the Frog Prince,' I said to the toad, letting it go so that I could hold Bogus. The toad attached herself to Bogus's neck and, supported by me, he stopped panicking. I wondered how long it would be before Bogus became waterlogged.

A shadow obscured the light. Above us on the parapet a

ginger cat sat looking down, his tail lashing from side to side. Bogus made a throttling, whining noise which in any other circumstances would have meant pleasure. The cat looked down with large, green eyes. Striped like a tiger, it opened its mouth and yowled a long echoing yowl, arched its back, the sun glinting on its stripes. Time for another shriek I thought and, closing my eyes, opened my mouth and screamed.

Suddenly Bogus was lifted up from the water. The water streamed off him into my eyes and the toad fell into my hands. Half blinded by the water, I looked up. Hands reached down, caught me under the armpits. I was lifted clear and put down, holding the toad guiltily in one hand, trying to wipe the water away from my eyes with the other. For a moment I saw a man, nearly as tall as Pa. He stooped to pat Bogus. I tried to see his face but it was hidden by the brim of a Panama hat. He was there, then he was gone.

The ginger cat vanished. The garden was empty except for me and Bogus, and the toad – uncomfortably squeezed in my hand making an orange mess. Trembling, I put her back in the clump of iris.

'It was Pa,' I said to Bogus who was rolling against a clump of catmint. But I knew it was not Pa as I tried to squeeze the water from my clothes.

I waited to experience terror. I expected extreme terror. I felt I should be in a state of terror, the natural thing to feel after being lifted from a well by someone who wasn't there. I felt no terror at all.

'Goodness, Bogus,' I said to him. 'I am not in a state of terror.'

Then I was afraid. My voice was not my voice, not the voice of a child but a deeper, older voice, almost the voice of a woman.

I ran.

I ran to Pa's loft. I had to see him. I raced up the steps leading to Pa's loft and pushed open the door. Pa looked up in irritation; it was unheard of to interrupt him at work.

'What is it?' He sounded ungracious. 'Why d'you interrupt me?'

'Pa . . . I . . . Pa, I fell into the well, Pa. I was fished out. Bogus fell in, too. I can't explain. There was a ginger cat, and a – a – man in a hat. Oh, Pa – '

Pa sighed. He had been painting Grandpa. He covered the canvas with a cloth.

'All right, Father, it's gone. Another day perhaps.' Pa's expression was strange as though he were elsewhere, not looking at me – dripping wet after nearly drowning. I looked from Pa to Grandpa and the covered canvas. Did Pa see Grandpa as I did now – a man of about fifty with a thatch of grey hair, elegant nose. beetling eyebrows, alert eyes?

Grandpa took my hand. 'Lisa, you are soaked.'

'Grandpa, you looked – '

'I know, I know, that's how I was feeling.'

'So much younger,' I blurted out. 'Hardly older than Pa.'

'Nothing to worry about.' The hand which gripped mine was the gnarled hand I knew, wrinkled with brown marks and swollen joints; his face looking at me old, leathery, not unlike the toad's. 'How did you get so wet?'

As we walked to the house I told him about the toad, the well, and Bogus falling in when I had shouted for help. I could not tell him about how I had been lifted out or by whom.

'There was a huge ginger cat.'

'A stray perhaps.'

'It didn't look like a stray, it looked – er – prosperous.'

'Some cats are. Old X-ray has recently grown prosperous. You say the bottom of the well was slippery,'

'Yes, like ice. I went under twice. I thought I was going to die.'

Grandpa laughed. 'You won't come to that that way.' He began to wheeze and stood to catch his breath. When we walked on a thought struck me.

'Grandpa, you've never let Pa paint you before have you? What made you change your mind?'

'This and that. Listen. Something's going on in the house. Listen to that racket.'

'It's Victoria again. I thought they'd gone to catch the bus.'

'Came back, said there was no bus, seemed to think there never would be a bus, said the postmistress says there never is a bus – '

'There is. I've seen it.'

'Well, they didn't. They jabbered about getting a fright in the churchyard? What were they doing in the churchyard?'

'It's very pretty.'

Grandpa laughed. 'So pretty they came running back, running all the way. Must have jogged that baby, churned up the child's dinner. Your mother smoothed them down, you know her clever way with ruffled feelings.' Grandpa wheezed again. 'Then she sent them up the ladder to rest. Wish I could get up the ladder – '

'But you can!'

'Don't trust it. Only been halfway. Haven't you noticed?'

'If you wanted to you could.'

'I sleep downstairs on the sofa. I'm waiting for the stairs; then I'll go up.'

'When you came out of the pub, and when Pa was painting you just now, you looked young enough to climb Everest.'

'Ah, but it doesn't always last.'

'So it's true you do get younger?'

'What's true varies. Come on, let's see what the hubbub is about.'

In the kitchen Victoria was screaming and shouting while Edward tried to calm her. David, Josh, and Mr Bailey stood around bawling excited questions. Ma stood watching. Baby bellowed, his face purple with the effort. Grandpa scrambled on to a chair with such alacrity I decided the ladder was a case not of 'can't' but 'won't'. He shouted above the din.

'What – is – going – on?'

Everyone stopped and stared up at Grandpa, agape. 'Well?'

'My beads.' Victoria was hysterical. 'My bean beads. They are gone – stolen.' She wrung her hands histrionically. 'They've gone – my beads, my beans.'

'Did you put them in the stew, my dear?' From the chair Grandpa looked down his beaky nose at Ma, his eyes flashing.

'That kind of remark is no help at all,' said Ma.

'Where did you see them last?' Josh was able to make himself heard.

'I wore them yesterday. They were by the bed this morning.'

'They'll turn up.' David, bored, turned and left the room.

'I know they won't.' Victoria weeping was beautiful.

'Sure they are not in the stew?' Grandpa stepped down gingerly from his chair, his hand on Josh's shoulder.

'Grandpa!' Ma spoke between clenched teeth.

'I was only trying to help.' Grandpa and Ma eyed one another.

'You can get other beans – ' Josh suggested.

'No. Mine came from Brazil. We must go back.'

'Back to Brazil,' Josh was staggered.

'It's a "façon de parler" ', said Mr Bailey. 'French for "push off 'ome".'

'Perhaps some clever dick's planted them.' Grandpa was laughing across the room at Ma.

'Don't – make – matters – worse,' she hissed at him.

A thought struck me. I left them and ran to the garden. In the stillness I listened, then I moved slowly, looking about me. Some earth was freshly tilled. I poked a finger into the earth and uncovered a pink bean. I squatted, looking down at the earth. 'All right,' I whispered to the still air. 'You know what you are doing.' I pushed the earth back over the bean and stood up. 'I shall forget you frightened me,' I said to the quiet air.

Later, Victoria and Edward left. Victoria carried Baby who waved goodbye with a fat little hand. Edward reached up to encircle Victoria's waist and hurried with short steps to keep up with her. 'It was bound to happen,' said Ma.

'I am sad,' I said. 'It is like a death.'

'A little.' Grandpa picked up Old X-ray and held her against his face. She looked away from him, twitching her tail.

'They left the van in the yard,' said Josh.

'They won't need it.' Old X-ray disengaged herself and dropped to the ground.

'Won't they come back?' I watched Victoria's skirt swishing into the wood.

'No, but your father caught her on canvas.'

'Oh, did he? In spite of the fuss?'

'Yes, wearing the hat.'

'The Panama,'

'He intends painting us all wearing that hat. "Hat Period" like Picasso's "Blue". The arrogance! I can still see them.' Grandpa peered across to the wood, his knobbly fingers shading his eyes.

'Oh.' Ma sounded distressed. 'Oh dear.'

Pa, who had been in the hall, joined us. 'What is it?' he said.

'They are stuck,' I said.

'Don't be ridiculous. Stuck? It's a trick of the light.'

I was right. Victoria and Edward were moving, but not into the wood or back to us. 'Go fetch them, Bogus.' Josh spoke low. 'Go fetch them.'

Bogus raced across the grass. We watched him bound through the slanting light to Edward and Victoria, jumping up and down, barking. But he jumped and bounded through them as though through a patch of mist. Mr Bailey, standing beside Grandpa, put his fingers to his mouth and whistled shrilly. Bogus hesitated, then came slowly back to us, his tail low, wagging apologetically.

'You don't want to lose the dog, do you?' Mr Bailey, watching Bogus, spoke harshly. I shivered.

'Come in all of you.' Ma was brisk. 'Lisa, you are wet. Go and change. Josh, go with her and see she puts on warm clothes. Andrew – ' She looked at Pa. I thought she was crying. Pa put an arm round her and drew her into the house.

Josh followed me up the ladder. 'Time you and I had a talk,' he said as we reached my room. 'Nobody else seems to want to.'

I pulled my shirt over my head. 'The tricks aren't all tricks of light. There's something strange going on.'

Josh sat on the side of the bed pulling his knees up to his chin. 'It's haphazard. You must have noticed it comes and goes, without any logical reason.' Josh handed me a towel to dry my hair. 'What have you noticed?'

'Promise not to laugh.'

'I promise,' he said gravely.

I began. 'There's an invisible gardener. I can hear him working, but I can't see him.' I paused. For a moment I wondered whether I could tell Josh about being lifted out of the well by a man wearing a hat who vanished. I decided not to. Josh might scoff. Whatever happened with whoever, it was my affair. 'He brings Ma vegetables.'

'Go on.'

'Grandpa from time to time looks as young as Pa.'

'I've noticed that, too, and Ma has changed.'

'Somebody waves from the window. I can't find the room.'

'I've looked, too. He wears the hat, or one like it.'

'There's something very odd about the village. The only people in it are Mr Pearce and Mrs Pearce.'

Josh frowned. 'There are other people but they don't talk. They wave or nod as they pass. They seem a little surprised to see me.'

'What sort of people?'

'Ordinary. There are people, at least I think there are. There's the bus driver. They don't speak. I *think* I've seen them.'

'Have you noticed something peculiar has happened with time? It feels as if we'd been here months and not days.'

'Yes. Angelique has grown up and Old X-ray is much younger. She was pretty ancient in London.'

'And Bogus. The Pearces call him Rags and behave as though he'd been here when Mr Hayco died in 1949. It's just possible Bogus might be another dog who looks exactly like Rags. It's possible that we only have vivid imaginations.'

Josh moved to the window and leaned out while I pulled on jeans. 'There's one thing I haven't imagined,' he said.

'And what's that?'

'There's a child's grave in the churchyard, no date on it. The child was called Arnold.'

'There are lots of Arnolds besides Baby.'

'It's a fresh grave, no proper stone.'

'Doesn't mean a thing.' I spoke more robustly than I felt. 'If we start imagining Baby's not alive which he *is*, we'll start thinking there's a staircase to be found.'

'I believe there is, and a person waving.'

'Oh Josh, just because that house agent said the house is haunted – '

'You've heard the gardener, seen the man waving – look at that.' Josh pointed out of the window. 'Something going on there.'

'Just mist rising.' I leaned beside him. 'It's awfully pretty.'

The mist was delicate as a Shetland shawl eddying in the evening air between the house and the wood, spiralling anticlockwise.

'Look.' Josh gripped my arm. 'See that?' The mist parted for a moment to show figures waving, then thickened. We could see arms reaching up, beckoning.

'It's Edward and Victoria. They need help.' Josh rushed to the door. 'Quick.'

We scrambled down the ladder to the hall. Bogus was standing at its foot. He barred our way so that Josh nearly fell over him.

'Out of the way, Bogus, out of the way.' Josh was impatient.

'He wants us to take the hat.' I snatched the Panama from the hatstand and crammed it on my head. Josh pulled open the front door and we ran out into thick mist.

Holding hands, a thing we had not done for years, we ran towards the wood, Bogus close on our heels. The mist deadened sound.

'We are coming,' Josh called. 'Where are you?'

'Here.' Edward's voice was anxious. We saw them standing close together, Victoria's head above the mist, she tall and spindly beside short Edward. She held Baby high on her shoulder. Edward had his arm round her. 'What's going on?' I tried to be reasonable, tried to be calm.

'We are trying to get away. We are stuck here, it's crazy.'
Edward was furious, afraid.

'I can't see, my glasses are misted.' Victoria was close to
tears.

'Wipe them.'

'I daren't let go of Edward and Baby.'

'Here then, keep still.' I took the glasses off her nose and
dried them. 'You don't need them anyway. They are only a
joke – you said so.' I replaced the glasses.

'I've needed them here, I really have. That's one of the
frightening things. But you wouldn't understand.'

'Try us,' I said. 'What d'you mean, you are stuck?'

'We can't get through the wood. It's been getting more
difficult every day.' Victoria sounded childish.

'Don't be so infantile,' Josh scoffed.

'We knew you'd never believe us if we told you. We are
infantile, that's just it.' Edward spoke with extreme exasperation.

'Tell,' I said.

'We wake in the night and find we are childrem,' Victoria
whispered. 'The first time it happened we didn't know each
other.' Victoria's eyes were enormous behind the pebble
glasses. 'Edward had spots.'

'And no beard.' I was beginning to understand.

'He wouldn't have a beard as a child.' Josh burst out
laughing.

'It's no laughing matter,' said Edward angrily.

I joined Josh in laughter.

'Don't you realize, you idiots,' cried Edward, 'we wake
up as children *and Baby isn't there.*'

'Oh,' we said, aghast. 'Oh.' Then with more understanding, 'You go back to before he was born?'

'Yes.' Tears were pouring down Victoria's cheeks.

'Come *on.*' Josh spoke roughly. 'Come *on.* We'll get
you away.' He snatched the hat from my head and put it
on Victoria's. 'Hold on to each other and to us. Let's go.'

We hurried them through the wood. Nobody spoke
until we reached the road.

'Did Pa paint you successfully?'

'*He* thought it a success.'

'You didn't?'

'I looked about six years old; it was gruesome. I had braces on my teeth and I wore glasses all the time then. One doesn't like to be reminded.'

'You are very beautiful now.' Edward looked up at her.

'You didn't think so the first time we woke up like that. You said – '

'Never mind what I said. I was upset, that's all. Unnerved.'

'All right.' Victoria was grudging. 'What do you think I felt?'

'We shall be at the bus-stop in a minute.' Josh was tactful.

'There isn't a bus.'

'Oh yes there is. We'll put you on it, see you safely off.'

'Really?'

'Yes, we promise.'

'You are going without your van,' I said tactlessly.

'You keep it,' Edward said kindly. 'It's had its day. You may find some use for the brass figures, but the engine's gone. I tried it and it's kaput. We thought we could escape in it but not since – ' He stopped.

'Not since what?'

'We saw something horrid in the churchyard.'

'Oh that,' exclaimed Josh. 'No need to worry about that. I've seen it, too. It's nothing to worry about at all.'

'The figures are super, thanks a lot,' I said.

We reached the bus-stop. Edward and Victoria looked relieved.

'I can hear the bus.' Josh turned his head and we all heard the sound of an engine. 'Thanks for the loan.' Victoria took off the hat and gave it to Josh. 'And you can keep these as a memento.' She handed me the glasses. 'I won't need them any more.'

Baby blew a bubble from wet lips. The spit ran down his chin.

'My baby.' Victoria kissed him, giving him a squeeze. Josh averted his eyes.

The bus drew to a halt. People looked down at us in silence.

'Climb aboard,' cried Josh. Victoria bent and kissed us. Edward clasped our hands. 'Goodbye,' they said. 'Thanks a lot. We'll be all right now. Goodbye.'

They climbed into the bus, Victoria's long skirts swinging out in the mist; Edward, thick-set, his arm ready to put round her waist when they found a seat. We watched them sit down. Baby pressed his face to the window, licking the glass, smearing it. The bus moved off. We waved. From behind the steamy, spat-on glass they waved back.

'That's a relief.' I patted Bogus as we watched the bus disappear round a bend. 'I feel happy.'

'Me, too.' Josh glanced at me. 'It's fine for Grandpa. It would have been rather nice to have them to play with if you think of it.'

'They were afraid of losing Baby.'

'Wouldn't have frightened me. Did you see him lick the window? Smothered it with spit. Ugh!'

'*They* love him.' I laughed.

'Let's take a peep in the churchyard.' Josh put on the hat and we climbed into the churchyard.

'Where is the grave?'

'I'll show you.' The pollen from the grass stuck to his jeans. There was no sound except of rooks cawing. 'It's here.' Josh rounded a corner by the tower.

'Where?'

'It's gone. How extraordinary.'

'Are you sure it was here?'

'Of course. A small grave, fresh earth and a black wooden marker which had "Arnold" in white paint. I swear it was here.'

'I believe you,' I said soberly. 'It looks as though we saved his life.'

'The hat did.'

'Okay, the hat.' Josh touched it.

'Baby Arnold's time had gone a bit wonky.'

'And Victoria and Edward's. They were not like us. This was a holiday for them, not real as it is for us.'

Our parents and David were sitting on the terrace watching the moon rise. 'They all look pretty normal,' I said. 'They don't look as though anything out of the ordinary ever happened, or even if they'd notice if it did. It's like a sneezing fit. The world seems about to burst, then it's normal again.'

'Tell you what isn't ordinary,' said Josh, looking up behind the house. 'I've been up that hill to look down on Haphazard and the house isn't there. No house, no garden, just a meadow with sheep cropping the grass.'

'Goodness, what did you do?'

'Ran home helter-skelter, and the house was here and he was waving from the window.'

'Perhaps you'd better wear the hat another time.'

'Perhaps I had. Look, he's waving.'

We waved back to whoever he was and ran across the grass to our parents.

'Have they gone?' Pa looked over the rim of his glass, sitting with his back to the house, long legs stretched out.

'Yes. Caught the bus.'

Pa looked thoughtful. 'I never really caught Miss Pin, try as I would. She sat for me and, blimey, what came on to the canvas was a plain child in pebble glasses with her teeth in braces.' He sipped his drink and sighed. 'Not the prettiest of sitters.'

'Didn't you try her in the hat?' Ma asked mildly.

'I thought of it too late. By then she'd seen my painting, taken offence and wouldn't pose any more. I shall have to rake my memory to get those sharp elbows, lanky hair, the swing of the skirts.'

'You should have tried the hat.' Ma had taken it from Josh and held it gently in her lap. 'If you'd worn it – '

'Could have worn his false nose.' Grandpa tossed the sentence over his shoulder.

'Grandpa, please,' Ma murmured. 'Just when we are so peaceful.'

'Checkmate.' Mr Bailey moved his bishop.

'I think you cheated but I'll let it pass.' Grandpa set the men up again. 'Do best to get on with your portrait of me,' he said. 'I shan't be around for ever.'

'For a long time yet,' I said, 'the way you carry on.'

'Don't be impertinent,' snapped Grandpa, moving his queen's pawn. 'One is always conscious of death, and the view from the bathroom window is no help.'

'What do you mean?' Mr Bailey was anxious to join whatever conversation there might be.

'The window looks down on the yard. There's a hearse – disguised – but champing to be off.' Grandpa removed his false teeth and snapped them like a castanet. Mr Bailey recoiled. Grandpa replaced the teeth. 'Your move,' he said.

Mr Bailey made a move.

'They gave us the van as a parting present,' said Josh casually. 'Those figures will be useful somewhere. They don't really look serious enough for a hearse.'

'Who wants to be serious?' Grandpa moved a pawn. 'I rode down in it. The cats liked it. Be different in a coffin, I daresay.'

'You wouldn't know much about it in your coffin.' Mr Bailey moved his knight. 'I once put a ticket on a hearse. Irish people – having a wake.'

'If you put that hat on my coffin like a fieldmarshal's whatsit I might resurrect.'

'I don't find this conversation edifying.' Ma grinned at Pa. 'I'm going to get supper. How those two ate, just like children, and the baby hardly at all.' She went into the house. I followed.

'Baby didn't eat much because he wasn't here much,' I said, hoping to surprise her.

'I know, love,' she said, 'none of them was.'

'Did you like Baby?'

'Well – '

'Josh and I didn't. He dribbled.'

'Babies do.' Ma was noncommittal. 'He was teething.'

'I wonder whether Mr Bailey will catch it,' I said, collecting knives and forks from a dresser.

'I doubt it.' Ma cut some onions from the string. 'Oh, look what's come in.' She sounded delighted.

The table in the scullery was loaded with spinach, new potatoes and raspberries. 'All grown with love,' she said.

'I wonder whether he planted the beans with love,' I muttered.

'The what, darling?'

'Nothing,' I said, glad to see Ma so happy.

In my four-poster, Bogus at my feet, I lay thinking of Edward and Victoria. If they had stayed on we could have played together, presuming that they would have been the same age as us. Josh and I had never had many friends. I wondered what Edward, aged fourteen, would have been like. I tried, vainly, to imagine him without the beard. Victoria with pebble glasses and braces on her teeth was difficult, too. I kicked restlessly; Bogus grunted. I sat up, stretching out my hand to stroke his head. My room was lit by the moon. Idly I watched my hand stroking the silky ears. Puzzled, I looked at it; it was larger than usual. Startled, I felt my arms and my shoulders, kicked my feet about. My legs were longer than normal. I got out of bed and looked in the mirror. The girl in the glass was not me. I lifted my eyes to my face, pushing back my hair. I confronted her. She looked back at me with startled eyes. I wondered who she could be and waved. She waved.

'Bogus,' I called. My voice sounded different.

Bogus got off the bed and came to me, looking up,

wagging his plumy tail. In the mirror he stood beside the girl, looking up at her. We stood confronting ourselves. I felt my hair, my face, my body. I could see the reflection in the mirror doing the same. Bogus sat down and started scratching. In the mirror he scratched, too. I heard my name called, 'Lisa? Lisa?' I had heard that voice before.

I stared at my reflection. I could not answer though I wanted to. Somewhere in the house was music. My feet began to tap. In a moment I was dancing. I danced; so did the reflection. A voice called, 'Lisa!' insistently.

The music stopped. I hurled myself into bed, dragging Bogus with me, pulling up the sheet, clutching Bogus. It was morning and my mother called, 'Lisa. Time to get up.' I dressed, scrambled down the ladder to the hall and ran to the kitchen. The woman standing by the stove was an older version of the girl in the mirror.

'What is it?' Ma smiled.

'A dream,' I said. 'I dreamed of music and that someone called me.'

'I called you,' said Ma.

'I thought it was a man's voice. I've heard it before.'

Ma said nothing, putting bacon on a plate, handing it to me. 'Eat it before it gets cold,' she said.

'Do you dream?' I asked her.

'I don't need to.' She sat opposite me across the table. 'Probably because I'm very happy here.'

'Oh Ma, were you not happy before? You had Pa, you had us.'

'Yes, but your Pa was not happy, nor were you children and your Grandpa was only kept alive by – '

'By what?'

'Cussedness, I suppose.' Ma grinned. She looked very like the girl in the mirror. I decided not to tell her, it might spoil her happiness. 'What keeps Grandpa alive now?' I asked.

'He's looking forward to something.'

'What on earth has he to look forward to at his age?' I exclaimed.

'Age is relative,' said Ma. 'The air here suits him as it did not suit Victoria and Edward.'

We heard Josh calling, 'Ma, Ma, look who has come to see us!' Walking towards the house came Josh with Sandy.

'Sandy!' Ma and I ran to meet them. 'Sandy, what brings you here? How nice to see you.' She sounded insincere.

'Business.' Sandy bent to peck Ma's cheek. 'You look pretty fit.'

'You are in time for breakfast. Come in.' I looked up. The person at the window, wearing the hat, waved mockingly. I waved back.

'I would have been here sooner,' Sandy was saying, 'but I had trouble with my car. As I was coming into your village I swerved to avoid a cat and the car stalled. Couldn't get it started again; had to leave it and walk. Luckily I ran into Josh.'

'Was it a ginger cat?' I asked.

'Yes. Huge brute, size of a tiger. D'you know it?'

'Sort of.'

'Couldn't find a soul to help me. There must be a garage.'

'There isn't,' said Josh.

'No *garage*? You *are* in the sticks.'

'No. Mini died.'

'Who was Minnie? Did she run a garage? Funny job for a woman.'

'Mini, our car.'

'That clapped-out old sardine tin? No garage could repair that.'

'She died in the village. Perhaps your car's dead, too,' Josh teased.

'Can't compare my Jaguar with your thing.'

Josh took offence. 'The village doesn't like cars.'

'He's only just arrived.' Ma hastened to make peace. 'It's great to see you Sandy, why have you come?'

'Andrew never answered my letters. I've written five.'

'I don't think he's had them, has he children?'

'No letters,' we chorused.

'That's absurd. I put the right address – Haphazard House, Coldharbour. It isn't an address you can get wrong, it is?'

'No,' we said. 'Not very easily.'

'I expect he destroyed them,' said Sandy querulously.

'He didn't get them,' said Ma. 'Tell us why you're here.'

'Time Andrew had another show. The public's crying out for another Andrew Fuller show.'

'But he's only just had one,' I said, 'in June, Derby Day. You must remember *that*.'

'That was years ago. He must have done some work since then.'

'Years?' I asked, puzzled.

'Yes, yes.' I caught Ma's eye. 'He's had plenty of time to paint enough for another show.'

'Ah, time,' said Ma, leading Sandy through the hall. 'Time to get you something to eat. You must be tired after your drive. Try and find your father, children.'

'I'll look in the loft,' said Josh.

'I'll look in the garden.'

'He won't be there.'

'He might be.'

In the garden Pa was sitting on the side of the well sketching.

'Hullo, Pa.' I sniffed. Pa was sketching some flowers.

'I hadn't noticed these before. Just smell them,' Pa said. The bean flowers were multicoloured, white, blue, yellow, pink, and the sweetest of all a strange colour, neither white nor green. Somewhere a person sneezed. 'The cats love them.' Pa went on drawing. Old X-ray and Angelique were winding and twining along the row of beans. Watching them I saw the ginger cat, then I sneezed so hard tears came to my eyes.

'Sandy's here,' I said. 'Come to pester you.'

'Oh bother! What does he want?'

'Pictures. He wants you to have another show.'

'Hah!' Pa flung down his pad and stood up in a rage.

'Ma is giving him breakfast.'

'She should have given him hemlock.'

'Now Pa, don't get worked up.'

Pa sneezed. 'It's the flowers,' he said. 'I wonder what they are?'

'Beans.'

'Rubbish. Oh, well, I suppose I'd better go in. Hide this for me.' He handed me the sketch pad. 'Put it somewhere safe where he can't see it.'

'I'll put it in the hat,' I said, but he did not hear me.

'The flowers are lovely. Thank you,' I called to the empty garden. There was no answer. I peeped in on the toads among the irises. Their sides moved a little as they breathed. I left the garden, the cats staring after me, unblinking, sitting among the beans, sleepy, luxurious. I had the feeling that someone other than the cats was watching me, too.

I rolled up Pa's sketch and put it in the hat where it hung on the stand. Sandy was tucking in to eggs and bacon, talking with his mouth full, looking up at Pa who stood leaning against the wall.

'Be reasonable,' Sandy munched. 'With a tumbledown place like this you need the money. Why, half of it has no roof.'

'That doesn't matter,' I said.

Sandy gulped coffee. 'The fire damage in the hall is frightful.'

'Could have been worse,' said Pa.

'You told me when you bought it there was no light, no mains water, no proper road, but this is ridiculous.'

'We like it that way.' Pa arched his back, resting his shoulders against the wall. I could see it annoyed Sandy, who was a short man, to be looking up at Pa. 'Why don't you sit down?'

'I like standing.'

'Listen,' said Sandy, 'be reasonable. Your public wants to buy Andrew Fullers. Suppose you give me all the work you've done so far and I'll take it up to London – organize another show for you?'

'I couldn't do that.'

'But you will need the money.'

'Will I? What for?'

'You have a wife, children, your father, hangers-on.' Sandy glanced at David and Mr Bailey who sat quietly eating their breakfasts. Pa said nothing. 'You can't have much left of your windfall. You need money to keep up this

establishment, such as it is.' Sandy's voice implied that the
Augean stables were on a par with Haphazard.

'Hah!' Mr Bailey uttered. 'Hah!' Sandy ignored him.

'You can't have much left. You'll never have a break like
that horse again.'

'Dear horse,' said Ma. 'What was it called? I forget.'

'False Start,' I said.

'Well?' Sandy looked at Pa.

'I haven't much time to paint.'

'You've had ages.'

'I've a new style. I haven't one canvas for you.'

'But you must have.'

'No must about it.' Pa's face was in shadow at the top of
his six-feet-four. 'Anyway, nobody's having what I'm
painting now.'

'What!' Sandy could not believe his ears. 'I come all this
way, take the trouble when you don't answer my letters; a
gallery laid on, all we need is the pictures. People want
Andrew Fullers.'

'Then want must be their master.'

'I'm your agent.'

'You *were* my agent.'

From his seat in the window Grandpa began to laugh.
'Hear that?' he cried. 'No more pictures. No more Fullers.
No more money for *you*.' Sandy looked put out. 'What did
you charge him? Twenty per cent? Twenty-five? The boy is
busy. Hasn't time for you. He's painting me; immortalizing
his aged father while there's time. He hasn't time for you.'

'I'm only – ' Sandy half rose.

'Only wasting time,' cried Grandpa gleefully. 'Isn't it
time you were off?'

'Grandpa, please,' Ma protested.

'Time, time, time,' Grandpa shouted, snapping his fingers
at Sandy. 'Your time is money, it's something quite else
here.' He sprang up, his halo of white hair bright.

'Come on, Father. To work.' Pa pushed himself away
from the wall and left the kitchen with Grandpa.

Sandy looked beseechingly at Ma. 'Can't you do something?'

She said, 'I'm sorry, Sandy, but it's over. All that bad time is over.'

'D'you mean he's stopped painting, got a block?'

'Oh no,' said Ma, 'oh no, not that. It's just – '

'What?'

'It's just that there isn't anything for you here. We'd love you to stay of course. Why don't you?'

'I've no time.' Sandy got to his feet. 'Thank you very much for breakfast but I'd better be on my way. I've no time to waste.'

'Oh, poor you.' Ma sounded sad. 'Unhappy man.'

'Perhaps I'll come later on and Andrew will have some stuff then.'

'Don't waste your time,' I said, feeling sorry for Sandy. 'You need your time, we have plenty.' As I spoke I wondered what I was talking about, what I meant.

'Well,' Ma spoke quietly. 'Lisa and Josh will see you back to your car.'

'It's broken down.'

'I daresay it will start now it's had a rest.'

'Jaguars don't need to rest. My car's not a horse.'

'Well,' Ma looked at Sandy then at Josh.

'Come on.' Josh caught Sandy's arm. 'It'll start if we push.'

We led Sandy away. As we left the house Josh took the hat from the stand. Ma called after us. 'If you see Mr Pearce ask about the Aga.'

'Okay,' we shouted as we moved off. I waved up to the window above the porch where a ginger cat sat sunning itself. Josh took off the hat with a flourish and bowed. Sandy looked up at the house. 'Who are you waving to?'

'We are just being childish,' I said, looking down at my legs in their old jeans. 'These wouldn't have fitted this morning.'

'What?' said Sandy.

'Nothing.'

'You lot are all crazy. This Haphazard dump has gone to your heads.' Sandy was vehement in his disgust and disappointment.

Sandy's Jaguar stood beside the pub. It looked very grand and out of place. The church tower seemed to be rearing away from it, offended.

'It just stalled.' Sandy put his hand on the bonnet.

'Cars do here. Get in. We will push you.'

'This has been a fruitless visit.' Sandy got into the driving seat.

'Scarcity will increase the value of what Fullers there are.' Josh tried to cheer him up. Looking at Sandy I remembered the sad days in Croydon when Ma had said to Sandy, 'If he could sell just one or two it would give him hope, give him time to work without always worrying about money.'

'Come on,' I said to Josh, 'push.' We pushed. Nothing happened. 'Have you got the brakes off?' I asked.

'Of course I have. I'd better push, too.' Sandy got out and began pushing from the side, his hand on the wheel to steer.

'Half the trouble with your father's pictures *is* their scarcity,' he puffed.

'There were three hundred in the show,' I said, remembering.

'More than half have disappeared. We can't trace them.'

'How's that?' Josh was getting red in the face from exertion.

'Some clever dick cornered the market.' Sandy stopped pushing. 'She's not going to move.'

'Oh yes she is. Get in,' I said, taking the hat off Josh's head and putting it on the Jaguar's bonnet. 'Try the starter.'

Sandy tried. The noble engine purred into life.

'There.' I stood beside him looking in. Josh retrieved the hat. 'Off you go.'

'Thank you.' Sandy suddenly looked happier. 'Thank you very much. I'm glad I came in spite of everything.'

'Glad? Why?'

'This is a magical place, so unexpected. I shall come again some day.'

We stood in the road waving. 'I think I'd better take the hat home. Just imagine if he'd driven off with it on the bonnet!' Josh held the hat against his chest.

'Here comes David,' I said, 'with Bogus.' We stood waiting for them.

'Your ma thought I'd better come up as Mr Pearce will be behind the bar, and you are too young to go into the pub.'

'I don't know that I am.' I remembered myself that morning in the mirror. Josh drifted away, carrying the hat. 'Anyway, I'd like a drink,' I said. 'No law against that.'

'I'll bring you a glass of wine.' David went into the pub, leaving me under the oak tree. I could hear the church clock above me and swallows whistling. The inn sign creaked. David brought me a glass of wine. He was followed by Mr Pearce.

'Morning,' said Mr Pearce. 'Hullo, Rags, how's tricks then?' Bogus thumped his tail. Mr Pearce patted him. 'Getting settled in then?' Mr Pearce sat beside me. He wore corduroy trousers tied under the knee with string, and a red handkerchief round his neck. He smelt of hay, sweat and beer. 'You like it at Coldharbour then? Getting settled in?'

'Yes, we love it. We are all very happy.'

'All?'

'Well, Edward and Victoria left.'

'They'd have to, wouldn't they? It was young Arnold. Couldn't stay after that, could they?'

'After what?' I said. 'After what?'

'David here says your ma is interested in an Aga.' Mr Pearce ignored my question.

'Yes, she'd like one please. She wants to keep the range though. What happened to Arnold, Mr Pearce?'

'Young Arnold?' Mr Pearce glanced briefly over his shoulder at the tombstones dancing their ballet. 'Tell your ma I'll bring the Aga tomorrow. She'd like a red one I take it? Look nice with all the copper.'

'When did young Arnold die?' I asked doggedly.

'Before you was born I should say. Rags was quite a puppy.' Mr Pearce fondled Bogus's ears. '*Nearly* died.'

'Did he recover?'

Mr Pearce looked vague. 'Time you went home. Tell her I'll bring the Aga.' The scent of beer receded as he went back to the pub.

David took the wine glass from my hand and put it on the step of the pub. 'Come on.' He took my hand.

We walked in silence through the wood, across the grass to the house, the midday sun in our eyes. The person at the window was watching. We both waved. The person waved back.

'It's difficult to see in this sunlight,' I said.

'In any light,' said David.

'Did you notice Mr Pearce's clothes, David? Weren't they a bit – '

'My credulity is elastic,' he said.

23

I climbed the hill behind the house. I wanted to test what Josh had said about the house not being there when he looked down from the hill. I wore the hat.

The way led up through beech woods. The trees towered above, grey boles, branches springing out, blocking the sky; here and there red and yellow fungus. The air under the trees was still. Above, the breeze rustled the leaves. The path zigzagged uphill. I was soon out of sight of the house. I felt I remembered the way and reproached myself for being fanciful.

A fox crossing a clearing paused and looked at me, its

eyes brightly interrogating. I reached the top of the hill, coming out on to a grassy space. I climbed on a rock and looked around. Unafraid of me, rabbits nibbled grass, sat up, washed their ears, lolloped to and fro showing white scuts. High up a buzzard screamed. I watched it circling on the warm thermals. It was joined by its mate. They circled the top of the hill until some rooks flew up to mob them, then drifted away. I looked down over the wood to the valley. Haphazard was reassuringly there below me.

I could see everything in miniature. In the walled garden Mr Bailey was sitting by the iris clump. The rows of fruit and vegetables criss-crossed the garden, each a different shade of green except for the row of Victoria's beans. The colours of the flowers fused like a rainbow. I saw my mother join Mr Bailey. She offered something, which he refused. I guessed that she had remembered to pay him for the taxi she had had to take from St James's Square the day we bought Haphazard. It seemed an infinity ago. Grandpa came briskly down the steps of Pa's loft. The sun shone directly on his head. I craned forward to see. Was his head bald or was it covered with iron-grey hair? Where the stream ran through the wood I could see the pool, Josh and David swimming. Bogus lolled against the front door. Old X-ray and Angelique basked at the kitchen window; smoke drifted gently up from the chimneys. I watched it, trying to see the exact point where the smoke became invisible. My eyes travelled up with it. Even here on top of the hill I had to raise my head. Unable to locate the invisible point, I looked down. Gone was the house. Gone my mother. Gone the kitchen garden, the cats, Grandpa, Mr Bailey, Bogus – gone Josh and David, only an open grass clearing below.

I felt that rare sensation of blood draining from my face. I shut my eyes, held my breath, listened, hoped. The buzzards screamed to each other. I kept my eyes shut. I was afraid. They had all gone, become as invisible as the man who tilled the garden, lit the fires, brought the vegetables, planted beans. Was I, too, invisible or was I sitting here on a rock on top of a hill with rabbits nibbling among harebells?

I whispered, 'Haphazard, come back. When I first saw

you in horrible Heath's waiting-room I knew we belonged to you. Haphazard, don't go away.'

I pressed my fingers to my eyes, not daring to look. Were my fingers the ones I had seen that morning in the mirror, Fear was choking me, it was hard to swallow. I opened my eyes and looked at my hands. I was so frightened I could not tell whether they were mine or that girl's. Someone was watching me. I stood up.

Below in the clearing a man looked up at me. He wore the hat.

But I was wearing the hat! I let out a yell from bursting lungs in dry-throated terror. Eerily my cry echoed downhill through the trees.

The man lifted his arms and waved the hat. He called my name, 'Lis-a-a-'

Trembling, I took off the hat, held it against my chest. I stared down at the man looking up at me.

A wind had risen, whisking my hair across my face. I brushed it away with angry fingers. The man was less distinct as I stared down, trying to see his face. His figure became hazy. I began to see the outlines of the house behind him, Mr Bailey alone now in the garden, Ma and Pa strolling out of the house, holding hands, Grandpa reading a newspaper. A newspaper! We had no newspapers, we had not seen a newspaper since we left London. Grandpa turned a page, giving the newspaper a shake. I could read the headlines.

'Tragedy of octogenarian in top floor flat. Mr Fuller, eighty-two, in his Bloomsbury home due for demolition – ' Grandpa flipped over another page. I could see no more. I tried to move but I couldn't. I struggled to get the hat on. The colours of the house and garden below were vivid. I could see the scarlet fruit of the irises, the many-coloured beans, Grandpa's white halo of hair, his polished head, the brilliant fur of the cats, the grass, Ma's teeth flashing as she laughed with Pa. The stranger had gone. I stood up. A hawk swooped like a bullet to snatch a mouse from the grass. I began to run, racing down through the trees, scrambling, jumping, tearing downhill to erupt beside my parents who were sitting, chatting idly.

'Hullo.' Pa looked up. 'Heavens, you look hot.'

'What have you been doing? You look dishevelled.' Ma held her hand to shade her eyes.

'I was looking down from the top. I – er – ran back when I saw you.' I sat down to get my breath, to still my trembling legs.

'That's nice,' said Ma.

'I thought I saw Grandpa reading a newspaper.'

Ma and Pa burst out laughing.

'A paper! Here! A *newspaper*! You were dreaming.'

'No papers,' said Ma.

'No television,' said Pa.

'No noise, no harrassment, no fuss,' said Ma. 'No aggro.'

'No creditors, no hurry, no bores to waste one's time,' said Pa.

'There was Sandy,' I reminded him.

'Oh, the poor fellow,' exclaimed Pa cheerfully. 'Came all that way with expectations only to go back empty-handed.'

'Not a sausage,' I said, feeling better.

'A shame really.' Ma smiled. 'Especially as you *are* painting.'

'No luck with Victoria. Couldn't catch that girl.'

'She wasn't really here to catch,' said Ma ambiguously. 'How are you getting on with your father?'

'Rather well. I am pleased so far.'

'The newspaper headline seemed to say – ' I began. Then I paused. 'Tragedy' it had said. Did not 'tragedy' usually imply death?

'Newspaper headlines always "seem" but are rarely true. Anyway you couldn't have read it at that distance.' Pa idly took the hat from my head and put it on.

'Of course I couldn't,' I agreed.

'I've changed my style,' said Pa to Ma. 'I'm painting really well.'

'It's you who has changed. You are much nicer since we got here. It's affected your work.'

It had been a dream, just a bad dream. I had enjoyed it in a way. I had felt happiness with the fear.

'Time for supper.' Ma got up, holding out her hands to

us. I had not realized how late it was. 'Sandy's visit was a bit – '

'Disturbing.' Pa tilted the hat. We joined Grandpa sitting with the cats.

'I saw you on top of the hill,' he said to me. 'What can you see from there?'

'Nothing.' I remembered my desolation. 'Nothing at all.'

Grandpa coughed. 'If there's nothing to see I won't go up, though my pipes are greatly improved.'

'If they are so improved you could climb up to bed like a civilized person,' said Ma, using slight asperity.

'Do you wish to kill me?' Grandpa stared at her.

'Don't speak of death!' I exclaimed, remembering my fear.

'Hush now.' Pa spoke briskly, reassuringly. 'We forgot our manners, we forgot to wave.'

We all ran backwards until we could see the window above the porch. We waved, and Pa doffed the hat. In the dusk the person waved behind the glass.

'He seems to have a cat.' Ma went ahead into the house.

'A marmalade cat,' said Pa.

'Ginger,' Mr Bailey corrected him.

'All right, if you say so.' Pa was amiable. 'I must admit my parent has a point. Stairs are usual. They are a convenience.'

'A catalyst,' said Mr Bailey.

'What's that?' I asked.

'Something that joins or connects things together, loose-ly. Stairs would connect the ground floor with your grand-pa's bedroom, see?'

'Yes. Mr Bailey, I had a funny dream on top of the hill.' I feld a need to confirm.

'Dreamed you was back in Croydon?'

'That would have been a nightmare,' I exclaimed. Again I remembered Ma speaking to Sandy long ago, well before Derby Day. 'Oh, Sandy, if he could just sell *one*.' Her face had been strained, lined, worried, unhappy, old.

'What was the dream, then?' Mr Bailey enquired.

'I don't think I can tell you after all.' I remembered the man calling my name. 'It was a nice dream, really.'

'That's good. Like me putting tickets on cars and dreaming of toads was it?'

'Something like that. It was something I want.'

I lay listening to the house waking. A mouse scratched under the boards, a bumblebee zoomed by. I got up and leaned out of my window, wondering whether the man two or three windows along the landing was also looking out.

Along the wall an open window enabled me to hear my parents waking. Pa yawned loudly. They laughed. I heard their door open and the sound of them going down the corridor.

From out of the wood Mr Pearce came leading a horse pulling a cart. On the cart, gleaming in the sun, was a red Aga. Ma walked out to meet Mr Pearce. I watched her. From the back anyone not knowing her age would take her for nineteen or twenty, not a woman with a son of fourteen and me, Lisa, aged eleven.

When I climbed down the ladder Mr Pearce, with David helping him, was lowering the Aga to a trolley. 'Easy now, easy.' It looked difficult.

The horse, its head turned to watch, wore blinkers. It had bright brasses on its harness. Ma stroked its nose. It mumbled her fingers with whiskery lips. 'What a magnificent colour.' Ma admired the Aga.

'I knew you'd want red. Goes nicely with the copper pots.'

'It certainly will.' Ma sounded pleased. 'Could we turn your horse loose to graze or will he go home?'

'He'll stay.' Mr Pearce unharnessed the horse who shook himself. The harness marks were dark on his light, bay coat. He smelt of sweat, and blew down his nose before starting to crop grass, mumbling among the sweet tufts with grey lips.

Mr Pearce and David began manoeuvring the stove through the front door. The trolley stuck. Mr Pearce pushed and heaved, his muscles bunched. David pulled.

'Come on, lass, youm going to like it here,' Mr Pearce addressed the Aga. 'Come on then, try.' After a while he began to wheedle. 'Just a little try. Youm being obstinate; 'tis here you belong to be.'

I climbed over the sill of the hall window, took the hat from the stand and put it on Mr Pearce's head. The trolley zoomed through the door, nearly knocking David down, and rolled sweetly along to the kitchen. I retrieved the hat, put it back on the stand and stroked the silky straw with my finger. My mother watched me.

By afternoon the Aga was installed beside the Edwardian range which Ma had blackleaded so that it shone, showing up its brass fittings. The copper kettles bubbled on the hob, thin lines of steam wavering to the ceiling.

Ma made tea while Mr Pearce stood back to admire his work.

'That's what was needed; ancient plus modern.'

'Absolutely.' Ma handed Mr Pearce his mug. 'My period.'

'Made it all nice; quite settled in.' He looked approving, then stooped to stroke Old X-ray who sat, feet together, facing the range, her eyes closed. 'Cat's happy.'

'Yes.' Ma offered more tea which was accepted, and cake.

'All happy then? Got a new bloke since I seen you, stopped to ask the way. "This Coldharbour then?".' Mr Pearce gave a fair imitation of Mr Bailey. ' "I'm looking for Coldharbour," he said to my wife; a cockney type.'

'He is from London. His name is Bailey.'

'He suited here?'

'Seems very happy. He plays chess, loves the country.' Ma sat at the table looking at Mr Pearce amiably. 'He's settled.'

'Your husband fixed up?'

'Very busy painting.'

'Father-in-law?'

'My husband is painting his portrait.'

Mr Pearce swallowed some tea, then said casually, 'Those two with young Arnold now – '

'They left. I told you,' I said. 'Don't you remember?'

'Ah yes, so you did. Couldn't have stayed could they? Bit of an error that was. A slip-up somewhere after what happened before.'

'Mr Pearce.' Ma looked him in the eye. 'Why are there no children in Coldharbour?'

'Well – ' Mr Pearce looked shifty.

'Well, what?' Ma asked briskly.

'We don't get many.' Mr Pearce was barely audible. 'Not these days. He was the last, young Arnold.' Mr Pearce spoke so quietly I barely heard him. Ma looked strangely at him.

'I thought as much. What about Josh and Lisa?'

'Oh they belong. They always belonged. You must have known that.'

Ma let out her breath in a long sigh and nodded at Mr Pearce.

'Ah, just look at that!' Mr Pearce exclaimed suddenly, his hearty self pointing at Angelique stepping proudly into the kitchen carrying a white mouse.

'Mouse!' David upset his tea and leapt at Angelique who let him take Mouse from her. 'Unhurt,' he said, relieved, 'but she's pregnant.' Mouse indeed tooked that way.

'Your mouse?' Mr Pearce looked interested.

'She was to have had experiments done on her.'

'Looks as though she's tried one on her own. Mr Hayco liked a good, white mouse. You belong here, young David, you belong. She'll have a pretty litter; piebald they'll be.'

'She nearly didn't.' David looked furiously at Angelique who was grooming herself. 'Horrible animal! She's not like her mother.'

'Old X-ray thinks she's an elephant. She's afraid of mice,' Ma explained. 'Put Mouse somewhere safe, David, in a box or something. Tell us more about Mr Hayco, Mr Pearce.'

'Nay. You can find that out for yourselves.' Mr Pearce assumed a mulish expression.

'I daresay,' said Ma lightly. 'More tea? No? The next thing we'd like you to help us with, Mr Pearce, is the stairs. My father-in-law can't get up and down the ladder. Didn't you say there were stairs? That Mr Hayco had some made?'

The blood drained from Mr Pearce's face then rushed back until he was purple with anger. He spoke harshly. 'I did not say anything about stairs.'

'You implied.' Ma stood her ground.

'I did not. 'Tis wrong to say so. I ain't got no power over stairs, I tell you. 'Tis up to you.'

Ma held her ground. 'I had rather gathered there had been some made, or planned.'

'I didn't say so.'

'Not in so many words. But you must admit we need stairs.'

'What's wrong with the back stairs then? I'll mend the few unsteady treads. I'll do that tomorrow.'

'And the others? Up to us you say?'

'No hurry.'

'But Mr Pearce – '

Mr Pearce crashed his fist on the table. 'I tell you there's no hurry, none at all.'

'I see nothing unusual in our having front stairs.' I had never heard Ma speak so forcibly. 'A spiral staircase. We'll set the figures from the van on the banister rail. It will suit Grandpa. He wants stairs. He says so.'

Mr Pearce glared at Ma, then got up and made for the door.

'I'll mend those treads.' His voice was his normal one, his rage gone. 'There's no need for haste.'

We watched him catch the horse, harness it to the cart and drive away, sitting stiff.

'What on earth made me say all that?' Ma murmured.

'About the stairs and the brass figures?'

'Yes. I must be mad. I saw them in my mind's eye quite clearly.'

'You weren't even wearing the hat,' I said.

'I see them spiralling up from the hall. The sun lights them up.' Ma made a circular movement with her finger, her eyes on her vision. This was the girl Pa had fallen in love with.

'I wonder why he says there's no hurry?' Ma's eyes focussed on me. She was herself again.

'Where were you, Ma?'

'Just then?'

'Yes.'

'Some place in my mind where that staircase is a fine place.'

❧ 25 ❧

I followed David to the library, Mouse in his cupped hand, her pink nose sniffing out between his thumb and finger.

'I don't think she's puzzled,' I said to David's back. 'I think she knows something, my Ma.'

'It's not like her to be so tough. She was tough with Comrade Pearce.' David opened a drawer in a kneehole desk and Mouse went in cautiously.

'Are you pleased he said you belong?'

'I knew I did.' David pushed Mouse with a gentle finger. 'You'll be all right there. You can breathe through the keyhole.' He shut the drawer. 'Safe from that Angelique. Diabolic I'd call her.'

'How did you know you belong?' I asked.

'I knew it in the back of my head. That's where thoughts which aren't quite ready lurk, haven't you noticed? Your pa has them about his painting, like the job he wants to do on Victoria. Some day when he's ready he'll get that girl on canvas, beads, elbows and all. He's just not ready.'

'Ma seems ready for the stairs.'

'Comrade P. isn't. Doesn't act ready, does he? Run along. I want to read.' David picked up a book and lay down on the sofa, withdrawn. He had even forgotten Mouse. I went to the kitchen, mixed bread and milk in a saucer and brought it to Mouse. She was busy shredding paper at the back of the drawer. David did not look up.

'David,' I interrupted.

David looked up, keeping his place in the book with a finger. 'What is it?'

'David, have you noticed what's going on here?'

'What's bothering you?' He looked ready to listen.

'Somebody's watching us.'

'The gent in the window? He isn't there you know. I've looked.'

'So have I, but he still waves, and we all wave now. It's only polite.'

'There isn't a room there.'

'I can't find it but it is there. I am certain.'

'If you say so. What else?'

'No papers, no post, no television, no telephone.'

'No communications – I like it. Suits me. Suits Mouse.'

'Somebody works in the garden. Somebody brings in vegetables.'

'Somebody also brings in groceries, eggs, milk and meat, sees to the fires, does the work, cleans the house. I have noticed.' Patiently.

'Ma cooks.'

'It's token cookery. She cooks when whe wants to, she does a sort of family cooking act. Have you seen her wash up?'

'No, not often. I can't remember.'

'Suits me. I hate chores. I like to read.'

I took the hint. 'I'll go in a minute, leave you in peace.'

'It's okay. What else?'

'Are you being watched?'

'No, not me or Mr Bailey.'

'Josh?'

'Sometimes, I think. It's possible.'

'I'm watched a lot. It's a man. He wears the hat.'

'One like it, perhaps. The house is supposed to be haunted isn't it?'

'Pa said it was a sales gimmick. The man called to me, too.'

'What's really bothering you? Didn't you answer?'

Afraid he would laugh at me, I told him how I had woken to find myself grown-up. David listened attentively and finally said, 'Um.'

'Also,' I said, since he hadn't laughed, 'Ma looks years younger than she used to. You must have noticed.'

'Country air?'

'Country air doesn't get rid of grey hair and lines. Then there is Grandpa. I have caught him several times looking about Pa's age – thick hair, David.'

'He's as bald as a coot.'

'Not always. And another thing. When we first got here Mr Pearce wore blue jeans and drove a tractor. Now he wears corduroy trousers tied below the knee with string and drives a cart and horse.'

'So you assume before long he'll be wearing a smock, a funny hat and touching his forelock.'

I giggled.

'He well might.' David was pleased to have made me laugh. 'It's all in the mind,' he said. 'Now push off and let me read.'

'Ma is not puzzled.' It occurred to me this was indeed true.

'Nor me. Run along, do. Leave me in peace.'

'Thanks for listening, David.'

'Goodbye,' said David firmly, burying his nose in his book.

I left him. Finding Bogus in the hall I went outside.

'Bogus, I've got thoughts in the back of my head coming forward,' I said to him. He cavorted with pleasure. On the way to the wood I looked back and waved. And he, or perhaps he didn't, waved back.

I planned a visit to the post office feeling that if I could get Mrs Pearce talking she might add a bit to my puzzle.

'You are an important bit of the puzzle,' I said to Bogus who wagged in appreciation. 'Ma and Grandpa look younger than they are.' Bogus turned aside to snuff in the grass. He jerked back as a frog jumped with a plop into the ditch. I watched it swim, then let its legs trail. 'Somebody waves from that window, Bogus, we all see him.' I walked on. 'It was something pretty fishy that made Edward and Victoria leave.' Bogus was unresponsive. Drops of rain began pattering through the trees, the wind was rising, the tops of the trees began to sway. 'Something about a staircase, and cars that don't work; its ridiculous.' Bogus looked up and barked. 'And they call you "Rags"; that's ridiculous, too.' Bogus barked cheerfully, not minding the rain, not threatened by ideas, not afraid. I wished I had brought the hat with me.

26

By the time we reached the village the rain was stinging my face. It hissed on the road, drove slanting against the headstones in the churchyard. I went into the post office, wiping the water out of my eyes.

'Good afternoon.' Mrs Pearce greeted me from behind the counter. The pearls gleamed on her bosom, pink as shrimps.

'I am afraid we are rather wet,' I apologized, as Bogus shook himself and sat down to lick his chest and stomach.

'People get wet when it rains.' Mrs Pearce gave the impression that she was imparting an erudite piece of information.

There was a stool by the counter. I hoisted myself on to it so that I perched, my eyes level with Mrs Pearce's.

'Mr Pearce brought us an Aga.'

'That's so. To suit your ma.'

'My father's agent came to see whether he had any pictures ready.'

'Went away empty-handed.' Mrs Pearce's pearls moved gently up and down her bosom.

'How did you know?'

Mrs Pearce indicated by the slightest twitch of an eyebrow that this question was a silly one.

I tried again. 'Victoria and Edward took Baby away in the bus.'

'Best way to go isn't it? Better than that hearse thing.'

'Have you see the hearse? It's a van now.'

'It won't be needed here.'

'I'm glad to hear that.' I wondered whether Mrs Pearce ever unbent or expressed surprise.

'Nothing surprises me.' Mrs Pearce showed a mouthful of teeth, threw back her head and laughed. The pearls clattered.

'Not since 1665,' I said boldly. Mrs Pearce's teeth clicked shut. 'Where is Mr Hayco buried? Which is his stone?' I waved towards the churchyard.

'Who said he had one? Like a toffee?' Mrs Pearce took the top off a jar of toffees and offered it – a friendly gesture. I took one and began untwisting the paper.

'That'll clamp your jaws.'

'Oh.' – my mouth was open for the toffee – 'are you suggesting I talk too much?'

'I'm saying it.'

'About 1665? The Plague? Mr Hayco? What else?'

'The Plague.' Mrs Pearce looked through me.

'What was it like?' I put the toffee in my mouth.

'You can read all about it in your history books.'

'But here, here in Coldharbour?' I forced out the question. Speech was possible in spite of the toffee.

Mrs Pearce waved a hand in a circling motion. 'This was a very big village, almost a town. That's why the church is so big. Nearly everyone died.' Mrs Pearce looked out through the rain at the church.

'The tower looks like a dog,' I said, prising the toffee from my teeth with a fingernail.

'He said that he called it "Guardoggod".' Mrs Pearce smiled grimly. 'Profanity really. One shouldn't laugh.'

'But you do. Was "he" Mr Hayco?'

'Might have been,' she said evasively.

'Either it was Mr Hayco or it wasn't.' I tried to appear

polite, not to let exasperation sound in my voice. I fished what was left of the toffee out of my mouth and offered it to Bogus.

'Let him have one of his own.' Mrs Pearce unwrapped a toffee and handed it to Bogus. 'He's a good dog is Rags.'

'Not a guarddoggod? That's the sort of joke Grandpa makes.'

'Irreverent, too, is he?'

'I suppose that is what he is.'

'They get on well?' Mrs Pearce's eyes defied me not to know her meaning.

'I don't think they've met yet.' I felt the blood rising to my face, my heart thumping. Had Grandpa and Mr Hayco met, did they know each other? Explosive thoughts crowded my brain. I stared at Mrs Pearce.

'Have another toffee, dear.'

Tears began to roll down my checks.

'There's nothing to cry about,' Mrs Pearce brought her face closer to mine, the pearls swinging towards me, 'just takes a bit of getting used to. 'Tis all natural.'

'It isn't – ' I sniffed. Mrs Pearce reached for a box of tissues and handed me one. 'Blow.' I blew my nose and wiped my eyes.

'It isn't natural,' I said. 'No children, no people, cars don't work. Not a soul about. Grandpa looking young; Ma too. Bogus – '

'Rags.'

'Victoria and Edward, they had to leave.'

'Baby Arnold. 'Twas sad that.'

'And someone waves from the window.' I had not meant to let this escape me.

'He waves does he? That's good. Good afternoon, Mrs Fuller, what can I do for you?' Mrs Pearce swung into full postmistress splendour as my mother came into the shop. I felt relieved to see her as though she had snatched me back from something I was not ready for.

'Good afternoon, Mrs Pearce.' Ma smiled in a friendly way. 'Have you such a thing as a scrubbing brush and a bar of soap?'

'Found something needs cleaning?' Mrs Pearce was startled.

'Yes. The house is spotless as you know.' Ma smiled. She knew and I knew that there was no reason to suppose Mrs Pearce should know how spotless Haphazard, empty for so many years, could be. 'We've come across some – er – glass which needs careful cleaning.'

'Glass.' Mrs Pearce spoke as though Ma has said a bomb which needs defusing.

'Yes.' Ma glanced round. 'Ah, that brush will do beautifully and this.' She picked up a bar of soap. 'How much is that?' She put a pound note on the counter. Mrs Pearce gave her change.

'Glass.' She was shaken.

'You shouldn't eat too many toffees darling; they ruin your teeth.' Ma took my hand. 'The rain has stopped. Come Lisa, come Bogus. It is kind of you to let them shelter. See you soon Mrs Pearce. Goodbye. Thank you.' Ma drew me to the door. 'We shall be late.'

'Late for what?' I ungraciously removed my hand from my mother's.

'Late for the unearthing, the unwatering. Come on.' Ma walked quickly along the road.

'The what?'

'Mr Bailey has found the stairs. They are as I imagined them.'

'Where? What stairs?' I hissed. 'Where?'

'At the bottom of the well in the kitchen garden.'

'I must have been standing on them when I was fished out. That's what I slipped on.'

'What on earth were you doing in the well?'

I explained. 'Poor toad,' said Ma. 'They don't like water except to spawn in. It was cruel of you.' She could not have made a worse reproach. 'What were you gossiping about with that old witch?'

'Is she a witch?'

'She might be.' Ma was matter of fact. 'Quite easily.'

'I was trying to find things out.'

'Did you?'

'Nothing that makes sense. Mr Hayco doesn't seem to have had a funeral. She knew Baby. How could she have?'

'I don't know, love.'

'He was rather disgusting, Ma.' I remembered the bus driving away. 'He licked the window of the bus, smeared it with his goo.'

'You were a baby once and licked all sorts of things; babies do.'

Ma was hurrying. When we reached the wood she began to run. I was hard put to it to keep up with her. 'Not all of them particularly nice, either.' I let this comment pass, it being as unlike my ma to be unkind as it was for her to run so fast, besides which I was bewildered to notice she was outdistancing me. She shot out of the wood, across the grass and round the corner of the house. I caught up with her in the garden.

Grandpa, Pa, Josh, David and Ma were round the well, leaning over the parapet, their bottoms forming a ring. I could hear Mr Bailey's voice booming up from the well.

'They're here, all of them, I can count them: stacked but hard to shift.'

'How on earth did he find them?' I, too, leaned over the parapet. Mr Bailey stood in the water at the foot of a ladder.

'He was poking about after toads,' Josh murmured, 'and he slipped.'

'He heaved up one bit but it fell back. Your pa is sure it's part of a glass stair,' David whispered in my ear. As David spoke Mr Bailey climbed up the ladder, then, like the rest of us, leaned over and stared into the enigmatic water, a dark mirror reflecting our faces.

As we leaned there was a flash of lightning and a crash of thunder. The rain came again, stinging our necks, lashing our shoulders.

'Indoors,' Ma shouted. 'Indoors all of you; it's dangerous.'

We followed her into the house to gather wetly round the kitchen range which Ma raked until the coals glowed, casting a red light on our faces.

'We must wait.' Ma looked up at Pa standing so tall I could not see his face. He took off the hat, shook it free of rain and laid it on the kitchen table.

The storm battered the house. The wind howled like a pack of demon wolves wailing round corners, yowling in the chimney, gusting, snuffing, grunting against the doors, thundering down from the hills across to the wood where, roaring angrily through the trees, it boomed like the sea in winter. Nobody spoke. We stood facing the fire, our backs to the storm. Old X-ray and Angelique pressed close to Grandpa, the hair on their backs raised, tails twitching. Bogus pressed his nose into my mother's hand. She stroked his muzzle with nervous fingers. Mr Bailey, standing further from the fire than the rest of us, pulled open the flap of his pocket and peered in. He took out a sizeable slow-worm and held it towards me. As I stroked its smooth length it curled, wrapping its pale brown body round his wrist.

We listened, alert, afraid, uncertain. My parents were holding hands, like children. I put mine in Grandpa's; his bony fingers closed over mine. David looked about him nervously then left us to return carrying the drawer with Mouse in it. Now we were all there, all our company. The wind abated slowly, still making angry gusts. We could hear the rain separate from the wind, drumming on the cobbles in the yard, water gushing down the gutters. It became possible to hear sounds in the house, coal shifting in the grate. The wind died suddenly, the clouds parted and the moon came out. We must have stood there a long time. In the village the church clock was striking, and in the house a clock whirred and began to strike.

Ma sighed. 'There are no clocks in the house,' she said.

'But I've heard them,' I said.

'But not seen them.'

Pa picked up the hat and put it on.

'Time was angry,' I said, not knowing why I said it or whether it was true.

'Come on all of you. Coast's clear. All's well,' Pa said.

We followed him to the well. Around the valley, disturbed by the storm, rooks circled by the light of the moon to find their roosting places, cawing raucously. Pa lowered himself over the parapet. 'Oops, it's cold!'

Pa stepped off the ladder into the dark water standing up to his waist where I had stood up to my neck. He tipped the hat to the back of his head and leant down carefully.

'We shall need ropes.'

David and Josh went to find some. Pa came up to sit on the parapet, his legs hanging down. We stood round him in silence listening to the drip of water from his jeans. He began to sing quietly, 'Long ago and far away – '

'No hurry now.' Ma leant beside him. 'Look at the people over there dancing.'

'I see nobody.' Pa's eyes followed her pointing finger.

'Nobody,' I said. 'No dancers.'

'Mrs Pearce is among them. I know her by her pearls. I hadn't realized she was so young.'

'Dreams,' grunted Grandpa. 'Stuff.'

'People in dreams are often far more real than in life, especially as you grow old.'

Grandpa looked in the direction Ma had pointed, his bald head gleaming by the light of the moon, framed by the frill of white hair. 'What I see,' he said, 'are sheep and a shepherd and his dog.'

I looked towards the wood but couldn't see anything.

'Long ago and far away,' sang Pa. 'Ah, here come the boys.' Josh and David arrived carrying ropes.

'These do?'

'I think so.' Pa lowered himself down the well. 'When I've got the rope round the first step I'll say "Haul" and you pull up gently.'

We waited as he fumbled in the dark water. He had stopped singing and muttered to himself.

Ma went to the house and returned carrying a candela-brum, all the candles lit, the flames steady.

'They had their say, then gave up.' Grandpa eyed the candles.

'Who?' I asked.

'The elements. Some call them the Furies.'

'The elements don't speak,' I said.

'Then you cannot have listened, little fool.'

I felt huffy looking at his craggy face where age had carved clefts and folds on cheeks and jaws, pleating the skin round his lips and neck. He had the appearance of a tortoise, quite unlike the man I had seen Pa painting, a man with bold eyes, large nose and iron-grey hair.

'I saw you though,' I whispered. 'I saw you when Pa was painting you.'

'Yes,' said Grandpa. 'In my prime.'

'Haul!' Pa shouted from below. 'Haul!'

David, Mr Bailey and Josh hauled while Ma guided the rope. Bogus peered over the edge, the cats looked down, ears alert, paws neat. Up from the well came a wedge, heavy, dripping.

'Careful, it's slimy.'

The first find was laid reverently on the soft earth. 'Don't let it spoil the plants!' I cried.

'It's just earth,' said Ma. She wiped the slab free of mud with her hand. 'It's glass all right, it needs a good scrub.' We all looked, standing round as she held up the candelabrum.

'Hey, I'm not getting any warmer down here.' Pa's teeth were chattering. We turned back to work.

Twenty-five slabs came up, giving little resistance. The candles grew short and the moon sank. I counted the slabs laid on the vegetable beds, narrowly triangular like the petals of a sunflower, forming a circle round the well. I stood alone as the others helped Pa climb, exhausted, up the ladder. From somewhere nearby I heard a throat cleared, then a laugh.

'I hope we are not intruding,' I said to the invisible person who did not reply. This time I was not afraid. Pa stretched aching limbs, his dripping arms reaching up to the sky. 'You look like a scarecrow,' said Ma. 'Come indoors before you catch your death.'

'He catches you.' Pa put his arm round Ma's shoulders. They went into the house. Pa hung the hat on its stand.

'Maybe some time we shall also find the banisters and the central pole, or whatever it's called.'

'The sun's rising,' called Josh. We all turned and looked from the doorway.

'The music's stopping,' David murmured. Faintly, from the far end of the house, I heard the last bars of a dance. I stood still trying to hear the music. My family talked and laughed in the kitchen, a robin sang suddenly loud from a lilac bush.

'Always up first.' Mr Bailey was beside me. He took the slow-worm from his pocket and put it down. It slid away into the Mediterranean daisies.

'Come and see Mouse's mice,' David called. 'Come quickly.'

'No need to 'urry.' Mr Bailey was ahead of me. 'They won't push off until they can see. Oh my,' he said peering into the drawer held open by David, 'you 'ave to be a real animal lover to like that lot – ugh!'

'They'll be very elegant.' David was defensive. The infant mice reached their puny paws towards Mouse.

'Ma said she would have Supermice,' I said.

'Quite right,' granted Mr Bailey. He put out his finger to stroke Mouse who bit him sharply. 'Can't call that no dream.' He sucked the injury. 'I didn't see no dancing nor hear no music but I feel yer bite. You're a good mother I'd say, got the right idea – that there X-ray ain't going to care for this lot.'

❧ 28 ❧

Ma made Pa change into dry clothes while she got breakfast. Josh and I laid the table, David stoked the fires. Grandpa and Mr Bailey sat side by side in the window seat, their backs to the light. They looked tired. Neither spoke. When we were all sitting at the table, Ma looked round at us.

'Will you all listen a moment.' The sound of munching stopped.

'I just want to say – ' She sounded nervous. 'I just have to tell you that before anybody does anything to those glass stairs we must all get some sleep.' There was a babble of protest.

'I mean it.' Ma reached for the hat on the table behind her and put it on. 'If from carelessness due to tiredness we crack or break a glass tread we can never replace it. So sleep is an order.'

'Order! Giving me orders are you?' Grandpa was angry.

'Yes.' From beneath the hat's brim Ma's eyes flashed.

'At my age! Accusing me of senility! At my age!'

'The reverse.'

'An infantile geriatric?'

'Not exactly.'

'What do you mean by that?'

'You know as well as I do.' Ma quelled him. 'Age is a rather dodgy subject, let's not discuss it. We must get some sleep. The stairs won't disappear.'

'Somebody should guard them.' Pa sounded exhausted.

'No need. Everyone to bed, please. Lisa can help me to clear breakfast, then we'll go to bed, too.'

They trailed away grumbling. Ma and I stacked the plates and washed up without discussion. We felt we had to.

'Nobody knows they are there. Stop worrying, Lisa.' Ma passed me a plate to dry.

'The gardener does.'

'Was he watching us?'

'Yes, if it *is* the gardener.'

'Well.' Ma rinsed the sink. 'Let's take a look before we sleep. We can shut the garden doors; that should satisfy you.' We walked to the walled garden. Ma still wore the hat. Bogus and the cats came with us, nosing at the door. Ma pushed it open. The slabs of glass, drying in the sun, lay splayed round the well. All was quiet.

'No gardener,' said Ma.

'I've never seen him, only heard,' I said, looking at the neat rows of vegetables, the orderly fruit. 'This is where the toads live.' I showed Ma the irises. Ma peered down. 'Dear things.'

'This is where he's planted Victoria's beans.' I showed Ma the glorious, multicoloured flowers.

'Victoria's beans? What do you mean?'

I told Ma.

'Well,' she exclaimed, 'I call that going too far. Poor Victoria, poor girl, she was so upset.'

'But she got away, she and Edward, Baby, too.'

'What makes you say that?' Ma was sharp.

'I don't know,' I said, 'I really don't. Sandy got away as well. They all *wanted* to. They didn't really belong here.'

'Oh yes, I see that. Perhaps they will come back later on. Come on, bed for both of us.' We bolted the door and walked round to the front of the house. I looked up at the window above the porch and so did Ma.

'Not there this morning,' she said, hanging up the hat.

'I didn't know until yesterday you saw him, too,' I said.

'We all do. He's a friend.'

'Does he wave and beckon?'

'He waves,' she said dryly and sent me to bed up the back stairs.

I heard music somewhere, whether in the house or in my head I did not know but I danced and twirled along the passage to my room, dreaming that I wore full skirts which swung out as I danced through the sunbeams. I cast off my clothes and went to draw the curtains. As I looked out I saw a circle on the grass where many people had trod. I scrambled into bed, wishing I had seen them dance, joined them perhaps, got to know them, made friends.

In my sleep I dreamed I was in bed at Haphazard, that it was time to get up, but I thought in my dream, I *am* in bed and it can't be time to get up. I am tired. Ma has just sent me to bed even though it is daylight. I turned my face away from the light so that I could sleep. I heard someone come in and draw the curtains. The sun shone into my room. The rooks were cawing in the wood as they do in early autumn when they fly round oaks burdened with acorns, pecking at them, springing about the branches, cawing, 'Acorns, caw, what shall we do? Caw. Winter is near – here – caw.' A scratching and whining. I got up to let Bogus in. I was drugged with sleep. Back in bed I pulled the bedclothes round my head. Bogus did not settle as usual, laying his head beside me, pushing his body against me for warmth. He pawed at the bedclothes, scraping them off my face. I flung out an arm to hold his neck, to keep him quiet. He sat up. I could feel his tail waving, little gusts of air round my face. He sat, ears pricked, listening. Listening to what? I sat up and listened, too.

Down the passage to my room someone was walking. Who? I knew all my family's footsteps. These steps were shorter than Grandpa's but firmer. They did not diminish as they would have done if someone were just passing my door. Whoever it was was marking time. Marking time? Whoever it was gave a cough, cleared his throat. 'I am asleep. I am dreaming. This is horrible. I must wake up.' I held my head in my hands shaking it from side to side. Bogus jumped off the bed and ran to the door, wagging his tail. 'I am asleep. I am dreaming,' I assured myself out loud as I watched the handle of the door turn. 'I am afraid. I must forget this. It isn't happening – I must forget,' I shouted out loud in panic. 'I *will* forget.'

'Rags?' A voice called. Bogus scratched to get out.

'Bogus,' I whispered. 'I am dreaming. Come back.'

Bogus clawed at the door, lying on his side digging at the door, making throaty, gasping noises. The footsteps stopped.

'Rags?' said a man's voice.

'Bogus, oh Bogus, don't go. *Please.*'

I was out of bed, running to hold Bogus back. Terror such as I had never experienced, or will again, exploded. Bogus wriggled through the door and leapt up, overcome with joy.

'There boy, there. Steady, my beauty, steady. It's been a long time for me, too.'

Bursting through the door Bogus had kicked it back at me so that I sat back abruptly, defenceless, looking up.

'Hullo, Lisa.' Mr Hayco held out a hand to help me to my feet.

'I am asleep, I am dreaming,' I said through clenched teeth. 'I want to wake up. I want to wake up at once. I shall forget this.'

'Not this time.' Mr Hayco wore a Panama hat. 'This one is mine.' He smiled. My heart thumped. 'Heart thumping?' he was watching me as he gentled Bogus.

'Yes,' I whispered. I began to cry, tears splashing down the front of my nightdress. 'I'm asleep,' I said, a grain of spirit returning.

'Then it's time you woke up.'

'Time – ' I whispered. Then, not knowing why, I said aloud, 'I hate time.'

'Nothing to hate. Time is a bit askew that's all.' Mr Hayco sounded perfectly reasonable.

'Why?' My heart was thumping less. Bogus was calming down.

'I think I can explain it.' Mr Hayco lifted his hat and smoothed his thick white hair before replacing it on his head. 'Though I'm not a scientist, Lisa.'

'How do you know my name?'

'I do. I always have.'

'You call Bogus "Rags".'

'You call Rags "Bogus".'

'I hadn't thought of it that way.'

'So I noticed.' Mr Hayco looked amused. 'To me he is "Rags", to you "Bogus" – excellent name, wish I'd thought of it myself, but at that time – '

'What time?'

'The time when he was a puppy, neither particularly ragged or bogus.'

I was silent. Mr Hayco said, 'I am trying to stop you being frightened.'

'I'm not frightened.'

'Oh, but you are.'

'No.' I got to my feet.

'Well, be that as it may. Have you had anything to do with clocks?'

'Certainly not.'

'Well, you might have, you might have seen your elders winding them even though you are not allowed to touch them yourself.'

'Of course I've seen them being wound.'

'Well then,' he said. 'Seen a grandfather clock wound?'

'Yes, of course I have.'

'Seen what happens if the weights are taken off?'

'Yes,' I said, 'It goes mad, the pendulum races.'

'That's right. I call it askew, an agreeable word, askew.'

'Perhaps it is.'

'Don't be so grudging.' Mr Hayco laughed wheezily. 'It's a lovely word – askew – positively Shakespearean. D'you like Shakespeare?'

'Don't know much of it.' I was feeling better.

'Well, Lisa, that's it. That's just what it is.'

'What is what?' I was no longer afraid.

'That's better,' Mr Hayco said easily, 'you're feeling all right now, so stop being pert and take in the fact that here at Haphazard time is askew.'

'It's been askew ever since Pa bought that hat,' I said.

'I bought mine in 1949,' said Mr Hayco. 'At that time I thought it extravagant.'

'Time,' I said irritated. 'What has time, askew as you call it, what has it to do with hats?'

'Hats are timeless, ours are anyway. Now to time. Your

grandfather might call it an element. We live in it we suppose – '

'And it's gone funny like a grandfather clock with the weights off?'

'Round here it has – round Coldharbour.' We were strolling down the passage, he in his hat, I in my night-dress, Bogus between us.

'Josh would call it a Time Warp,' I said, inspired.

'Ugly expression.' Mr Hayco frowned. 'I have something to show you.' He took my hand.

We were in the passage along which I had danced to bed. The window at the far end let in shafts of sun in which fluttered a butterfly.

'It can get out.' Mr Hayco followed my gaze.

'Josh and I let one out of the church.'

'Commendable. Geraldine thinks they are the souls of the dead aspiring to heaven.'

'How soppy. Who is Geraldine?'

'Geraldine Pearce at the post office. You have met her.'

'Geraldine.' I rolled the name round my tongue, spinning it out.

'Yes, it's unsuitable.' Mr Hayco turned the handle of a door. 'Come in here,' he said. 'This is my room. Step inside.'

I walked across the room to the window. It was immediately above the porch.

'You wave from here?'

'Yes, and I beckon.'

There was an armchair by the window. In it, curled up in a ball, a marmalade cat. 'This in Gingerpop.' Mr Hayco picked up the cat and laid him, still curled up, on another chair. 'Night-time is his time, he hasn't much use for the daytime.'

'Is his time askew?'

'Difficult to tell with cats – think of Old X-ray and Angelique.'

'Do you know them?'

'Of course. Now sit and watch time passing.' Mr Hayco pulled up a chair for me. 'Are you cold?' He wrapped a shawl round my shoulders. 'Look out of the window, Lisa.'

At first all I could see was the grass between the house and the wood, the soft, yellow-green of late summer. As I grew used to the view I saw the sheep Grandpa had remarked on. 'I see sheep, a shepherd and his dog.'

'A relative of Rags, a good dog.' Hearing his name, Bogus thumped his tail.

'Bogus,' I said. Bogus thumped again.

'Don't quibble. Keep still and watch.'

From the wood drove Mr Pearce in his lorry, jolting across the grass. He waved up at the window, Mr Hayco waved back.

'He brought the Aga in a cart,' I said, 'though the first time he came it was in the lorry.'

'He finds lorry-time more exciting. It's a matter of taste. He's not like his wife.'

'What is her time?'

'Haven't you guessed?'

I tried to guess at Mrs Pearce's time. '1665? The year of the Plague?'

'Yes, She's come on, of course – had to – but she harks back. Some people love disaster.'

As I thought of Mrs Pearce I saw unhappy people, frightened, sick. I saw the village as we had first seen it when we arrived in the van, when Josh had exclaimed at his first view of the house.

'How sad,' I said, watching the people creeping from their wretched little houses, collapsing in the road to die. 'Oh,' I clenched my hands together. 'How gruesome.' A cart loaded with bodies went slowly along the road. 'How terrible that time was. Did everyone die?'

'No. The Pearces escaped, and I did.'

'You?'

'Yes, me.'

'Who clsc? Edward and Victoria and their baby?'

'Poor young people. They fled from the Plague in London but they brought it with them. When they recovered they left the village. So did all the villagers except the Pearces.'

'No wonder they had to get away this time,' I said, not understanding what I tried to say.

'Look – ' Mr Hayco chuckled. Swiftly from the wood came Sandy driving up to the house in his Jaguar. We watched him get down at the front door, ring the bell, listen, then stand back and look up at us.

'Does he see us?'

'No.'

'Why not?'

'Not time yet.'

'Time again.' I was irritated. 'Time askew I suppose.'

'Yes, he's early.'

Sandy got into his Jaguar and drove away. I watched the car drive through a crowd of people who were gathering by the wood to dance round a fiddler. 'What are they dancing for?' I was not bothered that Sandy had not seen them.

'They celebrate. Sometimes it is Waterloo, sometimes Agincourt, now and again it is 1919, the Peace.'

'I like their clothes.' I held the shawl tightly round me. 'Those whirly-twirly skirts would be fun to dance in.'

'You did, you do, you shall.'

'Where shall I dance next?' I felt Mr Hayco should be humoured.

'Men like to be humoured,' said Mr Hayco. 'Come, Lisa, and see the time you shall dance in. Enough of that view.' He picked up Gingerpop. In his arms the cat yawned, showing the mauve of his mouth. I thought fleetingly of Mouse. 'Gingerpop is not the world's greatest mouser. Come along.' He took my hand in his. I looked at our hands. My hand was the hand of the girl in the mirror, his the hand of a young man. I wore a long dress with narrow waist and full skirts. I looked up at him and saw the face of the man who had called up from the valley, 'Lisa'.

Gingerpop and Bogus walked ahead, tails high. The passage widened into a gallery leading to the landing. All along the wall hung Pa's pictures. Ma in a deckchair, me doing a handstand.

'Haven't had time to hang it the right way up and now I like it as it is.' Mr Hayco was laughing at me. 'Why don't you call me by my proper name?' he asked.

'I don't know it. Are you Hayco's ghost? Shall I call you Mr Hayco?'

'Oh no. I am Haphazard Hayco of Coldharbour. My mother called me Haphazard. So must you.'

'Haphazard,' I said. It sounded right.

'Listen.' He stopped, pushing back the hat to hear better.

From the village came the sound of a band. 'Time to dance,' he said, whirling me along the gallery to the head of the stairs. 'Let's show our paces. This is our time at last. The ball is beginning.'

I looked down into the hall and gasped with delight.

Looking up at us were Grandpa with Old X-ray and Angelique; stretching from them to us a glass stair. From the floor of the hall to the ceiling above us was a glass pillar – radiating from it the treads we had found in the well. They shone like silver, they shone like gold. A spiral glass banister swept up beside them. At the first turn Death with his scythe, then the Fat Lady, then the Harlequin catching up with the Fleeing Girl. The sun shone through the windows striking sparks from the twists and turns.

'It's like a wine glass,' I cried.

'A spiral mercurial twist to be exact, but better.'

'How?'

'Watch closely.'

Indeed this stair was better than any glass I had ever seen. The central pillar and the banisters were hollow and up them came bright beetles and butterflies, a green frog and a toad. A snake slithered down, passing a black mouse moving up towards Mouse who was pattering down, her pink feet skittering, her whiskers atwitch. Driven mad, Old X-ray and Angelique and Gingerpop leapt and pounced, tearing up and down, crazed.

'What a tease!' I cried and Gingerpop stopped and sat rather grandly at the head of the stairs by Bogus.

'He sees the future.' Haphazard bent and stroked him. The cat paid no attention. 'Bit snobbish today, Gingerpop. This is a party.' The cat looked away.

'Dancing time. Come.' He took my hands in his. 'Listen to the music and dance.'

My heart was full of music, my feet moved, my skirts twirled out. I held his hands and we danced at the head of the stairs. My body swayed, my hair swung free. We were not alone. Dancing along the hall came Ma and Pa, young and loving, Josh with a girl I had never seen, though Josh seemed to know her, and David and Mr Bailey dancing, too. Suddenly, with a shout, came Grandpa, swinging up the stairs to meet a lovely woman as though he had never heard of aches, pains or wheezy pipes. She passed us running to meet him, to catch his hands and dance, waltzing up and waltzing down. She had eyes for no one but Grandpa, looking so full of love that for a moment I was embarrassed that anyone so old could inspire such feeling, until Haphazard, dancing with me, fingers snapping, feet tapping, cried,

'Silly, don't look like that. That's your grandmother,' and I cried out, 'So he *is* in his prime. Then who are you?'

'Can't you guess?'

I tried to see his face, shaded by the hat. A face I knew I had always known. He was laughing at me, watching me from under the brim.

'Won't I do? Don't you like what you see?'

'Who *are* you?'

'Haphazard.' I knew that voice. 'I've been calling you.'

'Oh, Haphazard!' I cried. 'Why was I afraid? I have known all along. Are we in love? Shall we grow old? Are we dead?'

'Of course we shall. Of course we are.' He took off the hat and let it float down to Grandpa who crammed it on as he danced with my grandmother.

'Aren't they beautiful?' Haphazard held me. 'They are not afraid, are you?'

'No I am not. Shall I wake up? Shall I forget?'

'Not this time. Dance, Lisa. I have waited so long for you.'

We danced down the stairs, our hearts full of joy, through a crowd of people: Ma and Pa, Mr and Mrs Pearce, he red-faced and jolly, she with her pearls swinging out in an iridescent arc, past people I had known and would know. We danced out along the path to the garden where Haphazard snatched up a swathe of bean flowers, swinging them into a garland to hold us together as we danced, for we are dancing still.

If you find this hard to believe, look across from the wood to Haphazard House on a fine, still night and you will hear the music and see us dancing in the lights reflected from the spiral stair.

❧ Speaking Terms ❧

To Phyllis Jones

My elder sister Angela gave me a bullfinch in a cage for my birthday, before the laws were made to prevent people keeping beautiful wild birds in cages. The bullfinch was very wild, not unnaturally as he had been limed and his feet never really recovered from their injuries.

I loved him. I loved his fat pink stomach. I loved his black head. I loved his large wholly brown eyes.

Years passed and my bullfinch grew quite happy and contented in his cage. He flew about the room and made little piping noises. He puffed himself up round with affection when I came near him and he piped when he heard the wild birds outside in the garden.

'It is cruel,' I said to myself, 'to keep such a beautiful bird in captivity. He should at least have some freedom.'

For a long time I thought about this because Mr Bull, as I called him, had become part of my life and I did not wish to lose him.

One morning I cleaned his cage and fed him, giving him more hempseed than usual. Hempseed is not really good for bullfinches but they love it.

'Mr Bull, shall I ever see you again?' I asked, but he just looked at me with his enormous brown eyes and said nothing.

'Mr Bull, I'm going to give you a treat,' I said.

I carried him downstairs in the early morning and out into the garden. An almond tree was coming into flower. Its buds showed pink and my father was greatly looking forward to the full glory of the tree.

I opened the door of Mr Bull's cage and waited. Mr Bull, very fat, came and sat by the open door.

'Go on, Mr Bull,' I said. 'You can fly.'

Mr Bull spread his wings and flew into the almond tree.

'Please don't go away for ever.'

I stood holding the cage and watching Mr Bull, who began hopping about in the tree. Suddenly he put his head on one side and looked at a flower bud. He nipped it off the twig and mashed it between the two strong snippers of his beak.

'Oh!' I said in horror.

Mr Bull paid no attention but hopped busily about the tree nipping buds off, mashing them up and dropping bits on the ground. He went all over the tree, and before long the bits of bud lay all round me.

'Mr Bull.' I held up his cage. I was thinking of my father. Mr Bull paid no attention to me, not because he could not see me but because he did not want to.

'Mr Bull,' I called very urgently. 'Mr Bull, please.'

Behind me in the house I could hear sounds of people getting up and running baths, yawning and groaning as grown-up people do when they wake up and have to face the world.

Suddenly Mr Bull flipped his wings and flew directly into his cage. Quickly I shut the door and, carrying the cage with Mr Bull in it, I tore back into the house and into my room and shut the door.

'Mr Bull, I don't know what my father will say.'

'I do.'

For the first time since we had met Mr Bull spoke.

'You spoke, Mr Bull.'

'Naturally.'

'Mr Bull, you have ruined my father's almond tree.'

'Nonsense.' Mr Bull hopped down from his perch and drank a sip of water.

'What will he say?'

'He will say I have, or that some other bird has, ruined his almond tree.'

'But you have.'

'Nonsense.'

'Then what do you call what you have done?'

Mr Bull did not answer for a little time, but ate some seed. At last he spoke again, the husks of seed falling out of his beak as the almond buds had done.

'There was a bug in every bud,' he said.

'So you have done good?'

'Naturally.'

'Did you eat the bugs?'

'Yes.'

'How horrid of you.'

'Human beings eat oysters alive, don't they?'

'Yes. Mr Bull, I'm terribly worried about what my father will say.'

'He won't know it's me and next year his tree will flower beautifully.'

'Mr Bull, you have never spoken to me before.'

'It wasn't necessary. Go and have your breakfast.' Mr Bull closed his eyes, tightened his grip on his perch and spoke no more.

My father liked walking round his garden before breakfast to see how his flowers and trees had prospered in the night. He spent as much time as he could in the garden when he was not working at making money in his office in the nearby town. My father said gardening soothed his ulcers.

My mother said to me: 'Hurry up with your breakfast, Kate, or you will be late for school.'

I kept quiet and buried my face in my plate.

My father burst into the room. 'Have you seen the almond tree?' His voice was hoarse.

'No, not yet. Is it lovely' My mother was pouring out a cup of coffee.

'Lovely!' My father's voice rose. 'It's ruined. Some bird has pecked all the buds off it. Blast it!'

'Darling.' My mother made two faces at the same time, which was clever of her, and I decided to practise doing it myself in private. One was the face of loving concern because my father had been upset and was also upsetting his coffee, and the other was the face which meant 'mind the children.'

'It looks as though a blasted bullfinch has been at it. It's ruined. Every bud bitten off and just chucked on the ground.' My father took a great swallow of coffee and choked.

'There are no bullfinches in this district.' My mother was trying to be soothing, but she was apt to be right which never soothed my father.

'Goddammit, there must be.'

'Time for school,' my mother said quietly to my sister, and she and I left the room.

'Goddammit, we shall be late,' said my sister outside the room. 'Run.' And she began to run down the road to where we could see the car which gave us a lift each morning waiting for us.

'You are late,' said Andrew from the back seat where he was sitting with his brother James.

'Sorry.' My sister bounded into the car and I followed her. Our neighbour, Mrs Johnson, let in the clutch and drove off.

'Why are you late?' James was rather keen on punctuality. None of the rest of us minded.

'My father's favourite almond tree has had all its buds nipped off by a bullfinch,' said my sister Angela, knowing that just to make such a statement would apprise the Johnson family that our family would be in a state of hypertension and that by tonight my father's ulcers would be giving him hell.

'There are no bullfinches round here.'

Mrs Johnson was a keen bird-watcher, usually heard the first cuckoo, and could tell a warbler's song from a nightingale's. 'Such beautiful birds, I always think. When I was at school in Kent there was a girl who had a canary,' she said.

'Oh, canaries.' Andrew dismissed canaries.

'Didn't you have a pet bullfinch once?' Mrs Johnson called to me across the seat where Angela sat next to her.

'Yes, she had,' Angela answered politely.

I looked at Angela, who is two years older than me, and she did not seem any different from usual, but she had certainly said, 'Yes, she had,' not 'Yes, she has.'

We arrived at our school and Angela went off with Andrew, and James and I went into our part of the school, and all day I wondered whether Mr Bull had really spoken to me and what Angela knew. Lessons passed over my head and I had to depend on James for once, instead of his depending on me, because I am more like my mother than my father: I always know best.

At five we all four climbed into Mrs Johnson's car.

'What's that?' James looked at a book Angela was holding in her lap.

'Oh, just a book on birds.' Angela was rather offhand, as she usually is to people younger than herself.

Mrs Johnson took her eye off the road to look at the book, and we all went tense because we were terrified of accidents.

'Oh,' said Mrs Johnson, 'did you get it from the library? It's that book written by that dreadful man who says bullfinches destroy fruit trees. He must be mad. A whole book written against one small breed of birds. It's nonsense, of course.'

'Is it?' Angela looked sideways at Mrs Johnson.

'Of course it is.'

'Then I won't bother to read it.' Angela threw the book out of the window. Andrew, James and I gasped in admiration.

'Angela! That's a library book.' Mrs Johnson spoke reprovingly. 'We must find it.' She stopped the car and walked back up the road. We followed her, Angela bringing up the rear.

Mrs Johnson picked up the book, which was lying by the side of the road, with some of its pages dog-eared and muddy.

'Angela, you shouldn't do things like that.'

'But you said it was nonsense.'

'It is, but your parents would have to pay the bill for the lost book.'

'Oh, bills.' Angela shoved the book into the glove compartment of Mrs Johnson's car. Her voice sounded just like Andrew's that morning when he had said, 'Oh, canaries.'

When we reached home we both ran upstairs to wash our hands and comb our hair. We always did this if my father's ulcers were going to play him up. Angela came into my room. She looked up at the cage where Mr Bull sat in the evening sunshine, his fat stomach pink and his black head glossy.

'You had better tell me.' Angela stood looking at Mr Bull, who looked back at her sideways with his large brown eye.

'Later.' Mr Bull opened his beak and shut it, snap.

'I suppose this is late enough.' My sister came into my room where I lay in bed. Downstairs we could hear our parents talking.

'He is usually asleep by now,' I said.

'I'm not asleep.'

'Then what's all this about?' I got out of bed and took the cover off Mr Bull's cage.

'Ah.'

'What is it you want?' said Angela. 'Freedom?'

'Preserve me from that.'

'Why?'

'My poor feet.'

'The other birds would attack you,' I said hastily. I did not want to lose Mr Bull.

'Think so?' Mr Bull's chortle was rather offensive.

'He's lazy and greedy. He gets lots of food and care here. Why should he want to go?' said Angela.

'Only sometimes.'

'When?' I asked.

'When the wisteria is in bud, and the apples.'

'A man has written a whole book on how much harm bullfinches do.' Angela and I sat close to the cage. Mr Bull closed his eyes.

'You could go out sometimes early, like this morning,' I said.

'Our father has ulcers,' said Angela.

'Poor fellow.' Mr Bull sounded in no way sympathetic.

'Don't you like him?'

'No.'

'Why not?'

'He doesn't like bullfinches.' Mr Bull sounded very shrewd.

'What good could we do?' Angela suddenly switched her mood to one she occasionally had for doing good works.

'I don't want to do good. I want Mr Bull to have fun,' I said.

Mr Bull was looking at Angela seriously. 'We could warn the others,' he said. 'Hunting and so on.'

'Ah.' I could see Angela mounting a favourite hobby horse. 'Do the others understand you? All the animals and birds who live in fear?'

'Yes. You hunt, don't you?'

'Only because I like riding. Not killing. We shall have to bring the boys in on this. They always know about these things. Their father is a farmer,' said Angela.

'What things?' I choked with jealousy. Mr Bull and Angela seemed to be getting into a partnership which left me out.

'We wouldn't dream of leaving you out.' Mr Bull turned a large, loving eye on me.

'It's sabotage really, isn't it? I adore sabotage.' Angela sat close to the cage. 'The Johnson boys love animals.'

'Take a lot of organizing.' Mr Bull yawned and I felt probably Angela was right and that he was lazy.

'Not if we get help. I know Andrew and James feel as we do. They hate all the unnecessary killing. That's the only reason we like them. But we can't do anything without you.'

'No, you can't, can you?'

'Don't be so complacent just because you live in perfect safety,' snapped Angela.

'What about your cat?'

'With your help we will stop him coming and staring at you. If we can tell the Johnsons' dog not to chase him.'

'I don't like the way he sits and stares,' said Mr Bull. 'He covets me.'

'What are you getting at?' I said to Angela.

'I think she wants a sort of protection racket,' said Mr Bull.

'Protect the persecuted!' I exclaimed, thinking of last week's sermon on television which had so bored me.

'That's about it.' Angela got up and left the room and I heard her talking to our dog who sleeps with her in her room, and calling, 'Vice, Vice, Vice,' in a soft voice. She came back carrying Vice, our cat, in her arms, with Blueprint trotting behind her. Vice fixed Mr Bull with his staring green eyes and Blueprint got up on my bed.

'Stop that, Vice. We know Mr Bull can speak and so can you.'

'What about it?' Vice sounded in no way surprised but began licking his paws and combing his whiskers.

'We want you all to help each other and we will help you.'

'I don't need any help.' Vice went on licking his paws.

'You do when the Johnsons' dog chases you.'

Vice sneezed delicately.

'I'll tell him not to.' Blueprint spoke in a very educated voice considering his antecedents, which were half and half terrier and half and half spaniel.

'I can look after myself,' Vice said prissily.

'A lot of people can't,' said Angela. 'The birds who get nerves when the bird-watchers watch them, the deer, the foxes and the otters who are hunted, the badgers who are dug out of their sets, the birds who are shot.'

'We eat chickens and meat.'

'I know we do, but these things which are done for sport, we could stop those. All the things which upset us.'

'Upset the hunted more,' said Mr Bull coldly.

'I like hunting mice,' said Vice.

'If the Johnsons' dog stopped chasing you, would you stop hunting mice?'

'It is asking rather a lot,' Blueprint said in reasonable tones from my bed.

'It would be terrific fun,' said Vice suddenly. 'Just to upset things.'

'Then will you help?' Angela joined Blueprint on the bed.

'There's a mouse in the wainscot.'

'Then tell him he can come out and you won't hurt him.'
Angela spoke cajolingly and Blueprint raised his eyebrows.

'Mouse,' purred Vice. 'Mouse, come on out. I won't hurt you.'

There was a long silence while we waited, and then at last there was a faint scrabble and a very large mouse came out of a very small hole and climbed up Angela's leg on to her lap.

'Ow, you tickled.'

'Sorry.' The mouse looked round at us from Angela's knee and then said: 'I should feel happier in that cage with Mr Bull.'

I opened the door of Mr Bull's cage and the mouse streaked down Angela's leg and up the table leg, across the table and into Mr Bull's cage, where it sat panting, its little sides heaving and its whiskers twitching.

'Don't make a mess,' said Mr Bull to the mouse.

'Do you two know each other?' Angela looked at the mouse looking up at Mr Bull.

'Oh, yes. I eat, well we all eat the seeds Mr Bull scatters about sometimes.'

'Do you all know each other?'

'Only within a certain radius.'

'We shall need the boys to help us organize things,' said Angela to me. 'Their father takes the local paper and knows when and where the hounds are going to meet, and I'm sure he knows about badger baiting and the shooting.'

'Yes,' I said.

Outside we heard the owls hooting.

'They won't help,' said the mouse.

'They might in some ways.' Blueprint was an optimistic dog. 'I'll talk to the Johnsons' dog tomorrow.'

'I thought you always fought,' said Vice.

'It's only noise really, to keep up our status.'

'Status is going to be an obstacle to your game.' Vice finished licking his paws and sat crouched with his eyes shut.

'It will make a start. He told me yesterday that the otter hounds are meeting soon.'

'Where?' exclaimed Angela.

'Find out tomorrow,' said Vice. 'You people can read.'

'Yes. That will mean mounting quite an operation.' I let the mouse out of Mr Bull's cage and he vanished down his hole.

'No manners,' said Vice.

The rest of us said nothing. Angela and Blueprint left the room with Vice, and I covered Mr Bull's cage and snapped out my light because I could hear my parents coming upstairs to bed and my mother saying to my father, 'Do be quiet, you will wake the children.'

'May we have the Johnson boys to tea today? It's Saturday.' Angela sat at the kitchen table eating porridge and watching my mother cooking my father's breakfast.

'I thought you had a war on,' said my father, coming in from the garden.

'That was last week.'

'How fickle you are.' My father picked up the morning paper. 'Just like animals really, excepting dogs of course.' He stroked Blueprint's head. 'Dogs are never fickle. God's finest moral creation.' None of us paid any attention, because if my father had said that dogs were God's finest moral creation once, he had said it a hundred times. Blueprint, however, being of a charitable nature, wagged his tail.

'May we?' said Angela. My mother nodded.

'Now cats,' said my father, 'I admire cats.' He looked at Vice sitting sleekly in the window watching the birds eat the crumbs my mother had thrown out to them. 'Now cats are deep. Did you read last week of some cats killing a child? Remarkable.'

'Dreadful,' said my mother.

'I wonder what the child had done to them,' said Angela.

'I admire cats,' said my father again.

'Not murdering cats, surely, and you a pillar of the law.' My mother neatly slipped two eggs on to a piece of toast and put the plate in front of my father.

'One can have one's days off, I hope,' said my father, a solicitor in the town near which we lived.

'I hope Vice won't kill too many baby birds this year.' My mother looked at Vice who, in spite of his name and cleverness was not a great hunter really.

'There's a spotted flycatcher nesting at the back of the house,' said my father. 'You children are not to go near it. They are shy.'

We nodded agreement.

'Luckily it's quite out of Vice's reach.'

'How is the almond tree?' said Angela, out of pure spite I thought.

'Oh, it will recover. I wouldn't be surprised if it were better than ever next year.' On Saturday mornings, when he doesn't have to go to work, my father is angelic. 'It does trees and plants good to be cut back.'

Vice hopped out of the open window, landing on the path with a flop. The feeding birds did not look up.

'It's almost as if they knew he was not dangerous.' My mother sat down beside my father.

'They would fly off as he sprang and he would look a fool,' muttered Blueprint in a groaning voice.

My father gave Blueprint a piece of bacon.

'Honestly, darling, you shouldn't feed him at meals,' said my mother. Neither my father nor Blueprint paid any attention, and presently, while we reluctantly helped my mother wash up, we saw them going off together for a walk.

'It's absurd,' said my mother. 'He wants to talk to Mr Johnson and he daren't go near their house because the dogs fight.'

'Then he can telephone,' said Angela. 'May I go and ask them to come for the afternoon?' Angela left the kitchen before my mother could answer, leaving me with the washing up.

'She's left me with the washing up,' I said angrily.

'You two are just like animals yourselves.' My mother swished the water down the sink and wrung out the cloth.

'We can read,' I said to myself as I stacked the plates and watched Angela dash past on her bicycle with her behind stuck up in the air.

❧ 3 ❧

After lunch we walked through the wood which separates us from the Johnsons' farm. Blueprint crashed ahead of us, making a lot of noise in the undergrowth, his tail wagging and his whole body shaking from the sheer joy of exercise. Overhead the birds sang rather aggressively and the river rushed in all haste towards the sea.

'Do you think,' I said to Angela, 'that Andrew and James will believe us?'

'They'll have to, won't they?'

'What did you tell them this morning?'

'I just asked them to come for the afternoon and they said they would.'

'You didn't tell them about the animals talking?'

'No.' Angela looked embarrassed.

'Oh,' I said. 'You just asked them to tea?'

'Yes.'

'Oh.'

We walked on, Angela in the lead so that I could not see her face. Ahead of us Blueprint gave a series of excited yelps. We caught up with him to find him dancing rather clumsily round a tree, looking up. Above him, high out of reach, a shadow moved and Angela said crossly: 'Shut up, Blueprint. You mustn't chase squirrels now.'

'Sorry,' said Blueprint. 'I forgot.' He looked sad. 'I shall miss it, it's such fun.'

Blueprint spoke up into the tree. 'We are all going to protect each other and not chase each other any more. Except for fun.'

'Oh yeh?' The squirrel spoke from far above our heads.

'Honestly,' said Blueprint.

'What's up?' Joker, the Johnsons' sheepdog, arrived very silently through the bushes.

'The squirrel won't believe we can all help each other.' Blueprint lifted a leg in token of Joker's arrival, and Joker sniffed and did the same.

'That's because we don't need any help ourselves, or not much. Shall we fight?'

'No, no,' I said.

'Why not? We usually do when you are about.'

'Not now,' said Angela and sat down. 'Are the boys coming?'

'They are ambushing you and getting ready to leap out at you in a moment,' said Joker without turning his head.

'We are too old for that,' said Angela, and I remembered the time when our lives simply were not worth living because the Johnson boys continually ambushed us.

Joker sat down beside Angela, and Blueprint and I joined her.

'Come out, we know you are there.' Angela's voice trembled a little because her heart jumped when people leapt out at her.

The Johnson boys did not answer and Blueprint remarked: 'They know you can't see them. You tell them, Joker.'

Joker trotted off to a deep mass of dead bracken and burrowed in. We heard Andrew laugh and say, 'Oh, Joker, you spoiled it.'

'Come on out,' I called.

Andrew and James crawled out of the bracken and stood brushing bits of it off themselves.

'Why aren't the dogs fighting?' James spoke in tones of amazement.

'Come and sit down and we'll tell you why.'

The boys came and sat near us with Joker. Blueprint sat beside us, panting a little, his eyes half shut in the sunshine. There was a long pause and nobody spoke. The river cast itself against the stones and rocks, poured into pools, swung round corners, threw up little bits of spray, and all round us in the wood the birds sang heartily. I looked at Angela and she looked at me. The two dogs seemed to be grinning slightly.

A piece of stick fell on Andrew's head.

'Who threw that?'

'I did.' A tiny voice spoke from above our heads. Blueprint stood up and put his paws up a tree-trunk.

'If I'm not to chase you, you must not tease us.' He looked up the tree-trunk and spoke in a very reasonable voice.

Andrew looked at James and at us and then looked quickly away. Joker licked his face. 'It's all right. We all know.'

'All know what?'

'Well, Kate's bullfinch, having nothing better to do, has let on that we can speak.'

'How terribly awkward,' James exclaimed.

'Why?' said Angela.

'Well, our poor parents.'

'Our parents don't know, only us.'

'I mean, just think of the things my father says in front of the cows and the sheep, and as for the pigs – ' Words failed James.

'That's why we asked you to tea to discuss things,' said Angela. 'Awkward it certainly is in some ways, but most helpful in others.'

'Only you four know.' Blueprint rolled lazily on his back and made a sudden effort to catch his tail.

'It's a terrible responsibility.' Andrew looked at Angela.

'Rot,' said Angela. 'Just think of the fun we can have, preventing things.'

'Preventing what?' James could be very obtuse.

'Otter hunting, fox hunting, deer hunting, shooting, all sorts of things.'

'Shall we be able to stop the foxes eating my father's lambs?'

'We can try.'

'Badger baiting,' I said. I knew Andrew was terribly fond of badgers.

'That would be something.'

'And otters.'

'There are no otters here, alas.'

'Oh, yes there are. There's an otter with his wife and children only ten yards from where you are sitting.' The squirrel had come down the bole of the tree and hung downwards, poised.

'How marvellous!' Andrew exclaimed.

'Not if the hounds come this way,' I said. 'It won't be marvellous then.'

'We must save them,' Andrew said firmly.

'When are the hounds meeting?'

'Soon, I think. I heard my father say so. He said something about it only yesterday. He said they come over his land and make a lot of noise and they are killing off all the otters in the rivers.'

'Does he mind?'

'Not enough to do anything about it. He doesn't fish and he's very busy.'

'About time we got busy.' Andrew turned to James. 'Dash home and look at the paper and we'll wait for you here.'

'They bring the hounds in a van,' James said gloomily. 'And they all dress up in that archaic uniform and carry long sticks. The otters don't stand a chance.'

'Do go, James,' I said.

James hesitated and then ran off through the wood back towards the farm.

'How are we going to get in touch with the otters?' I asked.

'Ask Vice and Mr Bull,' Angela said crossly. 'They will know what to do. They hunt a whole long stretch of the river, miles of it in one day. There may be other otters besides these.'

'It isn't going to be easy,' I said.

'But it's going to be fun.' Andrew stroked Joker's head and Joker gazed into his eyes, saying nothing.

Presently we heard James coming back and the dogs wagged their tails and pricked their ears.

'Next Saturday at Overton.' James was panting slightly.

'Overton.' Andrew got up. 'Come on, we must see Mr Bull. Joker, you go home. We must keep up appearances.'

'Oh Lord, do you mean Blueprint and I have to pretend to fight every time we meet?'

'Only if grown-up people are there.'

'What a bore.'

'And Joker, please don't chase Vice any more,' I said.

'Not chase Vice!' Joker sounded shocked. 'I take care never to catch him. To be honest, I wouldn't know what to do if I did.'

'No cat chasing,' said Andrew.

'That means no fun.'

'Oh, we'll see we all get our fun.'

Joker looked doubtful, but then left us, and the two boys and Blueprint came back to our house with us. We all went up to my room where Mr Bull was sitting in the sun in his cage and Vice was lying asleep in a close ball on my bed.

'Mr Bull,' I said.

'Must you all come tramping in? This is when I have my nap.'

'Mr Bull, we want your advice.'

'Oh, do you?'

'Please, Mr Bull.'

'You forgot my groundsel today.' On the bed Vice yawned.

'Mr Bull, we find there is a family of otters by the river in the wood.'

'What about it?'

'The otter hounds are meeting at Overton next Saturday. They will hunt the river from there right past here.'

'I daresay they will.' Mr Bull spoke carelessly. 'Doesn't worry me,' he added.

'It worries us.' Andrew sat near the cage. 'How can we stop them?'

'You can't.'

'But they will kill the otters.'

'Not if they aren't there.'

'What do you mean?'

'I mean the otters must be hidden where the hounds can't find them. It's quite simple.'

'Is it?' Andrew looked anxious. 'Who is going to tell the otters?'

'I had better,' said Vice lazily. 'I'll tell them tonight on my prowl.'

'Our mother is trying to stop you prowling because of the young birds,' I said.

'Oh that,' Vice said rudely. 'I'll tell them and we must send word upstream and downstream too to other otters.'

'Who can do that?'

'The owls. They fly up the valley and down.'

'Can't we meet the otters?' Andrew asked patiently.

'It may come to that. I must think it out. Run along now and I'll give you all your instructions tomorrow.' Mr Bull closed his eyes, lifted one foot up among his stomach feathers and crouched down broodily. We left the room and went out and into the wood again.

'Old codger,' said James.

'We can't do without him,' I said.

'Did you see Vice just go to sleep again as we left?' Andrew was laughing.

Angela was watching a trout cruising slowly in the river. 'I think we had better leave it to Mr Bull and Vice to think out. We can try and think of a safe hiding place, if they will trust us.'

'Blueprint,' Andrew stroked Blueprint's head. 'Do you know where the otters are?'

'Oh yes,' Blueprint answered politely.

'Can't you show us?'

'No. They are afraid of me and of you.'

'Extra hemp,' I exclaimed suddenly.

'Yes,' said Angela. 'Bribery is the only thing.'

'Only a week is a very short time.' James's voice was reedy with anxiety.

We all sat on the bank brooding, worried to death for the otters we had never seen.

'Could we get at the hounds?'

'No, Andrew. They live too far away.'

'Tea-time,' said Angela.

We all got up and wandered towards our house.

'Tea is ready,' our mother called unnecessarily when she saw us. We all ate tea, politely passing plates to each other and thanking each other effusively. My mother looked at us suspiciously from time to time and I knew she thought we had quarrelled.

'Hullo,' my father said as he came into the room. 'Just going to cast a line. Coming, Blueprint?' Blueprint followed my father out of the room.

'Fish?' queried Andrew.

Angela nodded. We finished our tea and went out and leant on the bridge and watched our father walking down the river with his rod. Blueprint ran ahead of him and we could hear his barking voice shouting: 'Don't rise, don't rise.'

'*He* doesn't like eating them, *I* do.' Vice slipped past us into the wood.

Presently we heard my father cursing Blueprint and sounds of splashing.

'I think he's overdoing it,' I said.

'No, he isn't. It's good psychology. If the otters see the fish have been warned they will listen to Vice.' Andrew listened to my father 'Fine turn of phrase,' he added.

'It cuts both ways. The otters like fish too.' James spoke a little sadly.

'Let's all meet in the wood tonight,' said Angela. 'We can bring Mr Bull in his cage, then he will feel safe and wise, and you bring Joker. No doubt the cats will meet us at midnight.' Angela likes a bit of drama. We could just as easily have met at midday the following day.

We did meet at midnight in the middle of the wood. We had torches and so did Andrew and James. I carried Mr Bull's cage with a cover over it. Blueprint and Joker came with us and the boys respectively; Vice appeared out of the dark, and the Johnsons' tom cat. We sat down and I put Mr Bull's cage in the middle of our group.

'It's cold,' said Joker. 'Hurry up.'

'I've told the otters,' said Vice. 'They are going to think it over.'

'Think it over! Good Lord, they surely trust us?'

'No.'

'I told you they wouldn't.'

'They will.' Mr Bull spoke from under the cover of his cage and sneezed. 'It is cold,' he added. 'I shall get a chill.'

'What next?' Andrew pulled his sweater up round his ears.

'Keep still and listen.' Mr Bull let out several pipes and chortles and a low 'Whoo' came from above our heads.

'We won't eat you,' said Vice.

'What about my mice?' The owl sounded rather difficult. 'What do I get if I warn the otters?'

'I'll buy you something nice with my pocket money,' said Andrew.

'All right. I'll tell the owls to carry the news up and down the valley.'

'They need more than news. They must all be told to come here to be hidden.'

'They won't like it.' Vice sounded bored.

'That or the hounds,' said Mr Bull.

'That or the hounds.' A voice we had not heard before spoke from outside our circle. Blueprint and Joker craned their necks.

'No chasing,' said Mr Bull as though he could see the dogs. The otter sniggered.

'Cut-throats.' His voice scarcely reached us.

'The children are not cut-throats.' Blueprint was fair and reasonable. 'And didn't you see me warning the trout this evening?'

'Oh, I did. You looked a proper Charlie, and I had to go miles to get the wife and children's supper.'

'Anyway' – Angela ignored the unseen otter – 'will you spread the news?' She looked up to where she thought the owl sat.

'Okay.' We heard the owl leave its branch, and then there was silence.

'Every bird, every animal must be told. Now take me home. I'm cold.'

I carried Mr Bull back to the house and tried to speak to him as I went.

'Shut up,' he said snappily.

'Why?'

'I'm speaking to the bats.'

Angela and I slipped into the house with Vice and Blueprint at our heels.

'Will it work?'

'We can but try.' Angela sounded depressed.

In the morning I put Mr Bull's cage by the open window and got back into bed. Mr Bull started piping and chortling and before long the garden birds were flying past the window or sometimes stopping on the window-sill to listen. I watched bemused as chaffinch, sparrow, thrush, blackbird and tits visited in quick succession, and then with a flutter of wings a swallow followed by a martin.

'That takes care of the birds.' Mr Bull sounded pleased with himself.

'What will they do?'

'Each bird will tell its opposite number at the edge of its territory, and the news will spread like a ripple.'

'What about the animals?'

'Vice is going to tell foxes, rabbits, badgers and all farm animals.'

'Will they let us help them, Mr Bull?'

'Oh, I think so.'

'Would you like some extra hemp?'

'You know it upsets me.'

'What can I do then to thank you?'

'Let me out.'

'I can't for long. They will be getting up.'

'Just for a short time.'

I opened the cage and watched Mr Bull flip over the window ledge on to the wisteria which grew along the house. Snip, snip, snip went his beak.

'You'll give us away,' I hissed.

'Pick up the bits then.'

I tore down through the still sleeping house and ran round to below my window and as the bits of bud fell I furtively gathered them up.

'Victim of a small bird.' Vice passed me on the path and vanished among the bushes.

Presently I saw Mr Bull flit back through my window into his cage. Angela looked at me from my room, laughed and shut the window. I ran to the stream and threw the buds into it and then raced back to the house and dressed for breakfast.

'I hear the otter hounds are meeting at Overton next weekend,' said my father with his mouth full.

'Mr Johnson won't be pleased. His sheep haven't finished lambing.' My mother looked up from a letter she was reading.

'Silly waste of time and money,' said my father. 'There isn't an otter within miles.'

'One never knows. They are very secretive,' said my mother. Then she added: 'Have any fun last night fishing?'

'Not a rise. There are plenty of fish about though. I saw them. I shan't take Blueprint with me again. He acted like a lunatic, rushing in and out of the water barking.'

'Poor boy, he's not very bright.' My mother stroked Blueprint's head and Angela and I exchanged looks.

'Can't we ask these otter people not to go through our land?' asked Angela.

'Not really. There aren't any otters and they do no harm. Besides' – my father buttered a piece of toast – 'that fellow who is the M.O.H. does a lot of business through us. I don't want to offend him.'

'Easily offended?' enquired my mother.

'Oh, stuffy. He's quarrelled with every firm in the country except ours. I don't want to lose him. We have the girls to educate after all.'

'I love otters,' said my mother vaguely.

'I hate them being hunted,' said Angela snappily.

'Oh, live and let live.' My father smiled.

'Turn a blind eye do you mean?'

'Exactly.'

'What would you do if you saw an otter being torn to bits?' Angela was becoming aggressive.

'Be a bit late to do anything then, wouldn't it?' My father spoke casually.

'They are a lot of murderers,' I said.

'No, darling, they are not. Most hunting people are passionately devoted to animals. The R.S.P.C.A. depend on them, you know.'

'If I saw an otter being hunted and it took refuge in my house, say, I wouldn't open the door to the hounds,' said my father, helping himself to marmalade with his knife, which is a thing he knew my mother hated because she put a perfectly good spoon by the pot.

'Hardly a likely supposition,' said my mother, pushing the spoon too late towards my father.

'May we go now?' Angela got up.

'Yes,' said my mother unexpectedly, because usually she made us help wash up.

'We must get them into the house and hide them until it's safe for them to go back,' said Angela to me as we went upstairs.

'What about the smell?' I said.

'What smell?'

'The otter smell, stupid. The hounds will follow them to the house.' We went to my room.

'What can we do about the smell, Mr Bull, if we shelter the otters next Saturday in the house?'

'Carry them into the house.'

'Then we shall smell.'

'Wash in carbolic.'

'What a noise the birds are making.' Angela leant out of the window. 'Listen.'

I joined her and listened. All the birds were singing their hearts out and the swallows swooped in great arcs across the sky. High above us a pair of buzzards wheeled and screamed.

'Are they passing messages?' Angela looked at Mr Bull.

'Yes.'

We listened for quite a long time.

'They will need reminding all the time. They forget so easily.' Angela was looking at the ravaged wisteria.

'Look, here comes James.'

❧ 4 ❧

James waved from where he stood at the edge of the wood.
He wore gumboots, jeans and a thick jersey.

'What's up?' Angela enquired.

'Come into the wood.'

We followed James.

'James, you've got something odd under your jersey.'

'I'm not odd,' said an animal voice.

'Well, you show.'

The bulge under James's jersey shifted shape and said:
'That better?'

'No, you still show.'

'Have you got a kitten in there?' I asked.

'No, an otter.'

We gasped with respect and awe and watched the bulge
under James's jersey change shape until James seemed to
have one huge lump, then elongate itself until he looked as
though he had a French loaf under his jersey, then wriggle
again and a whiskered face peered out at his waist line.

'Isn't he gorgeous?' said James.

'Marvellous,' we whispered, watching the otter scramble
down James's leg on to the ground.

'I went to the otters and asked if they would conceal
themselves about our persons,' said James.

'It won't do,' said Angela. 'Mr Bull says they must come
into the house and we must overlay their scent with carbolic
or something smelly.'

'The house!' The otter sounded horrified. 'I've a perfectly
good house of my own.'

'The hounds will get you there,' I said.

'What does your wife say?' said Angela quickly.

'Oh, she's worried to death. The children are so small.'

'All into the house,' said James firmly. The otter looked disgusted.

'We are only trying to help,' I said.

'But the house, it's a terrible idea.'

'Not so bad as death,' said Angela.

'Almost.' The otter did not sound in any way grateful.

I looked at the otter. 'Are there other otters up and down the river?' I asked.

'Yes, but we don't speak.'

'Then they will be in danger too.'

'I suppose so.'

'We must save them.'

'Why, if you save us?'

'No otters should be killed.'

'Both lots upstream and down have better fishing and hunting than we do.'

'How can you be so selfish!' exclaimed Angela. The otter turned round and disappeared into the wood.

'Now you've offended him,' said James.

'What are we to do?' I ground my teeth.

'Ask the dogs to go up river and down and tell all the otters to come here. Then we will hide them while the hunt is on.'

'Blueprint!' Angela called at the top of her voice.

'Yes.' Blueprint appeared, as he always did, looking cheerful and eager.

'Blueprint, will you and Joker go and tell the otters upstream and down to come to us on Friday night and we will shelter them while the hunt is on?'

Blueprint did not answer but thundered away through the wood towards the Johnsons' farm.

'Our father does business for the Master of the Otter Hounds,' said Angela gloomily.

'Well, my father is in the middle of selling him a cow.'

'Our father said if he had a house full of otters he would turn a blind eye,' Angela said loyally.

'Well, he's a lawyer,' said James, and I wondered what the Johnsons said about our family in the privacy of their house.

All that week we were rather distracted. Only Mr Bull seemed perfectly calm when we came home in the evenings.

Andrew spent some of his pocket money buying steak which he put in the wood for the owls. My mother complained that Vice was prowling at night and had an argument with my father who said it couldn't be helped and it was 'cat nature'.

'Don't look so fussed. They have all been warned,' said Mr Bull.

'Which room shall we put them in when they come?' I asked.

'If they come.'

'Surely they will?'

Angela went to the village on her bicycle and bought some Jeyes fluid.

'Mother will be furious,' I said.

'I will roll in something she thinks really foul,' said Blueprint, 'and then you can wash me in the Jeyes.'

'Oh, Blueprint, you are heroic,' I said, because Blueprint couldn't stand baths.

'I'll get Joker to do the same.' Blueprint swelled with pride at being called heroic.

'I shall get the tom cat from the farm to help me,' said Vice mysteriously.

'What does he mean?' Angela's anxiety was dulling her intelligence.

'Nothing like a tom cat for sheer stink,' said Mr Bull.

'Our poor mother,' I said. 'And my room,' I insisted. 'Then they will have Mr Bull and they can feel they can climb down the wisteria if they must.'

'All this is pure hypothesis,' said Mr Bull.

'What do you mean?'

'They are unlikely to come.'

'Why? We've warned them enough.'

'Oh, warnings.' Mr Bull went to sleep.

'The hounds are meeting at ten-thirty. They should get here about twelve.' Andrew pointed with his finger at the winding river on the ordnance map. 'One or two of us should go to the meet, one of us should stay here and one walk up river with the dogs.'

'But all the otters will be here.'

'Mr Bull doesn't think so. I agree with him. If they come at all it will be at the last possible minute.'

'Don't be so pessimistic, Andrew.'

'I'm realistic.'

'Vice,' I said, 'what do the otters think?'

'They have all been warned, but whether they will act is another thing.'

We cast lots and it fell to James and Andrew to go to the meet, to Angela to walk up river and for me to wait near the house to admit the otters.

'They should all come the night before,' I said.

'They won't,' said the mouse who had joined us. 'They are not house-minded, not civilized.'

'We can only hope for the best.'

Blueprint laid his heavy head on my knee and groaned.

On the morning of the Saturday we saw Andrew and James go by, walking up the river with Joker. Angela followed them with Blueprint, and I went down to the river in the wood.

It was a beautiful morning. I just sat and waited, feeling tears of disappointment very close. No otters had come the night before, it was already eleven and the hounds would be moving downstream, nosing in and out of the banks, egged on by all those people carrying long sticks to block the way of any otter trying to escape with its life through the shallows. I looked at my watch. Eleven-thirty. Vice joined me, sitting with his ears pricked and paws neatly together.

'Here they come,' he said.

'I can hear nothing.'

'I can.'

'Then beg the otters to come.'

Vice went off with his tail in the air and I sat rigid.

Presently in the water I saw a ripple and an otter's head peered at me from behind a stone.

'This the sanctuary?'

'Yes. Do hurry.'

A pair of otters slipped out of the river on to the grass and followed me through the wood. I led them to the back of the house and upstairs to my bedroom.

'Get into the cupboard,' said Mr Bull. 'That's right. Be sensible.'

The otters climbed furtively into my cupboard and I shut the door.

'Where are the babies, Mr Bull?'

'Oh, that's not our lot. Those come from miles down-stream. Our lot have three babies who are too small to leave.'

'Why didn't they say so?'

'Can't expect everything,' said Mr Bull.

'I'll fetch them,' I said. Far up the river I could hear the sound of the hounds baying.

'Our lot think themselves clever. It's a great drawback.' Mr Bull pecked at his seed and drank a sip of water.

'Mr Bull, how can you?'

'It's not me they are hunting.'

'Vice has gone to tell them,' I said.

'They don't care for Vice.' Mr Bull, safe in his cage, was complacent. I left him and hurried back to the wood where I met Vice sauntering towards me with his tail in the air.

'Vice, where are they?'

'All in their hole.' Vice yawned and rolled on his back, stretching out a paw towards me.

'Vice, please show me where they are.'

Vice got up and led the way through the trees to the edge of the river. 'Here,' he said.

I saw a hole I had passed a hundred times.

'In there?' I was incredulous.

'Yep.'

'Otters!' I called.

There was a long silence and then an otter's voice said: 'What do you want?'

'I want to hide you and your wife and family. The hounds are coming. Can't you hear them?'

'Oh yes, we hear them.'

'Do come.'

'Where?'

'I already have two otters safe in my room with Mr Bull. Do come.'

'I'll ask the wife.'

I waited. The water carried the sound of the hounds downstream, and I seemed to hear Blueprint's voice and Joker's too. I wondered whether they could have become over-excited and joined in the hunt.

'Here we are.'

Two otters, each carrying a very small baby, emerged from the hole.

'Hurry,' I said.

'One more,' said one of the otters, and vanished down the hole again, reappearing quickly with the third baby.

'You'll have to let me carry it.' I snatched the baby from the ground and hurried up the river towards our house. Behind me Vice's venomous voice said: 'Hurry, you fools.'

On the bridge by our house our mother and father were standing looking upstream. I heard my father say: 'It disturbs the fish.'

'I should think it would disturb the otters more,' my mother said acidly.

'Oh, there aren't any otters on this stretch of river. I asked Johnson and he ought to know.'

I ran across the lane and into our house and up the stairs to my room. I reached it at the same time as the otters. Vice brought up the rear.

'Put them in the chest of drawers,' said Mr Bull.

'Why not with the others?' I said.

'They aren't on speaking terms.'

I opened the bottom drawer and the female otter leapt in with the baby in her mouth, followed by her mate. I shoved the third baby in after them and shut the drawer. Vice was already leaving the room. I saw him dashing downstairs. As I went out of the side door I had come in by I smelt a fearful smell.

'Was that you, Vice?'

'Yes. The Johnsons' cat has done the front door.'

'My poor mother!'

'Who do you want to please?' Vice ran off into the wood.

I joined my parents on the bridge, my heart thumping. Upstream, coming down quickly, we could hear hounds, and Blueprint and Joker barking.

'Sounds like Blueprint,' said my mother.

'He went out with Angela,' I said.

'He'll try and fight the hounds,' said my father. 'They will massacre him.' My father had pride in Blueprint's fighting capacities.

'Oh, the poor otters!' I said.

'But there aren't any, darling. It's just a lot of show.'

I thought of all the otters in my bedroom, and the family Mr Bull said lived upstream. They certainly would be dead.

Angela came walking down the river bank her eyes shining. She hurried into the house and I went after her. 'Ooh, what a pong! Where are the otters?'

'One lot in my cupboard and one in the chest of drawers,' I said.

'Okay.' Angela fished under her jersey and brought out two tiny otters and put them into the middle drawer.

'You babies keep quiet,' said Mr Bull.

We shut the drawer and ran down the stairs. 'Where are the parents? Are they dead?' I asked.

'No. Andrew's got them in his gumboots. Hurry.'

We reached the bridge in time to see the pack of hounds milling round and under it and among them Joker and Blueprint barking their heads off. Above the clamour I heard Blueprint shout into a large hound's ear: 'Louder, louder, and carry on downstream.' The hound, who appeared rather a jolly sort of animal, gave a tremendous bay, throwing up his head as he did so. All the other hounds joined in joyously.

'I wonder what they think they are hunting,' shouted my father to my mother.

'Otters,' shouted my mother to my father.

'Rubbish,' shouted my father. 'I told you Johnson says there are no otters on this stretch of river.'

'So you did, darling,' my mother mouthed. 'Here come the Johnson boys. Oh, poor Andrew, what's happened?'

Andrew, his feet bare and jeans wet, limped along the bank. 'Tally ho! and all that lark,' he said. He was carrying his gumboots. 'I filled my gumboots.'

'Go into the house and borrow mine,' said my mother.

Andrew went barefoot up the short bit of lane and into our house. 'What a stink! Where are the babies, Angela?'

'In my chest of drawers,' I said.

'What a stink,' he repeated, handing his gumboots to Angela, who hurried upstairs with them.

'It's the cats' contribution,' I said, watching Andrew put on my mother's boots. 'What happened?'

'We got them just before the hounds. Angela grabbed the two babies and I put the grown ones in my boots.'

'Where are the human hunters?' I asked.

'Coming along nicely,' said Andrew.

We went out and rejoined our parents by the bridge. Some three dozen people, some dressed in hunting uniforms carrying long sticks, were moving about. My parents were pointing downstream towards the distant sound of hounds baying.

Blueprint came trotting home panting, his eyes shining and his tongue lolling.

'Blueprint has rolled in something terrible,' said Angela.

'Oh Lord, we must bath him and he does so hate it.'

'The whole house smells,' remarked my father. 'Very curious. I'm going out.'

'He's afraid of being asked to bath Blueprint,' said my mother. 'Give me a hand, Angela, and Kate, will you open the windows, the smell is rather much.'

Angela and my mother took Blueprint into the scullery. Andrew, James and I dashed upstairs to my room.

'Better let them all go now while your father is out and your mother busy,' remarked Mr Bull.

We opened my cupboard and the drawers and the otters streamed out and down the stairs. I carried the extra baby in my hand as far as the otters' hole, put it down and turned away. None of the otters had said 'thank you'; they had just slipped away into the river.

Far away downstream the big hound was baying.

'Those hounds think this the funniest thing that's ever happened,' remarked Joker in a superior tone, and he trotted away towards the farm.

My mother went out during the afternoon to see Mrs Johnson. Angela and I walked down through the wood towards the Johnson farm.

'An ungrateful lot,' said Angela.

'They had their mouths full of babies,' I said.

'Even so.'

'Even so I would help them again.'

'What we need is a car,' said Angela.

'Why?'

'Well, I don't altogether rely on the birds and animals. A car to get about in is what we need.'

We met the Johnson boys sitting by the river, both silent.

'You look glum,' I said.

'We missed so much.'

'What do you mean?'

'We missed my father having a tearing row with the hunting people for disturbing the sheep.'

'The sheep knew. Joker told them.'

'They acted disturbed and my father was worried to death. What he said to the man who fell in the river would blister the paint off a battleship.'

'How lovely,' we said.

'Why did the man fall in the river?'

'Joker tripped him for fun.'

'Good for Joker.'

'What we need is a car,' said Andrew.

'Just what I was saying,' said Angela. 'The animals are too frivolous.'

'It isn't that. The real trouble is that they all seem to hunt each other and simply do not worry about others, only themselves.'

We all became very thoughtful.

'None of us is large enough to drive,' said James.

'I shall go and speak to Tom Foley,' said Andrew.

'Andrew!' we all exclaimed with one voice.

'Well, why not?'

Why not indeed. We all looked at each other in horror.

'Father says he's an intellectual.'

'He can drive, he has a car, he's – well he's the sort of person who would help. What's an intellectual?'

We all sat and thought about Tom Foley. Tom Foley so often fined for poaching salmon. Tom Foley up before the magistrates for driving an unlicensed car. Tom Foley and sheep – he had a funny way with sheep. Had we not all been brought up to keep out of Tom Foley's way?

'He has a dog,' said James.

'He has carrier pigeons,' said Andrew.

'He's got a girl friend,' said Angela.

'Never!' I exclaimed.

'He has,' said Angela.

'Who is it?' said Andrew.

'Nobody we know.'

'I think I'll go and see him just the same,' said Andrew.

'We are not allowed to talk to him,' said Angela.

'That wouldn't matter. Didn't you notice today that only the dogs were reliable? Tom's dog would be reliable.'

'She couldn't drive a car,' said James. 'When Tom's drunk,' he added. 'Or being intellectual. I don't think it's a disease.'

'Or even if he were not,' I said.

'The village is too public,' said Angela.

'Then I must see him at home.'

'Don't be stupid. None of us knows where he lives.'

'He always says "roundabout" when anyone asks him.'

'Some animal or bird would know.'

'Would they tell us?'

'Good heavens, now that we saved their lives!'

'That isn't what they think.'

'They don't think we saved their lives?'

'No. Blueprint says the last thing he heard from the otters was one otter saying to the other that our behaviour was unwarrantable interference.'

'I thought so,' said James sadly. 'They all think we are cranks.'

'All the more reason to get Tom Foley to help. He's a crank if ever there was one.' Angela got up from the long grass she was sitting in and felt her damp behind. 'It's damp,' she said.

'Who said Tom had a girl friend?' I asked.

'My father,' said James. 'Long ago, some time last summer, I heard my father telling my mother that Tom Foley had been thrown out of the pub because he was tipsy.'

'What's that got to do with a girl friend?'

'I don't know, only my father laughed and said Tom cursed them all in the pub and said he was off with his girl friend.'

'He doesn't seem to me the type to have a girl friend.' Andrew stood up too.

'That's what my father said.'

'Have any of us seen her?' I asked, looking round.

'No,' the others all answered at once.

'What do we know about him?' James could be quite good at sticking to the point.

'We know he lives somewhere near here,' said Angela.

'We know he hates the law.' I spoke as a lawyer's daughter. 'Our father says he's a law unto himself.'

'We know he's marvellous with sheep,' Andrew continued. 'He always doctors ours and he always helps with the shearing and he's a dab hand with delicate lambs.'

'Yes,' I said.

'We know he has a car, a vintage car.' James spoke respectfully.

'I believe he only works to get the money for its petrol and oil,' said Andrew. 'These boots are your mother's. I must return them. Lucky she has large feet.'

'It's a Bull-nosed Morris,' said James, who adores cars.

'He could make a lot of money if he sold it,' I said.

'But we want to use it.'

'Well, then, first we must find him. Would Mr Bull know?' Andrew queried.

'I'll ask him,' I said. 'If he doesn't he could find out.'

'I'm puzzled about his girl friend.' Andrew didn't trust many people.

'She's called Floss,' said Joker, who had joined the boys as we talked.

'Floss what? An odd name for a girl.'

'Floss,' repeated Joker, looking intelligently down his long nose. Joker is one of those black and white collies who go creepy-crawly round the sheep and bemuse them into going into pens.

'Floss,' he said again and yawned.

'I'll go and ask Mr Bull now,' I said, and I left the others and went home and up to my room.

Mr Bull was sitting in his cage with the afternoon sun shining on him, so that I could see and admire his glossy black head and deep pink stomach.

'You look beautiful, Mr Bull.'

'I am.'

'Mr Bull, do you know where Tom Foley lives?'

'He gets drunk. He's peculiar. He writes, so they say.'

'We know that's what they say, but he might help, Mr Bull. He has a car.'

'Very old.'

'I know it's old but it works. Do you think he would help us?'

'You could ask him.'

'Where does he live?'

'Everyone knows.'

'We don't.'

'You have been told to keep away from him. I heard your mother – '

'That's because of his language, Mr Bull. The boys know him.'

'But not where he lives.'

'No.'

Mr Bull opened his beak and let out a series of chortles and pipes, then stopped and seemed to go to sleep.

'Do tell me, Mr Bull.' I felt that if Mr Bull went on being so complacent I would do something nasty to him.

'No, you wouldn't.' He opened his eyes.

'Wouldn't what?'

'Do anything nasty.'

I began to laugh and said: 'You are too clever, Mr Bull. Too clever by half.'

'By half what?'

'Tell me, Mr Bull – please.'

'Tom Foley lives in the big wood on the hill above the Johnsons' farm.'

'But that's National Trust. A nature reserve.'

'Doesn't make any difference.'

'It's huge. How can we find him?'

'Get Joker or Blueprint to lead you there. They know.'

'What devils not to tell us,' I said.

'Perhaps you didn't ask them.'

I found Angela and the two Johnson boys standing where I had left them. Joker was sitting beside them and Blueprint with his ears pricked and head on one side. As I reached them Vice came sauntering down the path licking his lips.

'Vice! What have you eaten?' Angela asked suddenly.

'It fell out of the nest,' Vice answered casually. 'Only a young thrush, nothing rare. They are at their best before they can fly.'

'I don't call that helping each other.' Angela was furious.

'I was helping myself.' Vice sounded in no way perturbed. 'And the thrushes, of course. It had hurt its wing falling, poor thing. It makes one mouth less to feed for the parents.'

Vice sat down beside Joker and closed his eyes, his long white whiskers spreading out from beside his nose like the strings of a lyre.

Andrew shrugged his shoulders and said: 'Did Mr Bull tell you where Tom Foley lives?'

'He said everyone knows,' I said rather spitefully. 'Everyone except us, of course. He said Joker would lead us there. He lives in the High Woods above the Johnsons.'

'Joker.' James looked at Joker, who wagged his tail, rolled his eyes and looked amused and contrite all at once.

'We none of us asked him,' I said.

'Nor did we.' Andrew stroked Joker, who was standing up against him now with his paws on his chest, trying to reach his face to lick.

'You didn't ask me either.' Blueprint pressed his rather barrel-shaped body against my legs.

'And Vice knows too, I suppose,' said Angela.

'Naturally.' Vice purred more to himself than to us as he sat in the sun with his tail wrapped round him, absolutely still except for the tip of his tail which went flip, flip gently.

'Andrew looked at his watch. 'If we went now?'

'Yes, at once,' said Angela. 'You dogs lead us, and you,' she turned suddenly on Vice, 'you go home.' She bent to look into Vice's face. Like lightning he shot out a paw and scratched her cheek, then with his tail in the air he ambled off towards home.

'Never mind,' Blueprint said to her. 'We will lead you to Tom Foley.'

We followed the dogs past the Johnsons' farmhouse and waved to our mothers who were sitting on the doorstep in the sun.

'Going for a walk?' my mother called.

'Yes, sort of,' we waved back. My mother is a town person and has never realized that country people do not ever go for a walk. They walk for a sound purpose. Joker and Blueprint, their tails high, led us through the Johnsons' pasture, past the sheep who scarcely stopped munching grass to look at us, and up into the High Woods.

A cart-track led for a quarter of a mile to an old quarry. Ahead of us up the hill the wood stretched, oaks and beeches, larch and hazel, with a thick undergrowth of bramble and bracken. We had often played in the quarry and knew it well, but the wood was so thick and the brambles so thorny that we had not often gone far into it.

Joker led the way up the hill, in and out of the undergrowth, the white tip of his tail held high. Blueprint followed, sniffing the air. We followed in Indian file, only hearing the sound of the dry twigs crackling under our feet and the birds high above us in the trees. Somewhere a cuckoo cuckooed boringly and incessantly and a woodpecker startled us with a loud shriek of laughter.

Suddenly we were standing on the edge of a clearing, the four of us in a row, and the dogs standing by us wagging their tails and panting slightly.

'It's a badgers' set,' said Andrew under his breath.

All round us were well-established badgers' sets. In the middle of the clearing was a patch of grass, and lying on his back, with a very old brown hat over his eyes, a man asleep. His left hand and arm lovingly encircled a small dog who was watching us with very bright intelligent eyes peering down a sharp pointed nose. Her ears were pricked and her expression enigmatic. Above us the woodpecker let out another shriek of lunatic laughter and a pair of jays began to tease. The man stirred, automatically stroking the dog's silky flank.

Joker trotted down towards the man and appeared to be saying something friendly to the little bitch. She bared her teeth in a silent snarl and laid back her ears. Joker retreated a couple of yards and sat down.

'It's Tom Foley,' said James.

The man sat up, rubbed his eyes and looked up at us.

'Well?' said Tom Foley.

Joker wagged his tail.

'May we come and talk to you?' Andrew stepped forward.

'Free country.' Tom Foley stroked his dog. 'In parts,' he added. 'Not many parts left.'

'It's that sort of thing we wanted to talk to you about.'

'Yes?' Tom Foley was not exactly forthcoming.

'We need help.' Angela walked down into the hollow and sat beside Joker.

'Ask your father, he's a lawyer.'

'It's not a legal matter. No need to be huffy.'

Tom went on stroking his dog, who went on looking at us with her very bright eyes.

We all drew close to Tom who was now sitting up and looking at us with amusement down a long wandering nose, out of small eyes, which curiously resembled his dog's. We all

stared and sat silent. I appraised Tom Foley's clothes. The
hat I recognized at once as Mr Johnson's. He called it his
Milk Marketing Board hat, and there had been consider-
able uproar on the last occasion he had wished to wear it
and no one had been able to find it. The suit puzzled me as I
knew I had seen it before.

'Parson's country gentleman Honest to God Christian
outfit,' muttered Blueprint in my ear, and went on, 'shoes
from Lobb's, shirt Marks and Sparks, tie from the jumble
sale.'

'Who is Lobb?' I whispered.

'Everyone knows that,' grunted Blueprint in an unconvincing voice.

'Know me again, won't you.' Tom Foley grinned.

'Sorry,' I said.

'Liberty Hall.'

'Sorry,' I said again.

'Tom.' James crept close to Tom. 'We've found out all the
animals can talk.'

Tom Foley groaned and lay back, covering his face with
his hat.

'Tom, we messed up the otter hunt and we want you to
help us mess up other hunts and badger baiting and
shooting.'

'That's war on respectability.' Tom spoke from under his
hat.

'Just up your street,' said Joker.

'You leave my street alone,' said Tom from under his hat.

'We need your help and your car,' said Andrew.

'My car.' Tom Foley sat up again.

'Yes, if your girl friend will join us,' I said, feeling rather
wily.

'Who is your girl friend?' Andrew could be fearfully
clumsy.

Tom Foley began to laugh rather like the woodpecker.
'Oh, my girl friend,' he said, wiping a hand across his eyes.
'My girl friend,' and he laughed again. 'This is my girl
friend.' His encircling arm closed tighter round the little
dog. 'Floss,' said Tom Foley. The little dog's expression

changed entirely as she looked into his face and her bushy
tail moved.

'Can you speak too, Floss?'

'Yes,' said Floss.

<h1 style="text-align:center">❧ 6 ☙</h1>

Andrew told Tom Foley about Mr Bull, the mouse, the
birds, the other animals and the result of the otter hunt.
Tom Foley and Floss listened. Andrew finished and we all
looked at Tom.

'Well?' said Tom.

'We thought you might help us,' I said.

'Did you?'

'We thought with your car and carrier pigeons you would
like to help,' said Angela.

'They are not carrier pigeons, they are ordinary wood
pigeons.' Tom Foley showed his teeth in a slight smile.

'Oh,' Angela looked taken aback.

Tom Foley appeared to relent. 'You *might* call them
carrier pigeons if you stretched a point.'

'What point?' said James.

'I've taken their rings off. They have retired, so to speak.'

Somewhere in the wood a pigeon began to coo drowsily.

'They don't like the long train journeys in baskets, see. So
they retire.'

'And you help them,' Angela said quickly.

'Yes.'

'We want to help more than otters and pigeons. Think of
badgers,' Andrew said.

'Ah well, badgers. As you can see, I'm more or less a
lodger among the badgers. Go find a badger, Floss.'

Floss left Tom Foley and trotted to the nearest set and
went down it.

Tom looked at us. 'Fond of badgers?' he asked.

'They are marvellous,' said Andrew. 'They do nobody any harm. They are terribly clever and civilized and people dig them out and torture them. It's disgusting what people do to badgers.'

'What about cows, sheep, pigs and the like?' Tom queried.

'That's awful too, but they are not persecuted for sport.'

'No.'

Behind us a huge badger heaved itself silently out of one of the largest sets followed by Floss.

'What's going on, and in daylight too?' said the badger. 'I can't see a thing.'

'Well, old man, these children have found out you can all speak and they want to help you, stop you being tormented, and other animals too, for sporting reasons.'

The badger blinked in the sun and we admired his wonderful markings.

'Nobody ever comes here,' said the badger.

'They might,' I said.

'They mucked up an otter hunt this morning and they want to save the foxes and deer and so on as well as you.'

'Foxes eat sheep and chickens.' The badger looked doubtful.

'Not always,' I said.

'Need a lot of organizing. I'm sleepy,' said the badger.

'Were the otters pleased and grateful?' There was a trace of malice in Tom's voice.

'No, not at all. They thought we were interfering,' said Angela.

'Can't expect them to like you all of a sudden,' said Floss, in a rather high whining voice. 'I don't,' she added, with a sidelong look at Blueprint.

'With your car, Tom, we could travel long distances and give the animals warning,' said James. 'It's a beautiful car,' he added.

'And your pigeons can travel great distances,' said Angela. 'Once the animals know, we could just send them messages and they could cover their tracks and hide, or something,' she added lamely.

'This great wood could become a sanctuary,' I said, suddenly inspired. 'As it's meant to be.'

'It's going to cost money and make a lot of work,' said Tom.

'Surely it's worth it?' Angela looked frustrated. 'Think of all the things we could do without money.'

'Such as?' said Andrew.

'Teaching trout not to rise to a fly and foxes not to worry lambs. They hardly ever do anyway.'

'What about cats and mice? What about me and rabbits? What about squirrels eating pigeon's eggs?' Floss whined and snarled.

'Oh, you are all so difficult,' exclaimed James.

'It's a difficult subject,' said the badger.

'But will you help?' I said.

There was a long pause.

'Tell you what, we will think about it.' Tom Foley put his hat over his eyes again and lay back. Floss curled herself against his side and watched us.

'A lot of thinking is needed, not just enthusiasm,' said the badger.

'May we come again?' Andrew's voice was disappointed and sad.

'Oh yes, any time.' The badger left us.

We all felt tremendously let down.

Floss was looking at us with her beady eyes.

'The car has no petrol.' She made the statement flatly.

'Would it help if it had?'

'Certainly.'

'Would you?'

Floss grinned. 'Certainly.'

'So it boils down to money!' exclaimed James.

'Yes,' said Floss.

'Nonsense!' Tom spoke unexpectedly from under his hat. 'There is a lot can be done without money, though if we use the car we have to have petrol and oil.'

'Oh, Tom!'

Our hearts leapt.

'Oh, Tom, you are marvellous!' Angela sprang to her feet.

'We need the foxes' help badly,' I said.

'There's been a vixen sitting behind you ever since you came, listening.'

'Why didn't the dogs let us know?'

'They know, but don't know whether you should know.' The voice from under the hat was lazy and sleepy.

'Why doesn't she come forward?' Andrew sounded rather pompous.

'Would you if you'd fed your family on a Johnson lamb for several days?' Tom's voice trailed off into a gentle snore under the hat.

'Oh, dear, how complicated it all is,' I said.

Floss looked at me with a sneer and, lying close to Tom, closed her eyes.

'That lamb was a weakling. My father said so,' said James. 'He said the foxes were welcome to it if they didn't make a habit of it.'

'He isn't like most farmers,' a thin, high voice said behind us. 'He is odd.'

'What do you mean, odd?' James turned with the rest of us and stared up the bank to where we could just discern a vixen sitting upright in the shade.

'Well, odd,' said the vixen, 'very odd. He cares when he sells a cow. He loves his sheep. He dotes on his pigs.'

'He says the most awful things to them,' James muttered.

'That's just to hide his feelings. You see, pigs are bright and there is nothing you can do with a pig except eat it. You can't milk it as you do a cow and let it have a reasonably long life, or shear it as you do a sheep for its wool, and sheep have quite long lives too.'

'Except when they are eaten,' said Andrew.

'Oh well,' said the vixen, 'you can't have everything.' She, too, yawned and disappeared in the shadows of the trees.

'All yawning and going to sleep.' Andrew got up. 'We must find the money for petrol and oil for Tom's car.'

'That will take years,' James grumbled. 'Where is the car anyway?'

'In the quarry.' Floss spoke without opening her eyes.

'Would he mind if we looked at it?' James stood up and I joined him.

'Not if you cover it up again,' Tom murmured from under his hat.

'Goodbye,' we said, but no one answered and we followed Joker and Blueprint down the hill.

Shadowed by trees and covered by a groundsheet, Tom's car was parked in a corner of the quarry. No one would have noticed it if they had not known it was there. We lifted the groundsheet and looked at it with admiration.

'A 1924 Bullnose,' said James.

'But hardly any petrol,' said Andrew, looking into the tank.

The Johnson boys and Angela and I had for a long time made merry over what we called our parents' daily moan when the post arrived. 'Bills!' they would cry. 'Nothing but bills. It is high time you children grew up and earned your living.'

Now it was for us to moan, worry and fret over money, and ponder over ways and means to collect enough to run Tom's car. We walked about frowning and scuffling our shoes as we walked, kicking stones ill-temperedly. The days passed and we grumbled. Between us we raised seventeen and eleven from our pocket money, which we put in a jar in a hole in the wood.

We shared our troubles with the animals and birds.

'Money has never worried me,' said Mr Bull, crunching his seed in his strong beak. 'Not so long as I get my food.'

'Money,' said the cow Mr Johnson was selling to the Master of the Otter Hounds. 'Money is going to change hands but I shan't see it. It only goes towards paying the vet.'

'Money,' said the mouse. 'We have some money.' And he and several other mice kindly rolled two shilling pieces, a threepenny bit and a halfpenny out of their hole by the electric light plug. That brought our hoard up to a pound and twopence-halfpenny. We thanked the mice.

Early one morning Angela came into my room. 'Somebody has left a huge sea-trout at the back door,' she said.

'That's the otters,' said Mr Bull. 'Sell it.'

Angela smoothed over the otter's teeth marks and sold the fish at the hotel. The owner gave her fifteen shillings. That brought us up to one pound, fifteen and twopence-half-penny, and we went to thank the otters but they were all out.

'Can't leave a note because they can't read,' I said.

'What can we do?' said Angela. 'What can we do to get more money?'

'I think we should ask the animals. It's no good asking Tom Foley because he spends everything he earns on drink and Floss doesn't stop him because she likes beer.'

We knew this to be true because my father had told my mother that he had seen Tom Foley pour beer into a saucer in the pub and Floss drink it.

'If we got enough we could run the car,' said Andrew.

'I will ask Floss,' said Joker, who was very fond of visiting Floss when he could slip away from the farm.

'It is time I took a hand in this,' said Vice. 'I shall speak to the dogs.'

We looked doubtfully at Vice, who had recently caught a mouse.

'This needs brains,' said Vice.

'It's terrible. The otter hounds keep meeting and in August they will start deer hunting and the cubbing begins.'

'All the rich men are fishing now,' said Vice, gazing ahead of him into infinity.

'We warn the fish.'

'That's not what I meant.'

'The otters don't care for the fish to be warned,' I said. 'It was good of them to bring us that sea-trout.'

'I should have liked it,' said Vice.

'Vice, you get more than enough to eat.' Angela, quite rightly I felt, did not think Vice was wholeheartedly on our side.

'I'll talk to the dogs all the same.' Vice went to the door and miaowed as though he could not talk at all. We looked at each other and sighed.

'Let's go and ask for more pocket money,' said Angela.

'It won't do any good,' said Mr Bull. 'Dash it, even birdseed has gone up.'

'Then logically pocket money should go up too.' Angela twanged one of the bars of Mr Bull's cage.

We went to look for our parents, who were sitting in the sun in the garden. As we approached them we heard my mother say: 'I hate you letting the fishing, darling, you so enjoy it.'

'A hundred pounds a month is not to be sneezed at. Johnson has let his. The girls have to be educated and both Johnson and I have had the best of the river, May and June. Besides — ' my father was dreamily watching Blueprint running after Vice into the wood, 'the fish simply are not rising this year.'

'Then it seems dishonest to let.'

'Not really. There are plenty of fish. These chaps may catch them. They have money to throw about. They may be lucky.'

'It doesn't seem honest to me,' said my mother.

'I told them,' said my father, 'but there it is. Fishing is hard to get. They are staying at the hotel. They said they were given a very good sea-trout their first evening there. I wonder where it came from. I'd bet anything we had otters nearby but I never see them.'

'There are no otters round here,' said my mother.

'None at all,' said Angela.

'What do you girls want?' asked my father abruptly.

'More pocket money,' I said.

'No!' my father shouted.

'What next!' exclaimed my mother.

Our father went crossly into the house.

'Who has he let the fishing to?' I asked tactfully.

'Oh, he and Mr Johnson have let the whole two miles they have between them to some men called Macintosh or Jersey or Raglan or some name like that. They are from London.'

'Cardigan,' said Angela, who was rather good at names. 'They are publishers, rather "avant garde".'

'When are they starting to fish?'

'Tonight, I believe. D'you know what "avant garde" means, Angela?'

Angela shook her head, laughing.

We went down the river into the wood. By the otters' holt I called: 'Otters!'

There was a sort of whispering inside. 'What is it now?' said one of the baby otters irritably.

'Our father and Mr Johnson have let the fishing to two city gents.'

'Oh, have they?'

'Keep out of their way, won't you?'

'Don't be daft,' another otter answered.

Blueprint joined us, wagging his tail. 'Just had a word with Vice and Joker,' he said. 'Joker is going to tell Floss. She will help.'

'Help at what?' Blueprint was looking too amused to be safe.

'Oh, never mind,' he said. My father whistled and Blueprint went tearing off, his ears laid back.

We spent the evening watching the two visitors casting their lines. Now and again a fish rose with a swish and plopped back into the water.

'There are lots of fish but they just don't seem to be taking,' said one Mr Cardigan to the other as they passed us.

'Try again early tomorrow,' said the second Mr Cardigan.

'Try away,' said Angela, as we went off to school the next day and saw the two men getting out their rods near the bridge.

When we got home we heard voices in our house and went in to find both the Mr Cardigans talking to my mother.

'Oh, hullo darlings,' said our mother.

'Hullo,' we said, and then 'How do you do?' to the two Mr Cardigans.

'I should ring the police if I were you,' my mother said to the Mr Cardigans.

'We only wondered if you had seen anybody,' said one Mr Cardigan. 'We were watching the river.'

'What's happened?' asked Angela. 'A nice murder?'

'No. Mr Cardigan and his brother have both had money stolen from their wallets which they left in their coats while they were fishing. The wallets were there but no money.'

'How odd,' I said.

'How much?' asked Angela.

'About forty pounds, between us.'

'Forty pounds!' My voice squeaked in astonishment. 'Are you the sort of people who carry forty pounds on your persons?'

'Don't be rude, Kate,' said my mother. 'You should certainly tell the police,' she said to the older Mr Cardigan, 'and we will get hold of my husband when he comes in. He is a solicitor.'

'He's hardly likely to have pinched it,' said Angela. 'Who has been up and down the river, mother?'

'Nobody,' said my mother. 'I've been here all day.'

'It's very queer,' I said.

'Go and wash before tea,' said my mother, who never remembered to say things like that unless there were people visiting. 'You will stay to tea, won't you?' she said to the Mr Cardigans. 'After all, it's our land you were robbed on.'

'What a drama!' said Angela as she walked upstairs, ran the water over her hands in the bathroom and wiped the dirt off on to a towel. 'What a lovely drama!'

We had tea. My father came in. He took the two Cardigans off to the police. The police came in a squad car and tramped up and down the wood by the river. The Johnson boys and Joker came with us, and my mother and father, and Mr Johnson when he had finished milking. We all crashed about a bit in the wood. The two policemen looked very wise and went away and finally we went to bed.

When the house was quiet Angela came into my room with Blueprint and Vice. 'Fancy us having the police,' she said.

'Yes, fancy,' said Vice.

'What do you mean – "Fancy" – in that tone of voice?' I asked.

'Only fancy,' said Vice, who was sitting staring at Mr Bull.

'Stop staring at Mr Bull,' I said.

'Oh-ho-ho-ho-ho!' Blueprint lay on his back, switching himself from side to side his eyes rolling.

'What's the "ho-ho" for?' asked Angela.

Mr Bull gave a cheerful pipe and Vice began licking his white stomach. We could hear his harsh tongue scraping through his soft fur.

'Forty quid,' said Mr Bull.

'We all know they think they lost forty quid,' said Angela. 'The police don't think so, nor does father. You could see by their faces they didn't believe the Cardigans.'

'But we've got forty quid,' said Vice.

'We have,' growled Blueprint.

'Who took it?' I said.

'Joker and Floss and I,' said Blueprint.

Angela laughed. 'Where is it?'

'Down the mousehole. Now you can buy all the petrol you want.'

'I have asked the Cardigans to tea,' said my mother at breakfast. 'It's high time the girls met some respectable people.'

'Oh,' said my father. 'Er – I suppose it is.'

'It's terrible that they should be robbed on our land,' my mother continued, eating her breakfast. 'Not that I like the police tramping about the wood in the nesting season.'

'No,' said my father. 'Only doing their job,' he added.

'They long for a bit of crime.' I helped myself to a banana.

'You know,' I said to Angela as we walked down the road to meet Mrs Johnson and the boys, 'stealing is a crime.'

'In a good cause.' Angela began to run, seeing Mrs Johnson bring her car to a halt at the corner. 'Besides,' she added, 'we can't get at it, it's down the mousehole.'

'What's down the mousehole?' said Mrs Johnson as we climbed into her car.

'Only an old marble.'

'They always find their way to mouseholes. It's most peculiar. I think they play.' Mrs Johnson drove rather recklessly along the road. 'I must leave a message at the pub,' she said.

'Who for?' said Angela.

'Tom Foley. We want to pay him what we owe him for the lambing. We never know where to find him except the pub.' Mrs Johnson stopped at the pub and Andrew went into the ironmongers'.

'What's he doing?' asked Angela.

'Buying a can.' James had a harassed look. 'We shall be late. A can for petrol.'

Andrew came out and got in beside his mother. 'Did you leave a message?' He carried a jerry can.

'Yes. They say they will tell him when they see him.'

Mrs Johnson drove off. I watched our local milk lorry hurtling towards us. We passed it with a narrow margin and Mrs Johnson looked pleased, though the lorry driver didn't.

James and I did rather well at school that day. We had a system of helping each other. He did the maths and science and I did the history, geography and anything else I knew about. He was very good at copying my handwriting. Andrew and Angela did the same thing in their form.

Driving home the two boys sat in the back and whispered with Angela. I didn't like this as I like to know what's going on. Outside our front door two rods were propped.

'The Cardigans!' Angela loathed visitors.

'I'd forgotten.' I looked at the beautiful fibre-glass rods and smart bags and creels.

'Ah, here you are,' said my mother. We shook hands.

'Found your money yet?' Angela was a born criminal.

'No, we haven't.' The elder Mr Cardigan spoke from a nice Queen Anne chair which Vice likes scratching.

'We have done the same thing before.'

'The same what?' My mother's hand was trembling with the weight of the teapot as she began pouring tea.

'We are old bachelors,' said the younger Mr Cardigan. 'We have lived together for so many years that very often either both of us do a thing or neither of us does it.'

'What's that to do with losing forty pounds?' Angela passed a plate of buns to the older Mr Cardigan.

'I can see you are a lawyer's daughter.' The older Mr Cardigan politely refused a bun. 'You see, we both think we cashed cheques.'

Our mother raised her eyebrows.

'If you are not careful you will both be paying our father and Mr Johnson for the fishing twice.' Angela took two buns and, forgetting to pass them to me, ate ferociously.

'Oh, your father and Mr Johnson would tell us. Anyone in this delightful place would.' The younger Mr Cardigan smiled winningly at Angela, who could not smile back because her mouth was full, and we did know that a mouth full of half-chewed bun isn't attractive.

'Cash down,' I murmured. The younger Mr Cardigan looked at me and quickly looked away.

'Well, we must be going,' said the fatter Mr Cardigan and they got up and thanked our mother very politely and collected their fishing tackle and went off down the stream, speaking quietly about the evening rise.

We helped our mother clear up tea.

Angela said: 'They pay in cash.'

'What do you mean?' I said.

'Evasion of income tax, stupid. They pay cash for everything.'

'Oh,' I said, 'How did you guess?'

'They don't want enquiries made and the police with their great boots and notebooks tramping round. They paid Mr Johnson in cash.

'Did they?'

'Andrew told me.'

'What about father?'

'They will give him a cheque because he is a lawyer.'

'I think you girls have very nasty minds,' said my mother.

'Well, they have paid the hotel cash in advance.'

'How do you know these things?' Our mother looked genuinely astonished.

'The hotel told me,' said Angela patiently. 'They were awfully pleased.'

Our mother hung the tea towel on the hook and left the room.

'Did they tell you when you sold them the sea-trout?' I asked.

'Yes. Nobody is really honest.'

'Hm,' I said and went up to my room where Vice was sitting watching the mousehole.

'Don't do that, Vice.'

'I must,' said Vice.

'Why?'

'If I go away they are quite capable of chewing up the money and making nests of it.'

'I feel terrible being party to a robbery,' I said.

'Rubbish,' said Vice.

'Don't be a hypocrite,' said Mr Bull.

I went and looked out of the window. I could see Blueprint and Angela walking down the fisherman's path. I stood watching the light slanting through the trees and listening to the birds and the monotonous screech, wind-in, screech, as the two Cardigans fished slowly down the river. Presently Angela and Andrew came out of the wood together, laughing. Andrew was carrying an open envelope in one hand.

'Now we need the cash,' he said as they came in.

'Come away from the hole, Vice.' Angela picked Vice up tenderly in her arms. 'Tell the mouse to shove up the money,' she said cajolingly. Vice purred and put up a soft paw to her face.

'Hurry up,' said Mr Bull.

There was a rustling sound and a five pound note came out of the hole.

'We need much more than that,' said Andrew.

We all watched as note after note appeared through the hole. Andrew counted them, put them into the envelope and licked it up.

'Oh,' I said. 'Petrol galore!'

'There is another one pound ten in the hole,' said Mr Bull.

'Shove it up,' said Vice in a nasty voice.

'Bedding,' a mouse said, just out of reach in the wainscot.

'Give them some paper,' said Mr Bull.

'But the thread would so amuse the children.'

'Shove it up,' said Vice again.

The last pound and ten shilling note came through the hole and I put two rolled sheets of writing paper down in exchange.

'Call a swallow,' said Andrew to Mr Bull.

Mr Bull piped several times and a swallow swooped near the sill and snatched the two notes from between Andrew's fingers.

'Why the swallows?' said Angela.

'Taking them to Floss.' Andrew tickled Blueprint under the chin so that he closed his eyes in ecstacy. 'Now Floss and Tom can go to the pub tonight and fill up the car.'

'Drinking is so vulgar,' said Vice.

'Some people call it an art,' Mr Bull piped.

'I think I shall go out for a while.' Vice slid through the door and was gone. We watched him slip into the wood and saw our mother make a dash to catch him. She came back alone, looking rather flushed.

'Do you think?' I said.

'Yes,' said Andrew.

'Do something, Mr Bull.'

Mr Bull piped a few times and the sound of the birds' songs changed into high scolding notes as warnings were carried down through the wood.

'Vice!' said Angela.

'Don't be silly.' Mr Bull was crunching seeds. 'You children are party to theft. Only I am innocent.'

Angela twanged a bar of his cage twice.

9

We went down to the Johnsons' farm to pick up James. We met Vice wandering up the path, his eyes wide and innocent and his tail in the air. He passed us, but we were used to rudeness from cats.

'Your father will be struck off the Rolls,' Vice leered over his shoulder.

'He drives a Ford,' James said.

'*Legal* Rolls.' Angela was aghast. 'We must give it back. All that lovely lolly – Blueprint, we must get the money back and post it to the Hotel.' Angela was almost crying.

'I'll do it tonight.' Blueprint spoke comfortingly and Angela sighed with relief.

At the Johnsons' bridge we sat astride the parapet and watched the two Mr Cardigans.

'One of them slipped and filled his waders,' said James.

'Too bad,' said Andrew. 'We are going over the hill to the Broughtons' land.'

'Why?'

'To look at the game larder.'

'It's beastly,' said James, and added, 'Joker is busy with father.'

We looked away up the hillside and saw a flock of sheep moving reluctantly towards an open gate and Joker running silently to and fro behind them, his head and tail down and ears attentive to Mr Johnson's whistle.

'I shall escort you,' said Blueprint, who feels rather bad sometimes about having no exact profession.

We walked quickly up the hill. It was beautiful land, but ruined for us because the Broughtons let it all for shooting and the syndicate who rented the shoot employed two gamekeepers. At the top of the hill we lay down in a row and watched.

'Feeding time,' I said.

One of the gamekeepers came out of his cottage carrying a bucket. Behind him trotted a labrador.

'I must get at him,' grumbled Blueprint. 'Or Floss would do it better.'

We watched the keeper walk slowly to the edge of the corn and call 'Cluck, cluck, cluck.' Out of the corn came a stream of pheasants, high-stepping cocks and elegant hens. The keeper scattered corn liberally and the pheasants pecked and ate. The keeper watched them eat and seemed to be counting them. Leaving the edge of the wood, he walked along the cornfield scattering grain, glancing behind him to see the partridges sneak out of the corn and start eating. We trotted quickly downhill to the back of the cottage.

'I shall go and tell that dog we are visiting.' Blueprint scampered away from us.

Behind the cottage we came to two long wire lines tied between trees. In different stages of decay there hung from these wires the corpses of stoats, weasels, squirrels, carrion crows, jays and magpies. The smell was horrible.

Blueprint rejoined us and said: 'He takes an hour over his tea and then goes round the traps.'

A tiny voice remarked: 'That's my mate, third from the left.' Third from the left a slip of fur hung greasy with rot. A weasel showed itself for a moment.

'Move over to the big wood,' said James.

'But there is such good eating here,' answered the weasel.

'We want to help you,' I said.

'So I hear.' The weasel disappeared.

'It's hardly likely to trust us, is it?' said Angela. 'Come on.' She led the way at a run.

'You help, Blueprint,' said James, and Blueprint dashed ahead.

'He can find the traps,' I said.

'They are illegal,' said Angela.

'You are a fine one to talk.'

Ahead of us we heard a muffled yelp and we ran towards it. We found Blueprint standing waiting for us with an expression of shame on his face, his paw firmly held in a gin trap.

'You clot!' said Andrew, releasing him.

'Are you hurt?' I asked.

'Not much.' Blueprint licked the paw while Angela examined it.

'Come on, there must be a whole line of them.' James trotted ahead and we heard him give an exclamation of pleasure as he sprang a trap. Walking cautiously, with Blueprint limping behind us, we found a long line of traps and sprang them by poking a stick at them. In the last we found a dead rabbit and left it.

'As foolish as you, Blueprint.' Andrew looked at the rabbit.

'Don't go on about it.' Blueprint looked hurt.

'Where are the bird traps?' I asked.

'At the very edge of the wood where the pheasants are fed.'

We turned back. The bird traps were also in a long line and each held its complement of grain-eating birds. We let them out.

'Watch out.' Blueprint crouched down and we all lay on our stomachs in the fern and listened. Through the wood we could hear footsteps and voices.

'Not a thing in the big traps,' said a voice. 'Just one rabbit.'

'Don't get much these days,' another voice answered. 'Myxomatosis has done for most of them. This one's empty. Funny. And all the seed has gone.'

'Gone from this one too. Can't make it out.'

'They seem all right.'

The labrador came and muttered something to Blueprint and then ran off.

'He says we should go now before they see us,' said Blueprint importantly.

'I'm thinking of writing a dictionary of oaths.' Andrew was listening to the gamekeepers with a beatific expression. 'I took the petrol to Tom. The car's ready.' A pair of foxes trotted together towards the Broughton shoot.

'Traps,' called James.

The foxes leered and trotted on. 'Don't worry us,' one said.

We came home through the village. The pub door was open and we heard voices rumbling and occasional laughter. Tom Foley, with Mr Johnson's hat on the back of his head, was standing with his back to us. At his feet sat Floss. We saw the landlord pass a saucer to Tom, who filled it and laid it down in front of Floss. Floss drank, lapping slowly. I had the impression that she could see us, but when the saucer was empty she deliberately turned her back, leapt on to the stool beside Tom and leant her chin on the bar. We said goodnight to the boys. Vice met us in the hall. 'You might at least have brought me the rabbit,' he said.

'How do you know so soon?' whispered Angela.

'Owls and otters pass the news.'

'Have you heard too, Mr Bull?' I combed my hair, which was full of bits of bracken, before going down to supper.

'Naturally.'

'We must warn all those pheasants and partridges that they are going to be shot,' I said.

'They are rather annoyed about you letting all the trapped birds go.'

'What?' I said.

'Well, they eat their corn.'

❧ 10 ❧

From my sleep I was wakened by a persistent tickling at my nose. I sneezed. A tiny voice squeaked: 'Don't do that.' The mouse came back near my face. 'You awake?' it said.

'Yes.'

'We've made a nice nest. The wife is very pleased.'

'You didn't wake her up to tell her that.' Mr Bull spoke rather nastily from under the cover of his cage.

'Well, in the summer we go down to the garden at night with the children and meet our cousins. It's a bit of a risk because of the owls, but we keep in the shelter of the plants.' The mouse clutched the sheet near my face, thinking of the owls.

'Go on. Get to the point.'

'Well, tonight the otters told us cubbing starts next week. The pigs told them.'

'What pigs?'

'Mr Johnson's pigs.'

I thought of the Johnsons' pigs – huge elephantine sows who each lived in a little wooden hut with a corrugated iron roof in a field.

'Why should the pigs mind?' I was now fully awake.

'Five of them are due to farrow next week. Hounds disturb them.' The mouse scrambled off my bed and scratched its way down the bedclothes.

'Time you did something sharpish,' said Mr Bull. I got up and went into Angela's room. Blueprint, lying on the greater part of the bed with his head on the pillow, thumped his tail. Vice, curled in a ball at Angela's feet, opened his green eyes.

'Aahh,' Angela groaned. 'What do you want?' She was lying straight on the very edge of the bed so that Vice and Blueprint should be comfortable.

'Wake up. The mouse says the pigs know that cubbing is starting next week.'

'The pigs?'

'That's what he said.'

'Action!' exclaimed Angela.

'When?' said Blueprint.

'At once,' said Angela. 'We will let you out now and you can go and tell Floss and Joker. Vice, you must go too.'

'Oh, not now.' Vice curled himself into a tighter ball and shut his eyes.

'Yes, now.'

Vice gave Angela a very nasty look and shut his eyes again.

'Go on, Vice,' I said in a wheedling tone.

Vice got up and arched his back, clawed at the bedclothes several times, and yawned.

'Let us out.' Blueprint trotted to the door. We opened the front door and they went out into the night.

'Mr Bull,' said Angela.

'Oh, not *again*.' Mr Bull woke up crossly.

'Mr Bull, will you warn all the birds as soon as it's light?'

'All right, but let me sleep now.'

'Tomorrow we must all go and see Tom Foley.' Angela went back to bed.

The mouse was wandering about my bedroom floor. 'Got any cotton wool?' he said. 'It makes a good lining for the nest.' I rummaged in my dressing-table drawer and found a bit which had been in the top of a Disprin bottle. The mouse pulled it into his hole. I went back to sleep, and at first light Mr Bull began to pipe loudly and the birds in the garden answered in a loud chorus.

When after breakfast we went down to the Johnsons' farm, we saw James crawling backwards out of one of the sows' little huts. He was laughing.

'Don't disturb those sows, you fool!' shouted Mr Johnson. One of the sows came grunting up to him. 'Peace and quiet is what you want.' Mr Johnson scraped a stick along the sow's side so that she closed her tiny eyes with pleasure and twisted her body with joy.

'They won't get any peace and quiet next week,' said Angela. 'Cubbing is starting on Saturday.'

'Not on my land it isn't.' The boys' father stopped scratching the sow. 'Five of these beauties are having families at any minute. I'm not having a lot of hounds and idiot fools riding over my land disturbing my pigs.'

'Tell the hunt then,' said Andrew.

'I might,' said Mr Johnson. 'Anyone seen Joker? I need him for the sheep.'

'No,' we said, and all four of us walked away into the woods.

We met Joker trotting towards us. 'Fixed the car?' he enquired.

'Yes.'

'Must go back, alas, to work.' Joker passed us and ran fast back to the farm.

'Joker is conscientious,' said Andrew.

We walked to the clearing and here, as before, lay Tom Foley and Floss. 'Don't disturb,' said Floss, baring her teeth. 'Bad enough having Joker and Blueprint.'

'What's the news, Blueprint?' Andrew pulled a bag of sweets from his pocket and handed them round.

'Can't wake Tom.' Blueprint crunched the sweet and looked as though he could do with another.

'I'm awake.' Tom spoke with his eyes shut.

'Tom, the hounds are starting cubbing next Saturday.'

'Well?'

'We must warn all the foxes.'

'Warning doesn't do much good.' Tom Foley still kept his eyes shut. 'Need somebody with a gift for organization.' He seemed to drift off to sleep again, and Floss coolly closed her eyes and put her nose under her tail. James trotted across the clearing and looked under a bush, and then stretched his arm into the lower branches. Tom Foley sat up.

'What's going on?'

'I was going to give you some Alka-Selzer.'

'Good idea.' Tom Foley caressed Floss, who snuggled up to him. James filled a mug with water and added two Alka-Selzer tablets and handed it to Tom, who drank, making a face, and then burped.

'Now what's all this about?' Tom Foley looked at us down his long nose.'

'We need you and your car and a lot of advice.'

'Badgers.' Tom was sitting up.

'Oh, we are listening,' a badger remarked from a set.

'What do you advise?' Blueprint spoke respectfully.

'The foxes must be told to come here and Tom can bring the smallest in his car. We don't mind lodging them for the day.' The badger came out into the open and blinked in the bright light.

'How do I collect them?' Tom seemed quite agreeable to the arrangement.

'I shall go with you and tell you where to stop.' The vixen we had met before spoke from a clump of bracken.

'That's all very well, but we don't want the hounds all over this wood all day. They will be a damn nuisance.' Tom Foley lay back again.

Floss raised herself and began talking into Tom's ear. He listened and then let out a shout of laughter.

'What did she say?' Blueprint gazed longingly at Floss.

'Floss will take care of the hounds while we take care of the foxes.'

'All those huge hounds?' Blueprint looked both jealous and shocked.

'Just that.' Tom was still laughing. 'Anyone knows any horses?' he added.

'I do,' said Angela unexpectedly. 'I belong to the Pony Club.'

'Good Lord, so you do!' said Andrew.

'You'd better join in the hunt then,' said Floss nastily.

'What do you ride?' asked the vixen.

'Old Bodkin's horse.'

'Oh, I know *him*.' There was a wealth of relief and meaning in the vixen's voice.

'Then that's settled.' Tom Foley lay back, covered his face with his hat and breathed deeply. The vixen had come very close to James. 'I don't mind you,' she said craftily.

'The pigs have volunteered,' said James slyly. 'One of those sows is a Holy Terror.'

'Even with my father,' said Andrew.

'Old Bodkin's horse and Floss will see to it that the hunting people enjoy themselves.' Tom Foley spoke sleepily.

'I wonder how.' Angela looked uneasy. Floss opened her eyes and gave her a long appraising look.

'There may be some unexpected allies.' The badger turned and went back into the depths of the ground. On my way home I leant into the otters' holt and told them the news. I did not see them but I heard laughter.

11

'I say, Mr Bodkin.' Angela and I leant on the gate beside Mr Bodkin. 'Will you lend me your horse next Saturday?'

Mr Bodkin, who was a long thin man with a sad face, stroked the horse's head between its eyes as the horse nibbled with blue-gray lips at his coat.

'No,' said Mr Bodkin. 'I'm riding him myself. You can ride that thing.' He pointed towards a thin, racy animal standing twenty yards away, her ears pricked and a look of nervous horror on her face.

'When did you get her?' Angela looked away from Mr Bodkin's tranquil horse to the bundle of nerves staring at us.

'Bought that cheap. She's unrideable. Uncatchable too. Catch her and you can ride her.'

'What on earth made you buy her?' I asked.

'She's pretty. Well bred too. Make a lovely child's pony.' Mr Bodkin spoke in jerks.

'But uncatchable,' said Angela.

'Yes, I was had, I was.'

'I suppose she bucks, kicks, rears, runs away with you and bites.'

'She'll get you off under a branch or against a gatepost,' admitted Mr Bodkin. 'You school her for me and I'll lend her to you for the Shows and the hunting.'

'Thanks,' said Angela ungratefully.

Mr Bodkin wandered away. The quiet horse nuzzled us over the gate while the nervous new mare snorted and blew down her nose. Angela climbed over the gate and the new horse broke into a wild ungainly gallop up the field, throwing out her legs and tossing her head. Blueprint, the old horse and I waited.

'I hear there's goings-on,' said the quiet horse. 'I like hunting myself.'

'It's unfair.' Blueprint sat beside me watching Angela who, reaching the middle of the field, sat down. We could see she was talking, the new horse stood twenty yards away from her with its back turned and ears laid back. After what seemed a long time the horse turned round and, walking slowly and edgily, tiptoed up to Angela and began nibbling her hair. Angela did not move but went on talking. Presently she stood up and she and the horse seemed to confront each other. Suddenly the horse gave a loud whinnying laugh.

'You see,' we heard Angela say as she walked back with the horse to the gate, 'I won't frighten you if you don't frighten me.'

'I shall just pretend then,' said the horse.

'Make a good show,' said the quiet horse.

'I'll make a show all right,' said the nervous horse.

'Don't overdo it. I hate falling off,' said Angela.

We heard both horses whinnying as we walked home.

'Made an arrangement?' asked Blueprint.

'Yes,' said Angela. 'There are no flies on that horse.'

'Circus act?' enquired Blueprint, who had seen many circuses on television.

'Yes.' Angela looked thoughtful.

We went into our house and saw our mother putting the telephone back in its cradle. 'Awkward for your father,' she said.

'What is?'

'The Broughton syndicate don't want the hounds going over their land. Your father acts for them.'

'The keepers shoot foxes,' I said.

'It's very awkward,' repeated my mother. 'Are you going out on Saturday, Angela?'

'Yes,' said Angela with a boot face.

'Pity you don't ride,' said my mother to me. 'You get to know such nice people.'

'Such as?' I asked rather rudely.

'Oh, all the hunting people and the Pony Club and, well, everybody.'

'All your friends?' asked Angela.

'Well, not exactly, but you know what I mean, darling.'

'Come to the Meet then on Saturday.'

'I might. But they disturb the birds,' my mother said weakly.

'What about the foxes?'

'They disturb the birds too. But the hunting people are – '

'Crashing bores,' I said.

'I'm a hunting person,' said Angela, twisting a short piece of my hair near my neck. I hit her.

'Now, girls,' said my mother.

'Little birds in their nests should agree.' Mr Johnson came into the house without knocking, with bits of mud slipping off his gumboots on to our clean hall floor. Joker came behind him and Blueprint let out a ferocious bark and hurled himself at him. In the narrow confines of the hall the dogs made a fearful noise, snapping, snarling and bashing to and fro. Mr Johnson shouted and we separated them.

'They never hurt each other,' said Mr Johnson.

'No, they don't,' said my mother. 'What can I do for you?'

'It's my pigs, really. Do you think we can ask the hunt to keep off my land until they have farrowed?'

'No.' My mother was looking crossly at the mud now well ground into the hall carpet by the dog fight. 'No, there is nothing we can do. Besides, your Betty is more than a match for any pack of hounds.'

'Yes. I'll station her near the pigs next week, then it won't look like me. I'm selling to the Master. I don't want to offend him. He is buying my hay.'

'Moral coward.' Our mother laughed and Angela grinned.

I felt something was going on which I didn't understand. Angela for a moment had looked like Floss.

I went up to see Mr Bull. 'Do you want to go out?' I asked.

'No, I don't trust Vice.'

'In this world everyone is afraid of someone,' said Vice.

'I suppose so.'

'I hear on the grapevine that Angela is going hunting.'

'Very brave of her,' I said loyally.

'Hope she enjoys it.' Vice began staring at Mr Bull.

'Stop it, Vice.'

Angela rode Mr Bodkin's new mare slowly and sedately round Mr Bodkin's field. She got off when she saw me. 'Everything is going to be all right on Saturday.' She took off the saddle and bridle and said to the horse: 'Show Kate what you can do.' The horse lashed out with both hind feet and kicked the gate with a clang. Then she reared up on end and, dropping on all four feet, did a series of ghastly twisting bucks. Then she dashed under a low branch of a tree and came back to us with her ears back, her eyes rolling and teeth bared.

'Very funny,' said the old horse sarcastically.

'Only a child murderer would buy you,' I said to the horse.

The horse looked smugly from under long lashes.

'Come on,' said Angela. 'There isn't really much time.' We went back to Mr Bull. On the way Tom Foley passed us in his old Morris, wearing Mr Johnson's hat. He waved but Floss, sitting beside him, didn't even glance at us.

On the following Saturday my mother drove me to the Meet. She was looking anxious because Angela had gone off earlier on Mr Bodkin's new horse, and my mother had seen them going past the house sideways at an uncomfortable jog. At the Meet Angela was carried round in a dancing circle by the new horse.

'Brave girl, that,' said a fat man to my mother. 'Aren't you afraid she'll get run away with?'

'Oh, Angela's a good rider,' said my mother.

'I always put my children on quiet ponies,' said the fat man. 'Don't lose their nerve that way.' He moved off and my mother looked snubbed.

I looked round me. Quite a number of people were getting quiet horses out of horse-boxes. A lot of children wearing elegant velvet riding caps were sitting loosely and confidently on their ponies, all ready to move off. The grown-up people, wearing ratcatcher clothes, were chatting to each other. Andrew and James, wearing dirty jeans and rather torn jerseys, came up to us.

'Can Kate follow on foot with us and Blueprint?'

'Yes, of course,' said my mother. 'Where is your mother?'

'She's at home. Father thinks if the hounds come near the pigs she can fend them off better than he can.'

'Where are you going to draw first, Master?' a woman asked in a high confident voice.

'Longmans Wood. There are always cubs there and it's not too big.'

I moved aside with the Johnson boys and Blueprint.

'Nobody's talking to my mother,' I said.

'Just our friendly country manner,' said Andrew. 'Look, the Cardigans are talking to her.'

'They are strangers.'

'The others are all right, just a bit uncouth.' Andrew looked at the array of glossy Jaguars, Landrovers and Minis. 'Hunting people,' he added.

'Look at Angela,' said James.

The new horse was sweeping an apparently helpless Angela through the crowd, its ears back and head down. As she passed a very beautiful car she shied and kicked. There were exclamations of – 'Mind out!' – Need a hand?' – 'Steady on, whoa!' as the crowd scattered.

'Do my eyes deceive me?' Andrew looked up the road.

'They do not.' James's face was expressionless.

Down the road came Tom Foley driving his ancient Morris. Beside him sat Floss, looking unconcerned. Tom stopped and several voices called out – 'Hullo, Foley'.

Tom sat easily at the wheel, looking at the traditional scene.

'Morning, Foley,' shouted the Master.

Tom got out of his car. 'And how are you today?' he shouted at my mother, taking off Mr Johnson's hat to her. 'Hullo, Vicar.'

'Good morning,' said the vicar, rather surprised.

'Only Angela riding?' Tom Foley approached my mother, absolutely ignoring everyone else.

'Yes,' said my mother, looking up at him.

'I had a suit like that once,' said the vicar.

'Oh, this old thing.' Tom Foley looked down his long length. 'Like me to give the children a lift?' he asked my mother. 'Don't suppose you want to follow this lot.' His voice was louder, clearer, more confident than I had ever heard it – insolent.

'Not much,' said my mother honestly.

'Call your nosey hounds off my car,' said Tom genially to the Whip, pointing to where the hounds were milling round his ancient car and sniffing at Floss, who sat in the front seat snarling down at them.

'Sorry, sir. Here, Bashful, Dauntless, Terrible.' The Whip rode towards the Morris cracking his whip. The hounds moved away regretfully. If animals could smile I would have sworn that was just what the hounds were doing as they gathered obediently round the Whip. I sensed that what Floss had snarled at them was no ordinary snarl of a small bitch surrounded by large hounds. She looked smug.

'Weren't you in the same house as me?' A man in corduroy trousers and a tweed coat with leather patches at the elbows came up to Tom.

'Don't recollect it.' Tom spoke rudely and said to my mother: 'Angela's got quite a ride, I see.'

'We were in Wickhams,' said the man, but Tom was looking away.

'I daresay.' Tom sounded so off hand I blushed. 'Hounds moving off. Come on, you lot.' Tom took off the hat to my mother and led us to the Morris. We all climbed in. I held Blueprint in my arms. Tom started the engine and edged through the crowd. He drove rapidly round the corner of the road to the edge of the wood. 'They'll put the hounds in there,' Tom said to Floss. 'Bustle, old girl.' Floss nipped out of the car and raced to the edge of the wood.

'Now,' said Tom, and drove us furiously down the road to the great wood. 'You may be amused to watch the hunt,' he said to Andrew and James. 'I don't think you will find it unrewarding.' He went round to the back of the car and lifted the seat. Out streamed an incredible number of fox cubs.

'Now you behave and follow Blueprint. No skylarking.'
Blueprint raced up the hill through the bracken, followed by
a long line of fox cubs.

'Where are the old ones?' Andrew looked puzzled.

'They came ahead on foot.'

'I see.' Andrew and James left me alone with Tom Foley.
We walked without speaking to the badger sets, where we
found Blueprint sitting alone.

'Everything all right?'

'Yes,' said a fox voice.

Tom whistled and pigeons flew down from the trees.

'Just fly on patrol and keep me posted,' said Tom. 'And
now,' he said to me, 'we can watch ourselves.'

'But where are the foxes?'

'All around us. You won't see them.'

We walked quickly down to the road and sat down on a
bank to watch the hunt approach. First came the hounds,
trotting ahead of the huntsman and the Whip. They were
followed by Mr Bodkin on his nice quiet horse, a large
collection of children on admirable ponies, and all the
people who usually hunt, riding fine horses and looking at
each other rudely as hunting people do.

'Why do they all look so rude?' asked James.

'Nerves,' said Tom Foley, watching the cavalcade.

'Where is Floss?' I said.

'In the spinney now.' Tom grinned wolfishly. Blueprint
hurried up to us.

'What's up, Blueprint?'

'The cubs are there and some of their mothers, but most
of the grown foxes are not.'

'I told them to go ahead,' said Tom. 'They will be about
somewhere.' He didn't seem worried.

'When they've drawn the spinney where do they go next?'
I muttered.

'Across the Johnson land, I hope,' said Tom.

'Father will be livid. He's been up all night with
Gertrude.'

'The prize sow?' Tom looked amused.

'Yes. She farrowed.'

'Just look at Angela.' James admired Angela.

We watched Angela on the new mare bringing up the rear of the hunt. The mare was giving an excellent imitation of a rocking horse.

'She looks hot,' said James.

'Got a good grip on that animal's mane.' Tom grinned again. 'Listen.' We listened to the sound of the horn as the huntsman urged the hounds into the spinney. 'If we climb a bit higher we can get a better view.' Tom began loping up the hill and we followed. The huntsman blew his horn again. 'Now,' said Tom.

Almost immediately pandemonium broke loose in the spinney. Hounds bayed, people cantering alongside shouted, Angela went by far too fast, and a child we did not like much fell off his pony. The pony wheeled round and clattered off home with the loose stirrups swinging and his reins dangling. The child began to cry and a forceful woman jumped out of a Landrover to comfort him.

At the top of the hill Tom sat down and the boys and I sat beside him in a row with Blueprint.

'We can see home from here.' James pointed to the Johnsons' farm. 'There's mother leaning over the gate of the pig field.'

'That's our mother with her,' I said.

Below us in the spinney the hounds were giving tongue. A pigeon dropped at Tom's feet and said: 'Floss is in position.'

'Any minute now then.' Tom was smiling.

The hounds broke into full cry. They seemed to sweep round the spinney in a circle and then stream out of it across the fields towards the Johnsons'. Tom stood up and let out a blood curdling yell of 'Gone awaaay!' pointing towards the Johnsons' farm with his long arm. Below us the field gathered up their reins and clattered down the road. The Master was cantering ahead. We could see from where we sat that the hounds, although they had their noses to the ground, were chasing nothing. Floss ran a little way with them, then ran across the road and up the hill towards us. She arrived panting and wagging her bushy tail.

'Where did you send them Floss?' James looked respectfully at the little dog.

'They are calling on Gertrude first,' she said.

'Overdoing it a bit, aren't you, old girl?' Tom stroked Floss.

'Couldn't resist,' Floss panted.

We watched the hounds in full cry across the Johnsons' land.

'Father will be furious.' Andrew was standing up, hopping from one foot to another. We could see Mrs Johnson and our mother brace themselves by the gate of the pig field and Mr Johnson coming out of the farmyard with Joker.

'That ain't no cub, they must be on to a fox,' the huntsman was shouting to the Master.

'Then stop them.' The Master was having trouble holding his horse, and we saw Angela streak past him on the new mare, shouting: 'So sorry, so sorry, she's running away with me.'

In the corn stubble we heard derisory jeers, and when I looked round I saw eight or nine dog foxes crouching behind us. The whole field galloped past.

'Make them sweat. So bad for them when they aren't fit.' Blueprint is essentially kind and fair.

'Watch now.' Tom peered from under the brim of his hat. The hounds seemed to drown Mrs Johnson and our mother in a wave of white and tan and then charged up towards Gertrude's hut.

'Ah,' said Tom.

Furious and ponderous, Gertrude barred the entrance. The hounds milled round her. We could not hear Gertrude, but as suddenly as they had surrounded her the hounds reformed and streamed away.

Mr Johnson was yelling what I believe is known as 'a stream of epithets' at the Master and huntsman. Our mothers held fast to the gate and Joker ran behind the hounds, snapping.

'Father *is* in good form,' said Andrew.

'Yes.' James's eyes were shining. 'Ooh! Look at Angela!'

Angela was circling round the field. The new mare had her head down and was bucking with a twisting motion which brought her each time nearer to where the Master was apologising to Mr Johnson. As she finished her circle she kicked the Master's horse, making it rear up and nearly unseat the Master. The hounds were out of sight. We watched the field disappear after them and our mother and the Johnsons go into the farmhouse.

'Better not disturb her any more,' we heard the boys' father say, his voice hoarse with anger. Angela was lost to sight.

'Can't see anyone buying that animal in a hurry.' Tom got up slowly. We followed him into the wood, led by Floss. Apart from the jays and magpies making remarks on the edge of the wood, all was silence compared with the haunting voices of the hounds fading away down the valley.

Floss and Tom stopped at the badgers' sets. 'Everybody all right?' Tom enquired in a conversational voice.

A vixen came from behind a tree and fawned like a dog, grinning silently, her little sharp teeth bared, her ears laid back and her brush trailing low, and a whole multitude of cubs appeared from the bracken and out of the badger sets. A badger followed the last batch, remarking amiably: 'You smell.'

'Where are all the dog foxes?' I watched the cubs begin a game, flitting in and out among the trees, watched by bright-eyed vixens.

'Some were in the corn stubble.'

'We are here now.' A dignified fox trotted out from the trees.

'Enjoy yourselves?' enquired Floss.

'Very much.' The fox leered.

'Floss,' I said, 'what were you up to in that spinney?'

'Just warming them up.' Floss licked her chest and then, after scratching one ear hard, lay down.

'Next time they can manage alone, I daresay,' said Blueprint.

'I wonder where the other dog foxes are. There should be at least four more.' Blueprint looked at each in turn and tucked his tail out of the way of a cub who was creeping up on him to tweak it.

'Ah, here you all are.' Joker appeared suddenly in the clearing, followed by four dog foxes.

'Where were you all?' Blueprint asked.

One of the dog foxes began yelping with laughter and then rolled playfully on his back. 'With Gertrude,' he said.

'Gertrude farrowed last night.' Andrew sounded anxious. 'You didn't eat — ?'

'Oh, no, no,' said another fox. 'We got delayed so we popped in with Gertrude for a bit.'

'I wonder what my father would say.' Andrew looked suspiciously at the foxes.

'He won't know, will he?'

'I thought you smelt rather nasty,' a vixen snapped at one of Gertrude's visitors jealously.

'One wonders what has become of Angela,' murmured Tom.

'Yes.' James looked anxious. 'Can't you call a pigeon, Tom?'

From under his hat Tom whistled and a pigeon cooed above our heads.

'Won't come down because of the foxes.' Tom smiled.

'Quite safe for you all to go home.' A badger showed its striped nose from a hole. 'We like a bit of peace and quiet.'

Floss nestled against Tom. We stood up, feeling unwanted.

'You will all know your way another time,' said the badger courteously. 'Very welcome, of course.'

'The hounds know what to do in future.' Floss spoke complacently. 'Very handsome they are.'

We watched as the foxes gathered their families and moved off.

'Hounds get lost in this wood, it's so big.' Andrew looked down at Tom. 'Come on,' he said, and we followed Blueprint and Joker down the hill.

'Back to work.' Joker looked over his shoulder at

Blueprint, who looked embarrassed. 'I bet those hounds have fun.' Joker broke into a gallop in answer to a distant whistle.

'I should think everyone has had fun,' said James.

We accompanied the boys to their house and went into the kitchen, where our mother was helping Mrs Johnson.

'Hullo,' said my mother. 'Anyone seen Angela?'

'Don't worry,' said Mrs Johnson.

Mr Johnson came in and took off his gumboots. 'Gertrude *seems* all right,' he said.

'I'm sure she is.' My mother spoke soothingly.

'Nothing sure about it. That's a remarkable sow. She barred the entrance of her hut. Noble creature.'

'She's pretty savage,' said Mrs Johnson.

'So would you be savage if you had just had fourteen children, and a yelling pack of hounds tried to burst into the maternity ward.'

'It's an idea,' said my mother.

'I shall ring up the Master when he gets home,' Mr Johnson mused.

'Do,' said my mother. 'My husband has got to too. He's got to warn the hunt off the Broughton shoot.'

'Ha, ha!' said Joker from under the table.

'The Master's going to have a happy evening,' said Mrs Johnson.

'Well, Gertrude is a valuable animal.'

'From what I know of Gertrude she is quite able to look after herself,' said Mrs Johnson placidly.

I left the Johnsons' with my mother and we rejoined Blueprint, who had been tactfully waiting by the gate.

'Those poor men are still fishing,' said my mother as we walked up the river.

'Any luck?' my mother enquired kindly.

'No, none.' The fatter Mr Cardigan looked up as we paused above him. 'Plenty of fish about. One can see them all the time. But it's enjoyable even if you catch nothing.' The fat Mr Cardigan climbed up the bank and stood beside us looking down at the sun-flecked water. 'We've both seen so many birds and I thought I saw a pair of foxes and an otter.'

'Surely not with the hunt raging down the valley. Come and have tea, Mr Cardigan.' From my mother's voice I knew she felt guilty that the Cardigans had caught no fish.

'Thank you. We should love to and then perhaps we shall have better luck with the evening rise.'

'Perhaps,' said Blueprint.

As we reached home we heard the clatter of horses coming down the road and saw the Master and Angela riding slowly towards us.

'Had a good day?' asked my mother, who was not in the least interested.

'Remarkable, remarkable,' said the Master. 'Hounds ran right down the valley. Must have got on the scent of a fox.' He pulled up his horse and let the reins lie loose on its neck.

'Come and have tea,' said my mother affably. I could see she was relieved to see Angela all in one piece.

'I'll take your horse,' I said.

The Master got off, handed me the reins, and I led the horse round to the stable yard.

'Want a drink?' I asked.

'No, eat,' said the horse. 'I drank at the ford.'

I got the horse some hay and put it in a loose box.

'Had one hell of a day,' said the horse as I loosened its girths. 'I could do with a beer.'

I went into the house and opened a bottle of beer and took it to the horse in a bucket.

'Put up quite a show, didn't we?' The horse souped up the beer. 'No need for that mare to kick me though.'

'She overacts,' I said. I went indoors, where I could hear voises raised.

'What's up?' I said to my mother, who was making tea.

'The Cardigans have told him hunting is ridiculous,' said my mother with a faint smile. 'Take this tray.' I carried in the tray.

'Forms the character,' the Master was saying.

'Not like fishing, you need patience for that,' the thin Mr Cardigan said, rather nastily I thought.

My mother came in carrying another tray.

'Very rude, that Johnson chap.' The Master stood in front of the fireplace with his legs apart.

'Pigs,' I said.

'Ah, yes.'

'He's going to complain to you,' I said and left the room.

Upstairs Blueprint and I sat on the window-ledge beside Mr Bull's cage. 'Everybody will know exactly what to do next time,' Mr Bull piped cheerfully.

The mouse came out of its hole. 'Nobody got killed.'

'I nearly did.' Angela came into the room. 'Old Bodkin is furious. He says the whole neighbourhood knows what that "new thing", as he calls her, is like now.'

Vice uncurled and stretched on my bed. He scratched the bedhead violently.

'I'm aching from head to foot.' Angela started to undress. 'But it was worth it.'

'You and Gertrude seem to be the heroines of the day,' said the mouse.

'Don't forget Floss,' said Blueprint.

'Oh, Floss.' Vice began licking himself all over. 'Floss is wily.'

'More wily than me?' Blueprint leant heavily against me.

'Much more,' said Vice between long scraping licks. 'All the animals except Floss and me and Mr Bull here had to be told what to do.'

'What did you do?' asked Blueprint innocently.

'I directed operations.' Vice stared offensively at Blueprint.

'Did you now?' said the mouse, and before Vice could pounce vanished down its hole.

'Is Angela all right?' Our mother came into the room.

'Yes, just going to have a bath.' I saw my mother was frowning in a worried way.

'How is the tea party?' Angela started off towards the bathroom.

'Awful,' said my mother. 'Snapping each other's heads off like pekinese. You would think to hear them talk that they were hunting each other, not foxes and fish.'

Angela lay in the bath covered with soap, and Blueprint leant over the edge licking whatever bits of her he could reach.

'We should go and help mother,' I said.

'Why?'

'She's stuck between hunting and fishing.' Blueprint licked Angela's arm.

'All right.' Angela got out of the bath and dressed, combing her hair demurely behind her ears.

We went downstairs where Vice was sitting in the afternoon sun by the open front door. He was watching the birds whirling and circling in swoops which ended each time by my bedroom window. We paused a moment before joining the tea party to listen to the birds and Mr Bull's piping.

'They are having a good laugh.' Vice joined us and we went into the sitting-room where there was an awkward grown-up silence reigning.

'Had a good day?' The Cardigans greeted Angela.

'Yes, thank you.' Angela shot an angelic smile at the Master. Vice stalked across the room to where the two Mr Cardigans sat and began weaving in and out of their legs in an intricate pattern, bending his body sideways to press it against their shins and purring.

'Fond of cats?' I asked.

'Well, as a matter of fact they make us both sneeze, so we don't know much about them.'

'He means he hates cats,' said Blueprint, wagging his tail in a hospitable sort of way at the Master of Hounds, who instantly gave him a biscuit.

'Shall I remove him?' said my mother.

'Oh no, please. We both take antihistamine so it doesn't matter,' said the elder Mr Cardigan. 'One can't deny oneself all the joys of life just because they make you sneeze.'

'Do you hear that, Vice? You are one of the joys of life.' My mother laughed.

'Horses and dogs make us sneeze too.' The thin Mr Cardigan passed his cup politely to my mother.

'No need for you to go near horses if you are against hunting.' The Master used rather a hearty voice to be rude. 'Now, Angela is a born rider. You should have seen her on that wild creature of Bodkin's today.'

'I did,' said my mother.

'Natural hands and a beautiful seat,' said the Master.

Vice suddenly sprang at our father's favourite chair and scraped it viciously, lashing his tail and looking at my mother to see if she would try to stop him. Our mother went on pouring tea.

'Needs real courage to ride a thing like that.' The Master spoke with his mouth full of biscuit and a small shower of crumbs seemed to blow out with every word. 'Of course, he'll never sell it.'

'Well,' said Angela, with her mouth full, 'I'm going to hunt her this season.'

'Angela has volunteered to teach the younger children to ride.' The Master addressed himself to my mother.

'Oh,' she said.

'Is she mad?' I muttered to Blueprint, leaning down to give him a piece of cake.

'Crafty,' said Vice, passing me as he went to the window. 'Like Floss,' he added.

'I shall have to ask my husband,' said our mother. 'Oh, here he comes. I know he wants to see you, Master.' Our mother watched our father drive slowly past the window towards the garage. Blueprint began to shriek and yell and thump his tail as though he had not seen our father for a month.

'Time we went.' One of the Cardigans sneezed and the other stood up. They thanked my mother politely and gave a cold nod to the Master.

'Just the sort of people to have allergies. Too frightened to hunt and can't catch any fish.' The Master watched them go. 'Townees,' he added.

'I was brought up in London,' our mother said tartly. 'They know a lot about birds and fish.'

'Bet they don't shoot,' said the Master. 'Hullo, George,' he said as our father came in with Blueprint.

'Good afternoon,' said our father.

'What's this you want to see me about, George?' Hardly anyone calls my father George. He simply hates it.

'Shooting,' said my father, 'and hunting.'

'Shooting?'

'Yes. The Broughton Syndicate want you to keep off their land.' My father sounded rather pleased to impart the news. 'Your hounds disturb their pheasants and partridges. I act for them.'

'But that's ridiculous.'

'Quite legal.' Our father accepted a cup of tea from our mother and smiled.

'Legal be damned. It limits the field of the hunt quite dreadfully.'

'Why don't you try the Great Wood?' my mother asked soothingly.

'I can't. I always lose the whole pack in there.'

'Well, there it is,' said our father. 'It's trespassing and that Syndicate are a tough lot.' Our father flushed a little and our mother looked anxious, as when he got excited his ulcers hurt.

'A lot of company directors who shoot foxes!' exclaimed the Master.

'I thought you were a company director yourself,' I said.

'Help me clear away tea,' said my mother. Vice jumped on to our father's lap and Blueprint leant against his leg with his big head on his knee, gazing into his face.

'There is such a thing as tact,' said my mother to me in the hall.

'Listen,' said Angela. We stood in the hall, our hands holding trays of dirty cups and saucers.

'They come down at weekends and blaze off their guns.

They shoot foxes and I wouldn't be surprised if their keepers trapped them too. They are a bunch of Londoners who just come and throw their money about. They are just like that couple of old maids you and Johnson have let your fishing to, they – '

'I believe, er, Johnson would be happier if you kept off his farm,' our father said gently. 'I act for him too.'

'Happier!' Angela bumped open the kitchen door with her behind and we washed up without speaking, but each of us knew the others were thinking of the exchange of words Mr Johnson had had that morning with the Master.

'Why do we all call him Master?' I said. 'It's silly.'

'I must see he drinks milk tonight,' said my mother, which meant that she knew and we knew our father hated being called George and also hated rows so that his ulcers came to life.

'And I,' cried Angela suddenly, 'am going to every Pony Club meeting, every gymkhana. I am going to hunt twice a week.'

'Then you will be fully occupied,' our mother said drily. I went upstairs to see Mr Bull and refresh him with the news of the tea party.

'Can you get me some cheese?' said the mouse.

I went down to the larder and snipped a bit of Cheddar from a hunk of cheese. I gave it to the mouse, who hurried into its hole with it, and then I ran across the garden to join Angela.

'What's this about the Pony Club?' I asked.

'I can train them perfectly if I have them. That mare and I can meet all the horses and ponies from miles around.'

'What about it?'

'We can teach them too.'

'Oh,' I said, the light dawning. We walked on to the field Mr Bodkin kept his horses in. The new mare was rolling on her back, rolling and rolling and trying to get upright on the upward slope of the field.

'It's a perpetual challenge,' said the old horse, accepting a carrot. 'Enjoyed myself today,' he added, munching. 'Thought you two overdid it a bit.'

'Had to establish a reputation.' The new mare joined us. 'Nobody will dare buy me now,' she added smugly.

'I'm stiff all over,' said Angela.

'Come off it,' said the old horse. Angela laughed.

'We are going to hunt, go to all the gymkhanas and Pony Club meetings,' she said. The new mare whinnied. 'Someone may try and ride you, one of the judges or something.'

'I shall lie down and roll on him.' The new mare backed away and began to eat grass.

We walked home to find our mother leaning on the bridge parapet and looking downstream.

'How is father?' I said.

'Gone mad I think,' said our mother.

'Mad?'

'Yes, he let the Cardigans pay him for the fishing in cash and has now given it to the Master of Hounds for the R.S.P.C.A.'

'He's a great supporter,' I said.

'What about our education?' said Angela.

'Ah,' said our mother. 'Look, there's a woodpecker.'

'I saw a bullfinch today,' I said to test her.

'There aren't any bullfinches round here,' she said sadly. 'Only your poor creature in its cage.'

'He's perfectly happy,' I said.

'I don't like caged birds. Just look at all those fish, and those poor men catch nothing. It's funny.'

'Very funny,' said Angela.

After supper I went into the wood. The river makes quite a different noise at night if you listen carefully. An otter ambled along the bank and I said 'good evening'. The otter stopped. In the half-light I could see its whiskery face.

'You gave us a good laugh today,' said the otter. 'I like you.'

'Do you get on with foxes?' I asked.

'We don't speak unless necessary.'

'Do you speak to the other otters now?'

'Not necessary.'

'Why not necessary?'

'That Floss and your Blueprint and Joker told the hounds what to do.'

'Will they remember?'

'Oh, yes, they are pleased.'

'Why?'

'Well, if they *really* hunt us we bite them. Now they are just going to have jolly bathing parties along the rivers. Everyone will be pleased. Do you like slugs?'

'No,' I said.

'We eat a lot of slugs and mice and beetles.'

'What about fish?'

'Only on occasion.' The otter drifted into the shadows and I got up and walked on and out of the wood into the Johnsons' pig field. I went to Gertrude's hut. Gertrude's tiny eye glistened in the dark. I could just make out the shapes of her fourteen piglets lying against her flank.

'I wanted to thank you for what you did this morning,' I said.

Gertrude grunted.

'You were very brave.'

'Pigs are brave.' Gertrude's eye rolled a little.

'What is the meaning of life, Gertrude?' I asked.

'To produce bacon.'

'There must be something beyond bacon,' I said.

'Eggs.' Gertrude's bulk heaved at her own joke and all the disturbed piglets shifted and made tiny complaining grunts. 'No good being metaphysical on a farm,' said Gertrude.

'Do cows think the same as you?'

'More or less.'

'Bacon,' I said, feeling a tear roll down my cheek.

'Don't be a fool. Bacon, milk, eggs – we all live happy lives.' Gertrude grunted.

'Sheep,' I said.

'Wool and mutton,' said Gertrude. 'It's life.' She shut her tiny eye and I felt dismissed. I went to look for Andrew and told him about Gertrude.

'Ah,' said Andrew. 'Meaning of life my foot.'

'Will you come and see the badgers tomorrow?' I asked.

'Yes. I want to see Tom.'

But next morning when we had climbed up through the wood to the badgers' sets, Tom was not there.

'I wonder where he is.' Andrew looked round him and then went across to the bushes and peered under. 'Everything's gone.'

'Was the car in the quarry?'

'No, it wasn't, now I come to think of it.'

We stood uncertainly on the edge of the hollow.

'Pigeons?' I asked.

'There don't seem to be any.'

We listened to the silence and the faint noise of the wind in the trees. Andrew knelt down and spoke politely down a large badger set. 'Did Tom leave a message by any chance?'

'No message,' a grumbling voice answered.

'Oh, heavens!' I said. 'Here's a trapped fox.'

'Where?' Andrew joined me.

A young fox was lying on its side staring up at us. So fiercely had it fought when trapped that the chain to which the trap was attached was madly twisted.

'Keep still,' I said to the fox. The fox watched us.

'It's all right,' said Andrew, 'but you have twisted the beastly thing so much I can't step on the release.' Andrew strained with his strong hands to open the trap. The fox looked at him beadily.

'They usually knock us on the head with the butt of their guns,' it said.

'Keep still,' said Andrew, sweating. He forced the trap open slowly and the fox snatched its paw out.

'Where do you come from?' said Andrew.

'Not far.'

'We will carry you.'

'You smell,' said the fox.

'You must put up with it.' Andrew picked the fox up gently and waited while I went along the edge of the wood and let all the little birds out of the bird traps.

'Crazy,' said the fox.

'Anyone know where this cub comes from?' Andrew asked down one of the badgers' sets.

'Its mother is somewhere about,' came a sleepy answer.

The cub yelped and we waited. Presently the cub pricked its ears. 'There's my mum,' it said, and we saw a vixen watching us from the other side of the clearing. Andrew put the cub down and it limped away to its mother.

'Stupid fool, I told you not to go there,' she said.

'Doesn't seem to be much sympathy about.' Andrew dusted fox hairs off the front of his shirt. 'I wonder where he's gone.' He looked round the empty clearing. 'Does he live here all the year round?' Andrew asked down a hole.

'Depends on the weather,' came a sleepy answer.

'Just when we're getting organized,' Andrew grumbled.

'I know he comes and goes,' I said.

'Goes where?'

'I don't know.' Tom's disappearance gave me a sense of defeat.

'Don't be downhearted.' Andrew looked at me quite kindly. 'He'll come back.'

'When?'

'When will Tom come back?' Andrew asked down a set.

'Can't you leave us in peace,' a cross voice answered.

'The Cardigans paid my father for the fishing in cash,' I said, 'and he gave it to the R.S.P.C.A. He handed it straight to the Master.'

Andrew laughed. 'I posted them their stolen money,' he said.

'I must tell Gertrude,' I said. 'She seems to have a funny sense of humour. What is metaphysical?'

'I've no idea.' Andrew led the way downhill through the wood. 'Nothing to do with us.'

13

We met Angela riding the new mare. The moment she saw us the mare reared up, shied and put her head down.

'Don't be silly,' said Angela. 'I nearly fell off.'

'Sorry,' said the mare, but she didn't look it.

'What's her name?' asked Andrew.

'Mr Bodkin calls her "that thing".'

'She should have a name,' I said.

'I shall call her Margot Fonteyn,' said Angela.

'Why?' said the mare, turning her neck to nibble at Angela's foot in the stirrup. 'Who's she?'

'She's a dancer,' said Angela.

'Not as good as me, I bet,' said the mare. 'I'm sure she can't do this.' The mare gave a sideways leap and reared up on end. Angela fell off.

'You fool,' said Angela, getting up.

'Sorry,' said the mare, looking amused. 'Call me Marge.'

'All right, Marge.' Angela climbed back on to Marge.

'Marge! What an awful name.' Andrew watched Angela ride off through the wood. 'It's funny about Tom. I shall ask Joker. He's rather thick with Floss.'

We met Joker walking in a docile way behind Mr Johnson.

'Seen Floss?' enquired Andrew.

'Gone away. I'm busy now.' Joker glanced at Mr Johnson.

'If either of you see Tom Foley will you ask him to come and give me a hand tomorrow?'

'We haven't seen him,' we said.

'Then I shall have to manage on my own.' Mr Johnson walked on.

'I believe Joker knows,' said Andrew. 'And the badgers must too, but for some reason they won't tell.'

'Let's ask Gertrude.'

'Gertrude is busy. There's James. Let's ask him.'

But James did not know, and all the animals we met gave rude or evasive answers.

The weeks passed and we all went to the various gymkhanas to watch Angela and Marge perform. In the ring Marge would jump like a dream, play musical chairs and win races. But she was not popular with the judges who got nipped or kicked when they came up to pat her, nor with the admiring children who unwisely asked for rides. We all moved about among the children's ponies and Blueprint and Marge talked to them. When the hounds were brought to the Shows, Blueprint mixed freely with them.

'It is like canvassing for an election,' Blueprint explained. 'I brainwash them into thinking they do not like chasing foxes.'

'Any success?' I asked.

'Well, yes.' Blueprint enjoyed his encounters with hounds. 'The bitches think it's a good thing for their puppies to pretend, but the dogs want their puppies to be manly. They are on the Conservative side except for a few who would vote Labour or Liberal if they had the misfortune to be born human.'

'Misfortune?'

'Well, yes, having to work for their living like you all do. Just look at your father. Ulcers. *We* don't get ulcers.'

'I hadn't thought of it in that light,' I said.

'They all laugh though.' Blueprint looked pleased with his social success.

Angela and Marge went cubbing on Tuesdays and Saturdays and the rest of us watched the foxes, young and old, who gathered in the sanctuary of the Great Wood. Since foxes are highly intelligent, it soon became unnecessary to go ourselves. We just told the local foxes in our wood.

Our father was rung up one night by the Master, who accused his Broughton-shoot clients of shooting and trapping foxes. My father answered rather huffily and told the Master that if he made such unproven accusations he was heading for litigation.

'What is litigation?' I asked my mother.

'Litigation pays for your education,' she said ambiguously.

'Ah,' I said, none the wiser.

'The fact remains we haven't killed a single cub this season.' The Master had the sort of voice one could hear down the telephone from the next room, and our father held the receiver a yard from his ear.

'I hear that you are having very good days though,' said my father.

'Never see a fox. Can't get the hounds blooded.'

'Too bad,' said my father unsympathetically.

'Your daughter will tell you.'

'She seems to enjoy herself very much,' said my father, protecting his ear with one hand.

'Your daughter should join a circus.'

'That's an idea. Goodbye.' Our father laid the receiver back on its cradle.

'First of September on Saturday,' I said to Angela in my room.

'I'm hunting,' said Angela.

'Partridge shooting begins, you idiot,' I said.

'So it does.' Mr Bull looked at us wisely. 'You can't hide the partridges and foxes in the same place. It would be asking too much.'

'It would,' said Vice.

'The foxes will go as usual to the same place,' Blueprint remarked. 'You can't muddle them now.'

'And pheasant shooting begins in a month,' I moaned.

'If only Floss were here and Tom.'

'I will arrange it.' Vice looked incredibly sly. 'I know one of the keepers' cats.' He left the room and we looked at each other.

'We can't leave it to the cats.' Blueprint looked worried.

'You must,' piped Mr Bull.

'Blueprint, do you think Vice and the keepers' cat are the proper people to hide the partridges?'

'I will talk to Joker.'

'The shooting people all stay at the hotel for their weekends.'

'Good business,' said Blueprint.

'What on earth do you know about it?'

'I may not be able to read, but I can hear.' Blueprint went away looking very dignified. I went down to see James who, when I reminded him about the beginning of the shooting season, said: 'Oh, my, my!'

'I wish Tom would come back,' I said. 'He's been away weeks.'

We walked moodily to the pig field, which was now filled with immense sows surrounded by their rooting, romping families. Gertrude's were especially gay, cantering about in their jerky way like small people in bikinis. Gertrude watched them with her crafty eyes shining out of her great jowly face.

'Hullo, Gertrude,' said James.

Gertrude grunted.

'Father is going to keep all Gertrude's.' James looked at Gertrude with pride.

'He is keeping them for breeding.' Andrew picked up the thick stick his father kept near the gate for the special purpose of scratching his pigs and scraped it along Gertrude's side.

'Not bacon then,' I said, and looked at Gertrude with relief.

'Not this time,' said Gertrude.

' "Parting is such sweet sorrow" doesn't apply to farmers,' I said. 'They never see their dear ones again.'

'Sad,' said James. 'One shouldn't think of it.'

'Even if this lot are not to become bacon, their children will,' I said.

'Don't be so morbid, Kate.' Gertrude swayed her enormous flank closer to the stick. 'Even you will be buried one day,' she added maliciously.

Joker barked from the next field. He was rounding up a flock of sheep with Mr Johnson watching.

'I wish Tom would come back and give me a hand.' Mr Johnson watched Joker doing all the work as he stood leaning on his stick. 'They like Tom.' One of the ewes turned and glared at Joker and stamped her foot.

'Good wool,' remarked Mr Johnson. 'Should get good wool next year.'

'I don't mind the wool,' I said. 'It's the mutton.'

'You eat it,' said Mr Johnson without looking at me.

'Do you?'

'Not my own. How could you eat a bit of an animal you

had raised from birth, put a lot of love and work into, spent money you can't afford on, gone without holidays for, loved.' Mr Johnson's face was expressionless.

'Why are you a farmer then?' James looked at his father in surprise.

Mr Johnson laughed. 'I love animals,' he said. 'Look at that ewe annoying Joker. I give my animals very happy lives. Look at those pigs. Never do a stroke of work. Everything is provided for them. They don't have to sit in offices, do they?'

'No,' I said, visualizing Gertrude running an office.

'They don't get crushed in tubes and buses in noisy towns.'

'I can see Gertrude crushing a lot of people herself.' James began to laugh.

'Gertrude has brains,' said Mr Johnson, and walked up to close the gate Joker had driven the sheep though.

We went round a corner out of sight with Joker and told him about the cats and the first of September.

'I'm no wiser than you are,' said Joker. 'If Floss were here she would know what to do.'

'Floss isn't.'

'Then ask your bullfinch.' Joker lapped water from the trough and went into the farmhouse after his master.

'None of the animals are very helpful.' James looked disconsolate.

'I am.' Blueprint, who had been following at our heels all this time, suddenly left us and we saw him cutting across country to the Broughton land.

'He is friends with the keepers' dogs,' said James.

In my room Mr Bull was eating seed and the mouse was waiting for the odd seed to come his way.

'Vice and the keepers' cats are in cahoots,' I said.

'Don't care for cats.' The mouse nibbled a seed.

'Blueprint has gone to join them.'

'Why?' asked the mouse.

'He's made friends with the keepers' dogs, of course.' Mr Bull drank a sip of water, fluffed out his feathers, and jumped up on to his top perch.

'Angela has gone off to arrange a specially good hunt with Marge.'

The mouse tittered.

'It still leaves us with the terrible problem of where to put the partridges,' said James, stroking the mouse with one careful finger.

'Do you children feel left out?' Mr Bull had a nasty way of arriving at conclusions.

'Yes,' said James honestly.

'Then leave it to Vice. He knows what he is doing.'

Neither Mr Bull or the mouse would tell us any more, and in the woods and fields the few animals we met just laughed.

On the first of September we were worried stiff. Angela had gone off rather early, riding Marge. Vice had disappeared. James and I and Blueprint climbed the hill from the top of which we had a good view of the keepers' cottages and the Broughton shoot.

We had taken Blueprint to the hotel the evening before. The Syndicate arrived in their Jaguars, and Blueprint had had a word with a pair of smart labradors. We had seen the hotel-keeper help his guests carry in their guns. Blueprint had returned from his conversation with the labradors looking complacent, but had told us nothing, so as we three lay at the top of the hill both James and I felt rather cross with Blueprint.

It was not long before the keepers came and let their dogs out of their kennels. Both keepers carried guns and waited, chatting to each other.

'I wish I knew what Vice is up to.' James fidgeted.

'It's his joke,' said Blueprint, lying with his nose on his paws looking down at the keepers.

'I wish you would tell us.' James stroked Blueprint, who only rolled his eyes and wagged his tail faintly.

Presently we saw the Syndicate arrive, talk to the keepers and discuss how they would walk in line.

'They are starting,' I said.

The guns formed themselves into a line and began walking slowly across the nearest field of stubble. Blueprint cocked his ears as though he could hear them.

'It will be a massacre,' I said.

'Wait and watch,' Blueprint growled.

The guns walked across the first field and four pheasants flew up explosively.

'No danger for them for another month.' Andrew had joined us, crawling through the undergrowth at the edge of the wood. A stoat passed us and snickered.

'No need to laugh. The game larder has been empty for weeks,' said Blueprint. 'And small thanks to you.'

'Watch,' said Andrew.

The line of guns left the stubble and crossed a farm track into a field of kale. They carried their guns cocked.

'Look silly, don't they?' James was watching carefully.

We lay where we were for an hour, watching the sportsmen walk on in a line.

'Funny,' said Andrew.

'Very funny.' Blueprint was now standing up, panting.

'The partridges seem to have gone.' James looked very puzzled.

The guns wheeled in a wide circle and still no partridges rose in front of them. We saw the gamekeepers' cat sitting watching on one side of the cottage doorsteps.

'Funny,' said James, echoing Andrew.

'Funnier in a moment. Listen.' Blueprint and the cat below us both had cocked ears. Far away behind the big hill between us and home we heard hounds in full cry.

'Hounds,' I said.

We listened intently with our eyes still fixed on the Syndicate who were, one would imagine, getting hot and tired. The sound of the hunt swelled round the far side of the wood and we could see, though we could not hear, the Syndicate making angry signals to the keepers. Still no partridge rose in fearful covey, still the Syndicate walked on with guns cocked. Presently they stopped to confer. The hounds came nearer, and with joy we watched them running in a wedge about two miles away.

'There go Angela and Marge.' James had very sharp eyes.

The pack swept along the very edge of the Syndicate's lane. Sounds of angry protest came up to us from the sportsmen and we saw them get into their cars and drive off.

'Not a single partridge,' said James.

'Any point in waiting and watching now?' I could hear from his voice that James was hungry.

'None at all.' Blueprint rolled in the long grass, scratching his spine against a stick.

'I do think you are mean,' I said to him. 'You might tell us where the partridges are.'

'You will enjoy hearing the shooting people ringing up your father about the hunting people.'

'Gorgeous,' said James. 'You are lucky.'

We walked up through the woods, meeting small parties of foxes as we went, returning to their homes. They stood aside politely as we passed and we greeted them. Before we got to the Johnsons' farm we met Angela hacking slowly home on Marge.

'Enjoy yourself, Marge?' I asked.

'Yes. I'm going to have a red ribbon for my tail.' Marge nuzzled me nicely.

'Blueprint knows where the partridges are and won't tell us,' I said to Angela.

Angela looked furiously at Blueprint. 'How could you!' she said.

'You'd be frightened if I told you,' said Blueprint.

'Nonsense,' said Angela. Blueprint's tail dropped.

'Vice isn't frightened, nor was the keepers' cat,' I said.

'Vice knew you would be frightened,' Blueprint's tail was down.

'Is he bringing them back?' Andrew was practical.

'Oh yes.'

'And he isn't afraid?'

'It's his sort of place.' Blueprint sounded rather miserable.

'His sort of place?' Angela went white. 'Oh, NO!'

'Yes,' Blueprint whined.

'The haunted house,' whispered James.

Once long ago when we were small we had all four set out to visit the haunted house, but for perfectly good reasons which we all thought up, we had turned back.

'This time we must go,' said Angela. 'If Vice can, we can. We are older now anyway. Let's meet by the Johnsons' bridge after supper.' Angela trotted off on Marge.

After supper, which had been interrupted by Sir Some-body Something of the Broughton Syndicate ringing up my father and asking him to complain to the hunt, Angela and I with Blueprint went down through the wood carrying torches. We met the boys and Joker waiting for us.

'Anyone complain about the shoot yet?' James enquired.

'They certainly did, but father said if the hunt hadn't actually set hoof on their land he could do nothing.'

'There were no birds to disturb either,' said James.

'Come on,' said Andrew, and I could tell he was nervous. That house is not a place anyone goes to. All anyone knows is that it's a very old house in the Great Wood in a clearing and that it belongs to nobody. As I walked behind Andrew and Angela, with James and the dogs behind me, I tried to remember whether I knew anyone who had ever seen it and I couldn't.

'Does anyone know the way?' Andrew asked after we had been walking along the edge of the wood for some time.

'No,' we all said. 'It's secret.'

'I once heard my father say it is beyond the bend in the river,' James volunteered.

'Then it must be right back inside the wood.'

'Yes,' said James.

'Quite hidden.'

'Yes,' said James.

'Vice is the limit,' said Andrew presently.

'You tell him.' Angela was cross.

The river swept in a huge arc and then quite suddenly became wide, silent and dark under the trees, gliding oilily close to the woods. A water rat plopped into the river and we all jumped and stood still. It was dusk and in the wood the owls were beginning to hoot. Andrew shone his torch about him. 'There's no path into the wood.'

'Here's a tiny one,' said Angela after a time. 'It looks used.'

Andrew started walking up it slowly. We followed.

'Oh!' Andrew stopped suddenly. We stood in a row on the edge of a clearing and stared. On the edge of it crouched a low stone house. There was glass in the windows and the glass blinked back a reflection from the stars. There was absolute silence. Andrew and Angela shone the beams of their torches across the clearing towards the house. We stood hesitating. Suddenly there was a loud moaning yell ending in a shriek. We turned as one and ran. Andrew, running the fastest, tripped, Angela fell over him and James and I on top of them.

'Having trouble?' said Vice.

'You fiend,' said Andrew, shining his torch at Vice's green eyes. We all got up, ashamed and silent.

'This way.' Vice tripped lightly with his tail in the air across the clearing and round the corner of the house.

Shining their torches, Andrew and Angela picked out quantities of partridges crouched in the grass.

'I see,' said Angela. 'You wicked thing!' And she began to laugh. We all joined in and the dogs wagged their tails.

'I'll take them back later,' said Vice. 'And from October onwards the pheasants can roost in the trees.'

'Very jolly,' I said. 'And what's in the house?'

'The door is locked.' Vice sounded a bit annoyed.

'Then I'll unlock it.' Tom Foley spoke from behind us. 'Bit nosey, aren't you?' He spoke amiably. 'You the banshee?' He bent down to stroke Vice. The dogs wagged their tails.

'Where have you been, Tom?' Andrew wanted to speak quickly before any reference could be made to our recent panic.

'Scotland.'

'Why?'

'The Glorious Twelfth.' Tom was grinning.

'Grouse,' said James brightly.

'Yes. Taught them to lie still in the heather. That's about all I could do.'

'I read the season is rotten,' said Andrew.

'So it is.' Tom shoved a key into the lock and went into the house. 'Wait till I draw the curtains,' he said. 'Don't want any snoopers seeing lights.' We heard him moving about and presently strike a match and we watched him light an oil lamp. 'I like to be private.'

'Scotland,' muttered Andrew.

'Had a word with the deer in the Highlands.' Tom raised the lamp so that its light shone on us. 'Do I understand we have visitors tonight?'

'All the partridges from the Broughton shoot,' I said. 'And Vice wants to bring the pheasants when their time comes.'

'Good, good.' Tom was looking at us wolfishly. 'They can spend their weekends here if they wish.'

'Where's Floss?' Joker was looking up at Tom and wagging his tail.

'Ah, Floss. She's on her way.' Joker and Blueprint turned back to meet her. 'Come upstairs,' said Tom.

We followed him up a rickety staircase.

'He behaves as though it was *his* house,' muttered James.

'It *is* my house,' said Tom. He lit another lamp and we stared in wonder. The walls of the passage were lined with bookshelves and as he led us from room to room we saw books everywhere. Tom drew shabby but beautiful curtains across the windows as he went and lit candles and we stared at old lovely furniture. Pictures hung on the walls, and on the mantelshelves and in the corner cupboards we saw gleaming glass and china and unpolished silver. Paper was scattered over a writing table.

'Then you are not a tramp?' James could pop out with the most embarrassing questions.

'Oh yes, in a way, but a scholar too.'

'I thought you just lay about,' said Angela.

'I do. I do. Now here, I think, come the dogs.' Tom cocked his head on one side and Vice retreated under the bed.

'No need to be afraid,' said Tom rather maliciously, greatly raising our spirits. 'I went to the Farne Islands, too, you see. I have a plan to redistribute the seals.'

Vice came out from under the bed, which was a dusty four-poster with velvet hangings, extremely faded. 'You smell delicious,' he said. 'Fishy. Seals, I suppose.'

The dogs came in. Floss jumped on to the bed, curled up, put her nose under her bushy tail. I could tell she wasn't sleeping because her ears were half-cocked.

'How did you get here?' asked Tom, who was rummaging in a cupboard. 'Can I offer you a drink?' he said courteously to Angela, and without waiting for an answer poured brandy into a small glass and handed it to her. He did the same for me and the boys and poured out a tumblerful for himself. 'Drink up,' he said, eyeing us with amusement. 'Put a match to the fire, Andrew, it's ready laid.'

Andrew lit the fire. Vice sat immediately in front of it, staring at the flames as they leapt from one dry twig to another and set the logs burning.

'Where is the car?' I asked.

'In the quarry,' said Tom. 'I came the rest of the way on foot.'

'An otter caught a salmon,' said Floss.

'Dear me,' said Tom, adding rather hungrily, 'any left?'

'Plenty,' said Floss loftily. 'It said it had forgotten.'

'Then show Blueprint where it is, there's a darling, and bring it here. We all forget sometimes.' Floss got up and went out with Blueprint.

'What's the idea?' Andrew looked at Tom, who was looking at the flames of the fire through his glass, squinting down his long nose.

'The people who preserve the seals in the Farne Islands keep their numbers down, as they put it, by killing off a certain number every year.'

'I've read about it,' I said.

'We all have,' said James. 'It's disgusting.'

'Well, I thought so too, and as I was up that way I called.'

'Warning the grouse and the deer,' said Andrew.

'Yes, yes. I did that. It will cost a lot of money.' Tom gulped some brandy and laughed.

'Who to?' I said.

'All the people who have rented grouse moors and deer forests.'

'Good,' said Angela.

'And the seals?' Andrew returned to the point.

'Ah, yes, the seals. There is the north Devon coast, very rough and nasty. Quite a number of places in Cornwall. South-West Ireland, of course, and the coasts of Scotland. A lot of excellent places. Wales too. I shall tell them.'

'How wonderful that would be.' Angela's face was glowing.

'Yes.' Tom was sitting in a wing chair by the fire. 'Go and give the dogs a hand, boys.' Below us we could hear Floss being very governessy to Blueprint. The boys went out and presently came back carrying half a fish. They looked astonished and shamefaced.

'Surely not *our* otters!' I exclaimed.

'Well, it's dead now. We might as well eat it.' Tom pulled a sharp knife from his pocket and sliced the fish into steaks and impaled each steak with a stick. 'Grill 'em. They're delicious. I'm no saint. Nor are they.'

We grilled the steaks in silence and ate them pensively, pretending not to enjoy them.

'Father is looking for you to help with the farm,' said Andrew.

'Is he?' said Tom. 'Could do with some money. It was an expensive trip. Petrol and oil and so on.'

'Our father gave all the money he was paid for the fishing to the R.S.P.C.A.,' said Angela suddenly. 'We could have used it.' Tom nodded.

Floss looked at us and said in a nasty whining voice: 'Isn't it time you left? We are tired.'

We all stood up and said goodbye to Tom.

'What about the partridges?' I asked Vice.

'I'll lead them back.' Vice rose, arching his back.

We left the house with Blueprint and Joker and stood in a group in the moonlight, looking at the dark house behind us. A soft rustle came from behind the house. Round the corner came Vice, followed by a seemingly endless procession of partridges. 'It's not far as the crow flies,' said Blueprint.

'I think Vice is very clever,' I said.

'He frightened us,' said Andrew resentfully.

'Usually Tom gets a fox to cry out if anyone gets near here. Floss told me.' Joker stood by us waiting and listening.

'Time we went home,' James exclaimed and we hurried away. We reached home and our mother said: 'Where on earth have you been?' when we arrived.

'We were looking for a nightjar,' I said easily.

'There are no nightjars round here. They prefer sandy soil.' Get our mother on to birds and you are safe. 'Time you were in bed,' she said.

We hurried to bed and put out our lights. In the dark Angela came into my room. 'There's something funny about Tom Foley,' she whispered. 'Did you see all those books?'

'Yes.'

'That house, that car, his way of life.'

'It seems a nice way of life,' I said. 'Independent.'

'He drinks,' said Angela.

'So does the Master's horse when he gets the chance,' I said. 'He likes beer.'

'Get some sleep and don't disturb other people.' Mr Bull fidgeted in his cage. I could hear him fluffing up his feathers. The mouse climbed up on to my bed for a bit of conversation.

'Vice frightened us,' I whispered to the mouse.

The mouse tittered. 'He frightens us too.'

The following day I woke to Mr Bull's piping. Angela was still asleep and Blueprint and Vice lay on her bed in attitudes of deep repose. I wondered how and when Vice had got in.

My parents were breakfasting in the kitchen. I joined them. The telephone rang and my mother answered it. She listened.

'I'll see whether he is still here,' she said. My father turned the paper over and drank some coffee.

'I'm not here,' he said, gripping the paper. My father grinned and winked at me. 'White lies – useful.' He laid the paper on one side and helped himself to more coffee.

'Oh, how very interesting,' said my mother into the telephone. 'No,' she said firmly, 'I've no idea when he will be back. Why don't you ring him up tomorrow from London?' We heard her put the receiver back.

'Honestly,' said my mother, coming back into the room. 'Such a bad example for the children.'

'I won't be bothered on Sundays,' said my father, begging the question. 'Bad for my ulcers. Who was it?'

'That man who runs the Syndicate. He says their keepers tell them the Broughton place is alive with partridges, and there wasn't a bird there yesterday.'

'They can't shoot on Sunday,' said my father.

'That's why they are so cross,' said my mother.

'Hah!' My father laid his coffee cup back in the saucer and stood up, holding the paper. 'Useful clients. Top fees.'

'You are a disgrace,' said my mother amiably.

'Must educate the girls.' My father left the room.

'Living at home is an education in itself,' I said.

'I wonder what you mean by that?' My mother began clearing the breakfast things. I helped her.

'Who collects for the R.S.P.C.A. here?' I asked.

'The Master of the Hounds and the wife of the man who has the otter hounds,' said my mother in a flat voice. 'And,' she said, her voice rising, 'neither of them approves of stag hunting.'

'Surprise, surprise,' I said.

My mother began washing up. I went upstairs and woke Angela, who yawned and groaned.

'Let me out into the garden.' Blueprint trotted to the door. I let him out and went back to Angela.

'Stag hunting,' I said.

'Oh! I'd forgotten it. Will you and James find Tom?'

'All right,' I said. 'What do we say to him?'

'Tell him stag hunting is starting. He will think of something.'

I went down to the Johnsons' and found James. 'We've got to find Tom,' I said. 'He can send the pigeons.'

'Andrew is going to help my father.'

'What's he doing?'

'Rounding up sheep.'

'On a Sunday?'

'The sheep don't know it's Sunday.'

We went straight into the wood, skirted its edge to keep out of sight and walked, as we had walked the night before, to the hidden house. There was a slight misting rain and the trees dripped on us. We met a fox who said over its shoulder as it trotted into the wood: 'The keepers aren't half mad.'

'What are they doing?' James asked.

'Grumbling. They got no tips!'

When we reached the clearing we stopped and looked across at the house.

'No smoke,' said James. We walked round the clearing and tried the back door, which was not locked.

'He was tired last night,' I said.

'All the same we must tell him.' James held out a hand to me.

'Floss?' James called gently and enquiringly. There was no answer.

'Let's go up.' I followed him up the rickety stairs. He pushed open the door and again we listened. Outside the water was dripping from the gutters and pattering on the windows. We went into the room we had been in the night before. There was nobody. No Tom. No Floss.

'All gone,' said James and went across to the fireplace. 'The ashes are cold,' he whispered.

'We could lay his fire for him,' I said.

We took sticks from a big pile near the hearth and laid logs on them.

'Let's look round. We only saw it in the dark.' James was incurably curious. We looked round the room at the dusty bed and furniture, the books and china and the silver and the huge bed. We went into other rooms but there was nobody there. We went back to the room we had all sat in the night before.

'It's fishy, I mean it smells fishy,' said James.

'And of drink,' I said. 'Personally, I believe it's haunted,' I added, staring at a dirty old typewriter on the desk. 'What does he want this for?'

'I swear it's haunted,' said James. 'But only by Tom.'

'There's nobody here anyway,' I said.

We walked thoughtfully down into the village. From the pub we could hear a lot of talk and a good deal of laughter. As we passed the hotel we noticed that all the smart cars belonging to the shooting people had gone and only the Mr Cardigans' car was in the garage. One of the brothers was sitting in the garden reading. He waved to us and we went up to him.

'No fishing today,' he said. It was the older, fatter Mr Cardigan. 'It's Sunday.'

'Yes,' said James. 'You can't fish on Sunday.'

'Whether it's Sunday or any other day of the week, we still don't catch any fish.'

'You've been very nice about it,' I said.

'We've enjoyed ourselves. We still are enjoying ourselves. Not like those people who came down to shoot.'

'Didn't they enjoy themselves?' James sat down beside Mr Cardigan.

'No,' said Mr Cardigan, 'they did not. They expected a

lot of dead birds and they got none. We expect a lot of dead fish and get none. But we love watching the birds and animals. There's a difference.'

'My mother and James's mother watch birds,' I said.

'So do cats,' said Mr Cardigan. 'We've watched fish, too. There are plenty of fish in that water. It's very clear. It's a very odd thing.' Mr Cardigan gazed into the distance. 'The forty pounds arrived back by post.'

'How very odd,' I said.

'Yes. Local postmark too. Have a sweet.' Mr Cardigan offered a bag of peppermints. We said thank you and both blushed as we said goodbye. Mr Cardigan's face was expressionless.

'Even if he did know he wouldn't tell,' I said.

We walked on past the pub. On the step sat Joker.

'Father must be in there,' said James.

'He is,' said Joker. 'And Floss,' he added.

'Is Tom there?'

'Yes, he's hearing how there were no partridges to shoot.'

'Is that why they are laughing?'

'Yes.' Joker laid his nose on his paws and closed his eyes.

'Will you tell Floss we want to see Tom?'

'I might.' We knew from Joker's voice that he had been told to wait outside and was put out about it.

'Please, Joker.'

At that moment Mr Johnson, Tom and Floss came out of the pub. They all looked very cheerful.

'Hullo, you two,' said Mr Johnson.

'Hullo,' we said.

Mr Johnson and Joker got into his Landrover and drove off.

'What do you want?' said Tom. 'I'm busy.'

'Tom, the stag hunting has begun. Can you send your pigeons?'

'Easily,' said Tom good-humouredly. 'What do I do with the deer?'

'Oh, Floss can talk to the hounds and will you tell the deer to take to the forests?'

'Got to get them started.'

'You ask our mothers,' I said. 'They hate stag hunting.'

'Me?' Tom looked horrified. 'How could they help?'

'Money,' I said. 'They'll buy maize for your birds.'

'They think I'm a layabout in fact. It's better not to tell them.'

'You were at school with that awful man who was rude to mother at the Meet,' I said smugly.

'Blast you,' said Tom.

'We'll tell them you own the secret house.' James danced out of Tom's reach.

'Don't you dare!' Tom was furious. 'It's private.'

'We will,' I said, as Floss nipped me.

'Now, Floss.' Tom looked at the blood flowing freely from my calf and handed me a dirty handkerchief which I tied round my leg. James ignored my wound and pressed on with our advantage.

'I'll see.' Tom looked at James grumpily and added: 'It's blackmail.'

'What's blackmail?' The younger Mr Cardigan approached us from behind. Floss growled.

'Oh, the children are trying to blackmail me into protesting about stag hunting.'

'Stag hunting is disgusting,' said the younger Mr Cardigan.

'You are a fisherman,' Tom said rather rudely.

'Well, I fish, but the fish have choice. Hunting is quite different. However, there's always the hope that the people will break their necks,' said Mr Cardigan, smiling at his brother.

'Angela hunts,' I said.

'I understand there's every hope she will break her neck,' said Tom nastily. 'You are very Jesuitical.'

'Tell you what, Foley,' said the younger Mr Cardigan suddenly. 'You drive over and protest. Interrupt them.'

'Splendid idea, splendid,' said Tom acidly.

'Just exactly my idea of fun,' said Floss, standing up against Tom, wagging her bushy tail.

'What is Jesuitical?' I muttered, not wishing to show my ignorance. James shrugged his shoulders, equally baffled.

'They seem to know each other.' Blueprint, who had been shocked by Floss's behaviour, looked mystified.

⪼ 16 ⪻

After lunch that Sunday the four of us walked up to the quarry and Andrew and James lifted the cover off Tom Foley's car and gave it a good look.

'It's in marvellous condition for its age.' Andrew stroked the old paintwork.

'He doesn't use it much.' James stood on the running-board and peered inside before Andrew replaced the groundsheet reverently like a person covering a corpse he had just identified in a morgue.

'Is he really a tramp?' James looked at the sheeted car.

'I think so. Our father defended him last time he was had up for being drunk,' I said. 'He gets angry about things.'

'That doesn't make him a tramp,' Andrew said. 'And my father paid his fine.'

'I never knew that,' I said.

'Well, he helps father a lot on the farm. Father likes him.'

'Our fathers seem more human than we think,' said Angela. 'What about the poaching?'

'Perhaps he was hungry,' I said romantically.

'Don't be silly. He enjoys it,' Andrew said crushingly.

'He can't be a tramp if he owns a vintage car and a house,' James muttered. 'He knows the Cardigans.'

'He certainly looks like a tramp in that old hat of father's,' Andrew said.

'And the vicar's suit,' added Angela.

'He lives out.' Andrew tossed his head towards the badgers' sets. 'Sometimes.'

'Probably likes it,' said James. 'I would. No one to bother me. Why does he help us?'

'It amuses him, of course,' said Angela. 'Just as it amuses Marge and me to go hunting.'

'Oh,' we all said, heavily sarcastic, 'it *amuses* him.'

'There's more to it than that, of course.' Angela shifted from one foot to another.

'What?' I asked.

'I don't know,' said Angela. 'But just look what an inspiration he had about the foxes.'

'That was sheer genius,' said Andrew. 'Come on, we can't stop here.'

In the clearing Tom lay with Floss against him keeping a watchful eye open. She pricked her ears when we arrived and sat up.

'Are you asleep, Tom?' James asked respectfully.

'I was until I heard you all tramping up the hill.'

'We made no noise,' Angela said indignantly.

'My ears are close to the ground.'

'Sorry,' said Angela.

There was a long pause during which we sat in a row with Blueprint and looked down on Tom and Floss.

'Want to make plans about those deer, I suppose.' Tom spoke at last. 'The Cardigans will be amused.'

'Oh,' said Angela. 'So the Cardigans are with us?'

'In spirit, yes. I've sent the pigeons.'

'That will help,' I said politely.

'It isn't until Saturday. Can't you let me sleep?'

We felt dismissed.

'Do you really do nothing?' asked James, Floss sneered.

'As little as one can in this Welfare State.'

'You own a car and a house,' James said.

'I scribble.' Tom's voice repressed laughter.

'We are taught to write clear script,' James said. 'Some people learn Italic.'

'Really. How is the leg?' Tom addressed me.

'I shan't get blood poisoning,' I said tartly, feeling that we were all being made fun of.

'Time you left me in peace,' Tom said rudely.

We got up without speaking and went away to the Johnsons'.

'Do you like sheep?' Angela said to Mrs Johnson.

'Of course I do,' said Mrs Johnson. 'Earwigs are good mothers too.'

'What does she mean, earwigs?' I asked Angela as we walked home.

'She means earwigs and sheep are good mothers.'

'Then why doesn't she say so?'

'She's grown-up.' Angela gave a childish skip. 'I must go and talk to Marge.'

'Why Marge?' I found Angela very aggravating.

'Well, Mr Bodkin is going to keep her as a brood mare. She's engaged to a thoroughbred.'

'Heaven help him,' said Blueprint, who didn't like that word.

'How is the Pony Club?' I asked hurriedly.

'Never been better,' said Angela sweetly. 'They are much more confident.'

'Since they had rides on Marge, I suppose,' said Blueprint.

'That's about it.' Angela ran off.

'And none of them has seen a fox cub killed,' I said to Blueprint as we went home.

'Who bit your leg?' said my mother.

'It's just a scratch. I'll put a plaster on it.' I went up to Mr Bull.

'Don't you feel frustrated, Mr Bull, with all the birds getting ready to migrate?'

'Thankful I'm not,' said Mr Bull. 'No place like home.'

'Even bullfinches spout platitudes.' The mouse was peering out of its hole.

'You eat his spare seed, don't insult him.' I said.

The mouse sat up and began washing itself. 'I hear quite a lot is planned for Saturday,' it said, brushing its whiskers forward with its paws.

I looked at the mouse suspiciously, but it was squinting down its nose like Tom Foley. 'What do you know about Saturday?' I said. The mouse whisked back down its hole without answering. I went out to visit Gertrude.

Gertrude was lying on her side, keeping one eye on her porkers, who were rooting and playing round the field.

'Gertrude,' I said, 'do you know what is going on?'

'Yes,' Gertrude grunted without moving.

'Mr Bull and the mouse know something too.'

'Anything may happen.' Gertrude was enigmatic.

'Gertrude, you are a pig,' I said.

'True.' Gertrude's side heaved with laughter. I went away and sat in the sunlight until I saw our mother walking up through the wood with Andrew.

'Hullo,' she said. 'Andrew says you got bitten, not scratched. All you children are such ready liars. Your father says it will stand you in very good stead in later life.'

'How cynical,' said James, joining us from the farm.

'Lawyers have to be.' My mother smiled. 'It's not exactly included in law exams but they learn it. Andrew has been buying maize. I gave him an advance.'

James and I looked innocently at my mother, and Blueprint gazed ahead of him, his tail curled round his feet and his long ears drooping.

'Ah, here come the Cardigans.' My mother looked at the two brothers, each carrying a rod and creel, walking towards us. 'Come and have a cup of tea and tell us about the fishing,' she said to them. The Cardigans hesitated, then followed us to the house.

Angela got back a little later from cubbing. The Master stopped his horse-box near our house and let down the ramp. Angela led Marge down into the lane.

'Had a good day?' I asked.

'Lost the whole pack. I've left the Whip to look for them.' The Master sounded angry. 'I shall sue those people,' he said.

'What for?' I asked.

'I'll get your father to think of something.'

Angela grinned and helped the Master shut the back of his horse-box. 'Thank you for a lovely day,' she said.

The Master drove off waving goodbye. Marge lowered her head and blew down her nose at Vice, who recoiled and spat. 'Now then, Marge,' said Angela. But Marge suddenly darted away down the lane with the reins dangling and her head nodding high in the air.

'She overdoes it,' said Angela.

'She will stop when she gets to Bodkin's field,' said Vice.

'I know.' Angela went after Marge.

'I wonder what her foal will be like when she has one,' I said.

'Not a patch on its mother. Marge is a natural.' Blueprint shifted his weight against my legs.

Mr Bull was sitting in his cage by the open window listening to the birds singing and chattering outside, and I sat beside him watching the swallows and martins wheel and soar. Several pigeons flew past and into the wood.

'What's happening?' I asked Mr Bull.

Mr Bull hopped a little closer to the window. 'Let me out,' he said. I let him out and watched him flip his wings and swoop down and disappear into the hedge between our garden and the road.

'Leave the cage door open. He's gathering news.' The mouse was looking out of its hole and all I could see was whiskers and bright eyes.

'Come out,' I said to the mouse.

'No thanks.' The mouse stayed where it was. 'There's a lot going to happen,' it said.

'Rubbish,' I said uneasily. 'Floss will lead the deer to safety and Tom will be there.'

'When?' asked the mouse, peeping out of its hole.

'There is going to be plenty of trouble for the Syndicate because our constable is on to the traps. Tom said to meet him tonight,' I said. 'I suppose Floss will lead the deer to the sets.'

'No she won't.' The mouse poked its nose slightly further from the hole so that I could see the pink transparency of its ears.

'I've word from the pigeons,' Mr Bull piped as he came back. 'The deer have gone to the house – Tom's house.'

'What's going on?' Angela said idly as she came in.

'Evacuation,' Mr Bull answered at once. 'And they are making up a party in the next village to go badger baiting at dawn, and Floss will have all the deer at Tom's place.'

'They can't dig badgers!' I exclaimed.

'They can,' said the mouse.

'But nobody ever goes there.' Angela looked put out. 'It's secret. It's a Nature Reserve.'

'Quick, Mr Bull, send a message to Tom,' I said.

'The pigeons have gone. It's all right.'

'Blueprint,' I said urgently, 'can you go and tell Floss. It's Floss the badgers trust. We must tell her. I'm going to find Andrew,' and I went downstairs with Blueprint, who trotted away towards the woods and the badgers. I ran through the wood to the pig field.

'Gertrude,' I called. Gertrude grunted. 'Gertrude, you have brains. We hear there is a party on to bait badgers.'

'Ah,' said Gertrude. 'Leave it to Tom. Tell Andrew.' She closed her eyes and lay where she was, a huge mass of pink pig.

'Gertrude!' I said. Gertrude heaved a sigh.

After a long search I found Andrew sitting by the river with Joker. I told him about the badger baiting and he went quite white with rage. Joker licked his face.

'Oh!' Andrew cried out. 'Does Gertrude know?'

'I told her but she just lies there doing nothing.'

'She's thinking,' said Andrew defensively.

'Looks more like sleeping to me,' I said. 'Blueprint has gone to tell the badgers. So have the pigeons.'

'Good,' said Andrew. 'Floss will help. What time are they going to do it?' Andrew appeared to be keeping his head.

'At dawn,' said a voice behind us. We turned round and saw that we were being observed by a sheep.

'How do you know?' Joker asked arrogantly.

'The postman's dog told me this morning before you were up. It's a dirty business.' The sheep wandered away nibbling at the short grass as it went. 'It's supposed to be very sporting.'

'Hullo,' said the Cardigans as they passed us. 'Very peaceful, isn't it?'

'Yes,' I said.

'Back to the hurly-burly of city life next week,' the elder Mr Cardigan remarked.

'We shall miss the peace and quiet,' said the other.

'Really?' said Andrew.

'Earning one's living is a cut-throat business,' said the younger Mr Cardigan. 'You children wouldn't believe what city life is like after the charms of the country.'

'Don't forget we have to meet Tom tonight,' said Andrew. 'We must go there with Joker and Blueprint anyway. Let's all meet when our parents have gone to bed and go up to Tom's house.' Andrew was watching the Cardigans walking up the river. 'Cut-throat business indeed.'

'No use fussing,' said Joker. 'I want my dinner.'

I left Andrew and took the short cut home through the pig field. As I passed Gertrude's little corrugated covered house I said goodbye curtly. Gertrude still lay on her side but her tiny brown eye with a flash of red in it caught mine. 'Go away. I'm thinking,' she said. 'Tom is a poet.' I remembered the dusty typewriter and laughed.

At home the telephone was ringing as I went to wash my hands. 'I'm in,' said my father and went to the telephone and said, 'Jones here'. There was a long crackle in the telephone and my father listened. Finally he said: 'Very well, I'll see about it tomorrow. By the way, did you know your keepers have been using traps? Illegal, you know. You will be summoned for that. Heavy fines.' He put down the receiver and smiled.

'What does he want?' asked my mother.

'He wants retribution of some kind,' said my father.

'It's queer,' said my mother. 'The place is alive with game.'

'Traps too,' said my father as we went in to supper.

'Expensive litigation?' I asked.

'Oh, yes.' My father accepted a bowl of soup from my mother.

'What about the traps?' said Angela who had come in.

'They will be fined,' said my father. 'Against the law now.'

'I hope they get fined a lot,' said Angela.

'I expect they will,' said my father. 'The Master of Foxhounds is on the bench.'

The telephone rang again and my father answered it. There was a long roar down the instrument and my father listened with an expression of growing amusement.

'Well, well,' he said. 'It's not illegal, old boy. Somebody being funny, I expect.'

'Not on speaking terms,' we heard from where we sat. My father came back to the table and finished eating his soup. 'It appears there was some sort of mix-up with the shoot and the hounds.'

We told him and he laughed again.

'It's curious that you and the Johnson boys were all there,' he said.

'What do you mean, curious?' said Angela.

'I mean what I say,' said my father, giving Blueprint a small bit of cheese.

My mother looked out across the garden. 'I do wish Vice would leave the birds in peace,' she said.

'I expect he is just curious,' I said.

'What time shall we go?' I asked Angela as we went to bed.

'One o'clock should do.' Angela got into bed with Blueprint.

'Can you wake me at half-past twelve?' I said to the mouse.

'All right,' said the mouse, taking the bit of cheese I had brought for it. 'Where is Vice?'

'Gone out,' I said. 'Who is doing this badger baiting?'

'I'll find out,' said the mouse, and took the cheese into its hole.

'Will he?' I asked Mr Bull as I gave him fresh water.

'Yes, he will ask his cousins in the garden.'

'Will they know?'

'Well, mice are a gossipy lot.'

I went to bed and slept until the mouse woke me up by walking over my face. I sneezed and went and woke Angela. We dressed and crept downstairs with Blueprint and went out of the house. 'Party from the next village baiting,' squeaked the mouse.

Vice joined us, and as quickly as we could we walked

down to the Johnsons' bridge. Andrew and James were waiting for us with Joker. None of us said anything as we set off through the wood towards Tom's house.

An owl hooted twice in the wood and the two dogs stopped and listened.

'Fancy that,' said Vice.

'What did he say?' asked Andrew.

'Good luck and goodbye. Queer.'

We made our way to the hidden clearing. The house was grey, dark and silent, showing no sign of life. Vice led the way, on silent paws, followed rather furtively by the dogs.

'Come on,' said Andrew. But we all stood stock still and I reached for Angela's hand. Shapes were dotted about the clearing, shapes which disappeared silently into the wood or stood staring at us with great eyes.

'Deer,' said Andrew, letting out his breath with a sigh. 'It's the deer.'

'Only some of them.' Tom had come to the door of the house and stood in the darkness watching us.

'Oh, Tom!' James's voice was full of relief. 'Oh, Tom!'

'I've distributed the greater part of the deer among the Forestry lands. Only the larger stags are here.'

'What about the badgers?' James asked.

'They will be here presently.'

'How lovely,' said Andrew.

'Empty sets.' Tom chuckled.

'I asked the mouse to find out who they were,' I said.

'I know,' said Blueprint. 'Three men from the further village, the postman and the boy from the garage.'

'Five,' I said. 'They will get cold waiting.'

'Come in.' Tom led the way into the house. He lit no lamp

and everything looked strange in the moonlight. We kept close together. 'We must wait for the badgers.' Tom led us into the strange room with the big bed in it. He lay down on the bed and we all sat on the floor with Joker, Blueprint and Vice.

'It's promising, very promising.' Tom laughed an almost silent laugh. 'In fact, when people go to kill their fellow creatures they may get quite worried. Seals are highly intelligent. And Vice's idea about the partridges and pheasants is already catching on all over the country.'

'That's wonderful,' I said.

'The foxes and hounds have got organised as well,' Tom murmured. 'Of course there will be casualties, as no one can stop the fox's natural habits, any more than ours.'

'But hunting is going to get a boost,' said Angela. 'Hounds, horses and people are going to enjoy themselves tremendously.'

'Yes, I think they will,' said Tom.

'The Emperor has no clothes,' I said.

'Yes, but who is going to point that out? No one.'

'The otters, in spite of being so unsociable, are spreading the news as well, and the deer have undertaken to move off the moors every hunting day.'

'How will they know when it's a hunting day?' said James.

'We will send news by the birds.'

'Here comes Floss.' Joker spoke with his ears pricked and nose up.

We went to the window and looked out. Floss trotted into the clearing, her tail carried high and bushy, her pointed ears pricked and her bright white and brown markings showing clear in the moonlight. Behind her seemed to drift shadows which we only recognised as badgers when they ambled through a shaft of moonshine which showed up their heavily marked faces. We left the house and Floss came up to Tom, wagging her tail and her whole hind quarters, her ears lowered and her bared teeth grinning in the moonlight. Tom picked her up and held her against his chest while she licked his face.

'My darling,' said Tom.

'The keepers are joining in the badger dig.' Floss spoke in her usual whining voice.

'Are they indeed?'

'All the men are gathered about three, so that they can be at the sets at dawn.' A badger spoke from among the trees.

Tom stood thinking, and then we heard him murmur: 'Four children, three dogs, one cat and one man.' Floss, still in Tom's arms, put her nose up to his ear. Tom listened and laughed. 'Come on,' he said. 'Out into the clearing.'

We gathered in a group round Tom, who stood with Floss in his arms, looking round him. I could feel the ground cold under my feet and looked up at the moon. All round us we could see deer with their nervous ears cocked, watching with wide eyes. The badgers walked ponderously but silently up to Tom, paying no attention to us.

'They are short-sighted, almost blind.' Tom felt in his pockets for scraps which he gave them.

Several foxes began playing in the moonlight and Joker and Blueprint peered at them eagerly, then suddenly, as though unleashed, made a dash in pursuit and the foxes and dogs careered away in a hunt through the wood.

'No!' I exclaimed. 'They can't.'

'It is their nature so to do.' Tom quoted some poet we had never read. 'They won't catch them and they will go home. Listen.'

We heard the crashing approach of a large animal and presently Gertrude came waddling into the clearing and walked up to Tom, pushing her way through the other animals until she rubbed herself against Tom's legs. Tom, holding Floss, whose ears were pricked towards the distant hunt after the foxes, bent down and listened to something Gertrude was saying to him.

'Very well.' Tom smiled ruefully. Gertrude turned and left the clearing as noisily as she had come. As she went, the deer and badgers disappeared silently among the trees.

'Gertrude always knows best.' Tom stroked Floss, who licked his face. 'Gertrude is a thinker. Time you all went home, isn't it?'

We felt dismissed and, saying a subdued goodnight, we left the clearing as Tom went into his house with Floss, shutting the door behind him.

'The dogs behaved outrageously,' Angela said angrily.

'Quite naturally and harmlessly.' Andrew tossed the sentence over his shoulder rather crushingly.

When we reached the Johnsons' farm Joker barked and came bounding out to meet the boys, leaping up at them and wagging his tail.

'Where have you been?' Mr Johnson called to them. 'Give Joker a rub down, Andrew, he's been out hunting.'

'Sheep?' asked James in a voice which verged on the impertinent.

'Of course not. A fox, I expect, coming over our land. No harm done,' Mr Johnson's cheerful voice answered.

Angela and I cut across the pig field towards our house and as we passed Gertrude's hut I flashed my torch, catching her tiny red eye which gleamed like a ruby. 'You are a fraud,' I said to her. Gertrude grunted sleepily.

'Silence is golden,' she said.

'Nobody could call you silent,' Angela said from behind me.

'There's silence and speech.' Gertrude did not bother to move. 'We get on very well without your kind of speech.'

'But you understand us,' I said.

'Oh yes, but it's better to leave you guessing. We've decided.'

'Cheek,' said Angela, pulling me away. 'Absolute cheek. They are going to leave us out again.'

'It will save them a lot of trouble,' I said as we hurried home along the river path.

'It was a sort of ultimatum she made.' Angela was resentful. 'Do you suppose it will apply to them all?'

'We'll soon see,' I said and then stopped dead and pointed.

In a deep pool the otters were playing, the young ones chasing each other through the water and up on to rocks with incredible agility. On the bank their parents watched, making an occasional dive, tweaking one of their offspring under water. We stood watching entranced until the father otter reared himself up on his hind legs on the bank and stared at us. There was just enough light to see his bright beady eyes and twitching whiskers. He gave us a long appraising look then made a signal and slid silently into the water. There were one or two unusual swirls and eddies and then no noise except the noise of the river.

When we reached home my mother exclaimed: 'Really, girls, you must not stay out so late!'

'There is always a first time,' said my father, who stood at the top of the stairs in his pyjamas.

'And a last.' Angela took the full brunt of Blueprint's greeting as he hurled himself on to her chest and, overbalancing, sat down.

'Go to bed,' said my mother.

Upstairs, as Angela and Blueprint got into bed, I watched the mouse scuttle away into the hole by the electric light socket. I took the cover off Mr Bull's cage and gave him some hempseed which he took from between my fingers and crushed between his strong snippers.

'You started all this,' I said, looking into his large brown eyes. 'We shall always know that you can speak if you want to: that you can all of you speak but won't: that you can all understand us but we can't understand you. I suppose you are afraid of getting vulgarised and put on the movies? I suppose you want to keep the upper hand?'

Mr Bull did not answer but closed his eyes, pulling up one sticklike leg among his stomach feathers.

I put the cover back on his cage and got into bed with Vice, who was paying me an unusual visit as he normally preferred to sleep with Angela.

'Budge up,' I said to Vice, who was curled into a tight ball in the middle of the bed. 'You heard me.'

Vice yawned and stretched out a long foreleg, pricking me through the blankets with his claws. I laughed and made myself as comfortable as I could, listening sleepily to Vice purring and later having small dreams in which he made tiny mewing noises.

'Oh, do look!' exclaimed my mother at breakfast as she read the paper. 'Poems by Thomas Foley to be published by Cardigan and Cardigan. Can they be ours?'

'Yes. Couple of intellectuals,' said my father, plunging his knife into the marmalade. 'Poetry never makes money. I do though.'

'Litigation?' enquired my mother.

'Yes.' My father looked rather pleased with himself. 'The Cardigans have a sense of humour though.' He opened one of his letters and read it while we all watched him, especially Blueprint who was hoping for some scraps. 'They have reserved the fishing for next year and sent a cheque. Rather a nice way to put us at our ease since they caught no fish. They say it is to preserve the river for the otters.'

'There are no otters,' said my mother mechanically.

'No,' said my father, 'maybe not. Johnson says there are none.'

'Is Thomas Foley Tom Foley?' I asked.

'Of course. Didn't you know?' My father laughed and Angela and I looked at each other in outraged surprise.

'Another thing none of you know, as you were watching television' – my father grinned at my mother – 'and you girls were out doing God knows what, is that there was quite a battle last night in the village pub. The police were called in.'

'What about?' I asked.

'Well, I was having a quiet drink with Johnson and the Cardigans to say goodbye to them when a row blew up between the gamekeepers and the Huntsman and Whip. They started abusing each other because each thinks the other is to blame because there are no foxes or partridges about this year. They came to blows. Quite a battle.'

'I wish I had been with you,' said my mother. 'I am handy with an umbrella.'

'Johnson and the landlord put them all out in the street and they fought there.' My father answered Blueprint's gaze and gave him a rind of bacon. 'It wasn't fun,' my father went on. 'Several people got hurt. I never like to see people like that; it was ugly. Luckily the police came along. We shall have quite a case on our hands.'

'I thought you hated notoriety,' said my mother. 'You will get it, as the Master of Hounds is on the Bench and so is the Master of Otter Hounds.'

'I think it may go further than that. He's giving up otter hunting and like all converts is swinging the other way. He wants the protection of *all* Wild Life. We will get the girls educated yet. If I know these chaps we'll have a High Court case. Reporters prowling round and so on.'

'Oh, they will disturb the birds!' my mother cried angrily.

I went upstairs and put Mr Bull's cage by my window and sat down and told him the news my father had brought.

'Now you broadcast it,' I said when I had finished telling him and gave him some hempseed. Without haste Mr Bull crunched the seed and then, puffing himself up, began to pipe loudly, and in the garden, though the nesting season was long over, the birds answered him in chorus.

'What's he on about?' Angela came into the room with Blueprint.

'At a guess I should say he is telling them we are worse than they are,' I said. 'But from now on we must guess what's going on and tell them, mustn't we?'

'Floss will laugh,' said Angela, 'and Marge.'

❧ The Sixth Seal ❧

And I beheld when he had opened the sixth seal, and, lo, there was a great earthquake; and the sun became black as sackcloth of hair, and the moon became as blood.

Revelation vi.12

To W.S.

'Mama?'

Sam's quiet voice, which he'd affected since he was at Oxford, murmured in her ear.

'Oh, hullo darling, where are you?'

'In London with John Kelly.'

'Coming home?'

'Well, not immediately. We're going to Germany for a trip.'

'What fun for you. Whereabouts?'

'Just to look. You know it's all this pink snow and green stuff we want to see. Then we want to come home. Can I bring John?'

'Of course you can. Give him my love. When will you be back?'

'We don't know, but I'll telephone. We are motoring.'

Another affectation.

'Enjoy yourselves. Have you got enough money?'

'Yes, thank you. Goodbye Mama.'

'Goodbye, darling. Goodbye.'

Click. A dead line. How lonely she felt. John, Germany, coloured snow in July. Lonely sterile telephone. She banged down the receiver.

'Mum? Mum? Where are you?'

'Here, darling. Here, by the telephone.'

'Who was it?'

'Sam.'

'Is he coming home?'

'Presently. He's just going to Germany to look at that pink and green snow.'

'But it's in East Germany.'

'Oh.'

'Yes, it said near Dresden. That's East. How is he going to get there?'

'They get visas I think.'

'Paul, Paul, come on. It's nearly ready. Do buck up.'

'Okay. 'Bye, Mum.' Paul tore off to join the voice in the garden, leaving all the doors open as he ran.

Lonely. Silly. She had the two boys. Thirteen is a nice age she thought to herself as she laid tea on a tray. Nice to be thirteen and innocent. Sam was nineteen: John twenty-two and American.

The dogs followed her as she carried the tray up the garden to the extraordinary encampment the children had made. Her back ached.

'Mum, we can sleep here tonight, can't we?' Pleading.

'If you promise to come in if it rains.'

'We will. The rain would make an awful noise on the corrugated iron.'

'Pink snow wouldn't.'

'Stupid, it won't fall here, it's in Germany.'

'Blue then.'

'No snow. It's warm.'

'Oh, well.' Henry shrugged. 'England's dull.'

Henry looked so like Paul; dressed alike, hair alike, altogether the same colouring. Henry had done all the work of the camp, laying corrugated iron sheets found round about the farm across the brick-sided pond, which never had held water even when it was just built in the early nineteen hundreds as a small lily pond of all things. Dry it had always been, drier than the whole garden. Muriel looked with amusement at the iron covering, the mattresses and sleeping bags ready laid for the night.

'Mrs Wake, won't you join us?' Henry had a courteous old-fashioned way of speaking which he had picked out of some book. Muriel wondered which, as his mode of speech varied from month to month.

'Thank you very much, but I think not.' Muriel could see Paul's look of relief. He wanted his friend to himself. 'You see I have the dogs and cat sleeping with me. It would make rather a crowd.'

Paul said, 'Oh, couldn't they come?'

'Well, I might snore and keep you awake.'

'Henry snores. He sleeps on his back with his mouth open.'

Henry laughed. 'Let's have tea.'

They ate sitting by the camp and looking down over the moors to the valleys beyond.

'Pink snow.' Paul was jealous. 'How soon will we be able to travel alone – just to ring you up and say we are going?'

'Not long – about sixteen. That's when Sam started travelling on his own.'

'Where shall we go to first?' said Henry. He left big decisions to Paul sometimes.

'To wherever it's snowing or doing something out of context.'

Out of context, thought Muriel, pouring out tea and handing round buns. Where did that come from?

'Think of the floods in China.'

'Dreamy.'

'Those earthquakes in Africa.'

'Super.'

'Those pestilences in America.'

'Fab.'

'Plagues of Egypt,' said Muriel lightly. 'Listen to the Abbey bells. It must be a south-west wind.'

'Yes.' The two boys munched and held out their mugs for more tea.

'Look, Peg is dribbling.'

'Give her a bun.'

Peg ate daintily with an apologetic look at Muriel.

'When are her puppies due?'

'Oh, any day now.'

'And Charlie's kittens? I hope they have moustaches too.'

'Quite soon by the look of her.'

Muriel gathered up the tea things and sat for a moment looking down at the house, a grey stone hollow E, with the sun on it; the centre to live in, the east wing barns and lofts and stables, and the west wing garages with more lofts above them. Too large really, she thought, as she idly watched Charlie disappear up the steps into one of the lofts above the stable.

'She's made her nest below ground in the cellar,' said Paul, following her eyes.

'Well, so long as they aren't all born in my bed. Peg has her eyes on that.' Muriel picked up the tray and carried it back to the house, hearing an argument break out between the two boys as she went. The house was quiet. She could hear a mouse in the wainscot, and the clocks. She washed up.

'Tidy, tidy, so tidy, oh God.' She wandered from room to room, 'It could have been heaven,' she muttered. 'Self-pity,' she said aloud, picking up a photograph of a man, the man she had loved, Paul's father, and putting it on the log fire which burnt winter and summer in the drawing-room. 'If you are dead I'd rather not see you.'

Sam had given her no address. It was stupid not to have asked him. She wandered back through the hall and picked up a pile of letters, the morning's post which she had not bothered to look at. 'Heavens, what a lot of bills.' Just like Julian to put in oil-fired central heating and get enough oil for three years stored up here, and coal too, logs and coke for the Aga and oil for the electric plant. 'You never know,' he had said, and Muriel agreed one did not. He was killed three months ago now, she thought. Mustn't think of it.

The telephone again. 'Oh, hullo, Susan.'

'We are just leaving London, darling. Is Henry all right?'

'Oh yes.'

'Not being a nuisance?'

'You know I adore having him.'

Susan talked on about people, plays, films, clothes she had bought, Spain where she was going. Muriel hardly heard or listened.

'Yes, darling, yes, I'll see he gets to bed early. Yes, of course, not overdo things. Treat him as my own. Goodbye, Susan, have a good time, goodbye.'

Muriel went back towards the kitchen thinking it would be nice to have supper there, then watch the news on TV and that serial she liked, silly and unrealistic as it was, then an early bed with lots of pills to bring sleep so that she would not hear the shriek of brakes then the silence which underlay every waking moment.

She went across to the farm to fetch eggs and cream from Mrs Perryman who was preparing a colossal meal for her husband and son to eat after milking. She listened to the account of the birth of three new calves the night before, two heifers and a little bull. She enquired after the family, the hens, the sheep, the lambs, the ponies, the expected illegitimate babies in the village five miles away, and then, followed by Peg whose extended stomach swung rhythmically as she walked, she went back to the house and switched on the news and sat watching.

The announcer gave a lurid account of the road accidents on the A30 and A38: the traffic at a standstill for five hours on the Exeter by-pass; three more bank robberies in the City of London; the birth of triplets to a lady in Camborne; the unsuccessful search for the missing yachtsman off the north Devon coast; the weather forecast. 'Sunny and glorious, ever victorious,' muttered Muriel.

'More pinkish-red-snow is reported from East Germany and our reporter from West Germany says there are reports of heavy falls of green snow in the Bavarian Alps. From Stockholm there are unconfirmed reports of black snow in Finland and Russia . . . ' Muriel switched off. Disasters, she thought, but what about me? She went to the telephone and dialled the Abbey.

'Can I speak to Father Richard?'

A distant sighing voice said, 'Father Richard has taken the novices potholing. Can I give a message? It's Mrs Wake isn't it?'

'No, thank you. I'll try later.' I can't tell him I'm in a state of despair very well. Muriel laughed in the empty house.

'Mum! Mum! When is supper?'

'As soon as I can get it.'

'Come on, Henry, it's now. Then we can see Whirligig before we settle down.'

The children helped her with supper than sat rapt (watching a futuristic film of extreme violence) before disappearing in the dusk to their camp. Muriel let Peg out for a run, visited the camp and shouted, 'Are you all right?'

'Yes, it's wonderful. Cover us over will you, Mum?'

Muriel covered the last gap between the corrugated sheets with a board, called out goodnight and went back to the house. As she went in the stout figure of Charlie joined her from under a bush and together with the dog and cat she went up to her room.

Pills. Three perhaps. Muriel swallowed three. She undressed, put on her nightdress and got into bed. The dog and the cat settled themselves on the bed with her, so arranging themselves that either she had to lie curved like the letter S, or flat on her back with her legs apart. She listened to the noises of the night; the sheep on the moor, the ponies and cattle giving an occasional neigh or low, the owls from the barn crying as they set about their night's work.

Muriel sat up suddenly. 'What the hell does he want to go potholing for when I want spiritual advice?' She grabbed the telephone by the bed and heard it ringing unanswered for a long time in the hall by those ugly parlours. 'No answer. Of course, it's after Compline, they can't speak.' Muriel lay down and heard the clatter of horses' hooves and a man's Devonshire voice calling urgently. A woman's voice answered and, sleepily, she thought she heard Paul's and Henry's unbroken piping joining in.

'Curse it!' Muriel sat up and switched the radio on. Yehudi Menuhin was playing his violin, wailing, consoling, demanding. Suddenly he was interrupted. 'This is a News Flash. There has been a heavy fall of black snow in the mountains of Scotland and our correspondent from our northern studio reports yellow and green snowfalls in parts of Northumberland and Durham with heavy drifting. There are gale warnings all round the coast of England, Scotland and the Irish Channel.' Muriel switched off. 'Neopolitan ices – quite mad.' She curled up, taking sudden advantage of Peg changing position, and slept.

'If your mother heard that would she worry?' Henry propped up on an elbow, tried to see Paul in the dark. Between them was a small transistor radio.

'I expect she's asleep. There was no light in her window when we got back.'

'Do you think the animals have gone mad?'

'I can't think. Anyway we shut the ponies in and they can't run off and Mr Perryman has shut in those three cows and their calves and those five sheep with their lambs. He couldn't round up any others.'

'Perhaps he will in the morning.'

'Well, they've all gone to bed now. Lights out in the farm.'

'I wish your mother was here with us.'

'She's got enough worries.'

'I forgot.'

'My father killed – bills, bills, bills, no money. I don't think Sam ought to have gone off just like that. She was expecting him tomorrow.'

'Grown-ups are odd.'

'Not really. D'you know I found out a lot by reading her letters?'

'Paul!'

'Don't pretend to be shocked. I bet you read all your family's.'

'They lock them up usually.'

'There you are. You would if you could.'

Henry giggled. 'I listen outside doors.'

'Everyone does that.'

'One has to keep abreast. It's like not being told about sex and birth control.'

'Oh, I know all that but it's frightfully dull.'

'Well, all their plans, and "don't let's tell the children until we've made up our minds": that sort of stuff.'

'I can't hear anything now.'

'Let's listen.'

The two boys listened.

'Oh blast!'

'What's that?'

'Not very interesting. I'll tell you some time. Blow your nose and then you won't snuffle and we might hear something.' Henry blew. They listened.

'Absolutely nothing, and it said gales. Not even a breeze.'

'Paul.'

'Yes.'

'I'm frightened.' There was a long pause. Then Paul whispered, 'So am I.'

'What shall we do?'

'I'm going to put on a jersey.' They both put on jerseys and lay down again. The jerseys were prickly and the night very silent. Paul struggled out of his sleeping bag and stood up. The brick-sided pit was a good twelve feet deep and up one side they had a ladder. Without a word to Paul, Henry began tiptoeing up the ladder. Paul followed and held his breath while Henry cautiously slid open the corrugated iron trap door. They climbed out and stood listening. Not a sound. Not a breath of air.

'Damn all,' said Henry.

'Damn all,' said Paul.

'I'm going to see if Mrs Wake is all right.'

'I'm coming. I'm just as frightened as you.' They crept down the garden to the house and slipped in at the back door. Warmth from the Aga in the kitchen and the sound of Chap's tail wagging gently in greeting.

'Does he always sleep here?'

'Yes. He likes it.'

Both boys jumped as the cuckoo clock began to strike midnight, echoed by the Abbey bells in the distance.

'Will she be furious?'

'No, she's too unhappy.'

Chap got up and followed as the two boys crept up stairs. Paul opened his mother's door. 'Mum.'

From deep sleep Muriel came up slowly. She heard the shriek of brakes and silence, then her son's voice. 'Yes, darling? I was asleep.'

'Mum we're frightened.'

'Oh dear.'

'Could you come to the pit, Mrs Wake? And bring Charlie and Peg. Chap is here.'

Muriel switched on her bedside light. 'Okay,' she said matter-of-factly. 'Lead on.' Henry led.

Chap and Charlie got down the ladder by themselves. Peg made rather a fuss though appearing anxious to get down. Muriel and the animals settled on the mattress between the two boys.

'All the Perrymans' animals have run away.'

'So that's what I heard.'

'All except our ponies. Henry and I caught them and a few cows and sheep. It said snow was falling in England.'

'Yes, I heard it too, and Yehudi Menuhin.'

'Culture! Listen, planes.'

'Yes, going fast. It's the night run to Africa.'

'Mum.'

'Yes?'

'Listen to Henry snoring.'

'I'll come closer. Father Richard went potholing.'

'Crackers!'

'Let's sleep.'

'I can't.'

'Why?'

'My jersey tickles.'

'Take the damn thing off, it's as hot as the Black Hole of Calcutta now we're all down here.'

'Mum.'

'Let's talk a bit. I don't feel sleepy.'

'What about?'

'There are some more planes. Shall I switch on the radio? We might hear something.'

'We'd wake Henry.'

'Not Henry. There's Radio Albatross about now.'

'That's why you're always so hard to wake in the morning.'

'Shall I?'

'All right, but quietly. My watch says it's after one o'clock.'

'Listen.'

Radio Albatross said, 'If your mother seems worried and cross give her Super-white Everdry – washes whiter than snow, whiter than white – '

'Snow's green and pink now.'

'Whiter than the whites of a baby's eyes.'

Paul made a slight retching sound.

'And now the News. Our latest information is that all Europe is blanketed in snow, not only pink and green as previously reported, but in many varying colours. The resorts in the Alps are already overwhelmed with telephone calls for hotel bookings by winter sports enthusiasts. The floods in China appear to be unabated and the earthquakes in India, the Far East and the Middle East are continuing. The plague in America – '

'Plague!'

' – is spreading from the East to the West Coast and is reported as far north as Alaska and as far south as Mexico City. We have no further news of missing shipping.'

'No news!'

The news died away. Muriel fiddled with the controls of the small transistor but no more came. Paul was asleep. Henry snored in the dark. The three animals fitted themselves snugly to the curve of the human bodies. Charlie snarled under her breath. Peg sighed as her unborn puppies moved in her belly. Muriel felt, though she could not see, that Chap had his ears pricked. She slept.

Henry woke and in the twilight of the pit was aware of two things: an overwhelming desire to go to the lavatory and a glaring expression in the cat's eyes. She hissed at him.

'Puss, puss, Charlie.' Another hiss. Her whiskers bristled, her back was up, her white moustache seemed to flare at him against her black coat and the dim background of the pit.

'Oh, I *see*.' Henry saw slight humping heaving movements against her flank. He climbed out of his bag and, keeping well away from the cat and the recumbent forms of Paul and

Muriel—both asleep with their mouths open, he was glad to see — pulled on a shirt and his jeans and climbed out of the pit. Chap whined. Henry held the trap-door open while the dog scrambled after him. Once up, he opened his flies and in companionship with the dog watered an azalea. Much relieved, he stood thoughtfully looking about him.

Gorgeously quiet, thought Henry. He turned a somer-sault from sheer joy. Nobody nags here. He was hungry. He peeped down into the pit. Everyone was asleep except Peg who opened one eye and then buried her nose deeper into a rug.

Henry danced down the path to the house and went in at the back door. The clock was striking and died unwound with a gasp. Henry pulled up the chains with the metal fir cones on them and set the pendulum swinging. It cuckooed twice more. 'Must be dawn. You hungry too?'

Henry and the dog went to the larder. 'Ah, bacon and eggs!' Henry helped himself and fetched a frying-pan. The Aga! Hastily he riddled it and poured in fuel. He fried eggs and bacon and sat down to eat it out of the pan thinking of his mother. She'd have a fit, he thought happily. He scraped up the last of the egg and fat with a bit of bread and caught Chap's eye. 'Oh Lord!' In the larder he found dog meat and biscuits and watched while the dog ate. 'I bet Charlie needs something, and Peg.' Henry filled the bowl again with biscuit and meat, and filled another bowl with milk. Carefully he threaded his way in the sun to the pit.

'Still asleep. Gosh!'

Henry climbed down the ladder carefully with the bowl of dog food. Peg ate quietly, still lying down. Charlie glared.

'Oh, well —'

Henry climbed up the ladder again and fetched the milk. The cat drank ungratefully. 'Cats!'

Mrs Wake and Paul, the transistor between them, were snoring.

'Snubs!'

Henry went up the ladder again, replaced the trap-door and stood listening. Not a thing to be heard. He set off towards the farm. The farmhouse door was shut; he tried it, to find it locked. The Perrymans, he supposed, had gone off to round up their animals who had disappeared in that curious stampede last night. 'Oh well, they'll be back soon.'

Henry walked round the sheds to the silo pit. From the bottom of the pit three cows and three calves stared up at him, one cow in particular. The night before, he and Paul and the Perrymans' son had made a high wall of hay bales to keep them in, but they had no water. Henry remembered Mr Perryman saying, 'We'll let them get at the trough in the yard in the morning.'

'Forgotten I suppose.'

Henry dragged away the top bale and struggled with the others until he had made a narrow exit through which the cows and their calves pushed their way and rushed to the trough to drink deeply, then stared at him sighing, with water running out of their mouths as their calves nudged and jostled to get at their teats.

Henry remembered the sheep. 'Gosh, I need Paul's assistance.' He raced to the pit and whispered, 'Paul, wake up.'

Paul woke.

'The sheep.'

'The ponies.' Paul was struggling into his jeans.

'The cows are all right but the Perrymans must have forgotten them; they've gone out and locked the door.'

The boys ran together. The night before, so panic-stricken had been the sheep and lambs that they had fallen down the chute into the coal cellar. 'Let un be,' Perryman had said. 'They won't hurt. We'll get them out in the morning.' And he had slammed down the trap-door on them.

'They are there,' said Paul, 'but we need Mother.'

'Why?'

'Ever tried lifting one of these black-faced sheep alone? It takes a strong man.'

'I thought Mr Perryman beastly to leave them there.'

'Not really. They are quite safe and he was tired.'

'What about the ponies?'

'Let's look.' Paul led the way. 'You're very interested in animals suddenly. I thought all you Chelsea lot only liked them in their proper place and all that lark.'

'I like animals really. It's my family who don't. Besides a coal cellar can't be the proper place for sheep; even my town upbringing tells me that.'

'Sure.' Paul unbolted the top door of the first loose box and a delicate whinny greeted them. 'One is all right anyway, but do look at that.'

Both boys stared at a heap of bay horsehair lying in the rough shape of a horse, mane hair then long tail hairs.

'Christ!'

'Let's look at the others.'

In all six loose boxes the same pattern was repeated with variations: heaps of horse hair near the box doors and, standing looking at them, one or more ponies.

'How macabre. Let's let them out.' In all, five ponies came out where ten had been shut in. They hurried to the horse trough then stood in a group looking around them.

'Don't let them out of the yard yet. There's plenty of hay.'

Paul went back to the loose boxes. With the hair lay horseshoes, four to each heap of hair. He shut the doors.

'What about the hens? What could have made them all panic?' Henry, the boy from Chelsea who swore daily at cock-crow, remembered them. The boys walked, rather white-faced, to the barn where Mrs Perryman kept her large flock of free-ranging hens.

'Nothing but feathers,' whispered Paul. Then suddenly, 'Mummy, Mummy!' and he raced away from his friend, tore open the trap-door covering the pit, clambered down into it and gripped his sleeping mother.

'Mummy, Mummy, there's nothing but fur and feathers, fur and feathers, oh, oh,' he wept hysterically.

'Hi, what is all this?' Muriel surged up out of her deep sleep.

'Fur and feathers.'

'What?'

'It's true, Mrs Wake, at least almost true, and the Perrymans are out.'

Muriel got up, cramped, and Peg stood up beside her. 'Good heavens, Charlie has had her kittens and somebody's fed her.'

'Yes, I did,' said Henry. 'We found the cows and their calves and some of the ponies are alive but the others are gone. There are just heaps of fur and hair and horse-shoes left and the sheep we caught last night are in the coal cellar, that's why we came for you.'

'I'm coming. Help me with Peg.'

All three struggled to get the large bitch up the ladder. Muriel looked about her and up into the sky. Funny, she thought, no planes.

'Has the post come?'

'I don't know, but I've made up the Aga and fed Charlie and Peg and Chap.'

'Oh, thank you, Henry.' Muriel yawned.

'And wound up the clock and cooked myself breakfast. I hope you don't mind.'

'Splendid. Why should I? Where have the Perrymans gone, Paul?'

'To find their stock I suppose. They locked their door.'

'Let's look.'

Muriel, in her nightdress and slippers and Marks and Spencer dressing-gown, ran across the garden and up towards the farm. The boys showed her the cows with their calves and the five ponies, the heaps of feathers, the fur in the stables, the silent sheep standing with their lambs in the cellar, their yellow eyes blinking up at them.

'We'll have a game getting those out. I must put on some clothes.' In the house Muriel tore off her nightdress and put on jeans and a shirt.

'First the Perrymans,' she said. The farm door was locked. 'A ladder. Their window is open.'

'I'll go up.'

'No, Paul, I think I will. I'm quite spry.'

Muriel climbed the ladder and squeezed in by the Perrymans' bathroom window. 'Mrs Perryman? Mrs Perryman?' She opened the first bedroom door.

'Oh!'

On the pillow lay Mrs Perryman's red, too tightly home-permed hair, beside it Fred's dark straight hair; on each side of the bed false teeth in a glass of water on a small table.

Forcing herself, she shut the door and crossing the landing went into Abner's room. Here too the bedclothes were flat, the pillow dented, but just holding Abner's rather too long hair; at his feet a heap of rough, short, white hair. 'Nell.'

'Mum, can you find anyone?'

'No, I'm coming out.' Muriel climbed down the ladder again.

'Why didn't you come out by the door?'

'I didn't think.'

'Are they dead?'

'I suppose so.'

'They must be one thing or the other. Be logical,' said Henry rudely.

'It isn't logical. There's nothing there but their hair and false teeth.

Paul began to laugh wildly.

'Paul, you need your breakfast. The sheep must wait.'

They hurried to the house and Muriel, quick at the best of times, rushed breakfast on to the table.'

'Lunch really,' said Henry, as the clock struck.

'Yes, lunch.' Muriel drank coffee watching the boys eat. 'Now the sheep. We know they are alive.' They went up again to the farm.

'Jack is dead,' said Paul as they passed a ruffled heap of black and white hair beside a dog collar at the end of a chain tied to a barrel kennel.

Muriel forced herself up the ladder again and opened the door downstairs to the boys. 'Best get them out through the house.'

Half an hour later the sheep and their lambs were grazing in the orchard. Henry was covered in coal dust and Paul had a black eye. Muriel felt drained.

'Dial 999,' said Henry. Muriel went to the telephone.

'The line is dead. We'll have to walk down to Roberts and report it.'

'He has false teeth too, and Mrs Roberts.'

'Oh, Henry!'

'Well, we'd better be sensible about it, hadn't we?'

'Bags I break in.' Henry ran ahead, found a ladder, and by

the time Muriel and Paul reached the Roberts' cottage he was climbing in.

'Sleep with their windows shut,' said Paul.

Henry jabbed his elbow neatly at a pane of glass and, carefully sliding his small hand through the jagged hole, opened the window and climbed in.

Two minutes later he emerged quickly from the front door, shutting it behind him. 'Two lots of grey hair and two sets of false teeth.' Then he was sick. 'Sorry,' he said.

'We'll get used to it, won't we, Mum?'

Muriel looked at the boys bleakly. 'I think we should go to the village and report the telephone and see the police.'

'Yes.'

'All together in the Landrover and take the dogs.'

Before leaving the house they made a tour. Everything seemed as usual, the kitchen and larder, the dining-room, the large beautiful library lined with books from floor to ceiling.

'What colour are the curtains going to be?' asked Henry.

'White, very extravagant velvet.'

'Mourning colour in the East.'

'Yes.'

'Have you got the stuff?'

'Yes, and for all the chairs and sofas.'

'What colour?'

'Green and pink and red.'

'Same as the snow,' said Paul.

'Any yellow?' Henry loved colour.

'Well, just this little button chair.'

'Beautiful.'

'Yes. Come on.'

They looked in at the drawing-room. 'That must have been a mouse.' Soft, short, silky fur on the rug. Muriel looked away.

'We can Hoover it up. Does the electricity work?' Paul tried a switch and the lights lit up pale in the sunshine.

'That's something. And we have our own water.'

'Why?' said Henry.

'So far from any mains here. We have everything on our own.'

They climbed up the stairs and looked into all the bedrooms and bathrooms.

'Lots of mice,' said Henry.

'Oh, look, bats!' Paul pointed at a transparent outline near the window.

'They squeaked.'

'I like bats, their teeth are soft.'

Muriel tried a tap. The water ran normally. The tank in the hot cupboard was hot. 'We can all have baths when we get back.'

'I suppose we had better leave the door open in case anyone comes, and leave Charlie in charge.'

'Yes.'

'We shall meet anyone coming on the road; it ends here.'

They climbed into the Landrover and sat three abreast with the two dogs behind and drove quickly down the drive, past the Roberts's silent cottage, on to the road over the moor, which dipped after half a mile into the valley and led down to the village.

'No sheep, ponies or anything about,' said Paul. 'The Perrymans' stock must have run miles.'

The road led past the huge reservoir like a lake which drained off to supply the coastal towns.

'Stop a minute, Mum, by the moor gate.'

Muriel stopped at the gate which Paul held open for her, and she and Henry watched as he ran down to the dam and stood staring into the water. Presently he ran up the slope, shouting something which they could not hear.

'What?'

'Fish, masses of them, alive,' Paul gasped joyfully as he climbed in.

'Oh Happy Living Things!' exclaimed Henry.

'Culture!' Paul gave him a friendly jog and they all laughed as Muriel let in the clutch and they drove on down into the valley.

'Here's old Courtier's farm. Shall we just see if he's all right?'

'Yes. His telephone may be working. It often is when ours goes wrong.'

They stopped at the farm. The door was locked.

'I know where he keeps his key.' Paul felt under a stone. 'It's locked from the inside.'

'Oh.'

They looked at each other.

'You two look round the farm. I'll climb in,' said Muriel. The two boys went off to the yard and shippens, while Muriel waited before scrambling up a step ladder at the back of the house to squeeze in by a half-open window. Five minutes later she came out of the front door and met the boys.

'Nothing but fur, wool and feathers,' they said.

'Only hair,' said Muriel.

'No teeth?' asked Henry.

'He had his own.'

'All the better to bite you with.' Henry seemed to be feeling rather cheerful.

'What's that?' asked Muriel, looking at Paul's wrist. Paul held out his arm.

'The bull's nose-ring. D'you remember when he chased Mrs Perryman?'

'The telephone is dead in there too.' Muriel climbed crossly into the Landrover. 'Come on. I can't think why they are so slipshod about it.' They drove on.

'Nothing on the road,' said Paul.

'Never is much traffic.' Muriel braked violently as they rounded a blind corner. 'Old Bartlett's car in the ditch.' Paul jumped out and ran to look, peering in at the old car's side windows.

'Just teeth and a terrific smell of whisky,' he said when he climbed back into the Landrover.

Muriel squeezed past the wrecked car, scraping the wings of the Landrover, and drove on slowly without speaking.

As they came down into the village nobody spoke. Muriel parked the car in the square and looked up at the Church tower.

'Nearly four o'clock.'

'Nobody about.'

'No.'

'Where shall we go first?'

'The Post Office.'

'It's shut. I can see from here.'

'The Police.'

'Yes.'

They walked, with the dogs close on their heels, to Constable Halstead's house and banged on the door.

'No answer. Look.' Paul pointed at a heap of fur near the door. 'His cat. And I've seen several others.'

'And Foss was the name of his cat.'

'Shut up.'

'Let's try the telephone box.'

They walked back to the square and Muriel went into the box, taking money out of her pocket as she went.

'Annie loves George,' read Paul.

'Bugger off you,' read Henry.

'There's my mother looking green.'

'She is too.'

'No answer.' Muriel stepped out of the box. The boys were writing their names on the dusty glass panes with their forefingers.

'I don't think anyone will answer,' said Henry.

'Don't be absurd,' said Muriel.

'Well, there isn't anyone about here is there?'

'No.' Muriel looked round the village square. 'It isn't early closing is it?'

'Mum, you can't put it off.'

'No.'

'Well?'

The church clock struck four cheerfully but with dignity.

'I wonder how it's wound?'

'Why?'

'Well, it will run down.'

'Oh.'

'It lasts for a week. The sexton winds it on Sunday.'

'Why not Saturday?'

'I don't know. I'm hungry,' said Paul suddenly.

'So am I,' said Henry.

'We've brought nothing with us.' Muriel looked guilty.

'Let's help ourselves.' Henry suddenly smashed the fruit shop window and handed Paul a bunch of bananas. 'We had better load the Landrover,' he said.

Muriel looked curiously at the two boys.

'Dog and cat food,' said Paul. 'Mum starts all her lists with that. Then tea, coffee, sugar, soap, fruit, vegetables – except that we grow our own – meat, eggs – and we have our own eggs – '

'Not now,' said Henry.

'Okay then, eggs, butter, tinned fruit and so on and on and on until she gets to chemist and writes Disprin and s.pills. That's sleeping pills. Where shall we start?'

'That grocer.' Henry pointed.

'We don't go to that one. We go to the other one.'

'What does it matter now?'

'Nothing.'

'I must fill up with petrol,' said Muriel.

'The pumps will be locked,' said Henry. 'I'll come with you, Mrs Wake.'

'Thank you.' Muriel got into the Landrover.

'You start,' shouted Henry to Paul.

'Right.'

As Muriel drove out of the square to the garage she heard the sound of breaking glass.

'Here's the garage.'

'Nobody about.' Henry jumped down and looked round him. 'This will do.' He picked up a large spanner lying beside the pump and with great deftness smashed the lock off the nearest petrol pump. 'I'll fill her right up. There's a hand-pump.'

Muriel watched Henry filling the Landrover's tank with petrol, testing the oil and water and peering into the battery. 'Okay,' he said, wiping his hands on his behind. 'If you go back and help Paul I'll join you, Mrs Wake.'

'Ever courteous,' muttered Muriel, driving off.

In the square she found Paul surrounded by a vast heap of groceries. 'Ah, here you are, Mum. This is fun. We shan't get more than this lot in, allowing room for the dogs. Give us a hand.'

Muriel found herself hard at work loading boxes of dog food, cat food, tea and sugar, coffee, soap and an apparently endless stream of groceries.

'Have you made a list?' she asked.

'No, why?'

'We must pay.'

'Pay who? There's only Mr and Mrs Barnes' hair and teeth in the flat above the shop. I looked.'

'Dear God!'

'You're always telling me not to blaspheme. Listen!'

'A car.'

'It is. I swear it is. There *is* someone.'

Round the corner of the square rocked an Austin Mini, drawing up beside them.

'It's Henry!'

'I didn't know you could drive.'

'We Londoners – ' Henry got out of the Mini rather self-consciously. 'Let's load this too. I've filled her up.'

'It belongs to Mr Collins.'

'Well, he isn't here to say so.'

'You are too young to drive. You will get had up.'

'By whom?'

'Is there another for me?'

'Yes, several.'

'Come on then.' The boys raced off on foot. Muriel stood watching, feeling very tired.

'Curse it,' said Muriel. 'I need a drink.' She walked across to the Pig and Whistle, raised her elbow as she had seen

Henry do, smashed in a pane of glass in the door and reached in for the handle. Behind the bar she helped herself to a double Vat 69 and sat drinking it until she heard the sound of another car. Looking through the door she watched her son drive happily into the square and draw up behind the first Mini.

'That belongs to Mrs Carlisle,' she called.

The boys laughed and waved and then started loading the two small vans with tinned food. Presently they joined her.

'Drinking out of licensing hours,' said Paul complacently.

'Coke?' enquired Henry.

'Yes, please.'

'Before we leave I must wind the church clock.'

'I must see if the poor parson is all right.'

Henry shook his head gently. 'This is his.' He drew from his pocket a glass eye.

The wind rose to a gale as the three cars went back from the village on to the moor. They squeezed past the wrecked car, and Muriel admired the dexterity of the children's driving. Paul struggled to hold the moor gate open as his mother and Henry drove through, stopped and waited for him. Wind which had not existed that morning, or even at lunch, shrieked as it hurled itself up the valley. The moor gate fought to slam shut like a live thing, and Muriel drove Paul's Mini through for him as both boys held the gate open together. Driven by the wind came bunches of fleece, fur and feathers which stuck to their clothes. The lea of the tor gave a little shelter as they drove over the moor and up the drive. Muriel drove straight into the garage and got out and watched. The two children followed her in. All together they shut the heavy doors and ran to the house and stood gasping for breath.

'We must shut up the animals.'

Paul ran to the camp in the dried-up pond. All the corrugated iron sheets had been whipped away by the wind. Even in the sheltered bottom of the dry pond the sleeping bags and blankets were driven into a corner. Frantically he searched for Charlie and her kittens but found no sign. 'She must be here, she must,' he screamed, but she was not. He ran back to the house.

'Charlie is gone.'

'We must gather up the other animals; no time to lose.'

Leaning against the gale they held hands and walked slowly into the wind to the meadow where they had put the sheep. Chap crept under the gate but there was no need for his skill. No sooner was the gate a quarter open than the five sheep and their lambs, seeming to float on the gale, streamed past into the farmyard and into the shippen.

'Have they got water?'

'Yes.'

Muriel dragged the heavy door shut.

The cows and ponies were together by the gate and, as they watched, the weight of the animals pressing against it broke it down and the ponies, whinnying wildly, raced into the stables. Muriel and the two children fought the wind to get the doors shut on them, and then climbed over to fill buckets of water from the stable tap. Paul let hay down from the loft above and they turned without speaking to look for the cows. They found one calf penned by the wind against the yard wall, its mother, a huge Devon Brown, lowing beside it. Muriel and Paul dragged it protesting towards the silage pit where the remainder of the cows sheltered uneasily.

'If we build a wall of bales and fill the trough they'll be all right.' Paul's voice was carried away, but his mother and Henry understood.

The wind rose every minute and when they turned to get back to the house none of them could stand. They were penned against the yard wall. The fifty yards separating them from the house seemed enormous, a huge flood of railing wind. Muriel, her eyes filled with fear, looked at the two boys beaten against the wall. Suddenly Paul grinned. Inch by inch the dogs, flat on their bellies, were crawling across the yard, eyes half shut, snarling, their ears and tails streaming in the wind. Muriel and the children dropped on their stomachs and followed. Viciously the wind clawed at them, spitefully it filled their eyes and mouths with dust, but at what seemed long last they reached the back door porch and joined the dogs, crouching out of the wind. Muriel opened the door and they all rushed into the kitchen together, slamming, locking and bolting the door behind them.

'The windows.' Muriel could hear the gale leaping at the front of the house. They forced their exhausted bodies into action and scattered through the house, shutting windows, bolting them, nipping their fingers in their haste, moving from room to room, upstairs and down, until the air in the house was quiet behind the shutters. Standing at bay in the hall, their faces tear-streaked, their eyes full of grit, their clothes covered with sticky bits of wool and bramble, they listened.

'Charlie must have been blown away. Look at that.' Paul pointed at an angle through the library door and they watched through the window the great beech tree at the bottom of the garden heel over and crash like a capsizing frigate.

'She must have been blown miles.'

'Don't think of it. Come on, I'm going to get something to eat and then we can all have baths.'

'I couldn't eat.'

'Hot tea then.' Muriel boiled the kettle and made tea in the kitchen. They all drank.

'Thank you, Mum.' Paul was trying not to cry.

'Look at that!' Muriel stared out of the window which had grown dark.

'It's snowing or hailing.'

'The doors clapped to. The pane was blind with showers —'

Paul lashed out at Henry. 'Oh, shut up!'

'All right, sorry,' Henry muttered.

'Baths now,' said Muriel, 'and bed. It seems quite late.'

'Oh, just let me see the news.' Paul ran out of the room to the drawing-room where they kept the television set.

'No wonder it's dark. The snow is – yes, navy blue.'

'Henry.'

'Yes, Mrs Wake? Rather smart really.'

'Henry.'

'Yes?'

'Oh, nothing. Let's all have a bath.'

'Mummy, the television is dead.' Paul came back to the kitchen. 'But the lights work.'

'That's having our own plant.' Muriel switched the lights on and off in an irritated way.

'The refrigerator is working too. Listen to it humming.'

'Yes, it would. It runs off the plant. Try the telephone.'

Muriel tried it. 'Still dead.'

'Nobody could get to mend it in this gale.'

'No.'

'As for the television,' said Henry lightly, 'I don't suppose there is anyone left to broadcast.' He left the room.

Muriel and Paul stood looking at each other.

'Henry's parents,' said Paul flatly.

'We seem to be facing rather a lot of things at once,' said Muriel, looking out at the driving snow.

'Look, it's changing colour.'

'Yellow.'

'Getting dark too.'

Muriel absently wound up the cuckoo clock and made up the Aga, tipping the ashes into a large bucket. They walked upstairs together, followed by the dogs.

'I feel filthy.'

Muriel saw the dogs climb on to her bed and lie down sighing. They watched her undress, their noses on their paws. She opened her door and called down the passage to where the boys were undressing. 'Wash your heads.'

The roar of the wind outside and the sound of hail on the windows drowned her voice so she put on her dressing-gown and went to them. Paul was standing looking out of his bedroom window, and Henry was lying sunk in the bath with only his nose above water.

'Wash your heads.' She took a bottle of shampoo off the shelf.

'All those kittens too.'

'Stop it, Paul.'

'Four of them.'

'Stop it, Paul.'

Paul undressed and stepped into the bath companionably beside his friend.

'Lovely shiner you've got. Does it hurt?' They were all shouting to make themselves heard above the rage of the wind.

'No, I'm all right.'

Muriel wondered whether those were tears for Charlie or water from the sponge. She went back to her bathroom. In the bath her body felt beaten, scratched, bruised and empty. She forced herself to wash, wash her hair, and let the bath water out.

'Ugh, how filthy!' As she came back to her room Henry looked in.

'I'm going to get us all a hot drink,' he shouted and disappeared.

Muriel rubbed her hair with a towel and combed it through then stood, uncertainly, thinking of Henry.

The two boys arrived together with a tray. They wore pyjamas and were clean and neat.

'Ovaltine,' shouted Henry. He handed her a large glass.

'Sleeping pills' shouted Paul.

Muriel shouted, 'Thank you', but shook her head.

'What's that?'

Through the door left ajar by the boys slipped a very small black cat with a white moustache carrying a tiny blind kitten.

'Charlie!'

Paul spilt his Ovaltine.

Charlie jumped on the armchair where Muriel had flung her clothes, gave them a derisory kick and push, deposited the kitten and vanished. Three times they watched her return and each time she placed a kitten on the growing pile. Then she licked them all, arranged them neatly and deigned to drink some Ovaltine out of the top of Henry's glass. She blinked twice, then placed her chin on the faintly stirring heap of kittens and composed herself for sleep.

Henry looked at Paul. Paul looked away.

'Mrs Wake,' Henry shouted.

'Yes.'

'Mrs Wake, we feel it would be ungallant to leave you alone.'

'He means we are damn frightened,' shouted Paul.

Muriel laughed. The two boys slipped into bed, one on each side of her, the dogs shifted their positions, and Muriel switched off the light. Outside the wind hit the house with great whumps of air and the noise echoed down the chimneys.

'Harsh winds do shake – ' began Henry in a cheerful shout. 'Sleep I can get none for thinking of my dearie.' Henry turned suddenly towards Muriel and she took his hand. Beside her she could feel his body shaking with sobs. Her eyes filled with tears.

Paul switched on the bedside lamp. 'Let's all have a good cry,' he said, looking at his mother and friend, and tears began to spurt from his eyes.

'Handkerchiefs.' Muriel struggled out of the bed and snatched a box of paper handkerchiefs off her dressing table. They all three sat in a row in the bed and wept.

'Look at the animals,' sniffed Paul and his tears turned to laughter. Both dogs were staring at the three of them with amazement, while Charlie glared from her chair.

'Oh, I feel better.' Muriel mopped her eyes.

'I'm so hungry.' Paul wiped his tear-streaked face.

'We have none of us had a proper meal since it began.'

'The dogs and Charlie have.'

'They have more sense.'

'Come on.'

Muriel got up and led the boys down to the kitchen. The dogs followed patiently.

'Something hot,' said Muriel.

'Porridge,' said Paul.

'Why not? Everything is odd and porridge is easy.'

Muriel made porridge while Paul and Henry found sugar and opened a tin of Nestlé's milk. They sat down round the kitchen table to eat in silence.

'We shall have to milk the cows tomorrow.'

'I suppose so.'

'Gosh, we're *talking* not shouting.'

'So we are.'

All three listened. Outside the windows the wind was dying down, they could hear the cuckoo clock ticking and the grandfather clock in the hall chiming.

'What's the time?'

'A quarter to two.'

'Just about twenty-four hours since it started.' Henry looked at the clock. 'Open the shutters, Paul.'

They peered out of the window into the backyard.

'What piles of snow.'

Muriel opened the window a fraction. 'I must see if those poor beasts are all right.' She put on gumboots in the hall and took a torch from a chair where it was lying with a collection of letters, dog leads and a torn windcheater of Paul's.

'No, don't come,' she said to the two boys as she let herself out into the yard.

'Is she all right?'

'Oh yes, I think so. Quick, Henry, while she is out.'

'What?'

Henry followed Paul and watched him sweep the pile of letters off the chair, run into the library and snatch many more from the pigeon holes in the desk, seize a box of matches and set fire to the whole lot in the grate, cover them with sticks and nurse the fire alight until it caught enough to lay logs on.

'One thing less for her to worry about.'

'It smells good.'

'Apple wood.'

Outside in the snow Muriel went to the stables. The ponies blinked at her and one of them whinnied. The others were munching hay. The sheep in the shippen sprang to their feet and glared at her, their eyes green in the torchlight.

The cows seemed peaceful enough. Muriel turned back to the house, her feet sloshing now in the snow. All around her was the sound of running water; water running down drains and gullies, dripping off eaves, snow melting away as fast as it had come.

'Mum?'

'Yes.'

'Henry and I have made a fire.'

'How gorgeous.'

The smell of woodsmoke against the ticking clocks. The silence of the night. 'I honestly think we should sleep.'

'Okay.'

Paul stopped fiddling with the dead television set and followed his mother and Henry up the stairs.

'Still want to sleep with me?'

'Just for tonight.' Paul lay down in the bed and instantly fell asleep.

'You all right, Henry?'

'Mrs Wake, I hated my parents.'

'Henry!'

'It's marvellous really. I shall never see them again, like you and your bills.'

'What do you mean?'

'We burnt them all, you won't ever see them again, nor will I see my beastly father and quite vile mother.'

'Really, Henry —'

'Well, it's true, Mrs Wake.'

'The telephone is dead. It went click.'

'When?'

'When Susan rang off.'

'Ah.' Henry took her hand and held it. 'Go to sleep Mrs Wake.'

Paul and Muriel slept while Henry listened with the acute ear of a child to their breathing and the occasional sigh of a dog or sniff from the cat.

'But when night is on the hills, and the great voices roll in from the sea, by starlight and by dreamlight.'

Henry yawned and slept.

☙ 5 ❧

Paul woke first and wondered why his right elbow was sore. Remembering the day and night before, he lay very still and listened to the quiet. He wondered whether any of it had happened, wondered what Henry had done with the parson's glass eye, remembered the parson, a nice man, a retired naval chaplain. Paul smiled to himself. That eye. 'Not lost in some naval engagement but at an engagement party,' he could hear the parson's amused voice explaining. The sudden attack of a champagne cork, at his daughter's engagement party, resulting in the total loss of his eye. He hoped Henry had the eye safe; he must remember to ask him. Meanwhile he enjoyed the silence, the sound of clocks ticking, his mother and Henry breathing, and the bells in the distance striking.

'Tag rag merry derry, periwig and . . .'

Paul leant across his mother and poked Henry. Henry smiled broadly and finished, 'Hic hoc horum Gerritivo!'

'Wake up, Mum.'

'Well!' Muriel looked surprised and pleased. They all scrambled out of bed and dressed.

'Can you feed the animals while I get the breakfast?'

'Of course.'

Muriel flung open her windows to look at the blue summer morning. She frowned at the fallen beech tree and examined the view. She could see nothing move nor hear anything except the boys' high voices as they worked up in the yard. The view from her window was subtly changed. She looked closer, peering into the morning light, murmuring to herself, 'No sheep, no cattle, nothing moving.' Several tall trees besides the fallen beech were blown down, gates hung askew, and gaps which had not been there before showed in walls and hedges. Muriel dressed and went to the kitchen.

'Oh damn! No milk.' She picked up a jug and walked out into the yard. Paul saw her and called, 'Shall we let the sheep out?'

'Yes, they won't go very far. I'm going to try and milk a cow.'

'Try Muriel,' called Paul.

'Why Muriel?' asked Henry.

'Meant as a compliment,' said Paul. 'The Perrymans loved my mother.'

'Pity there are no eggs.'

'There may be a few laid in the barn. Let's look.'

Muriel found a bucket and approached her namesake firmly. A brief tussle ensued, but Muriel was victorious and succeeded in getting half a pail of milk from Muriel the cow.

'If we keep the calves in the cows won't go far.'

'True.'

Muriel went back to lay and cook the breakfast.

'Breakfast at lunchtime, breakfast at two in the morning, breakfast again, very nice.' Henry washed his hands and sat down to eat.

'What shall we do first?'

'Don't talk with your mouth full, Paul.'

'Okay, Mum.'

'The village again?' Henry seemed dubious.

'No, let's ride somewhere.' Paul looked eager.

'Why ride? We've got the Minis.'

'Yes, but trees will be down. If we ride we can see how far we can get.'

'That sounds sensible, let's do that. I'll wash up while you put the saddles on.'

Muriel listened to her oddly normal voice. The boys went out and she washed up. She picked up the telephone and wiggled it, listened and laid it back in its cradle, sighing.

'We'd better leave a note,' she said as the boys returned.

'Who for?' Henry looked at her.

'Well, just in case – ' Muriel's voice trailed away. The boys looked at each other with raised eyebrows as she wrote in pencil on a large sheet of paper – 'Gone out. Back Soon.' Weighing it down with the electric torch, she left it on the kitchen table.

'I'm leaving food for Charlie, and the window open,' said Henry.

'All right.' Muriel stood undecided.

'Come on, Mum.'

They mounted the ponies and rode slowly across the moor down into the valley in the bright sun.

'I think we must explore the village again.'

'Why?'

'Well, there must be someone . . .'

'As you please.' Paul shrugged.

'No moor gate,' said Henry. 'Blown away, and just look at the wood!'

The wind seemed to have cut swathes through the wood, but the trees had fallen in all directions, some uphill, some down.

'Must have been a whirlwind.'

'Mrs Wake.'

'Yes?'

'Very quiet, isn't it?'

'What do you mean?'

'Well, no planes, no helicopters, no traffic, nothing, only us.'

'Yes.'

They rode on down hill into the valley. Here and there a tree had fallen across the lane. The ponies either jumped over or the small party found a way round.

'We can bring the chain saw and clear the road.'

'Can you work it?' Muriel was doubtful.

'Oh yes, we know how.'

The village when they reached it looked wildly untidy: rubbish scattered in the streets, tiles strewn across the road and broken milk bottles from the stacks outside the dairy. Apart from the signs of the wind, the village was not changed in any way since their visit the day before.

'We should go separately and meet in an hour,' said Paul. 'Can I take Chap?'

'Yes, of course. Do you want Peg, Henry?'

'I think I would rather be alone, Mrs Wake.'

Muriel rode out of the village square to the council estate which was eerily quiet, empty cars, paper, fluff, cellophane, milk bottles, tins lying about the road, no sign of life from the houses. Her heart failed her. She rode back to the village where she could hear the boys' voices calling.

'Anybody there?'

'Only me.'

'Anybody there?'

'Only me.'

The echo threw back, 'There? There? There?'

Back in the square she found the boys together.

'It's too weird alone,' said Henry. 'There isn't anybody, Mrs Wake.'

'I'm going to ring the church bells,' said Paul suddenly. 'I've always wanted to ring out wild bells.'

'Ring out wild bells across the snow.'

'It's melted, stupid. Come on.'

The boys ran to the church, old, solid, beautiful, its clock with hands pointing to letters which spelt out, 'My dear mother', instead of numerals. Muriel walked across the churchyard to the vicarage, wondering how Henry had got in the day before. The back door swung on squeaking hinges. She went in. 'Anybody there?' As she searched the rooms, empty of life, she heard the bells begin to clang and clatter. Finding nothing, she went back to the church and in at the side door which was always open. At the foot of the tower, swinging on the bell ropes, she found the two boys. Muriel took a third rope and began to pull on it. Presently they stopped, breathless.

'Pouff! How far can these bells be heard, Mum?'

'It depends on the wind. Quite a long way I think. We hear the Abbey bells three miles across country.'

'We haven't heard the Abbey bells.'

'No. Oh dear!'

'We'd better leave a note here and ride over there and look.'

Muriel found the fly-leaf of a hymn book and wrote: 'We are alive at Brendon' and signed it 'Muriel Wake'. They took a pin from a notice which said: 'Choir Practice will be at 6.30 p.m. on Wednesday instead of 6 p.m.' in the Vicar's neat script and pinned the note to the outer door.

'How will they know how to find Brendon and know it's us?'

'It's marked on the AA map.'

'Like throwing a bottle overboard,' remarked Henry as he mounted his pony.

'Well, there's no post.'

'No, no nothing and no anybody.'

Muriel rode ahead not wanting to hear.

Across country to the Abbey was comparatively easy going. The gates were mostly blown down and the gaps made in the hedges convenient. They went carefully but steadily. She heard the boys talking ahead of her but her thoughts were far away. Sam. Where was Sam? And how queer, she thought, this morning she had woken for the first time from a dreamless sleep, no shriek of brakes, no silence. She had just woken to feel rested and peaceful, amused to hear the two boys talking across her as she lay dozing.

At the bottom of the valley, where the track joined the lane which led to the main road from Exeter to Plymouth, was a small pub, The Fisherman's Arms. The boys reined in their ponies and waited for Muriel.

'Shall we look?' Paul was already off his pony, handing the reins to Henry.

'We had better.' Muriel got off her pony and looked up at the quiet little country pub. 'About the only one I know which manages not to be folksy.' Julian's easy deep voice came into her mind from a long time ago. Three months perhaps?

The pub sat sleepy in the sunlight, its upper window half open, the sign of a leaping salmon hanging quite straight above the door which was closed. The boys went round into the backyard and came back carrying a ladder between them. Already, thought Muriel, we know better than to try the doors.

Henry climbed the ladder followed by Paul. Muriel waited, listening to the ponies breathing and the sound of the river across the field racing towards the sea. The boys looked out of a bedroom window together and waved.

'The usual,' said Henry.

'Oh.'

'Coming in a minute,' Paul called and vanished. Henry went on leaning out of the window, looking down at Muriel gravely.

'Got it all in a basket. Can you help?' Paul reappeared and the boys came down the ladder together carrying a large basket.

'What's that?' Muriel peered at the basket.

'Brandy, whisky, peanuts, crisps, olives and coke for us.'

'And an opener. You are practical.'

'We may find someone at the Abbey.' Paul did not sound hopeful.

'Yes, of course we will.'

Henry looked at Muriel and she looked away.

'Give me the basket and you ride on,' said Muriel.

The boys trotted ahead.

'That was a lapse.' Paul apologised for his mother to his friend.

'Oh, it's natural. It's a habit.'

'What's a habit?'

'Lying to children.'

'Yes.' Paul stroked his pony's neck. 'She hasn't lost hope. It's mortal sin. She tries to avoid them.'

'Faith, Hope and Charity and all that?'

'Yes.'

'What does she hope for at the Abbey?'

'She hopes to find the Abbey standing as it was last Sunday full of monks, and in particular she wants Father Richard.'

'Why?'

'To confess and get spiritual help and advice.'

'Confess what?'

'How should I know? But she was ringing up the Abbey the night before it happened. I heard when I slipped into the house to get those biscuits and she was asking for Father Richard. That means she wants advice, confession, et-cetera.'

'I wish I could get it.'

'Well, you aren't a Catholic like us, but old Father Richard would fix you up in a jiffy.'

'Old?'

'Not really. He is young. I meant old affectionately.'

'Oh. Not old.' Henry meditated. 'Paul, I feel great affection for your ma.'

'Good.'

'She was awfully funny when we all cried.'

'She can't help being funny. My father used to roar.'

'He was nice too. What is Sam like?'

'What *was* Sam like you should say. Now *you've* lapsed.'

'Yes. Sorry.'

The lane turned several hairpin bends and reached the main road.

'Heavens!'

For a mile in each direction a dual carriageway. All along it, as far as the boys could see, heavy lorries, vans, cars and all forms of transport had either run into each other or off the road and into the ditches, and the giant machines now rested silent. Muriel came up to the boys and gazed with them.

'All the night traffic,' she said. 'The police must have got those jams moving from the Exeter by-pass.'

'Nothing could get along it now.'

'Impossible. We shall be stuck in the lanes.'

Paul's face fell. 'I was so looking forward to racing in my Mini.'

'Mrs Carlisle's – '

'Yes, but – oh well, shall we look, Mum?'

'No, let's go back and get to the Abbey by the river path and the woods.' Muriel turned her pony's head and led the way.

'She didn't lapse that time.' Paul looked at his friend.

'No.'

'The woods are very quiet.'

'No birds.'

'And no birds sang,' Paul shouted suddenly at Henry.

'That's a ham one. It's the ones everyone doesn't know that count.'

'I only know the clichés.'

'I know. Come on, let's catch up with your mother and get to the bare ruined choirs.'

Muriel smiled when the two boys joined her and they trotted along the track through the wood.

'There's the tower.' All together, for no particular reason, they hurried their ponies into a canter and raced across the last field by the river to the Abbey.

'The clock is going – it's midday.'

'Then there should be the Angelus – listen.'

They got off their ponies and stood listening.

'Nothing,' said Paul. 'How do we get in? The great gates are locked at night.'

'Let's try them.' Henry rode up to the gates and shook them. 'Locked all right.'

'We can climb over quite easily.' They tied the ponies to the gate and climbed over.

'Quite easy really,' said Muriel, puffing. 'Let's try the doors.'

All the doors were locked. Muriel banged on the side door with her fist.

'No good, Mum. Let's make a tour.'

They began walking round the Abbey, calling out at intervals, 'Anybody there? Anybody there?' There was no answer. No jackdaws were startled from the tower, no swallows wheeled, no sparrows chattered, no starlings shone. They made the tour of the Church and Monastery and came back to where they had started.

'I'm going to look at the bees.' Paul raced across the Abbey lawns into an orchard. Muriel and Henry followed.

'No bees,' called Paul.

'It will be the same everywhere. Have a peanut, Mrs Wake.'

'Thank you.' Muriel accepted the peanuts and looked at Henry. He looked old.

'We'd better look at their farm.' Paul looked anxious.

'You look.' Henry sat down.

Paul looked undecided, then turned away from his mother and friend and walked away. They watched him cross two fields and reach the farm and saw him moving in and out among the buildings.

'Now he's lapsed,' said Henry.

'What do you mean?'

'Well, he won't and you won't believe what's under your noses. Nothing is left alive except us. You go on and on hoping.' Henry's voice rose to a scream. 'You two with your Faith, Hope and Charity. It's ridiculous.' Henry began to cry. 'I wish I had it.'

'I think you have.'

'It was taken away from me or never taught me.'

'Here's a handkerchief.'

'Thank you. I'm sorry, Mrs Wake.'

Paul rejoined them looking dejected. Neither his mother nor Henry asked him any questions.

'Let's go home.'

'I suppose so. We can't break in here, and if we did – ' Muriel looked away.

'Come on.'

Laboriously they climbed over the great gates and re-mounted their ponies.

'Let's go back past the quarry and home over the moor.'

'Very well.'

The track leading to the quarry led sharply uphill from the Abbey. 'It's a scandal really.'

'What's a scandal?'

'A scandal that they let these people go on quarrying into the hill, making it hideous and incidentally destroying the caves. They should have done something to stop them. They are so slow round here.' Muriel was talking to Henry, using an educative, explanatory tone of voice. 'If they are allowed to go on there will be no caves left. They are prehistoric and terribly interesting, natural caves enlarged and lived in, and they let them quarry away.'

Henry burst out laughing. '"They" and "them" aren't here any more. No more "they", no more "them", only "us".' Henry began to chant, 'No more Them, no more They, only Us,' to the tune of 'God Save the Queen'. Laughing, Paul joined in, and the boys broke into a canter up the track, singing at the top of their voices. Muriel followed, the basket full of loot from The Fisherman's Arms over her arm and the two dogs trotting by her. Peg looked rather too large for long expeditions and Muriel made a mental note that in future she must be left in the house until she had her puppies. When Chap stopped to sniff in the quarry at a lump of mud, and Muriel's pony shied, she nearly fell off. 'Steady,' she said to the pony, and then began to shriek. The mud was moving.

Muriel flung herself off her pony and ran towards the dog who was eagerly licking a man's face.

'Father Richard!'

'Oh, it's you, Mrs Wake. What are you doing here? Picnicking?'

'Potholing!' shouted Muriel furiously. 'You were potholing,' she accused.

'Yes, yes, we were. And I'm afraid brothers John and Peter are still in there.' Father Richard choked and spat. 'Sorry, Mrs Wake. It's the mud. There was a rock fall and we got lost.'

'Here, drink this.' Muriel, her hands shaking, uncorked a brandy flask.

'Oh, oh thank you, Mrs Wake. I was coming to get help. Father Abbot will be anxious — ' Father Richard sat up. 'That's much better, thank you. Do you always carry brandy like a St Bernard?'

'Father — '

'Yes?'

Muriel's voice was drowned by the clatter of hooves.

'Mum, what on earth?'

'Is it alive?' Henry approached cautiously.

'Very much alive.' Father Richard sounded tart.

'But nobody *is*.'

'I don't know what you are talking about, but brother John and brother Peter are in that cave and I must get help to get them out.'

'Alive?'

'Naturally.'

The boys looked at each other across Father Richard. Paul winked.

'Where are they?'

'Jammed in a crevice, a crack really. It's not the proper way out, but as I was telling your mother there was a fall of rock and we got lost and somehow by a miracle we found a way out. Now that's interesting. This way out must be quite a new way – quite a discovery.'

'Have an olive,' said Henry.

'Thank you. I'm afraid I'm spoiling your picnic, but could you, could one of you fetch help. You see they are in there and rather exhausted. It must be the day before yesterday – '

'How far in?' Paul spoke urgently.

'Not far, not far at all, but they got jammed. I am small, you see, so – '

'We'll get them. Come on Henry. Chap, quick! Will you tell him, Mum?'

'Yes.'

'Don't you think some of the stronger brothers – '

'No, Father. Here, have another swig and some peanuts.'

'Thank you.'

'Father, there are no other brothers, only us – '

'Only us?'

Sitting beside the exhausted little monk, Muriel told him all she knew. When she had finished he was silent for a long time.

'When we get brother John and brother Peter out, we must get to the Abbey.'

'We will help you.'

'Mum, Mum, got the brandy?' Paul came leaping down the quarry. 'We've got them out. We made them take off their clothes and squeeze.'

'Here.' Muriel handed Paul the flask. 'Are they hurt?'

'Oh, none of us is hurt.' Father Richard laughed. 'Here they come.'

Henry came down the slope of the quarry ahead of two tall young men smothered in mud from head to foot.

'Look you three get on to the ponies. We'll take you back. Can any of you ride?'

'Sort of.'

The children held the ponies while Muriel helped the three muddy men to mount and then, each leading a pony and supporting its rider, they wound their way down to the Abbey.

'And the earth shall be filled with the glory of God, As the waters cover the sea,' sang Henry.

'He was brought up an atheist,' said Muriel dryly to Father Richard.

During the long summer afternoon Muriel waited outside the Abbey. At intervals either Henry or Paul came out to see her.

'They have washed, changed and eaten.'

'We have gone all round the place with them.'

'They went potholing as a sort of treat. It's crazy.'

'Nobody else left. Just the usual.'

'We are all coming out to have tea on the grass with you.'

'A council, I think,' said the monk, sitting down beside her. 'I suggest that we all meet tomorrow. You have food and a few animals at Brendon. We have food here.'

'You should have half our animals,' interrupted Paul.

'That would be nice, but we only need a cow, if that.'

'You have two cows and their calves, and we will keep

the other. Tell you what, Henry and I can drive them over tomorrow.'

'Thank you. Then, Mrs Wake, we really should find out what is happening in Exeter and Plymouth, or go to meet the search parties from those centres.'

'Do you think there will be search parties?'

'Surely.'

'We don't,' said Henry. 'There have been no planes or helicopters and nothing can get along the roads. You and your two novices are just freaks.'

The monks laughed.

'I didn't mean to be rude.'

'I know. But I still think we should go and look. Now suppose two of us ride to Plymouth and two to Exeter while one person stays at Brendon and one here. How would that be?'

'Bags I Plymouth,' said Paul.

'Very well, Paul. You go to Plymouth with John, and Henry can go to Exeter with Peter. I will stay here. I feel I must. And your mother must stay at Brendon.'

'Why?' said Muriel mutinously. 'I feel left out.'

'Of course, but you can milk and so can I, so we must stay in those two places.'

'I shall jolly well see that Henry learns, at least as much as Paul.'

'Yes, but later.' The little monk looked very small beside his two tall novices.

'All right. This doesn't seem much of a council.'

'No, but everything is so simplified.'

'Probably only temporarily,' said Henry.

Muriel stood up uneasily. 'Come on boys, early start tomorrow then – '

The three men came to the great gates and waved goodbye and called out their thanks.

'Mind you ring the bells,' shouted Paul as he rode away.

'They are very hospitable, aren't they,' said Henry.

'They would have you to stay if you wanted to.'

'Would they?'

'Yes, of course.'

'Then I will stay with them one day. I want a long talk.'

'They don't talk after eight-thirty.'

'It's nearly six now. Let's hurry. Early start tomorrow.'

Muriel kicked her pony into a canter and sped across the moor for home. Then slowed up quickly, remembering Peg's condition.

'You go ahead,' she said, and watched the two boys and Chap diminish as they rode on over the moor. When she arrived half an hour later she found Henry smiling at her from a loft. 'I've found some eggs.'

'Good.'

'Do you think we could hatch any? We shall miss them.'

'I don't know the right temperature but put six in a box in the hot cupboard for luck. Where is Paul?'

'Seeing to the cows and sheep. He says we must take Diana and Flo to the monks tomorrow.'

'Very good. You do that.'

'And he says we had better winter all the cows at the Abbey.'

'You do look ahead.'

'I think we should. So does Paul.'

Muriel took the eggs. 'Would you like an omelette?'

'Yes, please.'

Supper that evening was quite convivial. All their spirits were high and Henry voiced their feelings. 'I feel fine now we know we have three friendly men only three miles away.'

They washed up and went to see that the animals were safe. The cows and ponies were grazing peacefully in the pasture, and the five sheep lying in a corner with their lambs.

'Is it safe to leave them out?' asked Paul.

'Yes, somehow I feel it is. None of them looks scared or restless as they did last night, and we shall hear if anything goes wrong. We can have our windows open and the dogs would bark.'

'Perchance my dog shall bark.'

'Henry, if you will stop quoting at us, so will we,' said Paul irritably.

'All right. Joke over.'

'You go to bed,' said Muriel.

The boys went into the house and Muriel walked slowly round the house, checking on the stables, the cowsheds, the electric engine, the garages. Everything seemed in order. She sighed, looking up at the quiet sky. 'Oh, well.' She went upstairs and into Paul's room.

'Good-night, my love.'

'Good-night, Mum. Don't worry.'

'Did you clean your teeth?'

'Yup, and I'll bring back all the toothbrushes I can from the big bad town.'

'Good-night, Henry.'

Henry was lying on his back with his arms behind his head. He put them up to kiss her and suddenly hugged her.

'I'm so sorry about your husband and Sam.'

'And I'm sorry about your parents.'

'I'm not, but I promise I'll tell you why. Not now though. I told that monk.'

'Goodness, did you?'

'Yes, he was extraordinary. He said my feelings were natural enough but I wasn't the only one and to look forward not back, or something like that, and I said wasn't I terribly wicked, and he said, "O, bless you no." I like him. I'll tell you all about it some day.'

'Yes, some day.'

'You know we may be gone more than a day, don't you?'

'Oh, no!' Muriel choked with dismay.

'Oh, yes. Think. Both lots of us have to ride twenty miles at least to get to Plymouth and Exeter. You must *not* expect us back in one day, Mrs Wake. Give us several, and don't worry. After all, we are each going with a large monk.'

'Henry, you sound fatherly.'

'Seems to me you need one – no offence meant.' Henry giggled.

'All right. I'll come with you two and the cows in the morning and we'll have a quick council and decide how long before we feel we should send out search parties.'

'You do that.' Henry snuggled into his pillow.

Muriel went to her room, undressed, got into bed and fell asleep almost immediately. The cat left her kittens, jumped on to the bed and, avoiding the dogs, came close to Muriel's face on the pillow. She twitched her whiskers, hesitated, and then went back to lie watchfully by her kittens.

Dawn was breaking as they drove the cows with their calves across the moor. They made a leisurely procession, stopping to let the animals drink at small streams. At the highest point of the moor, before the track turned downhill to the Abbey, they stopped.

'Look, the sea.' Paul pointed.

'No ships,' said Henry. 'I suppose they are drifting on the current.'

'Why?'

'Well, no *things* have disappeared, only people and animals. A ship with no crew will drift.'

'Gloomy.'

'Well, there will be lots tied up in Plymouth. Lucky you.'

'Our own private battleship,' said Paul. 'That would be fun.'

'But the Navy – ' began Muriel, and as she caught the boys looking at each other, she finished, 'No, I suppose not the Navy.'

They rode on down to the Abbey. Father Richard, wearing grey flannel trousers and a shirt, met them and they drove the cows into a field.

'Brother Peter was saying just now that motor scooters would be far quicker than ponies,' he said. 'He and Brother Paul have gone to the garage on the road to look for some.'

'How silly of us not to think of that. We can wind our way in and out of the debris.' Henry sounded delighted.

'Oh yes, let's go and meet them.' Paul and Henry darted off towards the main road.

'The children think they may be gone longer than a day.' Muriel looked at Father Richard.

'Oh, sure to be,' he saw she was anxious. 'Don't worry. If you leave a pony here with me, I can get over to you quickly if there is any news of them.'

'Oh dear, how long will they be?'

'It depends on the state of the roads and streets. It depends on what they find.'

'I don't like it.'

'Those novices are large and responsible.'

'I suppose so.' Muriel was doubtful now of the whole project.

'They must go. It is our duty to find out.'

'Very well. But I was just beginning to feel safe at Brendon.'

'Would you like to stay here?'

'No. I'll go back. I must. I must. Only I hope they won't be long. I wish we had the telephone.'

'Not even homing pigeons or the proverbial dove. I promise I'll come over to you and you must come to me if you are worried. Listen.'

From the direction of the main road came the popping sound of motor scooters, shouts and laughter, and soon they saw the two monks and the boys ride into the forecourt of the Abbey. They all looked happy and pleased.

'Ready to go?' Father Richard was brisk.

'Yes, yes.'

'Then go now, find out all you can, do not stay away too long because your mother will be anxious, and be careful.' He raised his hand.

'Come,' he said to Muriel. 'If we climb the tower we can watch them for their first two miles.'

Muriel kissed the children and watched them all ride their scooters out on to the road, then hurried up the narrow tower steps after the monk. When they reached the top of the tower the scooter party was already on the road. Muriel watched them part and begin weaving in and out of the wrecked vehicles on their separate ways, west and east.

'But whose scooters were they?'

'One of the brothers remembered the Scooter Club.'

'Oh.'

'Look, Brother Peter nearly fell off.'

'As long as it's only nearly – '

'There's quite a long stretch there with nothing to hinder them. With any luck there will be a lot of those.'

'You sound as if it were all a jolly adventure.'

'In some ways it is. The boys are enjoying it and the novices may have such fun they will lose their vocations.'

'I feel I may lose my reason.'

'Oh no you won't. Come on down now. They are all out of sight. You must have some hope and faith and keep yourself busy.'

'You too.' Muriel was rueful.

'Yes.'

When Muriel rode away up the hill she was thoughtful. 'This is going to be hard,' she addressed the dog. Then, 'Clothes' she said to herself and wondered whether she could somehow get the Landrover down to the village and stock up with clothes from the elegant shop called 'Hawkers' by the boys, but in truth 'Hawk', where they sold beautiful sweaters and sports clothes which she could never afford. As soon as she got back to the house she checked quickly that all was well, that the bitch and cat had food and drink, and went out again with Chap to the Landrover.

Later Muriel had to admit that she had enjoyed herself. For one thing, the ground was dry and the Landrover made easy detours from the road when it was blocked by fallen trees, and for another she enjoyed being alone. She wound her way in and out of fields back on to the lane, downhill to the village, only almost giving up hope when she reached the river, but even the river could not stop her for long when she followed its banks to a ford, crossed it and zigzagged back to the village.

The village was empty and sad as it had been two days ago, but curiously Muriel felt no horror. She smashed in the door of Hawk's and spent a useful hour collecting clothes for herself and for the boys, also for the boys to grow into. 'They will grow tall,' she said to the dog, 'and their feet will grow.' She moved the Landrover to the shoe shop and chose a variety of gumboots, sandals and slippers, also a large collection of socks. Then she walked slowly round the village looking at every shop intently. The butcher's was bare, so were the fishmonger's and dairy. From the baker's she collected huge sacks of flour, almost too heavy to lift, thinking that *she* must learn to bake bread. The vegetable shop looked sad; most of the vegetables were withering and the fruit rotting. She picked about until she found a bunch of bananas and then sat on the shop step eating them and some figs and dates from boxes. Chap snoozed at her feet in the sun. The church clock struck three. Muriel got up, went to the church and wound the clock as Paul had shown her. Her notice was still on the door, 'Alive at Brendon – ' She wondered whether the grass would grow tall and unkempt over the graves, and smiled because Sam had called them 'All the RIP's. Makes them sound like PTO or MFH or OMH or VIP or any old thing in this age of initials.' She wiped a tear from her eye. 'Goodbye, Mama,' he had said, and she had let him go when she so urgently wanted to see him.

'Hell!' shouted Muriel, 'Hell!' And then laughed because Henry would not have been able to resist adding 'Knows no fury etcetera'. She pottered round the churchyard thinking of Sam. Sam, tall and dark, her first child, Sam who was nineteen and so beautiful. Sam who had spent hours in this very churchyard when he was thirteen and emerged at last triumphant with the answer as to why this village so hated the next. 'These were Cavaliers – they were Roundheads,' which the vicar had corroborated. Six years since then. Three months since –

'Oh, Hell!' Muriel yelled. 'Hell, Hell, Hell!' Her voice echoed round the village. ''ell, 'ell, 'ell.'

'Who's that?'

From somewhere near came a disturbed croaking voice. Muriel jumped and stood still. Chap was standing over a freshly dug grave wagging his tail, peering down. Muriel tiptoed across the grass to join the dog.

'Oh!'

'Morning, Mrs Wake. This isn't your pitch. You belong to that new Abbey over the hill, not here.'

'It's rebuilt on the old foundations.' Muriel spoke automatically. Then, 'Mr Perdue! What on earth are you doing here?'

'Here, give us a hand, I don't feel quite myself somehow.'

Muriel knelt and reached down to the old man struggling to his feet from under a clutter of boards and spades, earth and sacking.

'I can't reach you.'

'Not surprised. This is a double grave, extra deep you know. That Mrs Willis, she's going to be buried on top of poor old Ned. Same in death as in life. She wants to be on top. Now don't tell anyone I said so.'

'There isn't anyone.'

'What's that? Where's my ladder?'

'Blown away I expect.'

'Them boys more like. They were larking about horrible, so I laid down to have a little nap.' The old man looked up at Muriel as he dusted his clothes.

'There's some steps in the vestry. I'll fetch them.'

'Don't let nobody see you.'

'There is nobody.'

'What's that?'

Muriel ran to the church and, finding a pair of steps in the vestry, carried them back and lowered them into the grave. The old man climbed up shakily.

'You need a drink,' she said.

'I don't drink,' the old man said huffily. Then, catching Muriel's eye, added, 'Only now and again when Fred Bartlett come to give me a hand with a big job like this. He was here last night.'

'Not last night. Three nights ago.'

'What's that? Never!'

'Yes.'

The old man muttered, 'My wife, she would have been proper angry.' Then he smiled. 'But she died. She won't be buried on top of me like Mrs Willis on top of Ned.'

'I think you had better come to the pub and I'll get you some food.'

'Never go inside the place. It's people like you who do such things, and football pools and horses and incense.'

'Let's leave the incense out for a minute, Mr Perdue. Come on.' Muriel led the old man across the churchyard to the inn.

'Where is everybody?' he asked. 'Blown away or what?'

'Blown away I think.'

'It isn't reasonable.'

'No. Will you sit here, Mr Perdue, drink this, eat that, and listen to me.' Muriel opened a bottle of beer, poured it into a tankard and handed the old man a packet of peanuts and a banana.

'Funny sort of breakfast,' he said.

'It's four o'clock. Now will you listen, Mr Perdue?'

'I'm listening. Don't hold with women in bars.'

'Mr Perdue, please.'

'All right, no offence, but it's laxity, that's what it is, incense and laxity. They go together.'

'Mr Perdue, will you shut up and listen? I have a lot to tell you.'

'If it's going to take long we'd better have another bottle.'

Muriel went behind the bar and poured out a whisky for herself and another beer for the old man.

'What's happened to the parrot?' He was peering into a large cage which had a notice, 'Please do not feed the parrot' wired on to it. 'Nothing but feathers'.

'That's what I want to tell you.'

Muriel began her story slowly, trying to remember the sequence of events, frowning, her eyes half shut. The old man listened without interrupting until she came to the bell-ringing, when he exclaimed, 'Ah!' I thought they was rung all wrong, like that scare in the 1939 war. Now that was something. Rung them all wrong they did, and it was a false alarm.'

'Let me finish.'

'All right.' He took a swig of beer sulkily. 'Women! They always interrupt.'

Muriel finished her story and said, 'Then you spoke from that grave.'

The old man burst into a roar of laughter. 'Hah! Hahahaha! Arrh!' He clutched his head in pain.

'Hangover,' said Muriel. 'Never!'

⁊ 7 ⁊

Mr Perdue stood up. 'I must see the Vicar and Mrs Willis.'

'You won't, Mr Perdue. I've told you there is nobody left.'

'Like to see for myself. They call me grumpy, but I'm thorough.'

'Just as you like.'

Muriel followed the old man across the square to the vicarage, up the stairs and waited while Mr Perdue knocked at the Vicar's bedroom door and, getting no answer, went into the room. She heard him walk round it and then watched him come out scratching his head.

'Gone,' said Mr Perdue. 'Clean as a whistle. Only his pyjamas in the bed, and his glass eye is gone too.'

'It's the same everywhere,' said Muriel hastily.

'Won't be with Mrs Willis. She wanted the grave hand-dug, she did. "No modern machine for me," she said. I have a proper good suction digger for graves, but she's old-fashioned, she is. That's why old Bartlett and I was digging so long. Ridiculous.'

Muriel followed Mr Perdue across the road and down a side lane to a row of pretty cottages.

'Here we are.' Mr Perdue knocked at the first door. 'Anyone up?' He raised his voice.

'We break in,' said Muriel. The old man looked shocked. 'I told you about it.'

'Yes, so you did. Housebreaking.'

Muriel shrugged her shoulders.

'Oh, all right.' Mr Perdue picked up a stone and smashed a front window. 'You nip in, Mrs Wake, and let me in.'

Muriel climbed in at the window and opened the door for the old man.

'I'm strong,' he said, 'for seventy-five, but not so nimble as I was.'

They walked upstairs. Muriel opened the door of the back bedroom. The bed was ruffled and on the pillow lay a mat of grey hair and curlers. The teeth, which were now becoming so commonplace, reposed in a glass beside the bed.

'She won't want any burying.' Mr Perdue stared. 'The coffin is in here. The funeral is today.'

Muriel did not bother to correct him but watched as the old man lifted the lid and peered in.

'His teeth, his hair, his wedding ring, nothing else but his clothes. She made the poor chap wear that ring even in death. She had her clamps on him and there was no need. He never looked at women, gardening was what he liked.' Mr Perdue replaced the coffin lid. 'Won't need burying now. All that heavy digging for nothing.'

They left the cottage and Muriel said quietly, 'Come up to Brendon with me, Mr Perdue, we would love to have you and we've masses of food and it's warm and light.'

'No, thank you all the same, I have my own house. There it is.' Mr Perdue pointed. 'Very comfortable it is and I have my cat and dog. I don't need anything else.'

'Let's go and look.' Muriel turned back up the road towards the sexton's house where Mr Perdue lived.

'Quiet,' said Mr Perdue. 'It's very quiet. My dog and cat won't be long in coming to meet me. My dog, he's old like me but he's company, and my cat she's good company too, better in some ways than the dog.' Mr Perdue hastened his steps and, fishing in his pockets for a key, went into the little house calling, 'Nip, Nip, where are you boy? Puss, come here, you must be hungry.'

There was a long silence. Muriel heard the old man moving about and clicking light switches and muttering. Waiting, she watched Chap scratching himself indulgently and listened to the silence of the street. The church clock struck five and Mr Perdue came out and sat down beside her. In his hand he held a dog collar and a bunch of fur.

'She was a tortoiseshell,' he said.

They sat together for a long time saying nothing.

At last Muriel broke the silence. 'At Brendon we have a cat with four kittens, Mr Perdue. Their father was a Siamese. He was killed in the accident which killed my husband.'

'I always said taking a cat in a car weren't natural.'

'And my dog is having puppies any day,' Muriel went on. 'Don't you think you could come up there for a while and give me a hand?'

'It wouldn't be proper.' Mr Perdue pursed his lips.

Muriel smiled and went on. 'The cows and calves, ponies and sheep need attending to too. It's rather a lot for me alone.'

'Nothing seems to work in my house,' said the old man. 'The power is gone, no light, no heat. It's mad, that's what it is, it's mad.'

'We have light and heat. We have our own plant.'

'Very old-fashioned.' Mr Perdue looked disapproving.

'My husband liked it. That way he said we were independent.'

'Nothing wrong with independence,' Mr Perdue conceded.

'We have fuel and oil for three years.'

'Have you now?' Mr Perdue looked obstinate. 'Isn't paid for I bet.'

'No, not yet. It's a big worry.'

'Don't see why it should worry you now.' Old Perdue stood up. 'Those kittens and that bitch shouldn't be left alone too long.' They walked towards the Landrover and got in. Muriel drove slowly out of the square.

'See that?' Mr Perdue was pointing.

'What?'

'The bank. Now's the time to rob it, no one about.' He laughed, adding, 'I still got my own teeth.'

'How lovely for you, so have I.'

'Well,' he leant back in the seat beside her. 'T'isn't decent, just blowing off and leaving things like that.'

Muriel said nothing but concentrated on her driving. She negotiated the ford and, changing into higher gear, set off up the hill. They passed the overturned car. Mr Perdue looked at it with one eyebrow raised. 'Poor chap!' he shouted in her ear. 'He drank. Steady on, look at that now.'

Ahead of the car in the evening light waddled a large female badger. She glanced over her shoulder and then vanished into the undergrowth of the wood.

'How queer.' Muriel stopped the car. Chap's eyes were bulging out of his head. She laid a restraining hand on his collar.

'Badgers!'

'They survive everything,' said Mr Perdue. 'Nice to see her though.'

Muriel drove on up over the edge of the moor to the house. Walking to meet them, her tail straight in the air, came the cat who at once began to wind herself in and out of the old man's legs, pressing herself against him. Mindful of Mr Perdue's feelings, Muriel went into the house and upstairs to the hot cupboard. The hot water tank gave a welcoming rumble as she took out clean sheets and pillowcases and went to the far end of the corridor past the boys' rooms to what had once, long ago, been called the bachelor wing, now two spare rooms which, with a communicating door, could be entirely separate from the rest of the house. She made up the bed, looked quickly in the chest of drawers and cupboard to see that they were clean and empty and went downstairs again. Mr Perdue was sitting steaming in front of the Aga.

'Heavens, Mr Perdue, you are soaking! I never noticed. You must have been snowed on.'

'Don't notice much, women don't. Now the cat, she did. Wouldn't sit on my knee.'

'I'm so sorry. You should have a hot bath and change, otherwise you'll get rheumatism.'

'Ain't got nothing to change into.' The old man looked not only cross but exhausted.

'I have masses of spare clothes.'

'Don't want women's clothes.' Muriel knew he was being annoying on purpose.

'Men's clothes,' she said firmly. 'Come and choose.'

Sulkily Mr Perdue followed her to her husband's room.

'Dusty in here,' he said.

'Well, I've not been in it for some time.'

'Not since he was killed I suppose. Were you driving?'

Mr Perdue looked through the drawers, picking out a shirt, underwear, a bright orange sweater, muttering as he did so, 'I like bright colours', a red neck scarf and green corduroy trousers, unworn and given to his father as a joke the previous Christmas by Sam.

Muriel steered the old man to his room.

'Here you are.'

'Does it lock?' He tried the door.

'Yes, of course. Now I'll get supper while you have a bath.'

She left him and went downstairs. In the library she threw some sticks on to the smouldering ashes and knelt while the fire kindled before she laid on logs. Among the ashes she saw a scrap of paper, rather charred. 'To account rendered' she read and smiled, putting the last trace of the bill on to the fire. In the kitchen she riddled the Aga, laid the table for two, fetched a can of soup from the store cupboard, and began to prepare supper thoughtfully.

After a few minutes she said loudly to herself, 'I will *not* be bullied,' and leaving the pans to simmer, she ran down to the cellar. As she came up carrying a bottle of claret she met Mr Perdue coming down the stairs wearing the dry clothes. 'You look wonderful,' she said, 'and you will feel better after a proper meal.'

Mr Perdue did not answer her but sat down at the table. Muriel gave him a bowl of soup and poured him a glass of wine. He made no comment. They ate silently and Muriel from the corner of her eye saw Mr Perdue sip his wine, hesitate, then drink. He smiled at her.

'That cat needs fresh food,' he said. 'She needs fish.'

'She's had masses out of the tins, and milk.'

'Not enough. She's nursing them kittens. They drain her strength.'

'Paul said there were fish in the lake – alive.'

'Did he now? Then tomorrow when I've seen to the farm I'll go fishing. That suit you, puss?' Mr Perdue and the cat exchanged an enigmatic look. 'Fishing is nice and quiet. A man gets away from all that jaw, jaw, jaw.'

'Then while you are fishing and looking after the place, I shall ride over to the Abbey and see whether there is any news of the boys.'

'And see that monk?'

'Yes.'

'Has he got a fish pond?'

'As a matter of fact there is one.'

'Ah.'

'And they are independent too. They get their electricity from the river.'

'Very old-fashioned.' Mr Perdue pursed his lips.

'Well, it works and none of the mains work, do they?'

'I grant you that, Mrs Wake. I was brought up differently, that's all. My mother liked everything modern and so do I. I like my mechanical grave-digger. I like cars and engines. I like the telephone and the telly.'

'Alas, they aren't working either.'

'Let's try un now.' Mr Perdue sprang to his feet, disturbing the cat. 'My cat was very fond of those nature programmes.'

Muriel led the way to the telephone.

'Try it yourself.' She stood by it watching the old man lift the receiver and jiggle the instrument.

'It's no good,' he said.

'Try the television too.'

'No, but I want to know why.' Mr Perdue sounded irritated.

'So do I,' said Muriel crossly. 'You think it out while you are fishing tomorrow.'

'I'll try,' he said, and went slowly away up the stairs.

8

In the morning, as she rode away over the hill, Muriel could see Mr Perdue sitting in a boat near the shore casting his line out where the breeze ruffled the water. Anxious now for Paul and Henry, she cantered quickly across the moor and down the valley to the Abbey. She turned her pony loose in the orchard to graze and went into the church to be met by the sound of a Hoover. Up by the great altar Father Richard was standing on a ladder directing the nozzle of the Hoover at the curtains round the altar.

'Good morning, Mrs Wake. It's all terribly dusty.'

'Don't you think, Father, that you should leave some spiders' webs for posterity? The time may come when people will not know what a spider was.'

'That's interesting.' Father Richard came down the ladder.

'I haven't seen any insects, but there are fish in our reservoir.'

'Are there? The fish are all right in our pond too.'

'We saw a badger yesterday evening.'

'We?'

'I must tell you. I found the village gravedigger lying at the bottom of a double grave in the churchyard.'

'Did you?'

'Yes, he'd fallen asleep drunk and knew nothing about anything. He's at Brendon now.'

'Well, that almost proves –' Father Richard wrinkled his brow.'

'Proves what?'

'I'm not sure yet so I won't say, but I'm beginning to think, to puzzle out a theory.' Father Richard looked at his watch. 'Time to ring the Angelus.'

'May I come up the tower with you?'

'Of course. When I have rung it we can look out and see if we can see any sign of the boys and the novices.'

'That's what I meant.'

Father Richard rang the bell energetically. 'One must keep some semblance of continuity,' he said when he stopped.

'Some symbol,' said Muriel. 'That awful old man has gone out fishing. He wants quiet.'

'He will get plenty of that.' Father Richard climbed ahead of Muriel up the stairs and opened the door at the top. They came out into the sun together.

'I should have brought field glasses. Muriel shaded her eyes, gazing down the road towards Plymouth. 'I can't see anything, only the wrecks.'

'In this stillness we would hear rather than see first,' said the little monk.

'I suppose so. Can I help you? I don't want to wait up here.'

'No, there is no point in that, and there is plenty to do.'

'At the farm?'

'Yes, at the farm, in the gardens and in the Abbey.' They climbed down the tower again.

'Who is this boy Henry?' asked Father Richard.

'He is Paul's best friend at school.'

'I thought it was term time.'

'It is but they are home as the school closed because of that odd disease so many children got. It didn't seem to hurt them, but some of the parents got panicky and of course the children were only too delighted to come home.'

'He told me he came from London.'

'He does, but his family have gone abroad.'

'I wonder if they will ever come back.'

'Father Richard, you really think – ' Muriel paused.

'Yes, I do. The last news was of odd happenings in Europe, very queer things in America and South America and floods all over Asia.'

'Sam went to look.' Muriel spoke flatly.

'Come and give me a hand with those cows,' said the little monk. 'If we are careful we can build up quite a herd.'

'Did Paul show you his bull-ring?' Muriel asked.

'Yes, he did, and one of the calves you brought over is a bull.'

'So he is. I must see which of our lambs is a ram, mustn't I, so that we can build up a flock. The boys want to bring all the animals down to you for the winter. They look ahead too. I wish –'

'Yes, you wish they would come back. So in a way do I, but they will not come today. Go back now, Mrs Wake, to your old man and see that all is in order at Brendon.'

'He's such a hypocrite,' exclaimed Muriel. 'The drunken old creature.'

'If he had not been drunk he might not have survived.' Father Richard spoke cheerfully.

'You speak as though his getting pickled was a virtue. He is disagreeable too.'

'I daresay he will mellow, and the pickling was a preservative.'

'The boys and I were not drunk, nor the cat or the dogs, nor the sheep, cows and ponies. What preservative had we?'

'We shall find out.' Father Richard looked at his watch again. 'Must do some work in the monastery I'm afraid.'

'Can't I help?' Muriel was loath to leave.

'Not in this.' He spoke gently. Muriel watched him go into the monastery and close the door. She called her pony and rode home, hoping that perhaps the boys had reached Brendon along the other road, the A30. How surprised and amused they would be to find old Mr Perdue in the house.

But there were no boys, only Mr Perdue, flushed from the sun, sitting by the Aga watching Charlie eating.

'Ah,' he said when she came in. 'I told you she needed fish.'

'How clever of you, Mr Perdue.'

'Not clever, just quiet I was. There are plenty for us too.'

'Mr Perdue, you *are* clever.'

'The one who is being clever is being clever all over your drawing-room sofa,' said the old man.

'Who?'

'Your bitch.'

Muriel ran to the drawing-room to find Peg lying blissfully quiet with four blind squealing puppies at her side.

'Torn the cover she has.' Mr Perdue had followed her.

'Oh, it doesn't matter. The boys will be thrilled.'

'Maybe, but if you'd had a proper modern sofa instead of this 'ere thing it wouldn't have got torn.'

'We like old things. She is hungry.'

'I'll get her some milk.' The old man went off.

Muriel sat stroking her dog, who lapped thirstily when Mr Perdue brought her a bowl of milk.

'Two dogs and two bitches,' said Muriel.

'Call them John, George, Ringo and Paul.'

'Why?'

'You remember, they was Top of the Pops.'

'Of course,' said Muriel vaguely, 'very nice names.'

Mr Perdue looked disappointed, so Muriel said quickly, 'How do you like your trout cooked?'

'I like 'em grilled, but with this old Aga thing you can't grill.'

'Yes, I can.' Muriel stood up. 'Did you milk the cows, Mr Perdue?'

'Yes, and I saw to the sheep and ponies too. Tomorrow I'll give your kitchen garden a look-see.'

Muriel thanked him and set to work cooking their supper.

'I enjoyed myself,' said the old man grudgingly.

Muriel smiled. 'If you did, I'll go over to the Abbey again tomorrow. The boys will turn up some time.'

'Don't fret.' Mr Perdue took the plate of fish Muriel handed him. Sitting at the table in his bright sweater, eating, Mr Perdue reminded Muriel of other times and other places.

'You look like an Augustus John,' she said.

'Who's 'e?'

'Or a Picasso.'

'What?'

'It's the bright colours. They were painters who loved bright colours and food.'

'Well, I like bright colours and food, but I never heard of them. My old mother she brought us up to be modern, contemporary she called it.'

'I wish I had known her.'

'Well, she'd be old-fashioned now, I daresay, but she'd never hold with what you've got here.'

'What do you mean, Mr Perdue?'

'All those chairs and sofas that's unwashable, that Aga thing and your own electricity, milking those poor cows by hand, and not even giving them no music, not having your own spin dryer, only cars and horses, ridiculous she'd have called it.'

'We liked it that way, and you must admit, Mr Perdue, it works.' Muriel felt rather annoyed.

'Works, I daresay, but tomorrow morning before I see to the garden, I'm going to fix the cows up with a bit of music. They'll give much more milk with a bit of music. No science 'ere at all.'

'No music either. The radio and television are dead. You will have to sing to them, Mr Perdue.'

'Sing?'

'Well, if you want some music for the cows, you will have to sing to them.'

'What I want is a bit of quiet away from all this chattering.'

'Then go fishing. I'm going to the Abbey again to see if the boys have come back.'

'They won't, not for weeks, not them boys.'

'How can you tell?'

'I know boys, they lark about and shatter the peace and quiet. Yes, I'll go fishing.'

Muriel looked with distaste at the old man, thinking how terrible it would be to be alone with him for long.

'Mr Perdue,' she said, 'I'm going now. Can you keep an eye on the animals? There's a full moon. The boys might come back.'

Mr Perdue made a contemptuous noise. 'You go,' he said. 'There's a record player in your library. I'm going to take it to the cowshed. Lots of old records too. Old-fashioned, but the cows won't know. Remind me of my old mother if I play them a bit of John, George and Ringo, a bit of Twist and Shout and they will milk lovely. Yeh! Yeh! Yeh!' he sang at her.

Muriel hesitated.

'You go,' said the old man more kindly. 'I'll see to things here.'

Still Muriel hesitated, thinking of Charlie and the kittens.

'I'll see to them.' The old man read her thoughts. 'They like a bit of quiet like me.'

Muriel left the house, feeling thoroughly unwanted, followed by Chap. She saddled a pony and rode slowly over the moor by the light of the moon. By the reservoir she paused to let the pony drink and looked around her. She saw Chap prick his ears and watch something up on the moor behind her.

'Sit quiet, Chap.'

The dog sat still watching, and Muriel strained her eyes. The pony raised his head and stood still with water dribbling out of his mouth. Turned in her saddle away from the water, Muriel tried to follow the dog's pointing nose. After a minute she was rewarded by the sight of a pair of foxes, silhouetted against the moon, trotting along the crest of the hill. She followed them with her eyes until they dropped out of sight behind the hill.

'Foxes and badgers,' she said cheerfully to the dog and proceeded on her way over the moor and downhill to the Abbey.

As she got near the Abbey Muriel began to feel rather ridiculous. She had, after all, only left it that evening, and here she was again coming back in the early hours of the morning, over-anxious about her son and Henry who were, she told herself, quite safe, each accompanied by one of the novices. The Abbey door was open so she went in. Chap, ignoring the notice pinned on the door: 'No Dogs Allowed', followed her quietly. Up at the high altar Father Richard was kneeling by what looked like a biscuit tin on a stand draped with a violet cloth. Muriel knelt too. Presently Father Richard rose and came down to join her.

'How good of you to come,' he said. 'This is Sunday and I am going to say a Requiem Mass and bury – ' he hesitated.

'Bury the bits,' said a voice behind her.

'Henry!' Muriel spun round. Henry was smiling at her.

'The others will be here soon,' he said.

'What others?'

'That novice chap and the people we found in Exeter.'

'We never heard you coming.'

'I don't suppose you did. We are on skates.'

'Skates?'

'Yes, roller skates. We got them in Exeter and simply buzzed along the main road. Ann and June are fearfully good on them, much better than us. They will be here in a minute. What's going on?'

'Father Richard is going to say Mass and bury – '

'Oh goodoh! Then we are just in time. Can I toll the bell, Father? Here they come.'

Henry appeared to be in high spirits and ran down the aisle to meet Peter and two girls who were standing in the porch taking off their roller skates. They all smiled at Muriel, and the novice hurried up to Father Richard and began to talk to him. The two girls put their skates down and shook hands with Muriel.

'Nice to meet you,' they said in chorus. 'What's going on? This is Ann and I am June.'

'Well, Father Richard is going to say Mass and then bury – ' Muriel looked helplessly at the girls who, she could see in the half light, were wearing track suits and were bare-headed. One seemed dark, the other fair.

'Well, there wouldn't be enough to fill a coffin, would there?' said the girl called June practically.

'Yes, it would be silly to have a coffin,' agreed the other girl. 'I'm Church of England myself.'

'Even the Church of England wouldn't fill a coffin, things being as they are,' said June. 'Henry told us about you, Mrs Wake. How can we help?'

'By just being here I think.'

Muriel looked up towards the altar where Father Richard was talking to Henry, who presently hurried off towards the Bell Tower, and within minutes the funeral bell began its tolling. Father Richard was joined by his novice in a surplice and began the Mass. The two strange girls knelt beside

Muriel and copied her movements, and all three slowly followed the little procession, made up of Father Richard, the novice and Henry, to the cemetery.

'Nice smell,' whispered June.

'That's incense. What's he doing now?' asked Ann.

'Sprinkling holy water.'

'Oh.'

They followed Father Richard back to the Abbey. 'You must be hungry,' he said. 'We will bring you breakfast in the parlour. Henry, will you help?'

Muriel led the two girls to the parlour. 'Please tell me – ' she began.

'Well,' said Ann, 'seems much the same thing happened in Exeter as it did to you, from what Henry told us. Snow and wind and that. June and I were staying in a basement flat. We were frightened and when we thought it was all over, the storm you know, we came out from under the bedclothes and we went out to look for other people.'

'But there were no other people,' said June.

'No, nobody,' went on Ann. 'Well, we stole food from shops and places, and we started shouting, but nobody came.'

'Not until Henry.'

'No, not until Henry. We don't know Exeter very well, you see. We are skating champions for the South West and we'd only come down for the contest.'

'What contest?'

'Oh, the championship contest.'

'I see.' Muriel did not see but wanted to hear more.

'Well, we couldn't find anything but messed up cars, lorries and trains, and we were in a fair state of nerves when yesterday we heard somebody shouting, "Anybody there? Anybody there?" so we screamed.'

'Then what?' Muriel bent forward on her elbows, looking at the two young faces with joy.

'Well, Henry and that novice chap came round a corner and we fell into their arms. It was lovely.' Both girls looked happily reminiscent.

At this moment the little monk and Henry came in

carrying trays of breakfast and the story was continued by
Henry.

'We hunted the whole city, the University, everywhere,
but the whole caboodle is blown away and there's an
awful mess.'

'Really nobody left?'

'Not that we could find. We thought you would be
getting anxious so we came back. It was Ann and June
who thought about skating here. It's even easier than the
scooters.'

'Once you have learnt,' said the young novice with a
grin.

'And I have found Mr Perdue and there are foxes and
badgers alive.' Muriel told her story.

'You two girls must come to Brendon.'

'We'd love to,' they said.

'We'll get another Landrover off the road somehow,'
said Henry. 'The moor is very dry. I'm sure I could get one
across country.'

'If you can roller-skate from Exeter I'm sure you can.'

'Oh, I brought you a present.' Henry left the room.

'We each brought a pack of clothes,' said June. 'Just in
case.'

Henry came back grinning. 'This is it.' He placed a large
jar of caviar in Muriel's lap.

'Henry! Where did you get it?'

'I broke into that posh hotel.'

'Well, it's gorgeous.'

'I brought this.' The novice opened his knapsack. 'We
broke into the hospitals and I took all the drugs I know
which I could find.'

'That was sensible.'

'Nothing makes sense.'

'It depends what you mean by sense.'

'Sense and sensibility.'

'Nonsense, sense is. Well, sense makes nonsense.'

They were all laughing and talking together, glad of
company, glad to be six people together and not just one
or two.

'By the way,' said Peter when they paused for breath. 'The Exe has changed its course and this part of England is completely cut off. As far as we could see, the sea has come right inland and flooded out all the low lying country.'

'So we can't get to London?'

'Not unless we fly or get a boat across and then try.'

'We shall have to soon.'

'I come from Australia,' said June suddenly. 'I wonder what has happened there.'

'The last news,' began Muriel, then added, 'Well, I suppose we all heard the last news.'

They all looked at one another and then at their plates.

'Is it the end of the world?' Henry's voice was quiet.

'Oh, no, I don't think so, Henry.' Father Richard's voice sounded very normal. 'After all, we are here. Something abnormal has happened, that's all. We shall find out in time what it is.'

'Our parents thought it was the end of the world in 1939,' said Muriel.

'1939?' Henry blinked. 'Oh, *that* war. How silly of them.'

'Then everybody thought it would be the end of the world if there were another war,' said Peter.

'My parents were CND,' said June, 'before they went to Australia.'

'Henry said you are absolutely self-sufficient, got all your own electricity, water, the lot, he says. Is it true?'

'Yes,' said Muriel. 'It's lucky really that my husband was so old-fashioned. He wanted to keep our house as it had once been. One can't, but he tried.'

'Henry says it's marvellous.' Ann turned to the little monk. 'What do you think, if it isn't the end of the world? Do you think it's a war?' She sounded incredulous.

'Oh no, some sort of accident or natural upheaval like an earthquake or something of that sort. I expect we shall find out.'

'Let's go and find a Landrover. I saw one not far off down the road.' Henry was impatient. The girls got up and set off with him.

Muriel went outside and stood chatting to the monk and his novice.

'I'll take those two girls home. Will you be all right here?'

'Oh, yes,' he said. 'We have plenty to do and Paul will be coming back here with John. They may have gleaned some more news in Plymouth than the others did in Exeter. I think it's only a matter of waiting.'

'I have no patience,' Muriel exclaimed. 'I want to know what has happened to Sam. I want to know about Henry's family. Waiting is not my forte.'

The men said nothing and they stood in the early sunshine looking about them at the blue sky, green grass, the grey stone buildings.

'I miss the birds,' said Peter.

'Look what a straight line those moles are making.' Muriel pointed at a line of mole hills erupting across the orchard grass.

'Moles!' The little monk looked eager. 'Moles. Those are fresh today. Moles – and you say you have seen badgers and foxes?'

'We saw rabbits too as we came along,' said Peter.

'Then – I think I am right.'

'What do you mean?' Muriel looked at the eager face.

'I cannot be sure yet. Ah, here they come.'

Ann drove a slightly battered Landrover into the courtyard. The girls and Henry loaded their packs into it, slung in their skates, said goodbye to the monks and set off up the lane to the moor. Muriel, too, said goodbye and rode off after them, thinking as she went that Father Richard's explanation of their present predicament as an accident was quite a remarkable understatement.

During the days that followed the people at Brendon fell into a comfortable routine. The two girls helped Muriel in the house, while Henry and Mr Perdue made expeditions down to the village to collect all the food, clothes and fuel and any household items they could find. These were all stored and stacked in the attics and lofts. Henry and the old man also brought loads of hay, cow cake, corn and veterinary medicines for the animals. They all wasted a lot of time playing with the kittens and puppies and just sitting in the incredible sun chatting and dozing.

'I've never known a summer like this.'

'It's like Australia.'

'Tell us about Australia.'

Muriel watched the young people lying easily relaxed in the sun, and the old man out on the lake fishing, and wondered why Paul had not come back and where Sam was. She envied them their ease.

'We have enough stores for years,' she said, interrupting the description of a duck-billed platypus.

'Yes, and they have at the Abbey too.'

'Are you worrying?' Henry looked at Muriel.

'Yes, and I can't bear it much longer.'

'You may have to.' Henry's eyes were on her.

'Sam – I can understand that Sam may never come back, but Paul should be back by now. It's nearly three weeks, Henry, since you went off to Exeter and he to Plymouth.'

'I know. Tell you what, let's go for a ride.' Henry was anxious to distract her.

'All right.' Muriel heard herself sounding ungracious and added quickly, 'Where shall we go?'

'Let's go to the holiday camp. It isn't far.'

'Why there? I always have thought it the height of bad taste to build a holiday camp just there near the prison.'

'Oh well, it makes an objective.' Henry picked up two saddles and bridles. 'No need to go inside,' he added.

'Inside used to have a sinister ring.'

'I know, but the camp is quite jolly now or was.' Henry caught two ponies and saddled and bridled them.

'Do you know the way across country?'

'Yes, I used to visit a man there years ago, in the prison.'

'Did you? How thrilling. What was it like? What had he done?'

'He was a burglar of sorts. It wasn't really interesting, Henry, only sad.'

'We are all burglars now I suppose.' Henry trotted beside her looking cheerful.

'Henry, you look very cheerful.' Henry laughed.

'I am cheerful. I'm enjoying all this, whatever it is. I like you, I like old Perdue, I like those two girls, I like this life.'

'So do I, except that I fret about Sam and Paul.'

'Paul will be all right.' Muriel noticed that Henry made no mention of Sam.

'What makes you so sure?'

'Well Paul has John with him and he was dead keen on going to Plymouth. I think he's found something there to amuse him.'

'I should go and look,' said Muriel. 'We are all being so apathetic in a way, storing everything at Brendon and not going far afield, only to the village and to rob farms of their food stores and to the Abbey.'

'Well,' Henry said soothingly, 'we are going somewhere now aren't we? We may find something. Let's go faster.'

Muriel cantered after Henry for a couple of miles across the heather until they stopped at the top of a hill.'

'There it is. The holiday camp and the prison.'

They looked down at the ugly shape of the prison, the terror of all criminals. It stood huge, star-shaped, near a dark wood of fir. Near it was the little town where the holiday camp provided rooms or houses during the summer months.

'It does look grim. Whoever thought of turning this into a holiday resort can have had no sensibility at all.' Muriel spoke with disgust.

'Some of us like that sort of thing.' Henry looked at her sidelong. They rode down into the little town and Henry raised his voice to cry – 'Anybody there? Anybody here?' His voice came back to them mockingly – 'Here, here, here.'

Henry got off his pony and handed the reins to Muriel. He ran ahead of her in and out of garden gates, peering into windows, looking into cars parked outside houses, vanishing suddenly into a house where the ground floor window had been left open. Muriel watched him as she rode slowly up towards the holiday camp.

'It's all "the usual",' Henry called from an upper window of a small house, 'except this. This is the first I've found.'

'First what?'

'First National Health wig.' Henry sounded pleased. 'Can't be too squeamish,' he added, joining her. 'Come on, let's get to the main gates. I've read about it but never seen it.' He loped ahead of her to the huge building.

Muriel rode up the little street seeing the now so familiar tufts of hair and fur blown into corners, the deserted cars, the empty windows. She wondered whether she liked Henry.

'Look, they left the gate open.' Henry opened the small door in the main gate. 'I wonder why?'

Muriel looked up at what had once been a terrible prison. She remembered the time not so long ago when she and her husband had tried so hard to get this place demolished, but had failed, and seen instead a tremendous tourist boom take place and a holiday camp built with flatlets with every modern convenience, with tennis courts and a cinema, with a swimming pool and a crêche for babies; 'No need to leave the premises during your stay' had been a nauseating sentence in the brochure of the camp. Muriel sat on her pony, looking at it with disgust. Inside the camp she heard Henry calling, 'Anybody here? Anybody there?' his voice bouncing back at him from the buildings like a squash ball, then dying away. She got off her pony and, slipping the stirrup leather through the rein, left it to graze by the road, did the same to Henry's and went in through the little gate by the main gate to find Henry.

Inside the main gate was a courtyard and across it another door. Henry had left the door open. She noticed that the gravel paths and intensely geometrical flowerbeds were the same as long ago, and the silence. Far away she heard Henry shriek. Muriel stood stock still wishing she had brought Chap with her.

'Henry!' she shouted. 'Henry,' the stone walls answered her on all sides. Henry did not shriek again or answer her.

'Henry! Henry!' Muriel began to run round the outside of the prison block and down the road to the camp nearby. 'Henry! Henry!' She ran on past another block of buildings and found herself standing by a large quiet swimming pool. 'Henry!'

'It's all right, Mrs Wake, we're here.' Henry emerged from a doorway followed by a very short, fat, middle-aged woman with a kind, wrinkled face who advanced to meet her holding out a welcoming hand.

'Very glad to meet you,' said the woman. 'I gave poor Henry here quite a fright.'

'Who are you?' Muriel took the warm friendly hand which was being held out to her.

'I'm Mrs Luard.'

'Mrs Luard?'

'Yes, dear. I'm here on my holiday. I'm an upholsterer from London.'

Muriel and Henry sat by the pool staring at Mrs Luard in silence while she smiled at them. After a long time Henry, who had been very white in the face, recovered and asked, 'Could you tell us?'

'Of course I can. Well now, there was a dreadful storm of wind and a lot of snow but it didn't worry me much because I was down in the basement watching the chicks hatch.'

'The what?'

'The chicks. Mr Linton who runs this place has a battery of hens in the basement and his chicks hatch regular as clockwork or they did do until the electricity went. He had, I should say, because I can't find any trace of him or anybody else and you can't say I haven't looked because I have. Nobody could say I haven't looked. I'm nosy by nature and this time I've had enough nosying to last me a lifetime I have.' She looked at Henry who was beginning to giggle and smiled. 'I've looked all over the place and there was nothing left but – '

'We know,' said Muriel,

'Well, there are the chicks – those I could save. I've always wanted to see chicks hatch out of their eggs and except on the television I never saw it. But Mr Linton, who was really kind, said if I liked I could sit in the basement and watch the little things hatch so that's what I was doing all that night. It was wonderfully interesting until all the lights went out and I had a terrible time getting upstairs. All I could hear was a cheep or two and when daylight came all the little dears were dead except for four of them and I put them inside my blouse and here they are.'

Mrs Luard paused, produced a box and brought forth four active chicks. 'I fed them on the chick mash I found,' she said proudly, 'and I keep them warm like a broody hen. That's how they were reared in the old days,' she added informatively, 'by a hen.' Mrs Luard put the four chicks beside her on the grass, smiling maternally. 'I'm going to bring them up to be free range chickens, the modern way,' she said proudly.

'We have, or had free range chickens,' said Muriel.

'Aylesbury ducks?' enquired Mrs Luard.

'All our poultry have vanished.'

'Then I can show you some.' Mrs Luard jumped up and with surprising agility ran into the prison block to emerge two minutes later with another box. 'Five ducklings,' she said with pride. 'Mr Linton had a battery for ducks, too, for us all to eat you know, only now there is nobody. I found an oil stove of course.'

'Has Henry told you about us?'

'I haven't had time,' said Henry.

'Mrs Luard, would you and your poultry like to come and live with us? There are five of us and I'm expecting, hoping, for my son to come back.'

Mrs Luard eyed her thoughtfully. 'I'm very independent,' she said. 'But maybe you've got a pond for the ducks?'

'We have a pond and everything for the chicks. You could have a room to yourself, Mrs Luard. Do come.'

'I've kind of got used to it here, but it's London I must get back to. My holiday is over and I must get back to my work. There are very few upholsterers left you know.'

'We don't know what has happened in London,' said Henry. 'Devon has become an island.'

'Has it indeed?' Mrs Luard did not seem particularly surprised. 'How can I get to your place anyway? I am fat.' Which was indeed true.

'I'll go home and get one of the Landrovers.' Henry jumped up.

'You are too young to drive.'

'The children seem to have grown up overnight,' said Muriel.

'All right then. You wait with me.' Mrs Luard laid a protective hand on Muriel's knee.

'Will you be all right?' Henry looked at the two women.

'Of course.'

Henry left them and presently they heard him clatter off on his pony and the sound died away in the still air.

Mrs Luard clucked and the young chickens and ducks gathered round her. 'They've been company,' she said, and a slow fat tear ran down her cheek.

Muriel felt it her turn to pat Mrs Luard's hand and did so. 'I think you were quite wonderful saving their lives,' she said.

'I never had anything to do with young birds before.' Mrs Luard looked happier. 'They need warmth, I could see that, so I lit the paraffin stove and kept it by my bed.'

'Mrs Luard, are you and the birds really the only people left?'

'Oh yes, I looked all right. I couldn't make it out at first, finding nobody, it didn't make sense. Then I thought it was some joke and then I just waited with my chicks. I don't mind waiting, that's what I'm used to. First my mum and I waited for my dad. He was inside here ten years. Then my old man was inside twice, first for eight years and then for five. He's dead now and when I got my holiday I thought to myself, well now, Norah – that's my name – you go and have a holiday at that camp, a kind of pilgrimage it was, but I didn't expect this to happen. Seems silly.'

'More than silly.'

'All a matter of proportion.' Mrs Luard patted Muriel's hand again. Muriel absently patted Mrs Luard's.

'When we can we must get to London. Henry's parents should be back.'

'They won't be. If they was they would have come to look for him wouldn't they?'

'They went to Spain for their holiday and left him with us.'

'Can't get back I daresay. You know,' Mrs Luard leant close to Muriel, 'there's been no post since that night, there's been no television, no aeroplanes, that means no communications. What an opportunity!' she exclaimed.

'Opportunity?'

'Yes. My dad and my old man they would have called this heaven-sent and made us all millionaires in a week.'

'We have been stealing food and clothes,' said Muriel.

'Ah, but think of the gold and diamonds, the fortunes that must be lying about for the taking. Not that I go in for the game myself, it was the men in our family who did that.'

Muriel hastily patted Mrs Luard's hand again to get in first.

'Ah, they were great thieves,' Mrs Luard said proudly. 'My grandad was a cat burglar. Did you ever hear of them?'

'I've read about them.'

'Well, my dad he specialised in safes in banks. He was very particular who he stole from.'

'I see.'

'My old man, now, he liked gold and diamonds but he lost his touch after we was married. I don't know why, and he was inside so much I had to take to upholstering. Now there's an *art*.'

'Old Mr Perdue who is living with us thinks it's very old-fashioned. He likes modern things.'

'Pah! It's antiques which are lovely. I love antiques.'

'So do I.'

'Got any antiques at this house of yours?'

'Yes, a great many.'

'Then I'll like that, make me feel at home. I like collections of all kinds, antiques, pictures, furniture, jewellery. Nice lot of things I have in London. Hope they're all right.'

'I'm sure they will be, Mrs Luard. It isn't the things which have gone, it's the people.'

'Well, I have nobody to miss. I have me ducks and chicks now.' Mrs Luard clucked and the little birds gathered round her, bright-eyed. 'Time for their tea.' Mrs Luard waddled off into the house behind the pool and came back carrying two bowls of food.

'Ducks,' she said. 'I feed them wet and the chicks dry.'

Muriel lay back in the sun listening to Mrs Luard's clucking noises and the small cheeps from the young birds. She wondered how long Henry would be getting to them in the Landrover and whether he would bring one of the girls with him. Presently she slept.

When Mrs Luard jogged Muriel's elbow she woke.

'Sounds like Henry.' Mrs Luard was listening. Muriel sat up.

'Yes, that's Henry crashing gears.' They went to the gate and found Henry with both the girls getting out of the Landrover. Muriel introduced June and Ann while Henry busied himself packing Mrs Luard and her chicks into the Landrover where she occupied the whole of the front seat, spreading her substantial thighs wide and clasping the box of small birds protectively to her huge breast. With Henry driving and the two girls walking beside Muriel on her pony, they wound their way slowly across the moor to Brendon. As they got near to the house Henry accelerated and, leaving Muriel behind with the girls, drove ahead into the yard tooting his horn. Muriel and the girls laughed as they heard the dogs bark in greeting and Henry shouting for Mr Perdue.

'I hope Mrs Luard and Mr Perdue will get on,' said Muriel.

'That's not very likely from what Henry told us.'

'Why not?'

'Well, Mr Perdue is so terribly virtuous and from what Henry said about Mrs Luard,' June hesitated, 'well, she seems more Henry's sort than old Perdue's.'

'Let's hurry and find out. She'll be dying for a cup of tea and company.' Ann broke into a run.

'I wonder whether she will.' Muriel turned her pony loose and walked towards the house with June. In the quiet of the warm summer evening they could hear voices coming from the house which suddenly rose to a crescendo of bass and contralto raised in argument.

'Oh dear!'

'It's sacrilege,' Mrs Luard was saying in a high voice.

'Not on that old thing. Ought to be thrown out it did.'

'What do you know about it, ignorant old man.'

'My old mother, she wouldn't have had such things near her, she was modern.'

'Collectors' pieces.'

'Now, Mrs Luard,' Henry's voice piped in.

'Get off it – look what they're doing – chewing it.'

Muriel ran into the house and hurried to the drawing-room where she heard the voices. Mrs Luard was standing glaring at Mr Perdue across the button sofa where Peg lay complacently surrounded by her puppies.

'Old philistine!' shouted Mrs Luard. 'Can't get these for love or money, let alone steal.'

'Mrs Luard!' bawled Henry as Muriel came in. 'There are yards and yards and yards of velvet to cover them just waiting for you.'

'Ah!' Mrs Luard stopped with her mouth open. 'And for the chairs too?' Her eyes were suspicious.

'Yes, yes, and curtains.'

'Then everything's all right. But that dog must get off. A job for an artist,' she murmured, 'and that artist is me.' Lovingly she stroked the chairs and the sofa.

⚜ 11 ⚜

Muriel settled Mrs Luard in the best spare room with a bathroom to herself. Mrs Luard prowled round the room, picking up objects and putting them down again, giving the impression of a suspicious goose being slowly mollified.

'Nice things you have here,' she said at last. 'Will you show me the whole house?'

'I would love to, but do settle in first and we will have supper. Come down when you are ready.'

'All right, dear.' Mrs Luard laid down a small piece of china she was examining and looked out of the window. 'Very quiet here,' she observed.

'Yes, that's why we live here. My husband and I loved it.'

'Is he dead then?'

'Yes, a car accident.' Muriel found she could speak quite naturally and without hearing the shriek of brakes and the silence after which had so haunted her.

'Was he the collector or was it you?'

'Oh, both of us, and a lot of things have been in the house for ever.'

'Cars shouldn't be allowed. Flying is much safer.'

'Yes, but this is a Nature Reserve. That's why we ride and have cars.'

'Nasty things horses. They give you such looks.'

Muriel laughed. 'You should meet my son Sam. He hates them. Or,' she corrected herself, 'he hated them.'

Mrs Luard advanced to pat Muriel. 'I'll soon fix those chairs and sofas,' she said kindly. 'It will be a pleasure, a real joy. Your dog can sleep somewhere else, can't she? I didn't mean to hurt your feelings but that old man was so rude.' Mrs Luard's hackles seemed to be rising again, 'No appreciation of good things.'

'He is all right really.' Muriel felt bound to defend Mr Perdue. 'He's been very good to us and he does like to be modern.'

'Not with me.' Mrs Luard was firm.

Muriel went downstairs deep in thought and into the kitchen where she found Henry and the two girls in a frenzy of activity.

'Here, try this.' Henry thrust an icy glass into her hand. Muriel sipped.

'Henry, it's marvellous!'

'It's to pacify.' Henry and both girls beamed. 'We mixed it for a treat. We just have to get one, just one, into old Perdue and Mrs Luard and all will be well.'

June laughed and said, 'Come and see what we've done.' She led Muriel into the dining-room which was in darkness and switched on the light. The table was laid for six with fine silver and glass, and candelabra waiting to be lit.

'The menu is clear iced soup, ham with mushrooms and Christmas pudding. Will you choose some wine, Mrs Wake?'

'How lovely! Of course I will. But what is old Perdue doing?'

'Getting a suitable box to put the little birds in by the Aga. He isn't so bad. We love your sofa and chairs too, you know, and I'm sure that gorgeous fat old thing will make a good job of them. Her eyes fairly shone when she saw them.'

'Where's a can of tomato juice, quick?' Henry was laughing and eager.

'Here's one ready cold in the ice-box.' June swiftly snatched a can from the refrigerator and opened it.

'Here comes Mr Perdue.' Ann wandered to the back door. 'Oh, Mr Perdue, can I help you?'

'No, you can't. You don't know nothing about young birds. You girls are just townspeople and that fat old geezer is another.'

'Well, Mr Perdue, she did keep them alive.' June spoke soothingly as she watched the old man put down a coop by the Aga.

'There, they'll be just right there. You get them a dish of water, girl. Alive by her bed! T'isn't sanitary. My old mother would turn in her grave. Disgusting, she'd call it.'

'Here's a dish.' Ann handed him a flat dish of water and the little birds began to drink from it.

'I expect you are thirsty too, Mr Perdue.' Henry advanced on the old man offering a large glass of tomato juice.

'What's this?'

'Tomato juice.'

'Tastes funny.'

'Well, speaking from a purely academic point of view, everything has been funny lately.' Henry sipped from his own glass which he took off the dresser.

'What's that you're drinking?' Mr Perdue looked at Henry with righteous suspicion.

'Oh, just a mild little drink Ann and June made for Mrs Wake and Mrs Luard. We are celebrating the arrival of Mrs Luard and her birds in the dining-room. High time we had a party.'

Mr Perdue finished his drink. 'Birds and parties used to mean something quite different in my day.' He laughed heartily and suddenly smacked June's behind.

'Henry, what did you give him?' Muriel pulled Henry into the passage.

'Three quarters vodka, one quarter tomato juice. Here comes Mrs Luard.'

Mrs Luard swept downstairs wearing a clean dress.

'Where are my chicks?'

'Safe by the Aga. Mr Perdue put them there in a coop. Have a drink, Mrs Luard.' Ann thrust a glass into Mrs Luard's hand. 'Coo, that's good! Now, where's me chicks?'

'Here, safe and sound. Got more room to move around than they had before.' Mr Perdue crouched by the coop holding an empty glass. 'Not that they was badly off before.' He eyed Mrs Luard gallantly.

'Let's have dinner as soon as we can. I'm starving.' June took Muriel's arm. 'Henry, for heaven's sake bring the food.'

Henry obeyed, sweeping into the dining-room carrying plates and dishes, while Ann lit the candles and put out the light. They all sat down except Henry, who toured the table filling wine glasses to the brim before taking his place beside Mrs Luard.

'My discovery!' Henry raised his glass and gazed up into Mrs Luard's face. Intently they drank a toast and then Mrs Luard whispered something to Henry who shouted with laughter and cried out, 'Oh, we will. Yes, let's.'

Muriel watched Mr Perdue refill his glass and drink gallantly to June. Then she turned to Ann. 'You had the right idea,' she said. 'I wish Paul and Sam were here to enjoy this.'

'Eat and drink,' said Ann. 'We have our lives to live.'

Muriel looked at Ann, at June, at Henry and at Mr Perdue eating and drinking and laughing together, and suddenly she no longer felt hungry, only tired. 'Excuse me a moment.' She slipped almost unnoticed out of the room. She passed the telephone, giving it a glance of hate, looked into the drawing-room where Peg lay comfortably with her puppies, and then walked out into the quiet night, leaving the sound of revelry behind her. Chap joined her, and in his silent company she walked down the hill to the reservoir, or lake as she and Julian had always called it, and sat down by the water to think. The water was very still except for the occasional plop of a trout rising. The woods across the water stood silent and enigmatic. Far away she heard a fox bark and Chap pricked his ears. It was very warm and Muriel wondered when it would rain.

'I can't think, I can't think.' She clutched her head.

'None of us dares.' Henry, who had followed her, sat down beside her. Chap wagged his tail.

'Henry!'

'Yes.'

'Henry, I can't think.'

'I can but I prefer not to.'

'Henry, what is all this about?'

'I've no idea.' Henry sounded cross.

'Are they all right back at the house?'

'Oh, yes. The girls are clearing up and old Perdue and Mrs Luard are bosom friends. Hail vodka!'

'The vodka was a good idea.'

'Yes.'

'Have I been here long?'

'About two hours.'

'It's so warm, it isn't natural.'

'Nothing is.'

'Henry, you don't think Paul has gone for good?'

'Oh no, of course I don't. He's too fond of you and of his home.'

'Henry, you can stay here for ever you know.'

'Thank you.' Henry put his arms around Muriel and kissed her. 'They found those six eggs I put in the hot cupboard had hatched,' he said. 'That's really what I came to tell you.'

'What eggs?'

'Don't you remember? I found some eggs in the loft and you said to put them in a box in the hot cupboard. Well, they've hatched. June spilt a lot of wine and went to get a clean cloth and she found them. Mrs Luard is drooling over them and so is old Perdue. It's been a funny evening.'

'Have they gone to bed?'

'I think so. The girls and I cleared up and Mrs Luard and Mr Perdue squabbled about the new chicks. She wanted them in her room but they settled them near the Aga. It's lucky you have the Aga.'

'Well, you know why.'

'Not really.'

'Sam and Julian decided we must be absolutely self-sufficient.'

'Why?'

'Well, in case of war. They said that if we kept our own power and warmth and lived here where it's isolated we should have more chance of survival. We have survived. Father Richard thinks it's accidental.'

'So do I. I bet my parents are blown away.'

'Poor Henry.'

'I didn't like them, you know I didn't.'

Muriel said nothing.

'I don't mind if they have been blown away.'

'Henry, you are drunk.'

'Not particularly. I love you and Paul and I like those girls and old Perdue and Mrs Luard and those chaps at the Abbey, but nothing could make me like my parents.' Henry paused. 'Look,' he said. 'There's something else left — otters.'

Muriel followed his pointing finger to where along the edge of the lake a pair of otters were playing in and out of the water. Henry was holding Chap's collar.

'Otters, foxes, rabbits, moles. You see, it proves what Father Richard thinks.'

'I don't see anything proved. Why do you hate your parents? I always rather liked them.'

'My mother loathes me because I am not her child and my father because I am not his.'

'Is this true?'

'Yes, I found out by listening at keyholes and reading letters.'

'I never knew.' Muriel was bewildered.

'They adopted me and then they found me a bore and I couldn't like the things they liked.'

'But that's normal between parents and children.'

'Yes, if you are parents and children, but we were not. You see, they are or were mad about politics. I adored literature. They said it was waste of time and intellect. They loved sport. I'm afraid of it. They loved travelling. Well, I'm like old Perdue's mother. I'm modern but not over-modern. Nothing would ever make them like me or me them. They are or were *inhuman*, Mrs Wake.'

'I suppose you know.'

'Yes, I do know. If they were here now they would be rushing round knowing what had happened, expounding theories as to why it had happened. They wouldn't have gone into a state of shock like you.'

'Is that what I'm in?'

'Yes. You were in a state of shock already over your husband's death. If you hadn't been you would be much worse than you are now.'

'Worse?' Muriel was indignant.

'Screaming worse.' Henry laughed. 'Come home to bed, Mrs Wake.' He took her hand and pulled her to her feet and then led her up from the lake to the house which stood very still and quiet in the moonlight. Henry led Muriel upstairs to her room and Chap followed.

'I moved Peg and her family up here before I came to fetch you.'

Muriel looked round her room at the cat and her kittens in the only comfortable chair, and at Peg and her family lying in a large basket. Peg thumped her tail in greeting. Muriel stroked her head. Chap jumped on to the bed and watched Muriel undress. Henry had gone.

'I can't think,' Muriel was muttering to herself. 'I can't think.'

'Far better not to.' Henry had come back wearing his pyjamas.

'You are so terribly grown-up, Henry, knowing so much.'

'I'm not grown-up, I'm frightened.'

'Is that why you brought Peg up here?'

'Yes. Somehow it's like that first night. Shall we take lots of sleeping pills?'

'Henry, you are tipsy.'

'No, frightened.'

Henry reached for the bottle of sleeping pills and handed it to Muriel. 'I've taken some already,' he said, and got into her bed and put his head under the bedclothes.

Muriel stood looking down at the boy, then round the room at the cat and her kittens, at the dogs, and then out of the window at the stars. She listened. The house was very quiet. She went to the door and opened it. She could hear nothing except the clock in the hall ticking. She wondered whether the girls were asleep and Mr Perdue and Mrs Luard. The clock downstairs struck one and the silence seemed more complete. Muriel shut her door, swallowed several pills and got into bed beside Henry. She put out her hand and touched him. He was alive and asleep. She wondered why he was afraid and where Paul was and Sam.

'I'm not asleep.'

'I thought you were.'

'I was pretending.'

'I was thinking.'

'We must explore, get further afield, Mrs Wake.'

'How?'

'Somehow we must get to London. Get to London and Paris. Mrs Luard wants to "get at the shops" as she calls it. Hatton Garden will do her for a start.'

'Or the Bank of England.' Muriel giggled.

'Yes, that will keep her occupied, but she told me she wanted to upholster all your chairs and things first before she goes off anywhere.'

'Will she come back?'

'She might. It depends.'

'I want Paul back and Sam.'

'Don't fuss. He'll come. My parents won't.'

'They only went to Spain.'

'Is that what they told you?'

'Of course.'

'They told me that too, but they were not going to Spain. I heard them planning. They said Germany, and "Push Russia and China into the Pacific, it's logical," my father said.'

'What on earth were they doing?'

'Planning to destroy and if it's not them it's someone else and whoever it is has succeeded.'

'But your parents must have been in the air, Henry, when it happened. It couldn't be them. You are imagining things.'

'No, I'm not. They were up to something. My father said, "What about Henry if we succeed?" and my mother said, "Oh, to hell with Henry, he's a bore." I heard them, Mrs Wake, through the keyhole absolutely clearly, and my father said, "Ah, well, good riddance," and they both laughed and I knew it was true because the next day before I left to come here I asked my mother for new shoes as I was growing out of my old ones. You know I've been borrowing Paul's since I was here?'

'No, I didn't.'

'Well, I told Paul not to tell you. The thing is, when I told my mother I needed shoes to grow into she said, "You won't need anything to grow into." So I put things together and now I know.'

'But they were in the air, Henry. They were flying.'

'Possibly, but they had the intention. That's enough.'

Henry seemed very small suddenly as he moved closer to her in the bed. 'Hold my hand.'

'Yes, I will. Don't worry, Henry.'

'Oh, I won't worry. I'm glad, glad, glad they are not my parents, or should I say were not?' Henry sighed and slept.

Muriel slept late the following morning and when she woke found Henry still asleep beside her. She lay still, not wishing to wake him. It had, after all, been about two or three when he had finally slept. She heard June and Ann moving about the house downstairs and once Mr Perdue call something and Mrs Luard's voice answer rather crossly.

Now, thought Muriel, I must get up, but she did not get up continuing to lie watching the sun trying to penetrate the curtains. She saw Charlie stir and jump up to the open window followed by her kittens. One after the other they went through the window and she heard their faint scrabbling descent as they climbed down the magnolia which spread across the front of the house to the ground. She heard Ann say, 'Here come the cats', and June remark,

'That poor dog must be bursting. I'll creep up and let her out'. Presently her door was gently opened and Peg went out followed in procession by all the puppies.

'June,' whispered Muriel.

June put her head round the door and smiled. 'I'll bring you some coffee.'

When she came back she entered silently, carrying a tray. 'I brought a cup for myself too.'

Muriel sat up carefully so as not to disturb Henry.

'Thank you, June. What's going on?'

'Old Ma Luard has started on your chairs. She won't let anyone near her.'

'What else?'

'Oh, nothing. Mr Perdue is tending the animals. What happened to you last night? We watched the summer lightning.'

'I saw none. I went and sat by the water. Henry joined me. We saw a pair of otters.'

'Can you think now? It was quite a party.'

'Yes, I can. June, what is going on? Why is it so wonderfully hot? Why are some of us alive and not others? Where is my Paul and my son Sam?'

'All those questions.' June sipped her coffee. 'No answers. Seems strange to us too. You saw coloured snow. We didn't.'

'I am sure we saw coloured snow.' Muriel was perplexed and stared at the girl.

'I should be worrying about my parents in Australia and all my relations and – '

'And what?'

'My fiancé. I was engaged but I don't feel engaged any more. Do you understand that feeling?'

'Yes.' Muriel put her cup back on the tray carefully. 'Henry said last night that I am suffering from shock. He may be right, but it feels more like release than shock.'

'It does to Ann and me too.'

'Release from everything except worrying about Paul and Sam.'

'It's hard for you. I'm sure Paul will come back. After all, what could have happened to him? Henry got back from Exeter.'

'Henry brought you, June, but Paul – ' Muriel sighed, listening to June's voice, gentle and reassuring. Muriel noticed that she said Paul would get back but made no mention of Sam.

'When you were out last night old Perdue and Mrs Luard had another row.' June changed the subject.

'Oh Lord, what about? Not the sofa again?'

'Not exactly, but he wanted some of the velvet.'

'What for?'

'To line a casket. He said Henry had told him your little monk at the Abbey had put all the bits he could find in a tin and buried them in the cemetery.'

'He did.'

'Well, Mr Perdue wants to collect all he can find in the village and bury them in the grave you found him in, but he wants Mrs Luard to line the coffin with velvet.'

'She could I'm sure.'

'Yes, but she won't, or rather she said she wouldn't unless there was enough stuff left over from the curtains and covers.'

'Did Henry put this idea into his head?'

'Who else?'

June looked down at Henry's innocent sleeping face. 'Henry said that your monk said a Requiem Mass and had incense and that the tin was covered with a silken pall.'

'So it was.'

'Well, old Perdue is madly jealous and he is going to collect all the bits he can and bury them in a velvet lined coffin.'

'He won't hear of church unity.' Henry's sleepy voice came up to them from the pillow. 'Any coffee for me?'

'Of course. Really, Henry, I suspect you of making mischief.'

'Oh, no.' Henry sat up. 'I've offered to help him. He can't possibly do the whole village alone.'

'Henry, you are a macabre child.'

'Depends how you look at it. I shall toll the bell too as I

did at the Abbey. For whom the bell tolls. Bells on her fingers and bells on her toes,' he sang.

'We must all go.' Muriel sat up angrily.

'Okay.'

'And if the poor man wants velvet he shall have it. But it isn't a joke, Henry.'

June laughed. 'Just imagine all those bits as you call them rising from the dead on the Day of Judgement.'

'You are as bad as Henry. I must go and see Mrs Luard.' Muriel got out of bed, put on her dressing-gown and went downstairs, hearing behind her June and Henry's laughter.

In the drawing-room she found Mrs Luard on hands and knees among the chairs and sofas, her mouth full of pins, a pair of scissors in her hand, snipping away at a great bolt of white velvet.

'Good morning, Mrs Luard.'

'Not one yard shall he have.'

'Please, Mrs Luard.'

'You're weak and who told you anyway?'

'June.'

'Ah, June. It's Henry who started it. If it hadn't been for him I should have been left in peace with my chairs.' Mrs Luard patted a small Victorian chair lovingly.

'I bought much more than enough and there is yellow and pink too.'

'He's not going to have any until I've cut out all the covers and the curtains.' Mrs Luard glared at Muriel who, recognising the look of the artist disturbed, retreated to the kitchen.

Mr Perdue was sitting on a chair by the Aga looking down at the little chicks and ducks.

'Good morning, Mr Perdue. How are they?'

''Ealthy. Much 'ealthier than they was. I'll get 'em out in the sun presently.'

'June and Henry tell me – '

'Ah yes, and that old woman won't give me a yard or two of velvet. She's an 'eathen.'

'I'll give you all the velvet you want. It is mine after all.'

'Not from the way she talks it isn't, nor them chairs.'

'She is an artist in her own line, just like you.'

'Trying to mollify me. Don't think I didn't hear that boy, I did.'

'When is the funeral?' Muriel hastily changed the subject.

'Tomorrow I thought.' Mr Perdue looked thoughtful. 'If you and those girls would help me we could make it tomorrow.'

'Then we must go down to the village now and start at once. We should have done this weeks ago, Mr Perdue.'

'Arr, time flies, but it won't matter.'

Muriel called Ann, June and Henry to her. 'Get boxes and baskets each of you.' Then, while they hurried to obey her, she went into the drawing-room, snatched the scissors from Mrs Luard, helped herself to at least four yards of white velvet while Mrs Luard watched her speechless, and said, 'You coming, Mrs Luard?'

'I don't hold with it,' Mrs Luard gasped, fat and furious.

'But I do.' Muriel swept up the velvet and went out to join the others. 'Here is your velvet, Mr Perdue. Come on all of you. It's shameful. We must clear the village.'

She led the way to the Landrover, jumped in, followed by Henry, and waited while Mr Perdue and the girls followed silently.

'I'm sorry we laughed,' June said gently.

'Well, none of us knows which to do, laugh or cry. It's quite natural.'

Muriel, having made a decision, felt better. She drove down to the village as fast as she could, not stopping until she reached the church. At the church the old man took over.

'You two girls collect,' he said, 'while Mrs Wake and I gets the coffin on to the Landrover and take it back to the churchyard.' Henry began tolling the bell which rang out slow and clear in the strong hot sun. Muriel walked round the village thoughtfully, leaving Mr Perdue to direct operations. When the bell stopped she went back to the churchyard. Mr Perdue, with Henry's help, had lowered the coffin into the grave where she had found Mr Perdue himself. The two girls had picked flowers which they threw in armfuls into the grave. The funeral was soon over and Mr Perdue looked relieved.

'Thank you for your help.' He looked round at them.

'We are all glad to help.'

'Not that fat old woman, she ain't decent.'

'She just has other interests,' said Henry. 'Shall we wind the clock while we are here?'

Henry and Mr Perdue went into the church.

'Let's go to the pub,' said Ann.

Muriel followed the two girls to the pub and sat on a stool by the bar with June while Ann poured them drinks.

'Is this going to be the pattern of our lives?'

'I think Mrs Luard will alter that.'

'She and old Perdue will make life unbearable. It's terribly kind of her to cover the chairs, but that occupation isn't going to last her for ever.' Muriel sipped her whisky.

'Young Henry will settle that. He has a plan.'

'Henry would have. That boy is resourceful. What is his plan?'

'I'm not sure yet. All I heard last night was something about "choosing the very finest of the period – collecting rare items" and something about "transport". After that they went into a huddle and whispered.'

'Oh.' Muriel looked at the girls thoughtfully. 'Are we really cut off from the rest of England?'

'Yes, there is a split right up what used to be the Exe valley and the sea has come in. You can't even see across.'

'Suppose the same has happened at Plymouth?'

'We think it's likely. June and I have been looking at maps.'

'I've been dreaming. I've only worried about Paul and Sam. I've only been thinking of myself.'

'It seemed natural to all of us.' Ann sounded reassuring.

'Well, it isn't. Another drink, please, Ann. Our lives can't go on like this, just looking after the animals, taking for granted we have no neighbours.'

'No, but it may take some time for us. Henry and Mrs Luard seem to be the only people planning anything. Mr Perdue is happy and busy with the farm animals. We have been very happy, thanks to you, and those two monks seem quite calm and very busy.'

'I think the trouble is,' June said thoughtfully, 'we don't know how to begin. We've done the obvious things like getting in stocks of food and clothes and you seem already to have had the idea of getting fuel.'

'That was my husband. He almost rebuilt the house too. He said we must. He must have had foresight.'

'Then you see we are all so used to the telephone, the post and communications of all sorts, we are paralysed without them. We have an enormous choice of cars, but we can't really get far. Our skates worked best.'

'We shall have to make expeditions to find out.'

'I must wait for Paul.' Muriel felt that she must no longer mention Sam. They all looked away when she did.

'Well, of course you must wait, but perhaps we shouldn't.'

'I'm perfectly happy to wait.' Ann sat down in a comfortable chair and put her feet up on another.

June laughed. 'You talk like the idle rich.'

'That's what I feel like, a sort of natural neutral beachcomber, happy and at peace with the world.'

'Old Perdue and Mrs Luard and Henry don't feel like that.'

'I would if – ' Muriel sighed.

'If your sons came home, if your husband was not dead.' June spoke slightly impatiently, then said, 'Sorry. I wonder what's keeping those two so long. It doesn't take all afternoon to wind one clock.'

'You would, if you had found a mouse in it.' Henry came cheerfully into the pub.

'Henry, what entrances you make!'

'Well, I was listening outside the door for a suitable cue. Mr Perdue has one mouse, I have another.'

'Let's see.' The girls crowded close to him.

'Aren't you afraid?'

'Of course not.'

'Tut, tut. Old Perdue will be so disappointed. He said, "Arr, these'll make those girls get a move on and that old witch".' Henry imitated Mr Perdue's voice. 'He is planning to set them on Mrs Luard.'

'We mustn't let Charlie get them.' Muriel took the tiny mouse and held it in her hand, watching the briskly twitching whiskers and large shining eyes.

'What were they doing in the clock?'

'Heaven knows. Give it a peanut. It's terribly tame.'

'Let's put them in a tin. Hullo, Mr Perdue. What a find.'

'Nothing keeps vermin down.' The old man absently accepted a glass of beer held out to him by June.

''Ere's t'other.' He handed a second mouse to Muriel who passed it on to Henry. 'That Mrs Luard and these 'ere mice —'ere's to them that was.' He raised his glass and drank.

'Mrs Wake?'

'Yes, Henry.'

'Do you mind if I go off and do a little trip on my own?' Henry looked innocent and eager.

'What sort of trip?'

'Oh, just a short trip. I'll be back for supper. I can go in the doctor's wife's Mini. It's all ready.'

'So you have something planned?'

'Well, yes.'

'You don't want to tell me about it?'

'Not yet. The plan may be no good. It's a present for Mrs Luard.'

'You are up to no good.'

'What is good and what is bad? This is diplomatic.'

'All right, Henry. But be sure to come back.'

'I will,' Henry handed the mice to Muriel. 'They like milk,' he said to June and slipped out of the pub.

'I wonder what he is up to.' Muriel went to the pub window and watched Henry running down the empty village street.

'Another drink before we go home?' Ann collected glasses and poured out drinks. They sat in silence until they heard the engine of a small car start up and die away.

'There he goes.'

'Time we went back. We must do the milking and I must have another struggle with making bread.'

The girls laughed, since both of them and Muriel took it

in turns to make rather unpalatable unleavened bread to eat with the tinned food and milk products they had at Brendon.

'How long before those chicks start laying, Mr Perdue?' Ann climbed into the Landrover.

'Six months, just about.'

'That will be the day.' June got in beside Muriel. 'I wonder whether any of us have lived so long without an egg.'

'It must have been done.' Muriel drove the Landrover on its winding way up the hill. 'You know, when the weather does change we shan't get even the Landrover down to the village. If you saw lightning that means rain.'

'If we could shift some of the tree trunks and old Bartlett's car we could use the road.'

'The breakdown truck in the garridge has a winch.' Mr Perdue spoke in superior tones.

'Then Ann and I can help you.'

'Of course.' Mr Perdue made a satisfied noise in his throat which Muriel and the girls recognised as purely male.

'You show us what to do and we will do it.' Ann spoke flatteringly. Muriel realised that the old man's vanity needed a bit of solace since the arrival of Mrs Luard.

'How do you imagine the mice got into the clock?' Muriel asked him.

'Climbed up to look at the view,' he said rudely. Muriel paid no attention but ploughed on.

'Climbed from where?'

'The crypt, of course. Boiling with mice the crypt used to be.'

'How clever you are, Mr Perdue.'

'Don't overdo it now. I can see what you women are up to.'

Muriel and the two girls laughed.

'It's that fat woman what's got no tact.'

'Here's old Mr Barlett's car. Do you think if we all gave it a heave we could get it a bit more out of the way?' Muriel spoke hastily.

'Yes, we could. Not that he was old. He was two years younger than me.'

'I spoke with — ' Muriel tried to think with what she had spoken — certainly not respect or affection.

'You spoke without thinking,' old Perdue snapped. 'Come on then, let's give it a heave. Not that I'm going to rupture myself, having just buried the doctor and the district nurse.'

'Quite a mild push should do it.'

They all got out and with a concerted heave levered the already lopsided car off the road.

'Now quite big things can get by.'

They stood looking at their handiwork with satisfaction before going on up the hill to the house.

Mrs Luard, surrounded by puppies and kittens, strolled to meet them. 'Had a nice time?' she enquired affably.

'That's one way of putting it.' Mr Perdue walked off calling, 'Muriel, Muriel, come on me beauty.'

'Muriel indeed! Where's Henry?' Mrs Luard was pettish.

'Gone exploring. It's for you he said.'

'Ah, he's a good boy. Reminds me of my old man, that boy.'

'Let's have tea.' Muriel smiled at the high praise given Henry. 'Shall we have it outdoors?'

June too was grinning. 'Yes, I like watching the evening sun.'

'You all smell like a pub.' Mrs Luard sounded in no way opprobious.

'I expect we do. Tea will steady us up. We've begun clearing the road to the village too.'

'I was thinking we would need that done.' Mrs Luard sat down beside Muriel and they waited for the girls to bring out trays of tea.

'We would be all right in the winter even if we did get cut off.'

'I shan't. I shall need the road.'

'Why?'

'To drive up and down, all being well.' Mrs Luard's mouth snapped shut.

Muriel poured out tea and handed round cups. 'What do you think of mice, Mrs Luard?'

'I love the little dears. It's one of the things I miss most just now, mice and men.'

'Henry and Mr Perdue found two.'

'Two mice? Lovely. Let's hope they aren't both female.'

'Mr Perdue will be disappointed.'

'Hoped I'd jump on one of my chairs and scream, did he?'

'Do it just to please him. We've got them in a tin.'

'Not me. I might break a spring, me being heavy.'

'Then he's doomed to disappointment.'

'Good.' Mrs Luard handed her cup to Muriel to be refilled.

'But you're not.'

June jumped to her feet. 'Look!'

They followed her pointing finger. Very high in the sky a tiny white object floated.

'A parachute!' shouted Ann. 'Where's the plane?'

'Not a sound of one – listen.'

The four women stood watching the tiny object grow slowly larger in the distance. Far away they heard a dull explosion, then silence.

'It's crashed.'

'Where is it going to land?'

'In the lake.' Muriel began to run.

'You're right.' The girls followed her, outpacing her with their long legs. The parachute, swinging slowly in the still air, grew larger rapidly until they could distinguish the human figure dangling.

'He's not much good at it,' Ann shouted.

'Or she.'

Muriel ran as she had not run for years, racing at an angle to the path the girls had taken, racing to where the boat old Perdue used for fishing was moored. As she reached the boat she heard the splash. She untied the mooring, grabbed the oars and rowed out into the lake with both Peg and Chap swimming strongly behind her. Glancing over her shoulder she could see the large, white parachute settling on the water like a jellyfish. She reached it and caught hold of it and pulled. Somewhere under the mass of silk was a human being. She pulled desperately at the silk and the boat tipped towards it suddenly, righting itself. She looked over her shoulder to see two hands gripping the side of the boat, followed by a brown face and a voice which said, 'Oh, thank you, thank you. I am not very good parachute.'

'Here, let me pull you.'

'Ah! Thank you, thank you. That is truly kind.'

Muriel leant back and pulled and got the speaker into the boat.

'Your dogs, kind lady, they want to come in too.'

Muriel caught each dog by the collar in turn and pulled them into the boat. They shook themselves, drenching her with spray, and stood balancing on their feet four square, wagging their tails.

'I am still tied to the parachute, lady.'

'So you are. Let me help.' Muriel helped the man off with the parachute harness. 'Where on earth do you come from?'

'From Afghanistan. This is Sweden I think?' The young man now sitting in the boat flashed her a brilliant smile. 'You speak very good English, almost as good as me.'

'This is England. I am English.'

'Oh! Then I am as bad pilot as parachute. The young ladies are signalling and calling.'

'So they are.' Muriel looked at Ann and June jumping and shouting on the shore.

'What do they want, those young ladies?'

'Oh, I expect they want to invite you to tea.'

'Tea, that would be nice.' The young man fainted against the gunwhale and Muriel rowed as hard as she could for the shore.

When three hours later Henry limped up the hill, nursing the bruises he had acquired when for a split second he had taken his eyes off the road and run into a tree, he found only Ann in the kitchen.

'Good heavens, Henry, you look a mess. What happened?'

'I saw a plane crashing and while I was looking I ran into a tree.'

'Sit down and let me look at you.'

'There was a parachute, Ann, I saw it.'

'So did we, it's here.'

'Oh, I missed it!'

'There was an Afghan hanging on it. Mrs Wake's taking care of him now.'

'Is he hurt?'

'No. Shocked I think.'

'Can I see him?'

'No,' said Muriel, coming into the room, 'not yet. He's asleep. Henry, what on earth has happened to you?'

'I ran into a tree when I saw the aeroplane.'

'Are you hurt?'

'Only bruised. I walked back. It's goodbye to that Mini though.'

'Oh dear, Mrs Lampson will be furious.'

'There isn't a Mrs Lampson any more.'

'Nor there is. Let me look at your bruises.'

'All right, but tell me about the Afghan.'

'We put him to bed.'

'I know, but where did he come from?'

'Afghanistan.'

'Are you being annoying on purpose, Ann?'

'Yes. Sorry, Henry. Drink this.'

'What is it?'

'Tea.'

'Treatment for shock – keep the patient warm and give him hot tea. It never said anywhere you must madden him with curiosity.'

'He comes from Kabul. He was flying to Sweden to see his sister who is or was studying there. He had never flown a plane so he got lost – '

'Almost a feat in itself these days.'

'Yes, and he had never used a parachute before either.'

'Seems like an intellectual!'

'He was on his way to Sweden because the Kabul Radio doesn't work any more nor their telephones or anything.'

'Any Afghans left?'

'He said quite a lot had disappeared in a disorderly way.'

'What does he mean – disorderly?'

'They left "bits" behind.'

'But there are some left alive?'

'He said some of the country people but not the townspeople, which accounts for him flying by himself.'

'It adds up.' Henry appeared satisfied. 'Will he be down for supper?'

'Not until tomorrow. I think he should sleep. I've given him a sedative.'

'How are the mice?'

'Fine. Mrs Luard says one of them is expecting. She put them down a mousehole to be safe from the cats.'

'Goodoh! Where is she now?'

'She's working on the chairs.'

'I've got good news for her.'

Henry put down his cup and left the kitchen, calling, 'Mrs Luard! Mrs Luard! It's all perfect.'

'Henry's bruises don't seem very bad.' Muriel picked up the empty cup.

'No, he's young. Running a Mini into a tree is nothing. I wonder how that Afghan got so far off course. As Henry says, it's almost impossible.'

'I'll go and see if he's asleep and if he isn't I'll ask him.' Muriel got up. 'I'll take him some tea.'

With Ann's help Muriel laid a small tray and carried it upstairs. She paused outside the room they had put their new visitor in and listened. Hearing movements in the bed she went in.

'Are you awake?'

'Yes, lady.'

'I've brought you some tea.'

'That is too much trouble for you.'

'Of course it isn't.' Muriel sat beside the bed and poured a cup of tea for the young man.

'Thank you,' he said, taking it. 'Thank you very much.'

'We were wondering just now how you got off course in your aeroplane.' Muriel smiled.

'My name is Akbar.' Akbar gave a little bow. 'I got off course, dear lady, because I have always had a pilot to fly me, dear lady, and when I noticed I had gone wrong there was no petrol left, so I baled out.'

'I see.'

'I am a professor of literature. I am not a practical man.'

'That explains it. Have some more tea. Does your head ache?'

'Oh no, I am very well. I am dry now and rested. I must find another plane to take me to Sweden.'

'That may be difficult, if not impossible.'

'Why so?'

'Well, here we are in a Nature Reserve and we are not allowed planes. Also things have happened.'

'What things?'

'Well, almost everybody but the people you have seen here have disappeared. We have no communications – '

'Not in Kabul either. Did you have snow, a lot of snow?'

'Yes, and terrible wind.'

'We too, a great storm.'

'And this part of England is cut off from the rest of the country by the sea. It's all very odd,' Muriel finished lamely, 'and the climate has gone mad,' she added.

'Tell me more if it is not too much trouble.'

Muriel told her new visitor all that had happened since that first night of fear, ending, 'I thought you might be able to tell me whether it's another war.'

'Oh no, not war, an accident of some kind.'

'That's what Father Richard says. He seems quite calm.'

'I, too, feel calm. Let us enjoy what has come to us.'

'Akbar – may I call you Akbar? – what has happened to us?'

'I do not know, lady. Maybe in Sweden they will know. They are very progressive.'

'Not if there are no Swedes left. It is over four weeks since we had our storm and everyone blew away.'

'Then maybe my sister she has blown away too.'

'Yes.' Too progressive, Muriel thought wryly.

'But here it is nice: nice house, nice climate, plenty to eat, pretty girls, why do you worry? I am here now. I will help you.'

'Thank you.'

'What is to be done first?'

'We thought we would clear the road to the village. Cut the trees away. There are not many across the road.'

'And make logs to burn?'

'Yes.'

'I would like that. I did that in my holidays as a boy.'

'We have saws and old Perdue says there is a winch at the garage in the village. We could begin at the bottom of the hill and work upwards.' Muriel felt enthusiastic with the prospect of something concrete to do.

'May I come in?' Henry came in, knocking as he did so. 'I am Henry.' Henry and Akbar shook hands.

'We were talking of clearing the road to the village. Mrs Luard is very keen on it too.'

'I can hardly see Mrs Luard as a lumberjack,' said Henry.

'No, but while we clear the road she can get on with covering the chairs and it will keep her and old Perdue apart. Then in the evening we can swim in the lake. What was the water like, Akbar?'

'Oh, warm, quite nice. Good for the health.'

'Are you a doctor?'

'Alas, no. I am a professor of literature.'

'There's a lovely library in this house.'

'Then I have fallen well.' Akbar seemed pleased. 'Two pretty girls, a kind lady and a library.'

'I think you should get some sleep and tomorrow, if you are well enough, we will all begin clearing the road.' Muriel looked thoughtfully at her new visitor, rose and went downstairs to join the girls.

'How is the Afghan?'

'Much better. He is pleased because there are two pretty girls.'

'We shall toss up for him,' Ann laughed. 'No sharing.'

'Hobson's choice.' June grinned.

Muriel felt irritable. All her visitors were so individual. Cross old Perdue, determined Mrs Luard, Henry full of secrets, the two girls so friendly and flippant. She went to the telephone and lifted the receiver. Nothing. She dialed 123. Nothing. She dialed 999. Nothing. She dialled all the numbers by which she had been able to get anything from the weather report to music. Nothing. She went out into the evening light and walked slowly round the house. The sun was setting and the sweet smell of flowers was all round her. Below her in the meadow the cows grazed and out on the moor she could see the sheep and ponies. In the farmyard Perdue was feeding the chicks, who were growing out of the attractive stage and beginning to look like miniature ostriches. She went up to the old man.

'How many hens and how many cockerels?' she asked.

'Three cockerels, the others hens I reckon, and three drakes among the ducks. We can eat two of the cockerels.'

'Are you happy, Mr Perdue?'

'I'm all right.'

Muriel went in to supper.

'Where's Henry?'

'He went out. He took sandwiches and said we were not to wait up for him.'

'Then I shan't.' Muriel ate and helped clear the table and then followed Mrs Luard into the drawing-room. There she sat down and watched the older woman resume her clever cutting and stitching.

'You have nearly finished.'

'Yes, soon be done now.'

'What will you do then?'

'The curtains, and when the road is cleared – ah well, I shall have plenty to do and no interference.'

'No, none. I rang 999.'

'What d'you want to do that for?' Mrs Luard was angry.

'Only to see if the telephone worked and it didn't.'

'No. Good job too. Wish my dad and my old man was alive, they'd have a laugh.'

'I suppose they would.'

'Take the salt out of it a bit though.'

'Why?'

'Well, not much fun in the profession when there's nobody to stop you, is there? They weren't like me and that boy Henry now were they?'

'No, I daresay not. But how are you and Henry alike?' Muriel stroked the velvet chair Mrs Luard was finishing.

'Ah, Henry and me we have higher interests, not that they are the same, mind you.'

'Henry has gone out.'

'Yes, I asked him to find me something I wanted.'

'What was that?'

'You'll know soon enough. Now you go to bed. I can see you're tired.'

'That Afghan –'

'Oh, the girls and I will manage him. You go to bed.'

'Mrs Luard, will you try and be nice to Mr Perdue?'

'I see no cause to be.' Mrs Luard looked obstinate.

Muriel sighed and left the room.

'I really felt happier alone with the boys,' she muttered to herself. She went upstairs, looked in on the sleeping Afghan, stood undecided for a moment on the landing watched by the dogs, and then went into her room and slowly went to bed. Lying stiffly in her bed, she heard the noises in the house. The girls talking to old Perdue and, what seemed very much later, all three of them going to bed. Somebody had a bath. The clock in the hall and the cuckoo clock in the kitchen struck midnight in unison. Far away she heard the village clock chime twelve, followed by the Abbey down in the valley tolling midnight too. Slowly she relaxed. The dogs sighed in their sleep and the puppies made snuffling noises. The night was so still she could hear the rasp of the cat's tongue as she licked a kitten.

14

'Mum, Mum, wake up.'

Muriel woke soggily. Paul was climbing onto her bed and hugging her. Both the dogs and an avalanche of puppies were greeting him. It was very dark and above the dogs' whimpers of joy she could hear a hiss and disturbances from the cats' chair.

'Oh, Paul! Oh, Paul! Are you safe?'

'Yes, of course I am. Has Peg had all these puppies? Let's have a light. Oh goodness! Charlie's here too.' Paul switched on his mother's bedside lamp. 'What a collection!'

'Paul, thank God you are back!' Muriel clung to him. 'I thought you had gone for ever.'

'Sorry, Mum.' Paul was stroking the dogs and the cat. 'Can I get in with you. I'm rather tired.'

'Of course.'

Paul pulled off his shirt and jeans and got in beside her. The dogs and the cat retired to their beds. The cat gathered her kittens into a bunch and turned her back on the light, and the dogs with their noses on their paws gazed ecstatically at Paul.

'I left John at the Abbey. Father Richard wanted me to stay the night but I thought you might be lonely.'

'Are you hungry?'

'Only sleepy. Father Richard said Henry was back and something about two girls.' Paul breathed deeply adding, 'We walked from Plymouth.'

'All those miles!'

'Father Richard and Peter fed us.'

Not wishing to show too much emotion, Muriel remained silent.

'Mum, you're crying.'

'Only because I'm glad you are back.'

Paul laughed and almost immediately fell asleep. Muriel listened to his breathing for a while, curled up beside him, and fell asleep again. She did not notice the dogs move uneasily and walk to the window listening. Chap stood alert by the window for the rest of the night while the bitch and the cat listened suspiciously by their broods. Muriel slept the dreamless sleep of profound relief.

When the Angelus sounded in the valley, Muriel stirred, looked at Paul still asleep beside her, slipped out of bed and, followed by the dogs, crept into the passage. She listened for a moment to the stillness broken by Henry's rhythmic snoring, Mrs Luard's loud breathing and an occasional abrupt snort from behind the door leading to Mr Perdue's bachelor wing. The dogs trotted down the stairs and stood by the front door looking up at her. Muriel crept back into her room, took an armful of clothes, dressed hurriedly and went downstairs. She opened the front door very quietly and slipped out after the dogs. It was dawn and she watched them throw up their heads and sniff, then begin to run north up the yard and on to the moor. Muriel followed, waiting until she got out of earshot of the house before she whistled. She did not want to wake her household so early.

Up on the moor in the increasing light she saw the dogs far ahead of her running with their heads up, already out of earshot. She saw their figures silhouetted against the sky for a second, and then disappear. Whistling at intervals, Muriel followed up the hill to the top from where she could see for miles around the moor. A long way off she heard the dogs barking. She shaded her eyes, and standing at the top of the hill looked westward to where the sound of the dogs seemed to come from. Advancing towards her from the direction of the holiday camp came a long line of tracked vehicles led by a ferret car flying a pennant.

Muriel stood in complete disbelief until the small vehicle drew up beside her. From beside the driver stepped down a trim figure in naval uniform who saluted.

'I am Commander James,' said the man, holding out his hand. 'Paul told you about us I take it, Mrs Wake?'

'Not a word,' said Muriel, taking the outstretched hand. 'He arrived exhausted. He is still asleep.'

'Wanted to surprise you I expect.' Commander James spoke easily. 'Paul and that monk fellow said there were people in the Abbey. I brought this lot across the moor. Navigation is easier. We spent the night in the holiday camp by the prison.'

Muriel looked at the calm young man and at a motley collection of people getting out of the tanks, jeeps and other army vehicles now stopped in a long line across the moor.

'Are you all from Plymouth?'

'Well, I am, and Petty Officer Coke here, and those people over there are from the marine farm off Fowey. We found them in Cornwall and I brought them over.'

'Over what?'

'Over the water. Cornwall is two islands now. It's split up the Tamar and at the far western end by Hayle. The Petty Officer and I were doing an underwater test when this thing blew up. It was pure luck your boy found us.'

'Paul found you?'

'Yes, he shouted down the blower from the ship and we shouted back. We'd been down twelve hours too long anyway.'

'We got the bends fearful.' Petty Officer Coke spoke for the first time. 'Pretty good at first aid that monk fellow was.'

Muriel was bewildered. 'Who are the others?' she asked.

'A job lot of people we found in Plymouth. Those girls are mostly telephonists or from the hospitals. They want to get to London.'

'I don't understand anything.' Muriel felt exasperated. 'What's going on? What has happened?'

'We don't understand either.' The young Commander sat down beside her. 'None of us knows anything.'

'Is there another war?'

'I don't think so. There's no enemy. It's a great big accident I think.'

'Father Richard said that.'

'Ah yes, they talked of him.'

'Are there a lot of people in Plymouth?'

'No, just this job lot. We thought we'd visit you on our way to London.'

'The bright lights,' said the Petty Officer, as though this explained everything.

'I doubt if you will find those. Nobody answers the telephone and there is no television or radio. There have been no planes.'

'We noticed that too.'

'Have you had breakfast?' Muriel looked at the crowd of some forty people.

'Oh yes, we ate before we started.'

'Why didn't Paul come back for all these weeks?' Muriel was suddenly angry.

'I'm sorry, Mrs Wake. He came out in a ship with the Petty Officer and me. He was a great help.'

'I thought he was dead.'

'He said it would be all right. Of course we were longer than we meant to be.'

'What about the monk?'

'He was helping to search the city. It takes time you know.'

'I think everything will take time now.'

'Do us good perhaps.' An oldish man stepped up to her from the little crowd. 'Don't worry, you have him back now.'

'We should be getting on.' A woman spoke up sharply.

'Won't you stay?' Muriel pleaded. There was a pause and uncertainty.

'I should like to.' The young Commander spoke quietly. 'There's nobody in Plymouth now.'

'I'll stay with you, sir.' The Petty Officer smiled at Muriel. 'Could make myself useful to you I've no doubt.'

'We should get back at once to the underwater station,' an oldish man in baggy trousers and a torn tweed coat said courteously. 'If we don't all our experiments of years may come to nothing, and with this curious upheaval there will be so much to record.'

'I'm afraid I rather insisted, sir.'

'Oh, not at all, that's all right. Just get us connected on the telephone when you have time. There are boats to get across the water.'

'We'll do that, sir.'

'Then we will go back at once. There's no point in waiting.'

'Will you be all right?' Muriel looked at the small group round the older man, three men and two girls.

'Yes, yes, of course. It's been a pleasure to meet you but we must get back.'

The little group smiled, waved, climbed into their vehicle and turned back the way they had come.

'Scientists!' said the Petty Officer.

'Even so they must have families or something.'

'They are wedded to fish. We were mad to have brought them. They have been very fretful.'

Muriel watched the departing scientists and laughed. 'We can visit them I suppose.'

'They look upon all this as a great opportunity to be left in peace. There was someone called Harbuckel at the Ministry of Agriculture and Fisheries who was always breathing down their necks. Now he can't.'

'Poor things.'

'They hope he is dead very fervently.'

'Do they?'

'Well, dead to their outfit. They say he visits them and wastes their time with red tape.'

'We want to go on.' An aggressive voice spoke from the crowd.

'Me too,' chorused the rest.

'How will you get to England?'

'Plenty of boats. I will see they get there.' A large man spoke up from the group. 'We are only down here on our holidays. I've got to get back to my office. There have been too many delays already.'

A chorus of approval met this statement.

'Will you take command, sir?' the young Commander asked the large man.

'Command, command? I'll lead them. Get them across the water and that sort of thing.'

'Then let's go.' The woman who had spoken first spoke again. 'I've got to get back to my shop. It will go to ruin unless I get back.'

The group dissolved, climbing back into their vehicles.

'Goodbye,' shouted the large man.

'Can't we stop them? Don't they realise?' Muriel appealed to the young naval officer beside her.

'No. It's a free country. They are fed up already. They won't believe until they see for themselves that there is probably nothing left.'

Muriel and the two men watched the column of vehicles move away jerkily, heading east.

'Better without them if you ask me,' said the Petty Officer. 'You and me going to run Plymouth, sir?'

'More or less.' The young man smiled, adding thoughtfully, 'I suppose.'

'Come to my house first.'

'Thank you, we would like to. Then we must go to this Abbey of yours and see whether they are all right.'

'I know they are because Paul got out to me in the middle of the night.'

'So he did. Wouldn't you like to come aboard?' Muriel climbed into the ferret car.

'Some of those people rather frightened me,' she said.

'Me too.' Petty Officer Coke started the engine. 'And I'm not easily frightened. Which way?'

Muriel pointed and with the dogs running alongside they drove down across the moor to Brendon.

'Those people seemed evil,' she said.

The sailors looked at her sidelong, saying nothing.

Only Mrs Luard seemed indifferent to the new arrivals. Muriel and the girls cooked a large breakfast while Petty Officer Coke told them all about Plymouth. His officer seemed tired and quite content to let him describe the events in Plymouth as they had seen them. He winced when Coke described the long wait in the underwater tank fathoms down in Plymouth Sound.

'We didn't get no response from the blower not for hours and we was just conking out, our oxygen run out, see, when a little voice came down the blower shouting, "Anybody there? Anybody there?" You should have seen the Commander wake up. "There certainly is," he said in his most prissy voice, "Heave us up."'

'Mum, it was very weird,' Paul broke in. 'We hauled them up and they collapsed at once, but we knew roughly what to do.'

'And that was roughly what they did.' Commander James spoke up. 'Saved our lives really.'

'Then what did you do?' Ann leant across the table towards Commander James.

'Do call me James, please.' He looked round.

'All right, what did you do then, James?'

'We couldn't believe what Paul and that monk fellow told us about the storm, the snow, everybody vanished and so on. We thought they were pulling our legs. We made a thorough search, but they were right. Everyone was gone.'

'No police?' Muriel questioned.

'The coppers! Hah! They was gone with the rest.'

'But who else?'

'Well, that big chap who took command so to speak and led the blooming lot we did find off across the moor, he was in the hold of a pub as you might say.'

'In a cellar?'

'Yes. Troublesome fellow that, uppish.'

'The people you saw,' James said slowly, 'came out of the ground like rats.'

'Will they get across to England?'

'I think so, but one of us should go and see that they do.'

'I'll go on my skates.' Paul spoke eagerly.

'Skates?'

'Yes. The roads are so difficult we can only skate or walk.'

'I'll go with you.' June got up. 'The sooner we go the better.'

'What's the hurry?' Mr Perdue asked.

'Those people. Well, those people are dangerous. I hope I'm not exaggerating.'

Muriel looked at James finishing his second breakfast.

'No, you are right. They are dangerous. They are frightened.'

Paul and June were getting ready.

'Get back as soon as you can, Paul. You only came home last night.'

'Okay, Mum, I will.'

'What do you two think?' Muriel asked her visitors.

'We think we are due for a spot of leave.'

'No joking. What do you really think?'

'What can anyone think? None of us knows more than anyone else. Akbar here says it's much the same in his country. We found nobody in Cornwall except the scientists in the Fish Farm, and as soon as they found they had plenty to eat for years they went down underwater again, except the ones you saw.'

'That was cool,' said Henry admiringly.

'Yes, they said they were seeing a lot of fish which don't belong in these waters and were making notes.'

'Who for?'

'For their own satisfaction I suppose. I don't think any of them thinks there will be anyone left to read them.'

'There may be in other places.' Muriel tried to sound hopeful. The two sailors said nothing but passed their cups to Ann who poured out more coffee.

'When will people come and look for us?' Akbar enquired.

'I don't know. I take it we must reconnoitre.'

Akbar sighed. 'Here it is so nice. Nice climate, nice people.'

'We are ready now.' Paul and June came in. 'We ought to go and we won't be long.'

'Don't let those people see you,' Petty Officer Coke whispered in June's ear.

'Why not?'

'Because it's better not.'

'We ought to go over to your Abbey.' James stood up.

'I'll come with you and show you the way.'

'Can we walk?'

'Yes,' said Muriel. 'Coming, Henry?'

'If you don't mind I think I won't.

'I'll get on with my chairs then.' Mrs Luard was helping Ann clear. 'You go, dear.'

'All right, but will you be all right on your own with Mr Perdue?'

'That Mr Perdue can see to the animate objects while I see to my chairs.'

Ann and James walked on either side of Muriel along the track leading down the valley. The Petty Officer and Akbar strolled slowly behind them.

'Mrs Luard doesn't seem to fit in with the scenery somehow.' James looked across the rolling moor.

'Her family were all professional thieves and we found her on a sentimental visit to the holiday camp to be near the prison.'

'Well, it's funny, the extreme tidiness of the place. Did she tidy up the bits by the way?'

'Yes, she told me she did. Why,' Muriel continued, 'did you go off taking Paul in a ship? I was worried to death.'

'I'm sorry. Paul said you wouldn't be expecting him back at once. The monk was busy looking for survivors, so we took Paul along with us. We went in an Air-Sea Rescue launch and I'm sorry to say we got stuck.'

'Stuck! I thought you were sailors.'

'We are, but no chart is any good any more, not round the coast of Cornwall anyway. We got stuck on a bar which has been thrown up at the mouth of the Fal. We took three days to get off it but after that we went more carefully.'

'Where did you go?'

'All round the coast. We landed at every port. Your son has a horrid way of chanting, "Anybody there? Anybody there?" by the way.'

'I've heard him. Gives you the willies. But what else can you do?'

'I used an old-fashioned loud hailer.'

'Was there anybody there?'

'No. Only the fishery people. They are a nice lot, but dedicated scientists only interested in fish. They can use the launch. We have several at Plymouth.'

'Did you go inland at all?'

'Oh yes, we went inland wherever we landed, pinched cars and so on and shouted, but it was useless. Not a sausage, not unless you count the bits.'

'Funny,' said Muriel, 'the way we all say bits, not pieces or remains or any other word.'

'We found,' went on James, 'that Cornwall is now two islands. We went right out to the Scillies. They have disappeared. They were very low. There's only a tip of rock where Bryher was and a tiny bit of Tresco.'

'Oh dear, they were so lovely.'

'They was my home,' Petty Officer Coke called out from behind them.

'There's the Abbey,' Ann pointed, 'down there among the trees.'

'Father Richard will be glad to have both his novices back.'

They walked down the valley to the Abbey in the sun. The silence was absolute.

'Where can they be?' Muriel began to hurry.

By the Abbey gate stood a motor scooter. 'I see he had to abandon his transport,' said James. 'He left Plymouth in a tank.'

'The roads are completely cluttered.' Ann spoke slowly as she watched Akbar at the Abbey door removing his shoes. He smiled at her.

'Atavistic,' he said. 'It's a holy place.'

Petty Officer Coke coughed and went in, crossing himself and genuflecting.

'What's *he* up to? He's a Methodist,' whispered James to Muriel.

They went in to the Abbey. A ceremony was just finishing. The two novices Peter and John were walking in procession. Father Richard followed. The monks disappeared into the Abbey and Muriel stood waiting with her companions.

'What's going on?' asked the Petty Officer.

'Haven't a clue,' said James.

'I have been ordaining the novices as priests.' Father Richard appeared beside them.

'But surely,' Muriel spoke hesitantly, 'only a Bishop can do that.'

'There *is* no Bishop.'

'In times of stress it is quite correct,' said Akbar, 'for a priest to ordain. I am a student of history as well as a professor of literature.'

'Yes,' Father Richard smiled. 'In Japan the faith was carried on for several hundred years.'

'Look! Look!' One of the new priests was pointing at the sky. High above them a vast flock of birds flew across the sky.

'Birds!' cried Muriel and fell silent.

They stood in a group watching as every minute or so a great flock of birds blotted out the light of the sun. James had a pair of binoculars slung round his neck and put them to his eyes. 'Swallows,' he said, 'martins, swifts, finches of some sort. These are duck.' His running commentary was the only sound as they gazed upward. 'And listen, here come the geese.' From a long way off and very high in the sky came the rhythmic honking which swelled and grew as a vast gaggle of geese flew down from the north, their wings seeming to ruffle the still air until they gradually disappeared into the south.

'If that isn't a sign now!' The Petty Officer was jumping from one foot to the other in his excitement.

'We have always been on the migratory course.' Father Richard spoke calmly. 'There, Father, you have the birds you so missed.'

The newly-ordained priest was standing murmuring to himself, his eyes filled with tears.

'What next!' exclaimed Muriel.

'Oh, lunch I think,' said Father Richard.

❧ 16 ❧

Long into the afternoon James and Petty Officer Coke and the priests conferred. Muriel wandered on a tour of the Abbey church, the grounds, the lake and the farm until they came out to join her.

'Made any decisions?' she asked.

'Yes. We think we will stay with you, if you will have us, and see you through the winter. Coke and I can get supplies from Plymouth.'

'What do you mean, winter? It's so hot.' Muriel looked at James.

'It may be now, but the birds have migrated. You saw for yourself.'

'Yes, that's true.'

'Coke and I can help you clear your way to the village and see you through the winter.'

'What about Plymouth?'

'Plymouth must wait.'

'What about all those other people? They frightened me.'

'I think there will be room for all wherever they go,' Father Richard said dryly.

'That's settled then. We clear the road to the village, we establish communications with you and the Fisheries and we divide up the livestock. After the winter we can spread our wings further.'

'Winter, winter, we never get much more than a few days at a time here,' Muriel snapped.

'This winter after this tremendously hot summer we shall, Mrs Wake. Coke and I are going into Plymouth as soon as we can to get skis and toboggans.'

'I think you are crazy.'

'Not if you work out what has happened.'

376

'I can't work out anything. I want Sam my son.'

'Naturally you do.'

'We have much to be thankful for,' Ann remarked parsonically.

'Oh, Ann!' Muriel could not help laughing. 'Henry pinched our village parson's glass eye.'

'Time we went back. Thank you for all you have done. Coke and I will connect you and Brendon up as soon as we can.'

James took Muriel by the arm and led her up the hill. Akbar, Ann and Petty Officer Coke followed.

'What do you mean, connect up?' Muriel knew she sounded querulous.

'Coke and I are going to set up radio communications between Brendon and the Abbey. We just have to get over to Plymouth for the equipment. We can fix up the Fisheries in Cornwall too.'

'Mrs Luard won't like that.'

'What's she got against the Fisheries?'

'Nothing. She likes privacy that's all.'

'She may be glad of them some day.'

'That would indeed be a miracle.'

'I'm glad we are here.' James looked round him at the beautiful country lying so peacefully in the sun. 'We thought we were going to die.'

'So am I, and glad to have you here. But this is my home. Won't you pine for yours?'

'I have no home. The Navy was my home and that doesn't exist any more as far as I can see.'

'What about the rest of the world?'

'We decided this afternoon and I honestly think we are right, not just selfish, to make your house and the Abbey a solid nucleus and then work outwards. We are all sure of it.'

'There must be masses of people cut off all over the place,' said Muriel.

'We don't know.'

'What about all those millions in skyscrapers in the States and South America? What about China? What about everyone everywhere?' Ann's voice broke in.

'Last news was plague and pestilence,' said James.

'There are lots of Afghans,' said Muriel.

'Yes. Anyway I am sure we shall find out sooner or later.'
James sounded tired.

'Bed for you when we get back.'

'You put everyone to bed,' Ann said.

'Well, they need it. I shall sit up and wait for Paul and
June.'

'Henry is out somewhere too.'

'Oh Lord, so he is. I don't think somehow that Henry is
up to much good.'

'But good may come of it.'

'That's true.'

'Yoohoo! Typhoo!' Boys' voices called from the hill.

'Henry and Paul!' said Muriel.

'And June,' said Ann.

'They've been damn quick.'

'That ancient family joke – ' Muriel began to hurry
towards the three figures running down the hill towards
them. 'How did you get back so soon?' she shouted. They
shouted something unintelligible.

'Sounds like June found a car.'

Petty Officer Coke cupped his hands and shouted up the
valley, 'Found a car?' in tones of brass.

The wind brought laughter faintly down the slope and
they saw Henry turning somersaults.

17

'What happened?'

'A terrible lot of things. You tell, June.'

'Well.' June looked at the little group. 'First, Paul and I
got as far as the main road in his Mini. Then after a hundred
yards or so it's blocked by two container lorries which have

crashed head on so we left the Mini and walked. Then we found a Landrover and a clear road. We fuelled the thing at a garage and I drove it to Exeter.'

'What happened then?'

'We hid it in some trees near the university because Coke had said to be careful of those people. Then we walked on to where the river used to be and where it's now sea and we saw all those people from Plymouth. It was horrible. They were quarrelling and fighting.'

'Why?'

'It looked as though they were drunk and that very big man was throwing his weight about and shouting. They had two boats, one towing the other, and they set off to cross to England.'

'Yes?'

'Well, there was a terrific tide running and the boat which was being towed capsized and everyone fell in the water.'

'Oh, my God! Were they drowned?'

'We think so.'

'Then what happened?'

'The people in the other boat started fighting again and it blew up.'

'Blew up?'

'Yes,' said Paul. 'Sky high and nobody was left, we could see that. Then just some heads bobbing and then nothing more.'

'How horrible!'

'I should not have let them go alone.' James sounded remorseful.

'Sounds a good riddance to me.'

'Henry, you are too truthful.' Ann was looking at him. 'They were human.'

'Not very,' James said quietly. 'There wasn't one among them who wouldn't have cut your throat.'

'Well, that's all,' said June rather too brightly. 'We drove back and when we saw Henry at the house we came on to meet you.'

They reached the top of the hill and walked down into the

dip to Brendon. In front of the house, with Mrs Luard at the wheel, stood an outsize maroon Phantom Rolls.

'My present to Mrs Luard.' Henry waved a careless hand.

Autumn began to colour the moor almost overnight. All the men, led by James, began the task of clearing the road to the village of fallen trees. The valley, lately so quiet, echoed with the harsh scream of chain saws and the creaking of the trunks as they were winched to the side of the road. Muriel and the girls cooked for the hungry men. Mrs Luard stitched at the velvet chairs. James seemed always to have his eye on the sky and one evening told Paul to take the sheep and one cow down the moor to the Abbey.

'Why so soon?' asked Ann.

'Winter may come any day now.'

'Since Henry drove the Rolls up here we are all used to strange things.'

'I'm not having me Rolls risked again.' Mrs Luard was firm. 'He might have broken an axle bringing it up over the moor.'

'We could keep it in the garage.'

'Not all winter. I want to drive it down to the village and –'

'And what?' Paul had taken to teasing Mrs Luard.

'That's my secret and Henry's.'

'You must do as you please.'

'I shall. Just as soon as I've finished the chairs I'm off.'

'Oh, Mrs Luard!' Muriel was hurt.

'You can't see me and Mr Perdue holed up together in one house for the whole of a winter now can you.'

Muriel acknowledged the strong feeling between Mrs Luard and Mr Perdue with a nod. It was undeniable.

Two days running James and June used the Landrover to

go to Plymouth. On the first day they came back with many more stores and another Landrover.

'The problem is where to keep them all,' said Akbar.

'Why? They are all right in front of the house.' Mrs Luard liked to wake in the mornings and go out and inspect them, smiling at the glossy Rolls among the Landrovers.

'They won't be all right in the winter.'

'Garn, we don't get much winter,' said Perdue.

'We shall.'

'One could be kept in the Dutch barn,' said Paul.

'What about the other?'

'I think the monks should have it. Father Richard can use it. They have a Dutch barn.'

'Okay, then we'll take them one tomorrow when we finish fixing their radio.'

Muriel and Paul listened to this talk without comment. Paul was tired from his wood-cutting and Muriel had reached a stage of sad bewilderment when nothing surprised her. All the activity disturbed her, though the young people and Mrs Luard seemed happy enough. Old Perdue, when not gazing in rapture at the Rolls, cherished the ducks and chickens which he now kept in what had once been the farmhouse kitchen. Muriel visited it on his insistence and found the once scrupulously clean kitchen covered with deep litter, a ramp leading up to the bathroom and perches fixed one above the other facing the now dead television set.

'If there is a winter like them chaps says there will be, then me ducks can get to the bathroom and me chickens can roost in comfort.'

Muriel inspected the curious arrangement and agreed that it was indeed comfortable. She sat down on a chair.

'Mr Perdue, what are Henry and Mrs Luard up to?'

'That boy, he's deep. He comes and goes when we are wood-cutting and he takes the Landrover and he's gone for hours but he don't say nothing.'

'Does Paul know what he's doing?'

'No. Just Mrs Luard. That old cow!' Mr Perdue spat.

'I can understand clearing the road so that we can get to

the village and cutting wood and getting in stores, but I can't understand Henry.'

'Henry is getting in stores too.'

'Well, I'm glad he's a help. I thought you said he went off though.'

'So he does, and it's not here he brings the stores nor the wood nor the coal.'

'Then where is it?'

'I don't know and I can't find out. He's a sneaky boy.'

'Oh, no!' Muriel felt obliged to defend Henry, but within herself agreed that sneaky was just what Henry was.

'He steals,' said Mr Perdue.

'We all steal.'

'Not caviar nor Rolls Royces. We steal what's necessary.'

'What about the Landrovers?'

'They'm necessary.'

'I suppose they are.'

'Why,' said Mr Perdue standing up, suddenly belligerent, 'does Henry keep an armalite rifle under his bed?'

Muriel made no answer but left the farmhouse and went straight back into her own house. Upstairs in Henry's room she knelt down and peered under the bed. There indeed, clean and gleaming, was an armalite rifle and beside it quite a number of boxes of ammunition. I must, thought Muriel, have a showdown with Henry. But other things happened to put Henry and his mysteries out of her head. As she went downstairs to lay the table for supper the telephone started ringing.

'Hullo? Hullo? Who is it? Who's there? Hullo? Hullo?'

Muriel held the dull dead telephone in her hand. She could hear the Landrover bringing back the men and boys from clearing the road.

'What are you doing with the telephone, Mum?' Paul looked at her with curiosity.

'It rang.'

'It can't have. James and Coke say we won't get the radio connected with the Abbey for three more days and Plymouth is going to take a week.'

'It rang I tell you.' Muriel stood holding the dumb instrument in her hand.

'And answer came there none.' Henry strolled up to her, took the receiver from her hand, smiled sweetly, listened, and put it back in its cradle.

'You must have imagined it.' He looked at her slyly.

'It rang I tell you.'

'I don't really think it can have.' James took up the receiver and dialled idly. 'No. Dead until we get the wavelength right. Imagination plays funny tricks.'

'Oh, hell!'

'Well, let's have supper.' June took Muriel's arm. 'We must ring the changes with the tinned soups. Ann and I thought mushroom would be nice tonight.'

'All right.' Muriel felt defeated by their common sense.

'Mrs Luard has finished the chairs.'

'How marvellous.'

'Come and look.'

They all trooped into the drawing-room where Mrs Luard stood alone in triumph among white, pink and yellow button chairs.

'Mrs Luard, they look wonderful.' James bowed.

'Very handsome I'm sure.' Mr Perdue spoke in neutral tones.

'This calls for a celebration. Got any champagne, Mum?'

'Of course. You and James get it.'

Muriel took Mrs Luard's hand and bent to kiss her fat face. 'My husband would have been so thrilled. You have made it just as he wanted it to be.'

'Let's all drink to Mrs Luard.' Paul was excited as he hurried up from the cellar followed by James.

'A party, a party!' Ann seized Mr Perdue round the waist and waltzed him round the room.

'Yes, yes, a party!' several voices exclaimed at once.

'And just look at the curtains!'

'Let's draw the curtains and switch on the lights.'

They drew the curtains, Coke switched on the lights and Muriel stood looking round her at the transformed room.

'It's gorgeous! How can I thank you enough.'

'Well, I enjoyed doing them.' Mrs Luard accepted a glass of champagne. 'Here's to you, Mr Perdue,' she said unexpectedly. Mr Perdue blushed, cleared his throat and drank.

'Supper's ready,' June called and they all trooped into the kitchen to eat.

As they were finishing their meal Muriel whispered to Paul who shook his head vigorously, so she turned to Henry who nodded and jumping up on a chair shouted, 'To Mrs Luard who has brightened our lives, I propose a toast.'

They all raised their glasses and drank. Mrs Luard bowed, raised her glass in turn and stood up.

'And I drink to you all,' she said, 'may you all live happy and free. And now that my work here is over I must leave you. I shall leave you with regret but I have my own house to care for and I hope that one day soon you will all come and dine with me there. I am going now since our naval gentlemen here tell me that the road is clear and I can drive down it. I have much to do settling into my own home before the winter sets in.' She paused and sipped her champagne. 'You will all,' she said, her eyes sweeping round the assembly, 'be more than welcome when I am ready. My thanks, my grateful thanks for all your kind hospitality here.' She bowed to Muriel. 'And help,' here she bowed to Henry. 'It was you who brought my car up here but it is I who shall drive it away.'

Mrs Luard rose, smiled once more round the table, and started walking with great dignity for one so fat towards the front door.

They watched Paul open the front door for her. They watched Henry hold open the door of the huge maroon Rolls, piled high, Muriel noticed suddenly, with her luggage. They saw her grip the wheel in her fat hands and, with a final bow and wave, drive away from them into the dusk, the engine of the Rolls inaudible.

'I saw *that*,' said Muriel.

'Of course you did,' they chorused, anxious to assuage her, and she knew then that they thought she had imagined the ringing of the telephone.

Henry was collapsed with laughter on the newly covered sofa.

'Henry! Where has she gone?'

'I gave her Willoughby,' he gasped.

'But it's a National Trust monument.'

'Not now. It belongs to Mrs Luard. Mrs Luard of Willoughby!'

'Mrs Luard with four sets of eighteenth century gold plate,' said Paul, awestruck.

'Mrs Luard in the finest example of seventeenth century architecture with a garden designed by Capability Brown,' crowed Henry.

'Those pictures,' Muriel whispered, 'a whole room full of Zoffanys.'

'That furniture,' murmured Paul.

'And the glass, the porcelain, the gold.'

'Henry, what made you think of it?'

'I think it's a very fine setting for Mrs Luard,' Henry spoke complacently.

'The old cow!'

'Now, now, Mr Perdue.'

'Has she anything to eat there?'

'Oh yes, I've stocked her up with all she needs. It was fun!'

Muriel drew James to one side. 'Henry has an armalite rifle under his bed.'

'Has he now? I'll go and look.' James slipped out of the room.

'More champagne,' cried the girls. 'Come on, Mr Perdue, she's out of your hair.'

'Thief!'

'Oh *no*, she is taking over for posterity.'

'And where did you find the Rolls then?'

'By chance in a side-road, quite unhurt.'

James came back into the room holding out his glass to be refilled. 'You must have imagined it,' he whispered.

'But Mr Perdue saw it too.'

'Oh, he wouldn't know the difference between a broken motor scooter and a gun.'

'But I would.'

'Have another drink.' James took Muriel's arm. 'It's getting quite autumnal. Come near the fire.'

Muriel gave in. 'I wonder how soon it would be decent to call,' she said.

'Give her a week.'

'We must fix her up on the blower, too.'

'I bet she would like one of the kittens and one of the puppies.'

'She said not until they are house trained because of the Aubusson carpets.'

'Henry, you know everything.'

'Well, it was fun. She wants Ringo, if it's okay by you and one of the tom cats.'

'You seem to have discussed it all with her.'

'I had to.'

'Will she be all right alone?' Ann sounded doubtful.

'She says she will. She has only one fear. She's afraid of burglars.' Again Henry began to laugh with helpless unrestraint. 'Burglars,' he giggled. 'Thieves breaking in! Burglars! Oh, Mrs Luard!'

20

'We thought you would like breakfast in bed.'

Muriel sat up and ran a comb through her hair and thanked the girls as they puffed the pillows behind her back and brought her tray, laying it across her knees. The smell of toast and coffee was delicious.

'Sit and talk to me.' Muriel looked at the girls who looked so young and cheerful. 'What is going on?'

'Well, James and Coke want to go to Plymouth to do whatever the final thing is to connect up the radio telephone with the Fisheries. They want June and Akbar to be here to answer it.'

'I don't want to be here when it first rings,' Muriel said violently, remembering the evening before.

'No need to be.' Ann looked out of the window. 'Lovely colours, the autumn really is here.'

'I think I shall go out with the boys.' Muriel buttered her toast.

'The boys went out very early. They left a note saying: "Expect us when you see us".'

'Where have they gone?'

'Gone to see Mrs Luard I expect.'

'I daresay. After last night they must be pining to see her installed. Where did Henry really find that Rolls?'

'He won't say. All he did say was that it was in perfect condition when he found it *and* it had a ginger moustache on the driver's seat.'

'That boy!'

'Yes.'

'I shall go alone then. Does anyone need me for anything?'

'What will you do, Ann?'

'Oh, potter about with Perdue, go for a swim, sleep in the sun.'

'Then you two, Akbar and Perdue will be here?'

'Yes.'

'Then I will take a day off. Do you think anyone wants me for anything?'

'No.' June put her arm round Muriel and kissed her.

'Right.' Muriel finished her breakfast, pushed the tray aside and got up. Half an hour later she was riding over the moor alone.

She rode first to the holiday camp and, leaving her pony in the yard, walked round it on foot. The swimming pool with the tables and cheerful umbrellas lay alone. The trim flower beds, still full of asters, were beginning to have a sprinkling of weeds among the flowers. Otherwise there was no sign of change of any sort, no breeze whispered in the passages, no doors opened, everything was still. Muriel picked up the telephone on the manager's desk and listened to nothing. 'Nothing, nothing,' she said to herself and went back the way she had come, mounted her pony and cantered over the brow of the hill towards the south. Far away she could see James and Coke in their Landrover dipping down towards Plymouth. She reached the Abbey about noon.

The priest who had been to Exeter was polishing the Abbey doorbell.

'Good morning. Can you tell me where Father Richard is?'

'He is seeing to the beehives though they are empty.'

Muriel walked back to where the beehives stood in rows by the orchard gates. 'What are you doing? There are no bees.'

'No, but there will be.' Father Richard shook her hand.

'How do you know?'

'That young man from Kabul told me that there are plenty of insects in Afghanistan. We shall get new bees from somewhere.'

'Father, do you think I am mad?'

'Dear me, no.'

'I heard our telephone ring and all the others say I didn't.'

'Perhaps they didn't hear it.'

'Do you think I heard it?'

'Naturally, if you say you did.'

'There's another thing. Perdue said Henry had an arma-lite rifle under his bed and when I looked there was, but when I told James and he looked he said I was mistaken and it was an old motor scooter. I am sure it was a rifle.'

'Then it was.'

'Henry has stolen a house too.'

'How comical.'

'Comical?'

'Well, you can't hide a house under your bed.'

'Then you think it *was* an armalite rifle?'

'I don't see why not. Henry is a collector.'

'He's a thief.'

'Has he stolen anything anyone wants?'

'No.'

'What about the house?'

'He gave it to Mrs Luard. He gave her Willoughby and a Rolls Royce.'

'Then he has set her up in style. Is she afraid of burglars?'

'Yes, she is, and Henry laughed his head off.'

'Well, it is funny.' Father Richard finished cleaning out the last hive and straightened up.

'You don't seem to take Henry seriously.'

'Oh, yes I do. I think Henry should be taken seriously.'

'In what way?'

'Loved.'

'Oh.' Muriel stood silent. 'I don't love him, he rather frightens me. After all, Henry is only thirteen, too young for all this –'

'His very youth may save him.'

'Do you think I am old?'

'No, but you were accustomed to matters as they were.'

'Matters? What matters? That priest is polishing your doorbell. Are you expecting visitors?' Muriel spoke crossly, feeling no wave of sympathy from Father Richard.

'We always expect visitors and he likes polishing.'

'James and Coke are going to connect you by radio to us and the Fisheries. They will have to connect Mrs Luard at Willoughby too.'

'If she wants to be.' Father Richard smiled.

'I'm going off for the day by myself, nobody seems to need me.'

Father Richard's face was impassive.

'I haven't been alone since the great storm. It seems silly when there are so few people.'

'It will do you good.'

'Can I look for anything for you?'

'No, thank you very much.'

'May I leave my pony here?'

'Of course.'

'Then I'll go, goodbye.'

Muriel unsaddled the pony and took off its bridle and turned her loose in the Abbey orchard. Up at the farm she could hear the priests Peter and John talking. She walked down to the main road and stood undecided. The huge dual carriageway stretched east and west, the wrecked lorries, vans and cars strewn along it. It looked sad and depressing. Muriel crossed the road, followed by her dog, and walked south downhill towards the sea. Chap ran cheerfully ahead of her sniffing the air, and Muriel's spirits rose as she walked on. She wondered a little about Paul and Henry and imagined to herself the pleasure they must be having at Willoughby with Mrs Luard. After a while she saw the long, low roof of a house she knew well lying in a dip by the river. She wondered what had become of old Mr and Mrs Bellew who had lived there. They had been kind to Sam when he was a child and taught him to fish. Muriel walked down to the house. There was no sign of life and all the windows and doors of the ground floor were shut.

Following what had become routine to her, Muriel searched until she found a ladder and carried it to the front of the house where she saw Mrs Bellew's window open. She climbed up and in at the window. The twin beds were slightly ruffled and a book lay open on one. She quickly collected the hair from the pillows and one set of teeth – Mrs Bellew had had her own – wrapped them in a face towel and walked round the house. As she had expected, there was nothing. The old couple had locked up and gone to bed. In the kitchen Muriel added a heap of Pekinese fur to her bundle and stood wondering what to do with it. Hitherto, with old Perdue's eye on her, she had buried what she had found in the nearest churchyard, or at very least in the garden, but at that moment she felt mutinous. 'Oh hell,' she muttered and shoved the bundle into a kitchen drawer. 'There,' she said, went upstairs, climbed out of the window, shut it behind her and went down the ladder. Chap was lying in the sun.

'Come on boy, old Bellew's boat.' She ran down to the river and there, as she expected, was Mr Bellew's boat moored to a little jetty. Muriel jumped in, followed by Chap,

THE SIXTH SEAL

and rowed into midstream to be carried fast and quietly down to the sea. The river ran fast and Muriel soon left the oars to sit in the stern and steer. This river, the Mecca of fishermen, ran smoothly here, unlike its rough turbulence where, smaller and more violent, it began its life on the moors. All along the banks prosperous meadows, once filled with cattle or sheep, slid down the valley to the water. Now the meadows were empty. Several times Muriel passed over a shoal of salmon swimming upstream to spawn, several times she saw otters in pairs or alone watching her from the bank without fear and her heart rejoiced. When the river swung round a bend through the great oak woods which stretched for miles across country, Muriel noticed how brown the leaves were already and how silent the woods and empty. Chap, usually so alert, came and lay at her feet and went to sleep.

The river joined the sea at what Julian had called The Sink of Iniquity, a large seaside town of blocks of sky-scrapers, flats, bars, circuses, bowling alleys, shops and huge luxury hotels along the sea front. Muriel steered the boat to a stop in the crowded marina and tied it up. She got out with the dog and walked about the town. For the first time she was not jostled by busy shopping crowds nor deafened by the loud talk of holiday-makers or the noise of traffic. The streets were almost empty, here and there cars had run into one another and crashed, but all around her was silence. The shops were shut, the corners filled with drifts of hair, human, feline or canine. False teeth champed alone in doorways. It was her own village again but on a larger scale. Muriel felt in need of a drink. She looked in the toolbox of a car and finding a large spanner walked quickly to the largest of the hotels. Here in the dead season in February her husband had brought her many times to lunch and look out at the sea from the restaurant windows. Here was an excellent bar. Muriel headed for it. She was slightly puzzled at finding no need for the spanner. The hotel doors opened with a swish as she went in. Chap began to sniff, his nose down and his tail up, but Muriel headed straight for the bar, went behind it and poured herself a large whisky. It was

391

when she had drunk half her drink that she noticed an odd smell and that Chap had gone. It was not the smell of the rich and scented which she was used to in this place, the mixture of women's scents, freshly varnished nails and make-up; it was not the smell of men's hair oil and tobacco, the clinging smell of cigars, nor was it drink or rich food.

'Chap,' Muriel called, 'Chap.' From the stool at the bar Muriel looked out at the empty sea, remembering the mass of blue, red, yellow and brown sails among the white which had delighted her in the summer. Uneasily she called again, 'Chap! Chap!'

Her voice became more urgent and questioning. That smell was in no way a luxury hotel smell. She got up, left the bar and went out into the hall.

'Who are you?'

A little girl was coming down the main stairs with Chap, her hand on his neck. 'Is this your dog?' The little girl stood looking at her.

'Yes, he is. Who are you?'

'My name is Patricia.'

'What are you doing here?'

'Taking care of the pigs.'

'Pigs!' Muriel now recognised the smell.

'Would you like to see them?' The child led the way to the stairs. 'This way,' she said.

Muriel and Chap followed her. The child ran upwards. Chap whined.

'He doesn't like hotels.' Muriel looked at the small girl.

'Oh, doesn't he? The pigs love them. This way.'

The child ran down the hotel passage to a door which she opened. The smell of pig grew stronger.

'Here they are,' she said proudly.

Muriel went into a large bedroom suite and stood rooted. Lying on a double bed were three young pigs who eyed her brightly from their small eyes.

'This is King of Copenhagen,' said the child, 'and these are Queen and Princess of Copenhagen.'

'What are you doing here?'

'Waiting.' The child suddenly looked anxious.

'Are you alone?'

'Oh yes. Except for King and Queen and Princess.'

'How did you get here?'

'We were here for the agricultural conference. My father brought me and them to the show.'

'Where is your father?'

'I don't know. I don't know where anyone is. We've been alone for so long.'

'We?'

'Me and them.'

Muriel looked at the pigs lying cosy and unconcerned on the bed. 'That explains the smell,' she said.

'What smell? They don't smell. They are terribly clean.' The child was indignant. 'They never foul the beds. They always go to the bathroom.'

'I'm sure they do.' Muriel looked at the child, small, pretty, determined.

'How old are you?'

'Eight.'

'Shall we go down and you can tell me all about it?'

'All right.' The child addressed the pigs. 'Like to come?'

The pigs jumped down from the bed. Muriel walked down the corridor with the child and the pigs.

'We only came to this floor yesterday,' said Patricia. 'We have lived on several floors but this one is quite nice.' She stood waiting for Muriel who was looking in and out of bedrooms as she walked towards the stairs. In each were drifts of dusty hair. The pigs trotted along, followed by Muriel, Chap and Patricia. When they reached the ground floor they sat down in the hotel lounge. The pigs wandered about before settling down to rest.

'Can you tell me what happened?' Muriel felt rather diffident.

'My father brought me down for a half-term treat with the pigs. He was going to show them at the show. Of course they are far too intelligent to make bacon from.'

'All pigs are.' Muriel looked at the three humorous faces.

'They love me.'

'I expect they do. Go on with your story.'

'Oh well,' Patricia seemed tired suddenly. 'My father had to go to this big dinner, the agricultural association or something, and I got bored in bed and went down to the underground garage where the hotel people had let my father put the pigs for the night in the trailer.'

'Go on.'

'Well, I got into the trailer with them and slept and in the morning there was nothing, nobody, just me and the pigs. We looked everywhere but everyone had gone.'

'Yes, I understand.'

'Do you?'

'Yes, it happened in lots of places.'

'Has it?'

'Yes. What have you fed the pigs on? They look terribly well.'

'Oh, cereals from the store cupboards and I've raided the refrigerators, but things are going bad in them now.'

'I bet they are.'

'Can you get me home?'

'Where is home?'

'London.'

'Oh, I don't know.'

'There's a helicopter station near here. Could you pilot one?'

'No, and I think London is, well I think London is like this.'

'Have you been?'

'No, but there's no telephone or radio or post or television.'

'I want to go. Please take me.'

'Honestly, Patricia, don't you think it would be better to come home with me? The pigs can be gloriously happy on a real farm. There's lot to eat and there are other people.'

'No, I want to go to London. I want my Mummy.' Patricia began to cry.

'Oh Lord! Don't cry.'

'This is the first time.'

'Then have a good one.' Muriel pulled a handkerchief from her pocket and put an arm round the child. Chap put his head on the child's knee and the three pigs came closer, their twinkling eyes growing grave. After what seemed a long time, Patricia stopped sobbing, handed a very wet handkerchief to Muriel and said, 'I'm sorry.'

'Where do, I mean did, the pigs live?'

'Norfolk.'

'We can't leave them here.'

'Then you'll take me?'

'Yes, but we ought to go at once.'

'Let's go early tomorrow and arrive for breakfast.'

'Why?'

'Well, if we go now it will be dark when we arrive. I hate the dark. There's a frightening searchlight.'

'All right, Patricia. Let's get ready and start early. We haven't seen a searchlight.'

'Lovely, and you can tell me your story too.'

'I will. Let's have tea.'

Muriel and the child found tinned milk and biscuits in the hotel kitchens. Muriel and Chap waded through empty packet after empty packet of breakfast cereals.

'The pigs eat here,' said Patricia unnecessarily. 'And I've been taking them for walks. Shall we take our tea outside?'

Muriel put the milk and biscuits on a tray and followed the child and the pigs to an arbour in the garden. The pigs began rooting contentedly in the garden and Muriel observed without making any comment that they had already ploughed and furrowed up the once trim lawns.

'Wouldn't it be much better if we took them to my home?'

'Perhaps.'

Muriel wandered round the side of the hotel looking for signs of life but found none. When she went back to Patricia she found her watching the pigs rooting through a flower-bed.

'The pigs will have to walk.'

'Must they? Oh, all right. Come on, time for your baths.'

Patricia galloped along a path towards the hotel swimming pool and the pigs followed her. At the pool they drank and then stood in the children's paddling pool while Patricia scrubbed each pig in turn with an enormous loofah.

'I found this in a bathroom. There's no water in the hotel now.'

'No light either, I suppose?'

'Oh no.'

'Then let's go to bed.'

They went to bed on the fifth floor, the pigs in one room and Patricia with Muriel and Chap in another.

'This is nicer than sleeping with the pigs really. They kick and snore a bit. Tell me all about you.'

As the light faded Muriel held the child in her arms and told her all she could remember of what had happened to herself and those at the Abbey and Paul and Henry.

'Where have Paul and Henry gone today?'

'I don't know, but they will be back now with the others.'

'I'd like to meet them one day.'

You shall, Muriel thought, poor child. It's tomorrow you will meet them, but she said nothing of the plan she was making to take Patricia and her pigs straight to Brendon.

21

Patricia shook Muriel. 'Wake up, please wake up.'

Muriel looked sleepily round the room and remembered. She yawned. 'There's no hurry.'

'Yes, yes there is. There is a hurry. If we start now we can get a long way.'

Muriel yawned again and caught sight of Chap who was outstaring the King of Copenhagen.

'If King tries to get on the bed Chap might bite him,' she said.

'Oh, Chap, you wouldn't.' Patricia flung her arms round the dog who, without taking his eyes off the pig, gave a little moan.

'Oh, do hurry.' Patricia was all eagerness. 'I've fed Chap

and the pigs, we are all ready. Mummy will be so thrilled.
We must get to her.'

Chap growled faintly at the pig's twitching snout so
near his nose. The pig turned and walked away into the
next room, switching his haunches to and fro.

'Patricia, I've been thinking. They will think I am lost at
home. I think we'd better go there first and then one of the
boys can come on to London with us. They will be anxious
about me.'

'What about my mother? Isn't she anxious? You promised. You did promise. Besides, if we go now you can leave
me with Mummy and you can come home again.'

'Did you say you were only eight?'

'Yes.'

'You are pushing me around.'

'You promised me.' Patricia's eyes filled with tears.

'No.' Muriel was suddenly firm. 'Before I take you home
I must tell my people what I am doing otherwise they will
be worried stiff.'

Patricia opened her mouth to speak but closed it again
in defeat.

'We must start now. We have a long way to go.' Muriel
grasped her advantage over the child. 'Yesterday I drifted
down in a boat but today we have to get back by road
unless you want your pigs to walk.'

Muriel left the child with her pigs, calling over her
shoulder, 'I'll be back soon,' and hurried out of the hotel
with Chap at her heels. It did not take her long to find an
empty Mini van parked in the street. Fastidiously she
brushed the seat free of some rather greasy black hair,
checked the fuel and drove back to the hotel. Patricia
stood on the steps flanked by the pigs who twitched their
mobile snouts to and fro and blinked their little eyes
maliciously.

'Can you make them get into the van?'

'They won't like it if they have no view,' the child said
petulantly.

'It can't be helped.' Muriel was determined to keep the
upper hand.

'Oh, all right.' Patricia went to the back of the van and waved the pigs in. Much to Muriel's surprise they leapt in one after another while Patricia's face assumed a smug expression.

'Every time we find the road blocked we shall have to walk or change cars.' Muriel put the car into gear and started off.

'They won't mind,' said Patricia.

Muriel drove uphill away from the sea along the main street of the town, dodging in and out among silent stationary cars. Sometimes she drove the wrong side of a traffic island and was amused at the pleasure it gave her to break the law. They had to get out and walk five or six times, changing cars, before they got free of the town, and Muriel choked down her impatience each time the child and the pigs got in or out of fresh vans or cars. At last, on the outskirts of the town near the railway station, she found what she wanted, a Landrover. Here the pigs had to be heaved into the back and quite failed to co-operate, kicking Muriel, squealing and generally making the whole operation as difficult as they could. Muriel was pleased to see Patricia lose patience and smack one of the pigs with quite a spiteful hand.

Once packed into the Landrover, Muriel drove doggedly inland along the road which led eventually to the Abbey. Patricia and Chap sat beside her and the three pigs kept up a commentary of squeals and grunts rising and falling in intensity as she drove along the flat road or took to the verge to avoid obstacles or, as on several occasions, she had to bump through fields. The distance was not very great, but great enough to exasperate, and when she finally came to a halt at the trunk road she was glad to get out and lead a silent Patricia through the piled up traffic to the woods surrounding the Abbey and find a path which led them in blessed silence to the doors of the church.

'Stay here,' Muriel said to the tired child. 'I can get us help and food before we go on.'

Patricia looked at her sulkily from under heavy eyelashes as she went round to the door of the Abbey and rang the bell.

Father Richard answered the door, opening it wide when he saw her and smiling.

'Father, I have found a child and three pigs in the town by the sea.'

'Gadarene swine?' Father Richard grinned.

'Far from it. Very civilised.' Muriel told the priest how she had found Patricia the day before. 'I must take them to Brendon,' she said.

'We must feed you all first, then one of us can drive you up over the moor.'

'I don't want to trouble you.' Muriel hesitated before leading the priest round the corner of the church.

'But they are gone!' she exclaimed. 'I left them here.'

'They can't have gone far,' said Father Richard with his eye on the church door. 'Sightseeing I expect. Your dog seems to think so.' His eyes followed Chap who was sniffing at the church door.

'Not in the church surely,' exclaimed Muriel.

Father Richard pushed open the door with one hand and, reaching out with the other to dip his fingers in the holy water, crossed himself as he genuflected like a duck dipping its head under water. Muriel did the same and stood looking up the aisle.

In the distance stood Patricia looking curiously about her while the three pigs meandered on delicate feet twitching their tails and snouts.

'Patricia, bring them out,' Muriel called in a low voice.

The child turned and came towards them slowly, followed by the pigs.

Father Richard suppressed a smile. 'So like,' he murmured.

'So like what?' asked Muriel crossly.

'So like the summer visitors,' Father Richard smiled. 'Visitors in shorts and tops who think us a rare species, but more like the wonderful man who gave us the mosaic flooring.'

'Was he like a pig?' Muriel found herself laughing.

'He was a tycoon. Those pigs bear a strange similarity.'

Muriel introduced Patricia and Father Richard smiled at the child. 'We will give you something to eat and drink and I will drive you up to Mrs Wake's house.'

'Thank you. I have to get to my mother in London.'
Patricia looked up at the monk.

'So Mrs Wake says. Would it not be better to wait a bit?'

'We've done nothing but wait.' Tears began to gather in
the child's eyes.'

'Tea, I think,' said the priest. 'Then you must decide. I
cannot decide for you, but I would advise leaving your pigs
at Brendon. They could not walk or swim two hundred
miles or more could they?'

'Oh,' Patricia's eyes wavered towards the pigs. 'I hadn't
thought of that.'

'Well then, tea first and then I will drive you over the hill.'

Father Richard was as good as his word, and after feeding
Muriel and the child drove them in his Landrover up the
track on to the moor and across to Brendon.

Old Perdue, pottering about in the farmyard, was the first
to greet them. 'Pigs!' he cried. 'Pigs! Why, they are worth a
month of anxiety. Ah, the beauties! Let me help now. Ah,
what proper beauties!'

June came running out of the house exclaiming, 'Gosh!
We've been anxious. We thought you'd had an accident.
We were going to send out search parties, and here you are.'

James and Coke followed by Akbar and Ann joined them
from the garage, exclaiming and extending greetings.

'Father, won't you come in?' Muriel said to the little
priest.

'Thank you, but I must get back. You are safe home now
and can rest.' He turned the car and drove away. Muriel
stood watching the Landrover disappear over the moor and
then let herself be drawn into the house.

'Listen, you must listen before you tell us anything. Coke
has been seeing things.' Ann held Muriel's arm.

'Seeing what?' Muriel felt very tired.

'Coloured streaks in the sky.'

'Cloud effects,' said Muriel.

'That's what I said,' James agreed with her. 'Or lightning.'

'They weren't no cloud effects,' said Coke firmly. 'Streaks
they was. Quite a lot of them too.'

'Tell us what happened to you,' said James firmly, pushing Muriel into a comfortable chair in the library and handing her a drink.

Muriel took the drink and sipped it, watching Patricia and the pigs settle themselves by the fire. She told them of her adventure, the discovery of Patricia and their return.

'The boys will be thrilled,' said June.

Muriel looked round her, suddenly noticing their absence. 'Where are the boys?'

'They went for a ride, that's all,' said James comfortably. 'They went off this morning.'

'But it's nearly dark.' Muriel felt the acid of fear racing through her veins. 'Where have they gone?'

'Nobody knows. To see Mrs Luard perhaps as they did yesterday. To look for you? They will come.' June looked at Muriel's worried face. 'Patricia and her pigs and Coke seeing streaks in the sky are much more exciting than the boys going for a ride. We can telephone Mrs Luard now. I'll do that if you are worried. That child should go to bed, she looks done in.'

'Oh dear.' Muriel looked at Patricia. 'Of course. Come on.' She led Patricia up the stairs followed by the pigs.

'Surely the pigs — ' Akbar began to speak.

'Oh, shut up,' said Muriel. 'We can sort that out tomorrow.' And she set to work settling the child in bed and giving her what solace she could. Everyone else seemed to be going to bed, running baths and calling goodnight to each other, so that when she went downstairs to the deserted library she found herself alone with her dogs, listening.

Much later, it seemed to her, she heard the sound of horses' hooves and running to the door saw Paul riding up to the house leading another pony.

'Paul!' Muriel gave a little cry and ran to meet him. 'Paul!'

'Hullo, Mum. Where did you go? We were anxious.'

'I'll tell you. Come in. Were you at Mrs Luard's?' She walked beside the ponies and helped Paul take off their saddles and bridles.

'No.' Paul pulled the bridle over his pony's head. 'No, we weren't.'

'Then where?' Muriel questioned.

'Mum,' said Paul, watching the ponies move slowly away into the field. 'Henry has gone.' He tried to see his mother's face in the dusk.

'Where?' Muriel's voice came in a harsh whisper.

'To London.' Paul spoke flatly. 'To London to find things out. We found a sailing dinghy and I sailed him across to the other side. It's miles, Mum, and the hell of a tide. That's why I'm so late getting home.'

'Go to bed, darling,' Muriel said absently. 'Go to bed now and so will I.' She crept up the stairs to her room and unthinkingly undressed and got into bed. 'Gone,' she muttered. 'Pigs, streaks in the sky and Henry is gone.' She felt as though the life had drained out of her, quite spent.

22

'Paul.' Muriel went into her son's room at dawn and woke him up. 'Paul, if Henry has gone to London, where in London has he gone?'

Paul looked at his mother sleepily and buried his face in the pillow without answering.

'Paul,' said Muriel sharply, 'answer me. Where has Henry gone? How was he going to get there?'

'He would go to his parents' house, wouldn't he?' Paul sounded unconvincing.

'No,' said Muriel, 'he might visit it but he wouldn't stay there.'

'Ask Mrs Luard or Father Richard.' Paul snuggled down in his bed and slept again. Muriel bent over and kissed his forehead and then left him to go back to her room, get into bed and lie thinking.

Later during the day she questioned the girls, James, Coke and Akbar and gradually became aware that none of them minded Henry's absence. Henry had made them uncomfortable. Mr Perdue openly rejoiced. 'Gone and good riddance, Mrs Wake. Sneaky boy, I told you. Not our kind. Let him go to London. We is happier without that Mrs Luard woman, now we'll be happier without 'im, you'll see.'

Muriel felt no happier, indeed less happy, if happy she had ever been since her husband's death, since the storm, since the disappearance of all her neighbours and the terrible loss of Sam. Restlessly she prowled round the house that day, looking askance at Paul who she suspected of knowing Henry's whereabouts, noticing a sudden intense friendship grow up between Patricia and Perdue so that Patricia quite stopped any reference to her mother or her past and slipped into a complete companionship with the old man and the pigs to the exclusion of everyone else.

At meals Muriel's eyes observed for the first time that June and Ann had paired off with James and Akbar and were behaving like engaged couples of long standing, treating her in her own house with bare politeness. Coke tinkered happily with the telephone, ringing up the Fisheries, the Abbey and Mrs Luard on the flimsiest of excuses just as though, Muriel thought, he had himself invented the telephone. A glorious toy.

'Coke,' Muriel suddenly addressed him. 'The telephone rang before you connected that radio telephone of yours.'

Coke raised his eyebrows and laughed. 'They said there was a great storm and coloured snow too. The Commander and I was under-water. Old Perdue didn't see no coloured snow.'

'He was drunk,' said Muriel.

'Them monks didn't see no coloured snow.' Coke spoke politely.

'They were underground. How could they have seen it?' Muriel resented Coke.

'Mrs Luard didn't see none either,' Coke went on.

'She was underground too, wasn't she?' Muriel walked out of the house into the yard loathing Coke and conscious of her unreason. She caught herself feeling lost and decided

403

that a talk with Mrs Luard would help her unease. As she drove down the hill to the village she wondered how Mrs Luard would be faring all alone in Willoughby and whether she would be lonely by now. She left the Landrover in the village and walked across the fields to the large house, followed by her dog.

A puff of smoke rose from one of the chimneys as she drew near, followed by a wavering line in the faint breeze. Muriel banged on the door and waited, looking at the gardens formerly so well-kept and now growing weedy.

Mrs Luard opened the door suddenly and Muriel jumped nervously.

'Oh, it's you.' Mrs Luard did not sound particularly welcoming.

'I'll go away if you are busy,' Muriel said hastily.

'What's the matter?' Mrs Luard peered into Muriel's face. 'Come in and tell me.' She led Muriel into a room off the great hall and made her sit down by a glowing log fire.

'Mrs Luard, Henry has gone. Paul says he's gone to London.'

'Ah.' Mrs Luard looked infinitely sympathetic and wise. 'Tell me about it,' she said,

Muriel told her of her expedition to the sea, of her finding Patricia and the pigs and of the present situation at Brendon. 'Paul knows something I'm sure but none of the others cares. Perdue is pleased. The young men and girls sit gazing into each other's eyes and Coke is in love with the telephone and, Mrs Luard, he doesn't believe there was coloured snow or a storm, or he thinks I am exaggerating. He – ' Muriel stopped.

'He doesn't know,' said Mrs Luard, staring into the fire. 'He doesn't know half what that boy knows, not half.'

'What am I to do?' Muriel asked the older woman.

'Let me show you something neither Coke nor those others know, but I do and Henry does. Come along.' Mrs Luard took Muriel's hand and led her out of the room. 'I love that boy,' she said. 'He and I have a lot in common, more in common than you would think.' Leading Muriel by the hand she waddled down the hall.

'This is something Henry hasn't told anyone but me. This is one of the reasons I am here.' Mrs Luard stood by a table in the hall loaded with drinks and glasses, looking at Muriel with speculative eyes. 'Henry can keep his trap shut,' she said.

'Of course he can. In fact Henry's the most secretive person I know. I never know what he's going to do next. I don't know whether I love him or hate him. I simply don't know Henry,' Muriel burst out passionately.

'No need to abuse the poor boy.'

'I'm not abusing him.'

'It sounded like it. Have a drink.' Mrs Luard waddled across to the table. 'Or would you prefer something hot?'

'Something hot I think. I'm sorry, Mrs Luard.'

'Nerves.' Mrs Luard took her hand. 'Come along and you can meet them.'

'Meet who?'

'Oh, some visitors.'

'What visitors? More pigs?'

'No, this lot are human. Henry found them and brought them here.'

Mrs Luard led the way followed by Muriel and the dog. The corridor was dark and long and Muriel remembered it led to the kitchens of the old house. At the end of the corridor a light shone under a door.

'Here they are.' Mrs Luard opened the door. 'Studying, poor things. Can't speak a word of English.'

Muriel walked into the old kitchen. Round a bare wooden table sat three men and three girls, their heads bent over books and a pile of foolscap on which they were making notes. These people stood up and looked at Mrs Luard questioningly. Mrs Luard raised her voice and said to Muriel. 'You 'ave to shout at them. Henry says they are Albanian but that may be Henry's little joke.'

'Where do you come from?' Muriel held out her hand in greeting.

'They are spies,' Mrs Luard remarked complacently.

'No. Submarine.' One of the young men held out a

dictionary open at a page which said 'Submarine. Underwater vessel. Gerundive – submersible.'

'Oh dear, they won't get very far with that!' Muriel exclaimed.

Sitting drinking cocoa with the crew of the submarine, Muriel gathered the gist of their story from Mrs Luard. Henry, driving his Landrover on one of his foraging expeditions in the late summer, had found them encamped sadly by the river up which they had walked from the sea. 'Or so he says,' Mrs Luard remarked.

Henry had taken them to Willoughby, taught them how to use the electric pump and light machine, installed them with plenty of food and come home to tell Mrs Luard. Mrs Luard's aversion to the law, and indeed to any form of uniform, had not made her anxious to tell James and Coke. Henry had installed Mrs Luard at Willoughby on condition she kept the whereabouts of the crew secret.

'But why the secrecy?'

'We thought the others would be nosy.'

'I daresay, but they all look very nice. Have they told you anything?'

'No, how could they?'

Muriel turned to the man who appeared to be the leader of the party and he produced a pile of drawings. The first was a rough sketch of a submarine. There followed a brilliant drawing of the ship sinking and the crew swimming ashore, a sketch map of England with a dotted line trail leading up the river inland from the sea, and a good likeness of Henry.

'Is there an atlas in the house?' Muriel asked Mrs Luard.

'No dear.'

'Then what's the idea?'

'Henry said I was to teach them English.'

'You don't seem to have got very far.'

'No, that's why I want Henry back, just as you do.'

'It all seems very improbable.'

'Oh, it is.'

'How did you hide them from Coke?'

'Coke doesn't demean himself enough to go into the kitchens and he isn't snoopy.'

'What next then?'

'Oh, we shall all be very happy living here for the winter, and they can keep me company.'

'I must talk to Father Richard.'

'Do by all means. He told Henry the laws of hospitality came first with monks.'

'Why do you call them spies?'

'Well, a submarine crew. Stands to reason doesn't it?'

'There is no reason anywhere.'

'Well, they all seem quite happy.' Mrs Luard looked round the room. 'Warm and happy. They talk to each other.'

'In what language?'

'I don't know. Look, they write like this.' Mrs Luard reached for a piece of paper.

'Kyrillic script,' said Muriel. 'I can't read it. I must get over to the Abbey. Father Richard will tell me what to do.'

'Ah, he said to leave them in peace. They came in peace. I telephoned to him.'

'Did you? But they might know something. Here they are, coming from a foreign country which may be full of people –'

'I hadn't thought of that.'

'Well, Akbar says Afghanistan is full of people.'

'He doesn't want to go back there.'

'I daresay not. He's in love with June. I'll get these people a dictionary. Look, Mrs Luard, you only have Modern English Usage here for them. That's no good.'

'That's all Henry could find. They didn't understand the French or German he brought them so he took them away again. Well, dear, do your best.'

'Patricia could come over and teach them.'

'That child you found?'

'Why not? She's very bright.'

'It means telling another person.'

'I think Patricia and Paul ought to know. You can't keep six people a secret can you?'

'I did when those two naval chaps connected me with the radio telephone.'

'I don't understand the secrecy.'

'It's just a feeling.' Mrs Luard looked round at the six calm friendly faces. 'Just a feeling.'

'But Father Richard knows.'

'He's a priest.'

'I thought you were anti-papist.'

'I'm not against that lot at the Abbey, not against them at all.'

'All right, Mrs Luard, but I'm going to tell Patricia and Paul. They won't tell anyone else. You know children, they won't give anything away.'

Mrs Luard nodded. 'Very well, you tell the children, but nobody else, and if Coke comes over this lot keep out of his way, and I will not' – here Mrs Luard thumped the table with her fist – 'I will not have that old man know.'

Muriel got up. 'I think I will go now,' she said.

'Won't you stay the night?'

'No, thank you. I'm restless. And if Patricia comes over she can bring you a pair of kittens and a puppy.'

'Very well.' Mrs Luard watched Muriel shake hands with the crew of the submarine and escorted her to the front door. The submarine crew stood beside her watching Muriel walk away.

She reached home late and went into the sleeping house and quietly to Paul's room.

'Paul.'

'Yes.'

'Paul, will you come and talk to me or are you too sleepy?'

'No, I'd love to.'

'Will you wake Patricia. I want to talk to her too.'

'Of course.'

Muriel waited for the children in her room and soon they slipped in quietly. Muriel hushed the dogs.

'What is it, Mother?' Paul and Patricia sat at the foot of her bed, their arms clasping their knees.

'Mrs Luard has a foreign submarine crew with her at Willoughby.'

'Where from?'

'I don't know. She says Henry found them and she has kept them secretly ever since she went there.'

'When did Henry find them?'

'Before Mrs Luard went there.'

'That's why she was in such a rush. That explains it.'

'Is nobody but us to know?' Patricia fondled a puppy.

'That's what she wants. For the present anyway.'

'Can I choose a puppy now?'

'Yes, of course.'

'Then I'll have this one. It came to me first.'

'That's George,' said Paul.

'Mrs Luard wants Ringo. Listen, Patricia, can you go over to Willoughby and teach that crew English?'

'Can't Mrs Luard?'

'No, she's hopeless.'

'I'd like that. When can I start?'

'Wait till after breakfast. I'm going to sleep a bit and then go to the Abbey. I want to see Father Richard.'

Paul lolled at her feet. 'What a skunk Henry is not to have told me.'

'Well, he's like that.'

'Let him wait till I get at him.'

'Paul, will you wake me early? And not a word, either of you.'

'As if we would.' Patricia kissed her and left the room.

Muriel fell asleep wondering about children who seemed to take everything for granted without fear or question.

❧ 24 ❧

'Here I am.' Father Richard came round a corner wearing gum-boots under his cassock. 'What can I do for you?'

'I want to tell you about Henry and the submarine crew and ask your help.'

'Certainly.'

'You know about the crew?'

'Yes. How did you find out?'

'Mrs Luard showed them to me. Patricia is going to teach them English.'

'That child you found? Give her something to do.'

'Yes. She's intelligent. Father, who are these people? Mrs Luard says they are spies and says Henry said they were Albanians. They use Kyrillic script.'

'So do several countries. They may be Russian.'

'Father, what do you think?'

'Well, I only speak English and Latin. None of them speaks either I gather.'

'Are they spies?'

'It doesn't matter now whether they are or not.'

'No, I suppose not.'

'What help do you want?'

'I want you to marry Akbar to June and Ann to James. They want to marry. You must talk to them.'

'I can do that. I will go and talk to them.'

'And, Father, I want to get to London.'

'Are you afraid?' The monk looked away from her.

'Yes. I am anxious about Henry.'

'One can understand that; he is young.'

'I think Paul could get me across the water to the mainland as he did Henry. Do you think I am being hysterical and over-anxious? Do you think, as Coke does, that I have imagined almost everything that has happened to us?'

'Those people are not Albanians,' the priest murmured to himself.

'My mind is not at rest,' exclaimed Muriel.

'Small wonder, after all.' Father Richard smiled a little. 'You do not like Henry, just as we do not like the truth.'

'The truth.' Muriel looked at him. 'They do not believe the truth. They do not believe what they cannot see. They do not believe the telephone rang and it did. I swear it did.'

'Then ring it did, and all of us who were underground or under very good cover like your cows and ponies have survived the storm and everyone else has blown away or, if you like, died.'

'Oh,' said Muriel, 'is it as simple as that? I had not reasoned.'

'The result is simple, but what began it? Henry has no doubt gone to find out and you would be right to follow him. He is too young to be alone.'

Muriel made her way up the hill towards her house. The appalling simplicity of survival so quietly mentioned had struck her dumb and she had left the Abbey with tears in her eyes. As she came up on to the moor she stopped and looked towards Brendon. Her son Paul was hopping and skipping along the track to meet her in company with the dogs. Seeing her he stopped and waved his arm skyward, and Muriel looking up saw flashes of light between the clouds, fleeting colours stabbing across the horizon from the east.

Paul reached her, calling as he ran, 'Do you see? Do you see?'

'Yes, I expect it is only the Aurora Borealis gone mad,' she said, and laughed at Paul's crestfallen expression.

'I don't believe it,' said Paul, 'one doesn't see the Aurora Borealis down here, only up north. The telephone rang again, Mum. Everyone was out. I answered and there was nobody. It was very strange and queer. Who can it be?'

'I expect Coke has made some mistake,' said Muriel sadly. 'We are limited to the Fisheries, the Abbey and Mrs Luard; that's the lot.'

'Well, anyway, there won't be a bill this quarter,' said Paul cheerfully. 'We can use it as much as we like. We can chat to Mrs Luard and the fish people, we can talk to the Abbey.'

'Yes.' Muriel looked at her son, thinking with amusement that he was still of an age when she could talk to him and be accepted. 'Thank God you are not adolescent,' she said.

'Why?' Paul looked surprised and then grinned in comprehension. 'Sam was pretty broody wasn't he?'

'Yes, and he had just grown out of it. Paul, I may have been rather mad since your father died and since the storm, but I am grateful to you and Henry. You heard the telephone; it brings us closer. You and I have both seen streaks in the sky, so has Coke. It may mean nothing at all. Old Perdue said Henry had a rifle under his bed – ' Muriel paused, seeing Paul flush.

'He took it with him,' said Paul. 'He said you had James and Coke and Akbar to look after you and Mrs Luard had her submarine crew, so he took it.'

'Where has he gone?' Muriel felt her moment of intimacy lost.

'To his parents' house I suppose.' From Paul's expression he was obviously lying.

'Darling, we must follow him. Can you get me across as you did him? We could take Chap with us.' Muriel looked at Paul's face, so like his father's.

'Of course we could get across.' Paul turned a radiant face to her. 'We can chase after him. He was going to follow the main road, not the motorway.'

'We will not tell anyone else,' said Muriel childishly, 'except Father Richard. He is the only person who would understand such an absurdity.'

'When shall we go?' Paul looked at his mother sideways.

'Tomorrow.' Muriel felt a rush of determination. 'I shall ring up Father Richard tonight.'

'Use the telephone?' Paul sounded taken aback.

'Yes, I am no longer afraid of it.'

'This means of locomotion is no longer currently fashion-able,' Paul said to his mother as he pulled up the sail of the small dinghy and sat down beside her. The wind filled the sail and the little boat heeled over and began to move in the water.

'Your father only said that because he was always seasick.' Muriel steered, peering across the water to the distant shore. 'It's lucky that I taught you and Sam to sail a boat.'

'Henry was sick all the way across. It gets very choppy when we get away from the land.' Paul's eyes were watering from the cold wind.

'Even Henry has his weaknesses.' Muriel smiled at her son. 'Personally I'm terrified of this crossing. You came back quite alone after getting Henry across.' Paul shrugged his shoulders and settled low in the boat, making the dog lie down at their feet.

Without speaking they manoeuvred the boat, working in unison as they had so often done before. The tide was contrary to the wind and the little boat rocked wickedly so that both Muriel and the child sat tense in concentration. It seemed a very long time before they reached the other shore and beached absurdly in a field where the water had stopped rising.

'We are very cut off.' Muriel looked back across the water.

'We had better tie her up and find the main road before it gets too dark.'

Paul helped her drag the dinghy up the field a little way and then rammed the anchor into the ground, furled the sail and lowered the mast as his mother stood looking around her, shading her eyes and trying to make out where they were. Far away across the water from where they had come she saw the dogged towers of Exeter cathedral standing against the backdrop of the sun. The wind whistled and moaned a little but otherwise there was no sound.

The dog sniffed up the hedge and trotted a short way up the field.

'Those pylons cross the road near here,' Muriel said to Paul. 'Let's go to them.'

Walking with the dog in the dusk they made their way across country until after a mile or more they met the road.

'Just the same as our side.' Paul stopped and looked up and down the road at empty lopsided lorries lying on their sides where they had left the road, mangled cars lying at all angles, so that it was not possible to know in some cases whether they had been coming west or travelling east.

'We must find somewhere to sleep the night.' Muriel looked at the lifeless countryside dotted about with houses and farms.

'A pub or a hotel would be best,' said Paul.

Muriel agreed and they began walking along the road not bothering to look at the wrecked traffic until they found a small hotel standing empty with its sign 'The Travellers Rest' swinging gently in the breeze. Muriel felt no fear of breaking in and was glad when they found an unused bedroom with the beds made up ready for the summer visitors who would never come.

'It's a double room. Shall we share?'

'Yes, please.' Paul looked much younger than he had during the past weeks.'

In the storeroom of the hotel they found some tins and ate, feeding Chap at the same time.

'Now let's sleep and hurry on tomorrow.' Muriel led the way up to the bedroom, switching the light on automatically.

'Damn!' she said.

'It's okay, I found some matches and a packet of candles.' Paul produced them.

'Oh.' Muriel felt foolish. 'Don't light them, Paul. Let's sleep in our clothes.'

'Beds damp?' Paul's voice was even.

'It's because we don't know,' said Muriel. 'The other side of the water we did.'

'All right.' Paul got into bed fully dressed and lay watching his mother. 'I suppose those ponies will find their way home,' he said.

'Oh, yes.' Muriel remembered the two ponies they had ridden from Brendon to the sea dividing Exeter from the mainland, standing looking at them with vague astonishment when she and Paul had taken off their saddles and bridles and left them to sail away in the little boat. One pony had whinnied and then turned away to graze. 'They may take some days to get home,' she said to console her son, 'but they will be all right.' She listened to Paul's breathing and to the silence all round them and lay wondering how long it would take them to reach London before she fell asleep.

Waking at first light she sat up in fear seeing Paul's bed empty. 'Paul!' she shouted. 'Paul!' The boy's footsteps came running up the stairs.

'Look what I found.' In his hands he held two young rats who eyed Muriel with curiosity. 'These are so young they must have been born after the storm.' Paul put them on his mother's bed.

'Yes.' Muriel stroked the small creatures. 'Were they in the cellar?'

'No, the bar. But I heard more. Chap wanted to have a hunt. May I keep them?'

'Why not?' said Muriel. 'Any sign of life is glorious.'

26

During the days and nights which followed Muriel never lost the feeling that she must waste no time but hurry after

Henry. She made no effort to define this feeling, but as they travelled it grew stronger rather than weaker and she felt a nagging fear. Their progress was jerky. Often they found a stretch of road which was empty and a car to travel along it. Now and again they found bicycles in villages or towns and used those. Sometimes they walked, always empty handed except for candles and matches and Paul's two rats which lived inside his windcheater becoming ever more tame. By day they raided shops for tinned food and public houses for drink. By night they found beds in hotels. There was never any sign of life along the road, just the grim silence of an abrupt stop to the machine age. Paul was on the whole rather silent and Muriel, setting her mind on her goal, managed not to let her thoughts wander to the many times she had driven up this road with her husband with gaiety and enjoyment and plans of what they would do together in London. It was only sometimes at the end of the day that she realised his death and then grimly she relived the accident in which he had died. Driving along a straight empty road his Siamese cat had leapt over her shoulder from the back of the car to land in her lap jerking the steering wheel from her hands so that the car careered into a tree. She remembered her foot pressing the brakes and the silence and seeing her husband dead and the cat.

Sometimes towards the end of the day on this journey with Paul she would brake suddenly if they were in a car and come to a halt. One evening she did this and Paul's face banged into the windscreen. Paul rubbed his head as she apologised and looked at her queerly.

'Mum, it was not your fault,' he said. 'Surely by now you know it was not your fault. Nobody ever blamed you, did they? We love you, you know.'

'We?' Muriel looked at the boy.

'Yes, we. Henry and I and all the people you have saved. We understand. We aren't idiots. We are old enough. You should talk to me about it. Tell me.'

'Tell you what?' Muriel drove on. 'Tell you that I loved your father? Tell you that I should have been more careful with the cat in the car? Oh, Paul.'

'Well, it's very silly now,' said Paul. 'It's very silly to go on about it. After all, Mum, by now you might just have his hair and nothing else left. He might be gone, blown away.'

'You speak like Henry,' said Muriel. 'Henry must be infectious.'

'It's funny that we've seen no sign of Henry yet.' Paul looked at his mother. 'And no more lights in the sky. Just this eternal junkyard.'

'Yes.' Muriel stopped the car where the road was completely blocked by an oil tanker in collision with a milk lorry.

'Out again,' she said, 'and walk. Thank God we haven't got Patricia and her pigs with us. Paul, when are you going to tell me where in London Henry has gone?' Paul blushed and grinned.

'When we get there.'

'London is so big.' Muriel hoped to trap some information.

'Yes, enormous,' Paul agreed.

Muriel sighed. 'We should reach it tomorrow. The last signpost said fifty miles and the roads get wider so travelling should be easier.'

'No need for signposts now.' Paul walked beside her. 'Does it irritate you that I look into the cars for bits and pieces? Does it worry you that I try telephones and televisions?'

'Oh no, of course it doesn't. It's a bit macabre that's all. I like to see you and Chap and the rats alive. I don't like dead telephones or a vanished population. I feel I am so alone. At home we had quite a collection of people and animals. This journey has been rather a journey of despair, hasn't it?'

'Let's stop at that hotel.' Paul changed the subject and began running ahead to break in. Muriel watched him run down the road with his hair flopping and she was sure the little rats zipped into his side pockets would be protesting.

Muriel knew the hotel well having often stopped there for a meal or a drink with Julian. She rather liked it. I must not think of Julian, she thought, but of the living, and she watched Paul go into the hotel with a loving eye. He came out almost as soon as he went in and he was laughing and calling to her. 'Come and look, quick, come and look.'

Muriel joined him and he took her hand and led her into the public bar and pointed, his eyes shining with amusement, at the blackboard by the dart-board.

'Look, Mum.'

Muriel looked and then stared at the board which, wiped clean, bore the cryptic message written in chalk:

'Henry was here.'

'Henry was here.' Muriel looked at Paul. 'He is not here now.' Wandering round the silent dusty bar, Paul looked away from his mother.

'It's near here there are those long miles of wired-in War Department installations with "Danger Keep Out" written in red on notice boards,' said Muriel, 'and air-strips which don't officially exist where they test prototype aircraft.'

'Tested,' corrected Paul.

'Ah, yes. Paul, I don't like this part of the world. Before it gets dark let's see whether we can find a car, shall we?'

Together they left the empty bar and began to search the garages of the hotel. After a while they found a Volkswagen with the keys still in the ignition and the petrol tank nearly full. Muriel tested the lights and started up the engine which, after a stutter or two, ran smoothly enough. By pushing and pulling they got cars parked outside the hotel out of the way and Muriel got the car out on to the road. A wind was blowing, whipping bits of paper and fluff about the yard.

'It's cold.' Paul climbed in beside his mother. 'We haven't driven at night yet,' he added.

'No. I'll go slowly.' Muriel drove into the dusk. 'The road

looks pretty clear,' she said, 'clear enough for us anyway.'
She looked at Paul sitting beside her, and felt comfort from
her dog on the seat behind.

'For aught we know Henry may have left messages all the
way up to London,' said Paul, 'and we just missed them.'

'I don't think so.' Muriel switched on the lights of the car.
'If he had wanted to leave messages he would have chalked
on the road. That message didn't seem a joke to me but a
warning.'

'Oh.' Paul was silent. 'Warning of what?' He added after a
few minutes, 'I don't know.'

Muriel drove slowly, puzzled by the fact that although
there were wrecked cars every so often the centre of the road
was clear as though a bulldozer had pushed the empty cars
aside to make room in the centre for a car. She mentioned this
to Paul who didn't reply.

Through the night she drove, and always there was a clear
way in the centre of the road.

'I don't like it,' said Muriel suddenly. 'This isn't natural, or
what we have come to know as natural. What shall we do?'

'Go on until you feel too unsafe and then we will walk.
Chap will let us know whether there is anyone about.'

'All right, I'll do that.' Muriel drove steadily on without
speaking and Paul fell asleep beside her. All the way into
London the centre of the road was clear and Muriel drove on
in the dark. Somewhere in the neighbourhood of Earl's
Court she felt it unwise to go any further and turned the car at
an angle to the road and stopped it. Paul was asleep but
behind her Chap was alert. Muriel switched off the engine of
the car and the lights and settled to wait until dawn, listening
with the dog who sat alert behind her, ears pricked.

Now and again Muriel dozed, listening to Paul's even
breathing. There was a full moon and it outlined the tall ugly
buildings of the district. Muriel got quietly out of the car with
the dog.

Apart from small rustlings of the wind the silence was
absolute. The growl of the great city in its sleep was gone.
Gone too the sound of the occasional passing car or heavy
lorry that she associated with sleeping London. Gone the

slow measured tread of a policeman on his rounds, the faraway sound of an ambulance or fire engine, the hoot of a ship going down river on the early tide. The silence was worse, far worse than the silence she had become accustomed to in the country where it was only comparative, since her house was occupied and sleepers turned in their beds or cried out and the few remaining animals moved on the moor, the mice found in the churchyard settled in the wainscots and the streams tripped towards the big river and the sea.

Standing by the car in which her son slept Muriel remembered telephoning the monk at the Abbey to tell him that she and Paul were going off in pursuit of Henry, and suddenly his voice rang in her ears and the curious sentence of farewell, 'Yes, do go. You must. And when you get back, if you do, you can tell me.' Standing with her dog in the street in Earls Court, Muriel went white and shivered. Then she leant into the car and shook Paul.

'Paul, wake up.'

'Where are we?' Paul stretched cramped limbs.

'Earls Court. Paul, it's light enough now to go on. Will you lead me? We must keep away from the main streets.'

'Oh, why?' Paul climbed out of the car, stretching and yawning, showing brilliant white teeth in the dim light.

'I would feel safer,' Muriel answered lamely.

Paul moved into the middle of the street to get his whereabouts.

'We must remember where we left the car.' Muriel followed him. Together they memorized the name of the side street and then set off in single file. Both Paul and Muriel wore rubber-soled shoes and the dog made very little sound.

Paul moved fast and Muriel followed. Neither spoke. They passed great blocks of flats and houses with closed doors, stepped over scattered heaps of clothing, made circuits round cars, and always Paul led east. Now and again he put his hand in his pocket to stroke one of the rats, but otherwise he stayed silent, moving fast.

It was growing light when they realised that many of the buildings they were passing were empty shells.

'Burned out,' whispered Muriel. 'There must have been a lot of fire.'

'Yes, and there's a funny smell.'

Muriel said nothing. She, too, had noticed an unpleasant smell every now and again.

They reached Kensington Gardens and walked through long grass to Hyde Park Corner noting constant signs of fire. At Hyde Park Corner Paul led her across the tangled skein of wrecked cars and lorries into Green Park.

'Are we going to Whitehall?' Muriel whispered.

Paul nodded, and twenty minutes later they passed the Cenotaph and Paul turned abruptly into Downing Street and ran to the steps of No. 10. He pushed at the door and went in. Muriel followed. How obvious, how childish, she thought, closing the door behind her and followed her dog who was running after Paul.

'This will be the Cabinet room.' Paul spoke out loud for the first time and then he began to laugh. Round the table sat in eternal session the Prime Minister and the cabinet, sitting portentously in dignified silence as they had been cast in wax at Madam Tussaud's.

'I thought Henry was – ' Paul began, grinning widely.

'I know Henry is truthful.' Muriel looked round the room in silence, at the waxworks.

28

Muriel and Paul explored the house, finding their way into the Prime Minister's flat which, compared with the desolate hotels they had been sleeping in, felt warm and lived in.

'It feels lived in.' Muriel was puzzled.

'It is. Look, unmade beds and in here unwashed dishes.' Paul darted from room to room. 'Oh, I'm so hungry.'

'Then have some breakfast.' Henry, materialising on silent feet stood behind them.

'Oh, Henry!' Muriel wondered whether she could conceal her relief and joy. 'Oh, Henry, we just followed and we never found any sign of you until we saw a message on a dart-board in a hotel bar.'

'That wasn't meant for you. Have you had anything to eat? There is plenty here. Did I leave the door open? That was a pity, except that you got in which is lucky. We use the back window.'

'We?' Muriel queried.

'Yes, a man I found. He is nice, an aerodynamics expert called Briggs. He was in the government deep shelter working on something when the storm hit London so he survived. He should be here soon, in fact that's him at the back window.' Henry left the room and Muriel and Paul heard him run down the stairs and voices talking.

'Why didn't you tell me where Henry had come?' Muriel said to Paul.

'He said not to.' Paul looked at his mother uneasily. 'He wanted it to be a secret, but when you were so lost without him I felt I had to bring you up to him. I am your son but it is Henry you love.' Paul spoke crossly but without any trace of jealousy.

Before Muriel could answer Henry came back into the room followed by a short fair man with a mild expression.

'This is Mr Briggs.' Henry waved an airy hand.

Muriel shook hands.

'Come on, let's have breakfast. Have you seen the Cabinet?' Henry appeared to be in high spirits.

'Yes,' said Muriel. 'A very bad taste joke.'

'But the truth.' Henry laughed. 'The truth is a waxwork. *You* should know.'

'I'm hungry,' said Muriel evasively, 'and tired, and so is Paul.'

'Well, we eat breakfast and sleep by day. There is a tremendous store of food here.'

Muriel followed Henry to the kitchen and soon she and Paul were eating round a table with Henry and Mr Briggs.

'Are you the only person left in London?' Paul asked.

'No,' Mr Briggs answered shortly.

'Who else is left?' Muriel enquired innocently.

Henry laughed. 'We are not sure of the numbers.'

'Oh.' Muriel looked from Henry to Mr Briggs, feeling puzzled.

'It is best not to meet them.' Mr Briggs looked at Muriel. 'We explore by night. I have been all over London since the storm. There were fires everywhere and since then – well.'

'Well what?' Muriel was impatient. 'I must go to Patricia's home and see what has happened there, and I have dozens of friends in London.'

'Have you?' Henry looked at her with an amused expression. 'I will take you to Patricia's flat. She gave me the key.'

'She what?'

'She gave me the key. She found it among her father's things.'

'And didn't tell me?' Muriel felt annoyed.

'Well,' said Henry comfortably, 'she saw me with my own latchkey so she gave me hers too. She thought you were a bit insensitive about the pigs.'

'But her parents were not pigs.'

'From what I hear Patricia has a parental feeling towards the pigs,' said Mr Briggs tactfully.

'Oh,' Muriel smiled, 'she has. She is very strong on the subject.'

'Well, the pigs are there and the parents are not.' Henry looked at Muriel. 'Come on and I'll show you.'

Mr Briggs raised an eyebrow. 'I'm going to sleep,' he said, 'and Paul should too. Come on and I'll find you a room.' He left the room followed by Paul.

Muriel rounded on Henry. 'Your parents,' she said.

'There's just the empty house. They had gone away. I've ransacked it. They left nothing of interest. Shall we go and see Patricia's flat if you must?'

'Yes,' said Muriel, 'I must.'

'Then follow me and do what I do.'

Henry led Muriel out of the window at the back of the house and then by devious routes through Westminster into Pimlico.

'It's getting bloody cold,' said Henry. 'We can't spend the winter here. We must get home, it's safe there.'

'Safe?' Muriel, walking beside Henry, decided that he was over-imaginative. 'Don't be silly,' she said.

Henry said nothing but walked on, keeping close to the area railings until they reached the block of flats Patricia's parents lived in.

'Upstairs, No. 303,' said Henry laconically, 'here's the key.'

They climbed the stairs to the third floor in silence and came to a stop outside the door numbered 303. Muriel paused.

'Go on,' Henry said roughly.

Muriel put the key in the lock and opened the door, calling softly, 'Anybody in? Anybody at home?' Henry sat down in the corridor with his back to the wall and waited.

Muriel walked into a quietly luxurious flat, noting good furniture and carpets, one or two good pictures on the walls and the light switches turned on, but there was no light.

'No light,' Muriel murmured to herself and opened a door which led her into a bedroom. The bed was slightly ruffled as though someone had been lying on it, and a mass of long fair hair lay on the pillow, nothing else. Muriel left the flat and rejoined Henry, feeling sick.

'See?' said Henry.

'See what?' Muriel flared up in hatred of Henry.

'See the truth of course.' Henry laughed in her face and then ran away down the stairs leaving her alone to find her way back to Downing Street.

Muriel walked proudly across the park and down Whitehall
towards the Cenotaph which she had passed that morning in
the dawn without paying it much attention. Now later in the
day she paused and stared at it with mounting horror.
Besides the conventional wreaths of poppies there were piled
against the foot of the monument shoes, hats, jewellery, a
bicycle, long strands of hair, bowler hats, umbrellas and 'Oh
God!' muttered Muriel, 'Teeth, teeth, teeth.' She broke into a
run and did not stop until she reached the closed door of
No. 10 Downing Street where she hammered like a child
with her fists until Mr Briggs opened the door.

'The Cenotaph,' said Muriel breathlessly.

'Ah yes. We found it like that.' Mr Briggs looked concerned for her.

'Who did it?'

'Who knows? Come in, it's cold.' Muriel allowed herself
to be led upstairs.

'Was it Henry?'

'No. I personally think people rushed there during the
storm. If you go to any church which is open you will find
much the same.'

Muriel felt calm slowly coming back as she climbed the
stairs.

'We must get out of here,' said Mr Briggs, 'and the sooner
the better. Ah, here comes Henry.'

Henry climbed the stairs after them. 'This is pretty, don't
you think?' He held out a diamond tiara to Muriel.

'Where did you get it?' Mr Briggs looked surprised.

'Cartier has had its windows bashed in.' Henry exchanged
an enigmatic look with the young man. 'I shall take it to Mrs
Luard.'

'I must look round a bit more. I cannot believe no one I love is left. I cannot.'

'It's snowing,' exclaimed Henry, looking out of the window. 'And freezing too.'

'I must go out.' Muriel pushed past the man and the boy.

'Let her go,' said Mr Briggs. 'She must see for herself, then she will come.'

'Then I shall go and get some sleep because we ought to go tomorrow before we are found.'

Muriel walked rapidly through the streets of Petty France and on towards Chelsea. She walked through the streets of Chelsea where her friends had lived and across to South Kensington. Every street was the same, empty, quiet, lifeless and full of rubbish, paper bags and sweet papers, cigarette ends and hair, empty cars and taxis and dusty shops. As she got near Gloucester Road, where some of Julian's highbrow friends had remained poised in top flats converted from the servants' quarters of giant houses of the late Victorian era, she felt a cold sweat break between her shoulder blades and the feeling that she was being watched. She tried not to walk faster or to betray her awareness but her heart began to thump and her eyes to flail from side to side of the street. As she hesitated over which direction to take, a shot rang out and she felt a bullet whistle past her head. At the same time a hand caught her ankle and she fell on the pavement.

'Lie still,' said a voice she did not know. 'Lie absolutely still.' Another shot rang out and a third further away.

'Someone is drawing their fire. Now run.'

A man she had never seen before pulled her to her feet and she found herself racing beside him through side streets. Suddenly, just as she thought she could run no more, the man stopped by a taxi standing by the pavement and, opening the door, pushed her in.

'Sorry to be so abrupt,' said the man, 'but it was the only thing to do. I wonder who is drawing them off. They were after me.'

'Trying to kill us,' Muriel gasped indignantly.

'Well, yes. My name is Waterford. What is yours?'

'Muriel Wake. What's going on?'

'Lie still. You are perfectly safe here. Where do you come from?'

'Devonshire. I got to Downing Street this morning.'

Muriel's rescuer was laughing. 'Sorry to laugh but it's such a funny combination. What is going on in Downing Street, if it's not indiscreet to ask?'

Muriel told the man about Henry and Mr Briggs and Paul and he sat thoughtfully on the floor of the taxi listening.

'And they did not tell you that it was dangerous to walk about in daylight?'

'I would not have believed them,' said Muriel truthfully.

'I suppose they knew you very well.'

'Henry does,' admitted Muriel. 'Please tell me what's going on?'

'Well.' Mr Waterford arranged long legs more comfortably. 'After the storm in July which eliminated nearly everyone, there were fires. You have probably seen the areas burned. Many people who lived below ground survived and they came out but, just as in the last war, they took shelter in the tubes because they were afraid. Others escaped — owners of gambling clubs, strip joints, the criminal fringe. They banded together under some clever fellow and they got a bulldozer and cleared the road west out of London. I hid and I watched. In my innocence I was glad because I thought those poor people hiding in the tubes would come out and we could live again.' He paused.

'We have lived again in Devon,' said Muriel. 'There was one very frightening lot who got drowned trying to get to London.' And Muriel told her new friend of her little community in the country. 'What happened to the people who cleared the road?'

'They came back,' said Mr Waterford gloomily, 'with some sort of gas and they have killed all the people who were in the tubes and anyone moving they shoot on sight. Of course it can't last long for any of us.'

'Why not?' said Muriel.

'Well, just think. Drains, typhus, plague and so on. The moment the weather gets warm all that will start.'

Muriel, sitting on the floor of the abandoned taxi, was silent.

'Lie still,' Muriel's new friend said suddenly and Muriel listened to the sound of soft footsteps approaching.

'Where is she, Chap? Find her.' Henry's cheerful voice spoke close by.

'Here,' said Muriel, standing up. 'Henry, I am here.'

Muriel and Mr Waterford got out of the taxi.

'I followed you,' said Henry. 'Who is this?'

'My name is Waterford.'

'Don't you think,' said Henry in conversational tones to Mr Waterford as he politely shook hands, 'that Mrs Wake should just peep into a tube station?'

'Why?'

Henry shifted the rifle he was carrying to his other arm. 'If she sees what's in the station she will believe and then we must all get out. That clot Paul has only just told me they came in as far as Earls Court by car. We can get out in it and old Briggs can fly us home. *He's* only just let on he can fly – that he actually holds a licence.'

'Tomorrow,' said Mr Waterford as they walked along.

'Yes, tomorrow,' said Henry. 'It wouldn't be safe at night. Here's a tube station, Mrs Wake. Just take a look for yourself.'

Mesmerised by Henry's casual manner, Muriel let herself be led down the staircase of a tube station.

'So that's the smell,' she said as she turned away and was sick until she could be sick no more.

'This is the gun old Perdue saw under my bed at Brendon,' said Henry, watching her with sad eyes as she walked slowly back to Downing Street. 'It's snowing,' he said cheerfully. 'The snow will keep them indoors.'

Later Muriel, lying on a sofa gulping hot tea, looked at her son and Henry and at Mr Briggs and Mr Waterford. 'Is there nobody else left?' she asked.

'We do not think so,' they said gently. 'We have searched very thoroughly. The time has come to go.'

Muriel listened listlessly to the men and boys planning their flight, for flight she fully realised it to be.

'If we can get unseen as far as London Airport we should be lucky enough to find a plane to fly us down to Devonshire.' Mr Briggs was quiet and unassuming.

'If not a plane a helicopter,' said Henry.

'I have never flown a helicopter. My experience is rather out of date anyway.' The young man spoke practically.

'Then we must walk,' Paul said cheerfully. 'Get back the way we came.'

'In this weather?' Henry's voice was flatly contemptuous. 'Look at it. Snowing and freezing. None of us would survive.'

'It may not last.' Paul looked at his mother lying resting on the sofa.

'It will. I can feel it in my bones,' said Henry. 'And while we wait all those dead people are fermenting in the tube.'

'Really, Henry,' Mr Waterford mildly protested.

'Well, I am right.' Henry stared out of the window at the falling snow. 'The sewage system will clog up. We did a paper on it once at school. All those bodies will be rotting away where they were killed. It's unhealthy, as old Perdue would say.'

Muriel got up and left the room to wander about the house in the grey light, opening and shutting doors as she went, knowing that never again would she see this house. In one room she stared blankly at a pile of pictures, portraits partially destroyed. She recognised past Prime Ministers in gold frames. Somebody had either slashed the canvases or put a foot through each. 'Henry, I suppose.' Muriel smiled in spite of herself.

The others moved briskly about the house talking in low voices. At a window commanding a view of the street Paul sat with Henry's gun watching the approach to the house.

Later in the evening Muriel made a meal of what she could find and they all ate in preoccupied silence.

At intervals during the evening the two men left her alone in the house with the boys.

'What are those two men doing?' she asked.

'Making sure we are not yet discovered, I think,' said Paul. 'We don't want to get ourselves shot or gassed do we?'

'No.' Muriel went and watched Henry playing idly with the telephone switchboard.

'Henry, Paul heard the telephone at home,' she said.

'So he told me.' Muriel felt a long divide between herself and the boy.

Late in the evening they all slept, though Muriel was aware that the two men took turns to keep watch. Outside in the silent city the snow fell steadily to cover the traces of human life.

At dawn Paul and Henry woke her. 'Come and fill some thermoses, Mum.'

Muriel boiled water and filled thermoses with tea and coffee and watched Paul feed his rats before zipping them into the pocket of his windcheater.

Mr Briggs cleared his throat. 'If you know where it is will you go with Henry to the car you left in Earls Court. The rest of us will follow if Paul will give us a lead.'

'Why can't we all go together?' Muriel asked.

'Oh Mum, you know whoever shot at you knows we are about. Don't be so dumb.' Henry laughed at Paul's rudeness.

'All right.'

Muriel with her dog at her heels slipped out of the house and set off, her feet crunching on the snow.

'Are you sure you don't mind me with you?' Henry spoke softly.

'No,' said Muriel, knowing that she was lying. 'No, I don't. I am afraid for the others.'

'They will go by different streets so that we don't leave a huge great trail to be followed.'

Muriel said nothing, hating the snow and the freezing wind, hating her fear.

'They are going to create diversions,' said Henry cheerfully. 'The first is the best.'

'What's that?'

'A gunpowder plot, a slow consuming fire in the Houses of Parliament. By the time it gets going we shall be gone.' Muriel looked at Henry unbelievingly.

'It's perfectly true,' said Henry, and hurried her on through the snow. 'If all Whitehall is on fire they will go there.'

'It seems mad,' Muriel said indignantly.

'But it's true.' Henry seemed in no way put out but led her as fast as she could walk on the long trail to Earls Court. When at last they reached it he said, 'Now, where's that car?'

Muriel cast about until she found the street and saw the car standing covered with snow in the side street.

'Now we wait,' said Henry.

'Henry, you know I hate waiting.'

'Maybe this is the last time.' Henry tried to cheer her. 'No, don't get into it, get into another and we will watch for the others.'

Together they got into an empty car and sat close together for warmth, listening. After a long time they heard far away the sound of an explosion and saw the sky grow red. Waiting, they watched the sky and the streets until at last, running as though they had run a long way, Paul appeared with the two men.

'Ah,' said Henry and slipped out of the car and stood waiting to meet them. Muriel joined him and looked anxiously at Paul who looked exhausted.

'No time to wait,' said Mr Waterford. 'Where's the car?'

Muriel pointed and the two men and the boys gathered round.

'Get in with the dog and we will push.'

Muriel obeyed, started the engine, and with the men and boys pushing the car through the snow, drove slowly out into the main road. Keeping in low gear through the snow,

Muriel felt the draught of the door opening as one by one the boys and the men jumped into the car as it was moving.

'Whatever you do, don't stop.' Mr Briggs was sitting beside her, 'And keep it, if you can, in the middle of the road.'

Muriel drove slowly, turning on the windscreen wipers and the heater, her heart in her mouth. The snow falling heavily made driving difficult.

'It may be difficult,' said Henry from the back seat, 'but the harder the snow falls the quicker our tracks will be covered.'

Behind her, a long way away, Muriel heard explosions.

'Don't look back, look at where you are driving,' Mr Waterford said dryly.

'What's going on?' Muriel asked.

'We set fire to the gas which is still in the tubes and the pressure is making explosions.'

'Why?' said Muriel angrily. 'Why destroy London?'

'Because it will flush out the people who are hunting us and distract their attention. Please do not behave like Lot's wife.'

'All right, I won't.' Muriel drove on.

'Of course if she did look,' Henry's cheerful voice remarked, 'she would see at last.'

'See what?' Muriel drove on.

'See what you have never seen,' said Henry airily.

'Time enough when we are airborne,' Mr Waterford said. 'I think, Henry, it would be best for you to shut up.'

Henry laughed. 'Couldn't she bear it?' he said.

'Not just yet.' Mr Waterford answered quietly.

'Very well.' Henry spoke gently. 'Drive on, Mrs Wake. You are doing very well.'

❧ 31 ❧

Muriel drove on doggedly, her heart in her mouth. The snow fell steadily but she managed to keep the car more or less in the centre of the road. Beside her Mr Briggs sat silent and behind her the two boys, Mr Waterford and the dog huddled in the back seat.

'What did you do in real life?' Muriel heard Henry asking Mr Waterford.

'I was doing research into the habits of Eastern peoples. The storm caught me underground and I have been dodging "the wreckers", as I call them to myself, ever since.'

'Now we have done some wrecking.' Henry sounded pleased.

'We had to save our lives,' Paul said reasonably.

'We must do some more at London Airport or they will follow us.'

'I don't think there are many people left,' Mr Briggs remarked from the seat beside Muriel. 'I have been watching them fighting among themselves. What is more, they are the kind of people who are afraid of the country so they will stay in the town and die.'

As he spoke the windscreen shattered and Muriel heard Mr Briggs grunt in pain.

'Don't stop, for God's sake,' Henry said from the back. 'Are you all right, Mr Briggs?'

'Give me a handkerchief or something. I've been hit in the shoulder. Go on driving, Mrs Wake. It's our only chance.'

From the back seat Mr Waterford leant forward and opened Mr Briggs' coat. 'You won't be much use as a pilot,' he remarked. 'The bullet's gone right through you into the seat. All I can do is stop the blood.'

'Go on, Mum, don't stop.' Paul spoke urgently. 'You know the way. Go on.'

Muriel smelt the smell of fresh blood and glancing sideways saw her companion looking very white as from the back seat Mr Waterford plugged a wound in the man's shoulder and without asking her took the headscarf off her head and fixed it in a sling to support Mr Briggs' arm.

'I won't die,' Mr Briggs said between his teeth. 'Drive on, Mrs Wake, drive on.'

Muriel drove as though in a nightmare through the snow, the sweat pouring down the small of her back and clogging her armpits.

'When we find an aircraft you will have to tell Mrs Wake how to pilot it.' Henry's voice was hard and clear.

'I can do that.'

'I have learnt to fly a little in good conditions. My husband taught me.' Muriel spoke with terror at the prospect before her.

'Then that will have to do.' Mr Waterford finished tying the sling and they were all silent until they reached the airport.

Muriel never very clearly remembered what followed except that she and Mr Waterford helped Mr Briggs out of the car and into shelter as the snow stung their eyes and blanketed all the neighbourhood. In the airport lounge they laid Mr Briggs in a chair and Henry ran to look for brandy which he found in a bar and brought back a bottle and some glasses. He dosed Mr Briggs and then turned to Muriel.

'Wait with him, Mrs Wake, while we find a plane. Don't let him move.'

Muriel sat beside the young man feeling very helpless, seeing the other man and the two boys run off.

'Does it hurt much?' Muriel looked at the white face.

'Like hell.'

Time passed slowly and Muriel fretted at the agony of its pace. At last the two boys and the man came back.

'Come on,' Henry exclaimed. 'We have found a plane. We must get it away. Come on, Mr Briggs.'

Mr Waterford and Muriel helped Mr Briggs up and slowly followed the boys and the dog.

'I found some morphia and I will give you a shot once you have told Mrs Wake how to get us off the ground.' Mr Waterford spoke as though promising a packet of sweets to a child. The other man smiled wryly.

The aircraft was small and Muriel recognised it as of the make Julian had taught her to fly in. They hoisted the wounded man into the plane and put him in the seat beside the pilot's.

'Now, Mrs Wake — ' Henry's voice roused Muriel's anger to the point of outrage, anger mixed with love. With a dreamlike determination she started the motor, hearing the boys and the dog settle behind her with Mr Waterford.

'Can you navigate?' she asked her wounded neighbour.

'I'll tell you the course to set once you get up,' the wounded man muttered. 'Just taxi off into the snow and I'll tell you what to do.'

The noise of the aircraft increased as Muriel taxied slowly along the runway. Then suddenly her confidence flowed back and they were airborne. She flew the aircraft as she had been taught long ago and circled the airfield. Below her she could hear explosions and see fires breaking out, but her mind was set on one thing only, to get home.

Mr Waterford came up from the back of the aircraft holding a syringe. 'Tell her what course to set, old boy, and then I'll put you out of pain.'

Mr Briggs began muttering and the other man interpreted to Muriel while she obeyed, setting the frail little aeroplane towards the west.

'Good. Keep her on that course. Now I'll jab the poor chap.'

Muriel, concentrating on the controls, felt her neighbour relax and sink in his seat.

'Nobody will follow us now,' said Henry's voice gaily.

'Nothing to follow in,' shouted Paul.

Checking her position Muriel saw from the cockpit, even through the snow, a great blaze behind and below them.

'It will all burn. Nothing like aviation petrol,' Henry shouted in her ear. 'Now you get us home, Mrs Wake, that's all you have to do.'

Simple, Muriel thought to herself as she flew into a sky full of falling snow. Behind her Henry was laughing and suddenly she knew fully and for the first time what she must tell Father Richard.

They soon lost sight of the ground and Muriel kept the nose of the plane pointing west as she flew it through the snowstorm. Beside her Mr Briggs, with the morphia beginning to work, lolled in silence like a corpse, his eyes shut. Behind her she heard her dog bark nervously and the two boys' voices raised high above the noise of the engine as they shouted at Mr Waterford.

Muriel wondered at Mr Waterford's calmness, the manner in which he had saved her life, his efficient way of dealing with Mr Briggs' wound and, smiling to herself, she remembered his very long legs like a spider which enabled him to bend from behind her as she sat in the cockpit and inject Mr Briggs with morphia. She heard Henry's voice shout above the engine, 'About two hundred and twenty miles', and Mr Waterford's head came between her and the unconscious Mr Briggs to look at the altimeter and the speedometer.

'Just keep on flying,' the young man's voice said in her ear.

'I say, care for a swig?' Henry's face replaced Mr Waterford's and she saw he was holding a paper cup of brandy.

Muriel nodded and drank as the boy held the cup to her lips.

'We are all getting plastered in the back,' his amiable voice said loud in her ear. 'Ever landed in snow?'

'No.' Muriel shook her head.

'First time for everything.' Henry still sounded cheerful.

'First time for death,' Muriel snapped and the boy grinned. She noticed that Paul and Mr Waterford each sat looking out on either side of the plane, seeing nothing she supposed but clouds and fleeting snow.

Either brandy or their desperate position exalted Muriel and she too glanced from time to time at the altimeter and tried to calculate how fast and far they were going.

'They call this "Going West".' Henry's voice was in her ear again. 'Paul and old Waterford are watching for the sea.'

'The sea?'

'Yes, we have passed Salisbury. Paul saw the tip of the spire. Keep it up, Mrs Wake.'

Muriel felt resentful that she should find herself in this ridiculous position, flying two children, two men, a dog and two rats through a snowstorm all because of Henry who had led them to the horrors of London. Glancing sideways she saw Henry sliding into the seat beside the unconscious man and begin to peer forwards through the clouds. He does not seem worried, she thought to herself, and then rebuked herself, thinking that he was only a child.

'You are not only a child,' she suddenly shouted at Henry. Henry nodded in agreement.

'Sea on the left,' Paul shouted in her ear. 'Mr Waterford says can you bear right a bit. We don't want to ditch in the sea.'

Henry laughed and looked at Muriel whose brows were knit in perplexity. She turned the aircraft slightly right and flew on.

'Will this ever end?' she said.

'Yes.' Henry seemed to have heard her.

'Fasten your seat belts, please.' Henry's voice was a dainty imitation of an air hostess. He fastened the seat belt round Mr Briggs who grunted in pain. Behind her she felt Paul and Mr Waterford securing themselves.

'There's the sea dividing Exeter from the mainland.' Henry pointed downwards through a gap in the clouds and Muriel saw angry sea horses chopping up the sea before the clouds cut off the sight of the sea which had once been the river Exe.

'Now watch out for the hills.' Muriel felt Henry's direction unnecessary as she peered through the clouds looking for the moor.

Now everyone was silent and Muriel knew that she and only she could bring down the aircraft. The clouds thickened and thinned giving her tantalizing glimpses of the ground below them. Each time she saw the earth she tried hard to recognise some land-mark. Suddenly, before she expected it, she saw the reservoir by Brendon below them and realised that she was overshooting her house. With the blood thumping in her head she banked the plane, hearing cries of protest from her passengers. She dropped height, the engines stuttered, the snow rushed up at them and before she could raise the nose of the plane it bumped, rose in the air, then bumped a second time to lie still in the snow, lopsided.

'Mum, you've done it.' Paul clambered up to her.

Muriel felt a great wave of relief followed by pain. Chap barked and she heard voices. The voices died away and surged back. She recognised Coke and James and the two girls chattering.

'Watch out, Mrs Wake is hurt, so is Briggs,' Mr Waterford was shouting.

'Get them out and clear before it catches fire.' Commander James's authority seemed to dominate.

'Patricia, get those damned pigs back to the house.'

Muriel felt herself lifted out, laid in the snow and then suddenly lifted again by Coke. 'It's all right, Mrs Wake, soon get you to the house.'

'Mr Briggs, Coke, Mr Briggs has been shot.'

'We'll take care of him.' Coke's boring reassuring voice answered. 'The Commander and the other chap's got him.'

Muriel fainted. Coming to she gasped, 'I'm terrified.'

'Too late to feel terrified now.' Henry, leaping through

the snow with Paul beside him, kept up with Coke sedately carrying her.

'I can walk,' Muriel said crossly. 'I'm not a bride to be carried over the threshold.'

'You've broken a leg,' Henry's voice cried cheerfully. 'Watch out, there she goes!'

Behind them, lying wrecked in the snow, the little plane burst into flames with a staccato explosion.

'We have a surprise for you.' June's face loomed up beside her.

'Best get her to bed and get her leg set first,' said Coke.

Muriel felt sudden warmth as Coke carried her into the house.

'If you can get her into bed I'll set her leg and give her some morphia.' Mr Waterford, his hair full of snow and his nose bleeding loped alongside.

'And who are you?' From beside the Aga old Mr Perdue rose with dignity as the cat jumped crossly off his lap her whiskers twitching.

'Waterford's the name. Can you get those girls to fill hot bottles for Mrs Wake and the other chap? He's been shot.'

'Arrh,' said the old man in disbelief.

Muriel, flinching with pain and half conscious, was carried up the stairs. June and Ann undressed her and listened to her muttering, 'My head, my head.'

'She's cracked her head,' said June to Mr Waterford.

'Has she? I'll give her a shot of morphia and see to the leg then I must see to poor Briggs.'

Muriel felt the prick of the syringe and great pain in her leg as the young man set it.

'She'll be all right. Get me something to make a splint. I expect she's got concussion too.'

'Lucky you know how to do all these things.' June's voice came through a dull haze. 'I wanted her to see her surprise.'

'It must wait. Let her sleep.'

Muriel felt pain, relief, the comfort of her own bed, and slept. Much later she woke and remembered the horrors of London, the terror of the flight. The watcher at her side took her hand and held it firmly as she cried out, sweating with fear.

'It's quite all right now. They are all safe and so are you. Don't worry any more.' The watcher leant over her and kissed her.

Muriel opened doped eyes and stared. 'My God,' she whispered.

'Yes, it's me. I'm sorry I couldn't get back sooner. I arrived the day you left.'

'Sam.'

'Yes, Mama. Sam. Go to sleep now.'

Somebody gave Muriel another injection, but the hand which held hers was the long-fingered hand of Sam. Her fingers relaxed and she slept.

Henry put his head round the door. 'Want to eat?' Sam nodded.

Muriel opened her eyes and saw Henry.

'I saw Sam.'

'You saw Sam. Go to sleep.' The child's face bore no expression as he watched her close her eyes and begin to breathe deeply.

Outside the house the wind sank to a whisper as the snow rose round the walls. June and Ann helped Coke shutter the windows, creeping silently round the house so that they would not disturb Muriel and Mr Briggs.

Mr Waterford lay in a chair by the library fire and stretched his long legs, relaxing for the first time for many weeks, comforted by the presence of a collection of puppies and kittens, made drowsy by the warmth.

Outside, struggling through the snow, James and the three children helped Mr Perdue feed and water the animals and shut up the poultry. They closed all the sheds and barns and made their way back to the house.

'How long will this go on?' one of the girls muttered.

'Winter, it's winter,' the old man said.

'Where is Akbar?' Henry asked suddenly. 'Jolly old Akbar.'

'In bed with a cold.'

Henry clapped his hand to his mouth and spluttered with laughter. June looked at him with disgust.

'Nothing funny,' she said.

'No, no, but so normal.' Henry's eyes filled with tears of laughter. 'In bed with a cold. How gorgeous.'

'It's the contrast,' said James dryly.

'He drops in on us from Afghanistan, marries you and catches a cold.'

'Well?' June bristled.

'Oh, nothing.' James looked at Ann affectionately, knowing that she too would find Akbar's cold funny. Ann smiled at him.

'I think it's nice and normal to have a cold,' she said firmly.

'I am going to have a small session on the blower,' said Henry and went off with Paul to the telephone where they spent an hour or more talking to Mrs Luard and then to the Abbey. On their return Henry remarked casually, 'Mrs Luard is okay and Father Richard is coming up with medicines as soon as he can.'

'Medicines?'

'Yes. He says not only Mrs Wake and Mr Briggs will need them but Sam too. He says Sam may have had some shock.'

'Haven't we all?' Paul glanced at his friend.

'Yes, indeed yes. He said mental as well as physical though.'

'Oh.' Paul looked thoughtful.

'And of course there is Akbar's cold,' Henry said cheerfully to June. 'He may not have an ordinary British cold but a fierce Afghan one.'

'Shut up,' said June, hating Henry.

'Shut up is what we shall all be in this weather. If it freezes hard enough we can go visiting.'

'It will freeze,' Mr Perdue said with conviction. 'Ah yes, it will freeze.'

'Suit Akbar then.' Henry looked at June who looked away.

'I believe most people catch cold on their honeymoon. It's a sign of love,' Henry said to June. 'I've heard it said often.'

'Rubbish,' said June and began to prepare a tray for Akbar's tea which she intended to share with him in their bedroom.

Watching her leave the room a few minutes later, old Mr Perdue turned to Henry and said bluntly, 'You are not to tease them as is newly married. They get touchy.'

'Oh,' said Henry, turning to Ann. 'Are you touchy, Ann?'

'No,' Ann answered, 'but I have a cold coming on. I think Akbar will give it to us all.'

'Sure to,' said James, 'since we are all cooped up together.'

'I should like,' said Ann, 'to find a house where we could live on our own, James.'

'June and Akbar want to do that too, but none of us can move in this weather.'

'I daresay Mrs Wake would like to be left alone now she has her son back. I'm going to move into the farm.' The old man spoke gruffly. 'And I'm not going to wait for the spring either.'

'I'll come and live with you,' Coke said slowly, 'company for me, company for you, see?'

'All right.' The old man looked at Coke. 'All right. We'll have a kitten and keep house together.'

James wandered away into the library and stood watching Mr Waterford asleep in his chair. He wondered vaguely how long the other man would sleep and how soon the monk would arrive from the Abbey with medical relief. Taking Ann with him, he climbed the stairs to look into the room they had put Mr Briggs in and were met by feverish eyes staring at them from a flushed face.

'How are you feeling?' James asked.

'Pretty dim.'

'Medical supplies on their way,' said James. 'We all need them.'

'How is Mrs Wake?'

'Not too good, but her son is back.'

'Paul?'

'No, her older son Sam. He was abroad when the storm hit us. He turned up the day she went to London.'

'Poor London,' Mr Briggs muttered, 'burned, ravished, infected, blown up.'

'Why?' James got no answer but Ann tugged at his sleeve and pointed out of the window. Joining her he saw the figure of a monk, very small, coming through the snow and Henry and Paul running to meet him.

'The rescue team.' James and Ann left the room and went downstairs to find Father Richard shaking snow from his habit in the hall.

'How are they?' Father Richard enquired.

'They all look as if they had come out of hell,' said James. 'There is Briggs with a shot wound. Mrs Wake is semi-conscious and has a broken leg. Her son Sam is back.'

'Yes, I want to talk to him.'

'And we all have colds.'

Father Richard laughed. 'I had better see Mr Briggs first. His wound must not become infected.'

'Do you know any medicine?' Henry enquired at his elbow.

'Enough,' said the small monk and began climbing the stairs.

'I thought souls were your métier.' Henry's sophisticated voice followed Father Richard.

'Oh, drop dead,' said Father Richard amiably, remembering the parlance of the Youth Club of former days.

～ 34 ～

Mr Briggs submitted to the firm but gentle treatment administered to him and then lay back comfortably bandaged and rather drowsy.

'Waterford gave me morphia,' he said to the monk who was preparing a syringe.

'One more jab won't make you an addict,' Father Richard answered. 'You will sleep. Your fever will go and you will be up in a few days, but you must take it easy.'

'All right. You seem to know. But do you think we have brought any infection from London with us?'

'I'll ask Henry and that other man.' Father Richard smiled at the anxious face. 'It's a risk we have to take. We have no vaccines here, only common medicines. I shouldn't worry.'

'Spiritual infections.' Henry spoke from the doorway.

'I should call you a carrier,' said the monk tartly. 'Now I must see Mrs Wake. Good-bye and go to sleep.' He drew the bed-clothes up round Mr Briggs' chin.

'Akbar has a cold.' Henry, not to be subdued, accompanied the monk down the passage.

'Really. Now where is Mrs Wake?'

'Here, in here.' Henry led the way.

'Hullo, Sam, feeling better?' Father Richard went into Muriel's room.

'Yes, thanks. My mother is rambling a bit though. Wants to see you.'

'She's wanted to ever since the night of the storm,' Henry said cheerfully.

'Now buzz off for a bit. Give yourself a rest.' Father Richard put a hand on Muriel's forehead and took her wrist while Henry watched. After a moment Muriel opened her eyes and stared at the monk. 'I must – ' she began.

'You must rest. Let your leg and head heal. Everything is all right now and there are plenty of people to attend to things. There is nothing you must do just at the moment.'

'Sam. Sam is back.'

'Yes, Sam is back and Paul and Henry are safe. You brought them back and two men. Everything is under control.'

'It isn't,' said Muriel. 'I am not.'

Father Richard gave her a shot of morphia and stood watching her with Sam and Paul and Henry. 'She must be kept very quiet,' he said gently, watching her drift into sleep. 'Come on, Sam. I want to hear more than you told me when you arrived. Let's go to the library.'

Sam and his brother followed Father Richard out of the room forgetting Henry who curled up in a chair by the bed and fell asleep with his lips slightly parted, his face white with exhaustion.

Downstairs in the library they all gathered round the fire, even Akbar in a dressing-gown sniffing and sneezing at intervals. Mr Waterford woke from his sleep in the armchair and stared at them as he rose stiffly.

'You are from London. Henry told me on the telephone what had happened there. Was he exaggerating?'

'No. Nobody could have exaggerated it. London became a combination of Dante's Inferno and Giotto's Hell.' Mr Waterford sat down again. 'Sorry. I feel a bit shaky on my legs. It's the relief of getting away. I never thought I would. Then those children and Mrs Wake appeared and we got away.'

'Could you not have got away before?' asked June.

'Perhaps I could, but all the time I felt there was something I could do to stop them. Stop the destruction. It was really the sight of Henry's waxwork arrangement which convinced me.'

'Children.' Sam spoke in a neutral voice. 'By the way, where is Henry?'

'Asleep in Mum's room. It's all right, he just feels safe there.' Paul looked at his elder brother. 'If she wakes up he will be there. She is *used* to him now.'

Sam laughed, looking round the group of faces. 'Nice,' he said and then, stretching his arms above his head, he remarked at random. 'Nice to find people alive and sane. Nice to find my mother and brother, my home and,' he hesitated, 'a house party.'

'We shan't stay for ever,' said James. 'Ann and I want to live within reach, so do June and Akbar. Old Perdue and Coke are setting up house together and the Abbey is still going, I take it. What about you, Waterford and Briggs?'

'I want to write a book and now I have the time. I can't answer for Briggs. He is the sort of man who will want to go and find out what's happened on the continent, when he is well again that is.'

'You can tell us about the continent, Sam. You were there after all.' Paul spoke with the envy of a younger brother.

'It is just the same as here,' Sam answered. 'Everybody is gone. Nothing left. I found my way home by boat from the Baltic coast. To be honest, I was so scared on land that I made my way to the sea and looked for a boat. When I found one I could sail I followed the coast until I got to Calais, then I crossed the channel on a quiet day and followed the coastline until I got home. Then I walked inland to the Abbey and found Father Richard and came home.'

'Did you see nobody? No planes, no ships?' James asked.

'Plenty of ships drifting, and many wrecks,' said Sam, as though the recollection were repellent to him.

'When the weather improves we shall have to go across the channel and see whether we can find any explanation,' said James.

'I think Henry knows some explanation but won't tell,' said Paul.

'Possibly,' said Sam. 'His parents were mixed up in something fishy.'

Paul got up and left the room to join Patricia who was lying on the floor in the drawing room with her pigs round her, slowly scratching their stomachs with a small stick.

'What does Henry know that we don't know?' Paul lay down beside Patricia who just looked at him without answering.

In the library Father Richard was getting ready to leave. He gave June and Ann careful instructions on the nursing of Muriel and Mr Briggs. 'I must go now or I won't be back before Compline,' he said and left them to walk over the snow-covered moor and down through the woods into the valley.

James, seeing the total exhaustion on Mr Waterford's face, took him upstairs and found him a bedroom and, amused, watched him undress and get into the bed in what seemed one movement and fall immediately asleep.

With his new wife he looked in on Mr Briggs who, too, was sleeping quietly. They noticed Akbar and June vanish into their room, with Akbar suppressing a sneeze as he went, then they tip-toed towards Muriel's room and opened the door.

Muriel lay sleeping alone with her dog at her feet, her face white and expressionless.

'Look.' Ann pointed to Henry sprawled in a chair.

'Leave him,' said James.

'Should we?'

'Why not?'

'I don't know why not.' Ann flushed.

'Don't be silly then.' James turned to Sam and Paul coming towards them. 'It's all right, isn't it?' he asked the brothers, who looked in at their mother.

'Will she be all right if she wakes?' Paul whispered to his elder brother.

'Yes. God, I'm tired. I am going to bed. You should too.' Sam closed the door and led Paul away. 'Come and sleep. We can talk later.'

In her room Muriel heard them whispering and stirred in her sleep. Henry opened his eyes and got up to watch her. Then he moved to the window to look at the falling snow in the dusk and, going back to the armchair, fell asleep again.

Muriel lay in her bed and heard the noises of the house. Her fever made her acutely conscious. Clocks ticked and outside her window the wind rustled. She felt the pain in her leg. The pain of her head made it impossible to think. Once or twice during the night she cried out and Henry, rousing himself, came to her side.

'Henry, what happened?'

'You flew us home from London and crash-landed in the snow. You will be safe now.'

'Safe?'

'Well, London was not safe.'

'Why were we in London? I saw Sam, Henry. I saw Sam.'

'Yes,' Henry said patiently, 'you did. Sam is back. He is very tired. He is sleeping but he is quite all right.'

'Where's Julian?' Muriel felt the empty space beside her with her hand. 'Julian, Julian,' she muttered. 'There was a storm. Somebody shot at me in London. I must get home. I must get to Father Richard to talk to him.'

'Presently,' said Henry, pulling the bedclothes up to her face, watching her go off to sleep again. 'I hope you don't stay bonkers,' he muttered and went to rouse James.

'Someone should sit with her, nurse her.' Henry, standing sleepily in the doorway of James and Ann's room, roused them. 'She is wandering in her mind.'

'I'll go.' Ann got out of bed and put on a dressing-gown. 'Make some tea, sweetheart,' she said to James.

'Sweetheart.' Henry followed James and helped him make tea.

'I don't need you,' James said quite kindly. 'Go and sleep, Henry.' The boy said nothing, but James found him curled up in the armchair when he came up with a tray. They all drank tea, watching Muriel sleep. James and Ann stifled their yawns and exchanged glances.

'Somebody responsible must sit with her,' Ann whispered. James nodded and settled in a chair beside Muriel's bed.

Muriel startled them all by crying out suddenly, 'The cat.'

'The cat's all right,' Ann reassured her.

'No, he's dead, dead.'

Ann looked at James who shrugged his shoulders.

'We must make a rota, this may go on for days,' he murmured.

Very early he woke June and Akbar and together they went to visit Mr Briggs who greeted them cheerfully.

'Better, I'm much better. Mr Briggs seemed to have lost his fever. 'How is Mrs Wake?'

'Rambling,' said James. 'We must sit with her in turns. I'm going to arrange it. She is alone at the moment with Henry.'

'Then she will be quite all right,' said Mr Briggs.

'Oh, is that your opinion? How odd. He's only a child. June and Ann and Sam and I can take turns to sit with her. I shouldn't think Henry would be of much use.'

'You lack imagination,' said Mr Briggs from his bed. 'She followed Henry all the way to London. Personally I am delighted she did, otherwise poor Waterford and I would have perished.'

'How?' James looked obtuse.

'Don't be a fool,' Mr Briggs snapped. 'London was bed-lam. People were terrified. The strong destroyed the weak. They took a lot of trouble. They cleared the road to the west and brought in gas and murdered people. They shot people. They ravaged and burned. They used chemicals and gas.'

'You make it sound like Belsen,' said James lightly. 'You have had a shock.'

'That's mild,' said Mr Briggs angrily. 'Ask Waterford, ask Henry.' James looked perplexed.

'Ordinary people don't behave like that,' James said.

'These were not ordinary people, they were terrified people, not dumb-bells like you who know how to behave.' James looked offended and Ann hurriedly broke in saying that arrangements must be made to nurse Muriel.

Muriel tossed and turned in her sleep and days, then weeks passed. Now and again she opened her eyes and saw Ann and James sitting beside her or Akbar and June sitting hand in hand on the window seat. She wondered who they were and where they came from and why her leg and head hurt so much.

Late one afternoon she opened her eyes and saw Mrs Luard sitting comfortably beside her, knitting.

'You are not wearing your tiara,' said Muriel with a flash of memory.

'No, dear,' Mrs Luard said reasonably. 'I'm keeping it for best.'

'What are you doing here?'

'Henry came to fetch me. Said you needed a sensible woman. Those girls are too preoccupied.'

'What girls?' Muriel remembered no girls.

'Ann and June. They are married now, you know.'

'Married? I don't understand anything.'

'I daresay not, but you will.' The older woman's presence was soothing. 'That child Patricia and your Paul are going to stay for a bit in my house and teach my crew some English.'

Muriel did not answer but lay still, trying to recollect.

'It will all come back.' Mrs Luard watched her face. 'My old man got a crack on the head once and he was out quite a long time. The pigs went too. Ever so funny they looked walking over the snow.' Mrs Luard laughed. 'Your Sam is a handsome boy,' she said, but Muriel's mind was far away and she was staring in horror at heaps of bodies piled up in grotesque positions in the tube.

'We must get out. Escape. I must tell Father Richard.'

Mrs Luard raised her eyebrows and went on knitting, her ear cocked to the sounds in the house, Akbar sneezing and that horrid old man talking to Coke in the yard. She was glad that nice Mr Waterford and Mrs Wake's older son had gone off more than an hour before to fetch the priest. Mrs Luard sat waiting beside Muriel, her knitting needles clicking with a soothing rhythm. Now and again she glanced at Muriel's dog who sat with his head pressed on the side of the bed watching Muriel's face, his ears laid back. Later Mrs Luard saw the dog's ears move and, hearing nothing, went to the window. Across the frozen snow walked Sam and Mr Waterford on either side of the little priest, slowing their long strides so that they should not outpace him. Mrs Luard and the dog listened to the three men come into the house and the sound of Henry's voice raised in greeting.

Father Richard came into the room with Henry and Mr Waterford. 'Let's see the leg. How is she, Mrs Luard?'

'Comes and goes,' said Mrs Luard lifting the beclothes off Muriel's leg. 'If you ask me, the longer she's gone the better.'

'I'm not going anywhere,' said Muriel clearly. 'I have broken my leg and it will heal quickly. I always heal quickly. I have banged my head too.'

Father Richard grinned and examined the leg. 'It seems to be knitting all right.' He put back the bedclothes. 'How does your head feel?'

'Muzzy,' said Muriel.

'Well, that will clear. Your leg is mending but will keep you in bed for a while longer. I've brought you some tablets for your head. They can't do you any harm.'

'Got any tablets for her soul?' Henry stood looking at Muriel. Mr Waterford suppressed a smile.

'I'll take the tablets.' Muriel shut her eyes.

'She's wandering off again,' said Mrs Luard and left the room with the others to speak to them. 'Do you think she will be herself again?' she asked the priest abruptly.

'Who was she?' the priest murmured and went down the passage to visit Mr Briggs who was quite himself again.

❧ 36 ❧

By the time Christmas came Muriel was receiving visitors. Each time someone came to see her Henry slid out of the door. Sometimes he was gone for hours on end and Muriel wondered where he went.

One afternoon when Sam and Mr Waterford were sitting in her room she said to them, 'Where does Henry go when he disappears for hours on end?'

'Oh, he visits the submarine crew and Paul and Patricia. He visits the Abbey. Last week he was gone two days visiting the fish people.' Sam smiled at his mother, glad to find her lucid.

'Can they speak any English yet?' Muriel asked.

'Of a sort,' said Mr Briggs. 'The children are giving them a crash course in basic English. They teach very well. They come from Dubrovnik, charming people. I have visited them too.'

'I wish I could get about,' Muriel said petulantly. 'I am mewed in and surely there are things to be done.'

'Not until the spring,' said Sam. 'When the spring is come Briggs and I and James, Coke and Waterford are going to get a boat and cross the channel and explore. If people were left, as Akbar says they were in Afghanistan, there will be pockets of people like us all over the world who have survived. We just have to wait for the snow to go and the weather to be good.'

'Sam, the snow was coloured. I remember the radio announcer said so and we all saw it here.'

Sam laughed. 'I know. It was an experiment. You know the Americans, they will try anything. Their experiment got out of hand, or into other hands, we don't know.'

'And death to nearly everybody. Was that an experiment too?' Muriel was angry.

'Very likely, but shall we ever know? It was a monumental disappearance, not like the calculated deaths in London.'

'Did your American friend die?' Muriel asked Sam.

'He vanished,' said Sam shortly. 'I met no one until I got to the Abbey when I was staggered to find little Father Richard alive and kicking. He sent me on here as I've told you.'

'I don't think any of it matters,' Mr Briggs said surprisingly, 'nor does Waterford.'

'Mrs Luard was a great find, Mama.' Sam wished to distract his mother.

'Coke, Paul and I saw streaks, coloured streaks in the sky, before we went to London.' Muriel's memory revived again.

'I did too,' said Sam. 'The French have, or had a warning system. I tried to use it. I tried to ring you up, but though I heard the bell ringing I got no answer, so I took it for granted you were dead.'

'Coke and James had already been fiddling with the telephone,' said Mr Briggs, 'that was why you got no answer.'

'Your suggestions are too pat.' Muriel looked at Sam and Mr Briggs. 'What is more, until I have thought it over nobody is going to try and find out anything. Nobody is going to risk what we risked in London.'

Neither her son nor her guest answered but exchanged glances over her head.

'Noises off,' said Sam. 'Oho, here come Patricia and her pigs.' He looked out of the window.

'Send them up to me.' Muriel knew why she was tired of her son's company but could say nothing. She sat alone waiting with Chap beside her, waiting to hear the trot, scuffle, trot of the pigs coming along the passage with the child.

Patricia knocked and came in answer to her call, followed by the pigs, Paul and Henry.

'How are you?' Patricia asked formally.

'Better, thank you.' Muriel looked at the little girl's face glowing from the cold air outside and realised that she was beautiful.

'You look rather cross,' said Paul, kissing his mother. 'What has upset you?'

'Oh nothing,' Muriel answered evasively. 'How are the rats, darling?'

'Never mind the rats, what made you cross?' Henry stood beside the other children, staring at her. 'You should not be cross now. You are much better. You are in your right mind. You have Sam back. What's the fuss?'

'Don't be so governessy,' said Muriel laughing. 'Or so perceptive,' she added. All the children laughed.

'Now we no longer have television we watch faces,' said Paul. 'Something has annoyed you. Tell us.'

'It is just that Sam and Mr Briggs have been visiting me and they are so rational.'

'Ah.' All the children looked thoughtful. 'Mr Waterford isn't,' said Henry, 'nor is Mr Briggs as a rule.'

'They try to allay my fears,' said Muriel. 'It's the falsity I hate.'

'Rather silly.' Paul sat down on the floor. 'I'm very chuffed about everything that has happened.'

'Mrs Luard takes it all very calmly. She loves her house, her possessions, her visitors, her new mode of life,' said Henry. 'Is it the spirit of scientific enquiry which annoys you, or just that you can't get about and boss us around?'

'Not that.' Muriel stroked a pig between its eyes and watched Patricia rub each pig in turn until they lay flat on the floor, their tiny eyes swivelling in their heads, watching the children talking to Muriel.

'Out of the mouths of babes and sucklings. Are they still sucklings?' Henry teased Patricia who hit him without animosity.

'You children are getting no education,' Muriel murmured.

'Oh, we are,' said Paul with emphasis. 'You'd be surprised what we have learnt from Mrs Luard's submarine crew. What the sailors get up to is *no*body's business.'

'Dear me,' said Muriel. 'And who else teaches you?'

'Akbar. We watch Akbar and June and James and Ann, but they aren't so amusing.'

'Old Perdue teaches us a lot too, and you, you most of all.' Patricia put her arms round Muriel and hugged her. 'You are better than the pigs,' she said.

The two boys laughed.

'I shall have to wear a mask.' Muriel laughed up at Paul, and then her laughter died as she caught sight of Henry's face which bore an expression of extraordinary sadness.

🔖 37 🔖

The day came when Muriel, with Sam supporting her, and using a stick, was able to leave her room and walk downstairs to sit by the library fire. Only Mr Waterford was in the room reading, and he stood up when she walked in.

'Don't go,' Muriel said to him as he moved towards the door. 'Please don't go.'

The man sat down again, smiling.

'One of my legs is shorter than the other now,' Muriel said conversationally.

'My fault for setting the broken leg badly.'

'No, I think you did it wonderfully well. I am lucky.' Muriel paused, looking from Sam to the other man. 'Isn't it time you told me what you know?' she asked.

'We know so little,' Sam answered her. 'We know that Henry's family were mixed up in some international plot which either never happened or went wrong. We know,' Sam flushed, 'that my father was too.'

'How?' asked Muriel. 'How did you guess?'

'Well, he made this house "warproof" didn't he? He almost rebuilt it. He laid in stores and supplies for years. It was a refuge. But then he got killed so it did not matter to him did it?'

'No,' said Muriel, 'it did not matter any more. But you, Sam, you guessed and I guessed too that he was up to something. Did you go to Germany to try and find out? Did you find anything?'

'Not a sausage,' said Sam.

'So,' Muriel looked at her son and her guest. 'So nothing that they planned happened, did it?'

'Oh, Mama,' Sam exclaimed impatiently, 'of course it did. I told you about the silly snow. I told you about the warning system in France. You must know that they were part of a conspiracy to destroy. To stop America, Russia and China destroying the whole world, they wanted World Government, you know they did. My father took precautions for his own family, he didn't want them involved. And Henry's family didn't care much about him. They just sent him down here to you. They were out to destroy.'

'Don't be so old hat,' said Muriel quietly. 'You are barking up the wrong tree, not seeing what's under your nose. What happened is much more old hat than that, older than time, older than anything you know about. You have experienced it and you will not see. You are stupid, my poor darling, stupid.' Muriel stopped, seeing Mr Waterford lying back in his chair with tears of laughter running down his cheeks. Sam angrily left the room, slamming the door.

'Fool,' said Muriel mildly. 'His father used to do that.'

Her guest, stretching his legs to the fire, laughed more than ever. 'Keep it up,' he said.

'I am quite sure there was no man-made catastrophe,' said Muriel.

'Maybe not. Mankind just added to it.' Mr Waterford watched Muriel's face with interest.

'For years,' said Muriel, 'we have lived under the threat of nuclear destruction. I see no sign of it. Destruction, yes, but nuclear no.'

'There were a lot of do-gooders plotting,' said Mr Waterford.

'Yes. My husband, Henry's family, scientists in America, in England, everywhere. But they didn't do good.'

'No, I can't say they did. A smart piece of work with

coloured snow, and a new communications system of coloured streaks in the sky, that was all.'

'The storms, hurricanes, plagues and other pestilences were not started by man.' Muriel looked at her companion.

'No,' he said, staring into the fire. 'No, those lunatics in London added to the disasters, but they didn't create them. They were a very frightened lot of people. It was curious. I watched them and Briggs tells me he watched them too. They got a bulldozer and went out of London to the experimental station where the poison gas is made, clearing the road. Then they came back and poisoned the people taking shelter. Then they started fires, then they waited.'

'And you waited?' Muriel asked.

'I waited and hid until the day I met you.'

'Rescued me,' said Muriel.

'We are getting away from the point.' Mr Waterford got up and put a log on the fire. 'The point is that none of this that has happened to us and all over the world apparently is man-made. It's not just a natural phenomenon either.'

Muriel was silent for a long time. 'What is that book you are reading?' she asked.

'Science fiction. Ray Bradbury. He's very good.'

'Who gave it to you?' Muriel knew quite well that it was one of her personal books which she kept in her bedroom.

Mr Waterford laughed. 'Henry, of course. He has got Briggs rereading H.G. Wells and Briggs is furious because he is only interested in aerodynamics and has found some books he wants to read in the shelves here, and Jules Verne is positively whizzing from hand to hand. That is, when hands are not being held.'

'What do you mean?' Muriel said obtusely.

'I mean what we see. James and Ann. Akbar and June and Mrs Luard's submarine crew. The procreation of man.'

'Oh. Is it going on much?' Muriel laughed.

'Of course,' said Mr Waterford. 'Of course it is, and all egged on by Henry.'

'Poor old Perdue.' Muriel's mind wandered to the old man.

'Oh, he and Coke are getting down to it too.'

'What!' Muriel was shocked.

'No, no. They have taken charge of the animals.'

'Oh.' Muriel looked abashed. 'What about Patricia's pigs?' she asked.

'The time will come when they will desert her. It's only natural.'

'I cling,' said Muriel, 'to the natural.'

'Do you?' Henry appeared by her side. 'Do you?'

'You are right.' Muriel looked at Henry. 'I have not clung enough. I was just screwing myself up to the point of being natural when all this started.'

'Oh rot,' said Henry. 'You have always been natural, you know you have.'

Muriel did not answer but looked out of the window at the imprisoning snow.

❧ 38 ❧

Muriel's leg grew stronger as she spent the days limping about her house, wandering from room to room and climbing up and down the stairs. Sometimes she telephoned to Paul and Patricia at Willoughby and talked small talk to them as her eyes looked out of the window of her room on to the vast spaces of snow so strange with all the hills rounded and softened. The children sounded happy and told her about the Yugoslavs, how quick they were to learn, how hardworking, how happy.

'The children say your guests at Willoughby are cheerful,' Muriel said to Mrs Luard whom she found sitting reading by the library fire.

'Yes, they are a jolly lot,' Mrs Luard agreed, 'not like this. It's sad. That child Patricia must not read it.'

'What are you reading?' Muriel had seen Mrs Luard knit but never read.

'A book about pigs written by a chap called Orwell. It would upset Patricia.'

'I suppose Henry gave it to you,' Muriel said flatly. 'Henry is insidious; he is making everyone in the house read science fiction.'

'I'm not a great reader.' Mrs Luard laid the book down. 'Now you,' she said quietly to Muriel, 'you limp, but you have no need to. Your leg is perfectly all right. No need to limp at all.'

Muriel limped away, cherishing her lameness, followed by her dogs. She felt nearer to her dogs than her children or visitors. Her dogs neither spoke, hinted, nor laughed at her, as she felt Henry did.

Henry is the devil, Muriel thought angrily to herself as she let herself out of the house by the back door and limped along a well-trodden path to the farmhouse and the cow byres. She sniffed the agreeable smell of cows and ponies and heard in the stillness caused by the snow the quiet contented clucking of hens and a bird suddenly fluffing out its feathers as it preened itself.

She knocked and went into the warm farm kitchen. Coke and Mr Perdue sat on either side of a wood fire. They were playing cards. Both men rose to their feet in surprise.

'First time out,' said Coke cheerfully. 'Still a bit on the lame side.'

The old man looked at her rather nastily Muriel thought. 'Is your head all right?' His voice, Muriel thought, sounded sarcastic.

'Perfectly,' Muriel answered, sitting down in the chair Coke offered her.

'Young Henry was here. He offered us books.' Coke spoke politely.

'Oh, Henry. It's Henry's latest craze. Muriel tried to keep her voice cheerful.

'Sneaky boy that. He wants something to happen.' The old man spoke gratingly. 'Something to happen, as though enough hadn't happened already.'

Muriel felt as though she had a hand on a doorknob which she could turn if she wished. 'I don't think my head is quite recovered,' she said. 'What do you think, Mr Perdue? Is my head all right?'

'As right as it ever was.' Mr Perdue showed his gums. 'No woman is right in the head. None.'

'Rubbish,' said Muriel, laughing. 'Oh, what rubbish you talk, Mr Perdue.'

Coke grinned and glanced at the cards he held in his hand, and Muriel saw that he was about to play a king to Mr Perdue's queen. 'I must go back now. It's been nice seeing you.' Muriel moved to the door and went out quickly, shutting it behind her.

'Hail!' Henry greeted her as she crossed the yard.

'Henry, you must not inflict all those books on everybody.'

'Oh, why not?' Henry walked beside her.

'You know perfectly well why not.' Muriel looked at the boy.

'Oh, well.' Henry looked deflated. 'I'm going to stay at the Abbey, Mrs Wake. I thought I'd better tell you.'

'Of course. I should worry otherwise.'

'I'll see you there then.' Henry began running away from her across the frozen snow and she stood watching his light figure trotting downhill, trotting so lightly that his feet left no imprint as he went over the moor and down the hills through the woods.

'Where will he see you?' Sam came up to her.

'At the Abbey,' Muriel said softly. 'I must get there when I can.'

'We could make you a sledge and tow you down if your leg isn't strong enough.'

'No, thank you. I shall go when I can walk there myself.'

'Very well. Come in out of the cold, Mama.' Sam took her arm.

'How well did you know your father?' Muriel asked him, limping beside him.

'As much as I wanted to.'

'What a funny answer.' Muriel was surprised. 'He was a strange man,' she said.

'Very,' said Sam.

❧ 39 ❦

Muriel went into the room Mr Perdue had slept in before he moved to the farm with Coke. One of the girls had cleaned it and left it unnaturally tidy. The furniture stood primly, the bed was made up but flat. Muriel went across to the writing table and opened a drawer. She was surprised to find it empty, freshly lined with clean paper. Her husband had always kept his papers in folders in this desk and files of letters ready to be answered. Now she found nothing. Puzzled, she went out into the passage and called Sam and Paul who came up the stairs together looking very alike.

'Your father's desk is empty.' Muriel looked at her sons.

'We emptied it,' said Sam. 'There was a lot of rubbish in it.'

'I don't believe you,' said Muriel.

'Oh.' Sam looked embarrassed.

'He had a life apart from you.' Paul took her hand. 'He didn't really mind about you.'

'He did not mind?'

'No. He was wrapped up in his pipe dream. His new world. His World Government. That came first.'

'But we had such fun together.' Muriel remembered the man who had been her husband, who had indeed been her life, as she looked at her two sons. Muriel closed her mind and left the room.

'You should not have said that,' Sam said to his younger brother.

'It is my association with Henry which makes me say these things. Henry has gone down to the Abbey and I don't think he will come back.'

'Good thing.' Sam looked thoughtful. 'Are you going back to the pigs?'

'Yes,' Paul said quickly. 'Yes, the pigs and Patricia and the submarine crew are good company. It's your turn here.'

Sam looked put out and went to join his mother who was in the library with James and Ann and June and Akbar.

'Where are the others?' said Sam.

'I don't know. They will come back. Sam, these two lots of young people want homes of their own. What houses near here do you suggest?'

Sam felt his mother was applying her mind to something which did not interest her in the least. 'The old Admiral's house would suit you, James. Everything in its place. I shouldn't think it would take you more than a few days to get it in order. Shall we go and see it? You can walk there.'

'Yes, I'd love to.' James was enthusiastic. 'Is it too far for Ann to go?'

'No.' Sam felt and could feel Muriel was feeling the same thing, that these people, strangers to him, wanted to leave. He resented them feeling this as his mother had done so much for them.

'And what house would you suggest for us?' June asked Muriel.

Muriel looked at the girl thoughtfully and then said, 'The vicarage in the village. That would suit you perfectly.'

'I suggest,' said James, 'that we get the houses ready and warm and clear of débris and then go as soon as possible.'

'Yes, you do that. Coke and old Perdue are settled. Why not you? It didn't take long for them.' Muriel watched the two young couples leave the room and sat thoughtfully by the fire.

Mrs Luard joined her half an hour later and sat down beside her. 'Funny, isn't it?' said the older woman.

'What's funny?' Muriel looked at Mrs Luard sideways.

'We all wants a home of our own, that's what's funny. But there is something else.'

'What else?'

'You know, they know, we all know that you have to be alone. It isn't only that they want to be by themselves and set up house. Henry dropped a hint before he left.'

'What about Mr Waterford and Mr Briggs?' Muriel's resolve to be hospitable reasserted itself.

'They are going to see me home and bring back Paul and Patricia. Then I think they will stay with you.'

'That's nice,' said Muriel brightly. 'I couldn't bear only a household of children.'

'We can all visit,' Mrs Luard remarked.

'I am going to bed to think.' Muriel got up and limped up the stairs followed by her dogs. Getting into bed she lay quiet and tired, unable to think at all.

During the following days she heard Mrs Luard's departure and the return of Paul and Patricia. She listened, too, to comings and goings about the house as June and Ann made their preparations. Now and again Sam brought her food but as often as not he found his mother asleep.

Muriel dreamed and woke dreaming of the empty writing desk and the house which without her help emptied itself of visitors.

In the library Mr Waterford sat by the fire reading and Mr Briggs wrote the book he never had had time to write and which he supposed nobody would ever read.

Days passed and clocks ticked and Muriel lay waiting for the moment, the moment in time when she would act. Waiting for the courage which she needed.

The house buried in snow, gripped by the intense frost, was deathly quiet.

Visiting Muriel as she lay in bed, Sam, Paul and Patricia reported that June, Akbar, James and Ann were happy in their new homes, that although the village was mostly buried in snowdrifts, it was easy to visit Mrs Luard and the Yugoslavs walking on the hard snow, that everybody seemed happy. Muriel got the impression that her household and neighbours in their state of semi-hibernation were satisfied, content even. But she was not satisfied. She thought of her husband Julian, and faced the fact that he, Henry's parents and in all likelihood many other people, had plotted for power, that what they had wanted had been dangerous, insane; that their schemes, going dreadfully wrong, had led to the catastrophe which Father Richard charitably suggested might be an 'accident'.

She searched her mind as to whether, if she had not been blind and complacent, she might have been able to prevent some of the horrors which had taken place. Although she knew that worrying was useless, since the explanation of what had caused the end of the world as she had known it would remain a mystery, she still fretted.

She wondered resentfully whether Sam and Paul had not been high-handed in sweeping away all evidence of their father's activities. She was aware that it was something she should perhaps have done herself. In the event her sons had been right. It was useless to dwell on a life which was gone, never to return.

Not prepared to lapse into the contentment and ease of those about her, Muriel retreated more and more to her room to lie wakeful, listening to the absence of sound in this frozen world, waiting for she knew not what as days and weeks dragged by.

On a night of full moon she listened to the muted sounds of Sam, Paul and Patricia, Mr Waterford and Mr Briggs going to bed. Her dogs lay at her feet and Charlie crouched in the armchair. From the farm the occasional sound of a hen's cluck, a pony's stamp in the stable, sounded loud as pistol shots. As sleep settled over Brendon, the quiet was so intense she fancied she might have become deaf. Then at last in the unearthly stillness came the suspicion of a sound.

The dogs raised their heads, thumped their tails, the door opened and Henry slipped into the room.

'Mrs Wake.' He kissed her cheek. His face was icy.

'Henry.' She held his cold hands in hers.

'Are you ready?' he asked in an urgent whisper.

'I will get dressed.' She got up and started putting on her clothes. 'I am ready. I won't be long.'

As she dressed Henry talked in a low voice looking out of the window. 'We must remember all the good things. We must think of the people and animals who have survived. They are all good. They are all important.'

'Yes.' She was excited, she felt new life in her veins.

'Put on several jerseys, it is still very cold.'

'Yes.' She pulled on a third jersey. Henry took her hand. They went down the stairs in stockinged feet followed by the cat and the dogs.

In the back porch they put on gumboots. Henry picked up Charlie and put her inside his windcheater. They stepped out into the moonlit yard.

'Listen.' Henry held up his hand. 'It's coming alive, waking.'

Muriel heard as once before the drip of water from icicles hanging from the eaves, the gargle in the drainpipes. She watched Henry run lightly across the yard to open the doors of stables and byres, moving quickly in a haze of sweet smelling steam from cows and horses and restive sheep. One of the ponies whinnied softly.

'Come on.' Henry took her hand.

'What about the others?' Muriel whispered.

'They will come when they wake. They will see our tracks.' He was leading her onto the frozen moor. She saw as they walked across the moonlit world that their feet and those of the dogs charted the course for the others to follow.

They hurried over the brow of the hill and down into the valley, speeding over the crisp snow. The moon was setting as they came over the hill and into the woods and all about them the sleeping world came alive. The snow melted, icicles cracked, the streams, long frozen, chuckled and gurgled to rush down the hills to the river, to the sea, to the world beyond.

As she followed Henry, Muriel felt a rush of emotion which she tried to analyse.

'Henry, stop!' she cried, for he was outdistancing her.

'What is it, Mrs Wake?' In the curious light before dawn, when moonset gives way to sunrise, Henry looked larger, taller, stronger than she remembered.

'What is it?' he asked again.

She said, 'Don't laugh, Henry, but I feel hope.' She feared he would mock.

'At last,' said Henry, staring at her. 'You had lost it, hadn't you? Even when Sam came back he didn't bring hope.'

'No,' she said, smiling at Henry. 'I had to find it for myself.'

'Yes.' He was serious, concerned.

'But you helped me find it,' said Muriel.

Henry looked embarrassed and amused. 'Come on,' he said, and led her through the woods, noisy now with snow dropping in dollops off the trees, water dripping, a fox barking in the distance, a badger moving across their path so that Chap barked and his bark echoed loud down the valley.

'You are not lame any more,' said Henry.

'No,' said Muriel, surprised. 'I am healed.'

They walked out of the woods, across the fields to the Abbey, golden and rosy in the dawn light.

'I made a collection for you, an exhibition,' said Henry. 'For other people too. I thought it would amuse you.'

'Will you show me? What is this collection?'

'Oh,' cried Henry, 'it is not really amusing. I collected gold and jewels, bits of hair, a bull's nose ring, your parson's glass eye, false teeth, deaf aids, badges, bottles of pills and always money, money, money. I thought – '

'What?' Muriel stood still and looked at Henry.

'I thought they would serve as reminders,' said Henry, speaking lightly in his most offhand manner.

'I see,' said Muriel. 'We may need reminding.'

'There is Father Richard waiting for you. You want to talk to him.' Henry pointed to the Abbey porch where the monk stood waiting to greet them. 'Paul said you were ringing him up, trying to reach him the night of the great storm long ago.' Henry pushed her forward.

'So I was,' said Muriel, remembering that night.

'Go on then. You cannot put it off any longer. I will wait for you.' Henry gave her another push and she walked on to meet the monk, leaving Henry sitting on the Abbey steps with Charlie on his knee, a curiously lonely figure.

Father Richard took her hand. 'So Henry brought you.' He led her into the Abbey. 'It's about time.'

'Henry came to fetch me. He has changed in some way.'

'We all change when we grow up,' said the monk.

'So that's what has happened to him.'

'You did not come here to talk about Henry, you wanted to talk about yourself. We can talk about Henry later.'

'He reminded me that I needed to talk to you the night of the storm, before what you call the accident.'

Father Richard laughed. 'As well call it that as anything. What was the trouble?'

'I wanted to tell you about Julian. I suspected – no, to be truthful I had found out before he died in the car accident he was plotting something horrible with other people, with Henry's parents. They wanted to rule the world, they were putting the blame on other nations. I could have tried to prevent it, I should have.'

'Maybe.'

'I loved him. I did nothing.'

'He was a lovable man.'

'But wicked!' cried Muriel. 'I did nothing to stop it. When he had the crash which killed him I should have done something. I did nothing.' Muriel stared at the priest. 'Should you not give me some sort of spiritual jog?' she asked resentfully.

'I should think you have had enough of those. What about – ' he paused.

'What?'

'I was going to suggest – er – looking forward, having a bit of hope.'

'Hope has come back. I realised that this morning.'

'Then stop blaming Julian. Remember you loved him.'
Father Richard sat down in the choir. They had been walking
towards the altar. 'There's an awful lot to be done,' he said
thoughtfully, 'and if we have hope we can get on with it.'

'Oh.' Muriel was mystified. 'Don't you think – '

'I am not in a position to judge. I do know that whereas
confession may be good for the soul, hope and looking
forward to what's to come is much more important. Ask
Henry.'

'Henry?'

'Henry represents the future. I know – ' the priest held up a
hand to quell her protest – 'I know you do not altogether like
him, but you trust him. Did you not follow him to London?'

'Yes.' Muriel remembered that long nightmare journey
with Paul.

'And he brought you back. It seems to me – ' Father
Richard stood up and started walking towards the porch –
'that you underestimate Henry. If you have rediscovered
hope, have a bit of faith too.' He sounded quite tart, Muriel
thought, as close to being reproachful as she had ever known
him.

Henry's voice startled them.

'Here they come,' he shouted, loud in the empty Abbey.

When they reached the Abbey door Henry was running
with the dogs to meet a crowd of people walking out from the
woods, their voices carrying cheerfully in the cold clear air,
mingling with the sound of rushing water.

Sam and Paul, Mrs Luard and the Yugoslavs, Coke and
Perdue, James, Ann, Akbar, June, Mr Briggs and Mr Waterford, the people from the fish farm, Patricia dancing along
among them, now talking to one group, now dashing to greet
another.

'It's a carnival,' exclaimed Muriel.

'It is Easter,' said the monk. 'Spring.'

Muriel stood with Father Richard watching the people
coming out of the dark woods into the sunshine.

A vast flock of starlings swooped from the east, moment-
arily blotting out the sun. They settled chattering and
whistling on the Abbey roof drowning the sound of rushing

water and human speech. As suddenly as they had come they flew off and the sound of their wings died away.

The people gathered in the sun looking up at Muriel, waiting for her to speak. She searched their faces, the faces of friends, strangers, her sons. She looked for Henry. He stood apart, almost, she thought, as if ready to take flight.

'It has been a very long winter,' she began. 'It is over now.'

'Until the next' – old Perdue's voice from the crowd.

Some people smiled at the interruption, some looked anxious, Paul laughed outright. Henry began to move away.

'Henry *wait*,' Muriel called to him, 'wait a minute.' She looked again at the crowd of people. 'There is no proper end to a new beginning,' she said, 'but we have to start as best we can with someone to lead us – '

'Oh,' cried the people, and 'Who?' they questioned. 'You?'

'No, no, I am too old, too tired. I suggest – ' Muriel summoned up all her courage. 'I suggest,' she said, 'that we elect Henry.'

There was a stunned silence. Muriel saw that Henry, white-faced, was edging away. The crowd began to mutter, to grumble, to discuss. Then someone cheered and suddenly they all cheered and a girl from the fish farm ran out of the crowd and caught Henry by the arm and pulled him forward. She cried in a loud voice which carried authority, 'We have all been annoyed by Henry. We have all been irritated by him. He has made us *think* and that has been infuriating. That is what a leader is *for*. Everyone with any sense complains about their leader. I vote for – ' her voice was drowned by cries of, 'Henry, Henry, Henry.'

Muriel ran down the steps and joined the crowd, thinking, This is what I have been waiting for in the frozen world of winter. And much later, walking home with Sam and Paul after a day of rejoicing, she said, 'There will be other Henrys in other countries,' and Paul answered, 'Henriettas also.'

They will be young enough not to be daunted, thought Muriel, remembering all the terrors they had experienced and that after the initial shocks Henry had shown very little fear and much wisdom.

'We shall have to keep our wits about us from now on with Henry in charge.' Paul sounded pleased with the prospect.

'It's a good thing everybody doesn't like him,' said Sam. 'Why?'

'We have seen what too much power can do,' said Sam. 'We need the unpredictable Henry represents.'

'We shan't collapse into contentment,' said Mr Waterford who had caught up with them. 'With that boy around we dare not be complacent.'